Praise for Connie Flynn's novels:

The Fire Opal

"Thought-provoking, mystical, and hauntingly moving. Ms. Flynn creates a steamy, sensual tale of faith, forgiveness, and love. . . . The love scenes are sizzling, raw, and exposed. . . . The imagery of the swampy bayou is so vivid. You can hear every hiss, smell every fragrant flowery aroma, feel every rain drop, and taste the damp humidity on your tongue. . . . Excellent!"   —*Rendezvous*

"Brilliant . . . a first-rate romance blended inside a frightening plot, proving once again that no one makes the para-world seem more like a perfectly normal occurence than the fantastic [Connie] Flynn."
                    —Harriet Klausner, *BookBrowser*

Shadow of the Wolf

"A rich, complex novel filled with powerful emotions, romance, and magic."   —*Romantic Times*

continued . . .

Shadow on the Moon

"Sensational! *Shadow on the Moon* has one of the most compelling heroes ever. I wasn't just entertained, I was enthralled from the opening scene."

—Suzanne Forster

"Enter another rising star with a knack for werewolves and the sure touch of a born storyteller . . . a moving portrait." —*Romantic Times*

"Fabulous . . . charming . . . action-packed and exciting. . . . A great supernatural romance that fans of the sub-genre and horror stories in general will enjoy to the max." —*Under the Covers*

"A beautiful love story . . . Stephen King or Dean Koontz or other writers of the horror genre would be proud to put their names on this story. This is real suspense. While I knew that a happy ending was imminent, I certainly wanted it to get here . . . soon."

—*The Romantic Reader*

"Convincingly written with measured, controlled prose. Many fans of Stephen King and Dean Koontz will be drawn to the superb *Shadow on the Moon*— and they won't be disappointed."

—Scottsdale, AZ *Life*

"A tantalizing page-turner." —*Romance Forever*

THE
DRAGON
HOUR

A Time-Travel Romance

by
Connie Flynn

AN ONYX BOOK

ONYX
Published by New American Library, a division of
Penguin Putnam Inc., 375 Hudson Street,
New York, New York 10014, U.S.A.
Penguin Books Ltd, 27 Wrights Lane,
London W8 5TZ, England
Penguin Books Australia Ltd, Ringwood,
Victoria, Australia
Penguin Books Canada Ltd, 10 Alcorn Avenue,
Toronto, Ontario, Canada M4V 3B2
Penguin Books (N.Z.) Ltd, 182–190 Wairau Road,
Auckland 10, New Zealand

Penguin Books Ltd, Registered Offices:
Harmondsworth, Middlesex, England

First published by Onyx, an imprint of New American Library,
a division of Penguin Putnam Inc.

First Printing, January 2000
10 9 8 7 6 5 4 3 2 1

 REGISTERED TRADEMARK—MARCA REGISTRADA

Printed in the United States of America

PUBLISHER'S NOTE
This is a work of fiction. Names, characters, places, and incidents either are
the product of the author's imagination or are used fictitiously, and any
resemblance to actual persons, living or dead, business establishments,
events or locales is entirely coincidental.

To Linda Style, Sharyn Liberatore, Judy Bowden,
Laurie Schnebly, and Christy Strauch.

Thanks for a great year.

Acknowledgments

To me, research is always time-consuming and tedious, robbing precious hours I could devote to writing. The complexities of *The Dragon Hour*, however, required lots of it, a task I couldn't have waded through without the help of the following people.

Denise Domning, Christina Skye (otherwise known as Roberta), and Diana Gabaldon for so generously sharing their knowledge of the past and, in Denise's and Christina's case, their books. Todd Templeton for getting me in touch with wonderful resources about Scotland. Ed Lindow for telling me everything he knows about physics, and helping me understand that time travel really is impossible. Linda Style for surfing the web and forwarding URLs to countless invaluable sites. Dr. Jay Style for taking time out of his busy day to help me save Randy from anaphylactic shock. Eve Paludan for providing books on everything medieval, from soup to candles. Last of all, although this isn't a person, to Encarta for putting thousands of facts at my fingertips.

PROLOGUE

Scotland
May 29, 1672

Oh, please, Father, let me come home!

It was the afternoon of Caryn Maclachlan's fifteenth birthday, but instead of being pampered as was her due, she found herself racing up the stairs, running higher, ever higher, running as fast as she could to escape the seething humiliation of her husband's latest scolding.

Life was too cruel. Shipped off to a far corner of Scotland! Married to a man twice her age! Cut off from her father, her brothers, the people of Invergair who adored her!

Tears brimmed in her eyes, but she refused to give in to them. Gregory didn't love her, nor did she love him, although she'd tried, for a wife was commanded to love her husband. But how could she love a man who chastised her so frequently, so publically, so harshly?

Her path ended at the roof. With nowhere left to

run, she walked heavily to the battlement, leaned against the cool stone, and let her labored breathing subside. The Earl of Lochlorraine would not break her, she vowed to herself. Never. She was of the Clan Campbell, the daughter of a marquess, and she would not bow to one who treated her as chattel.

A strong wind whipped tendrils of hair from beneath her cap, and she tucked them back as she gazed out on her new land. Thatched cottage roofs reflected prisms of dancing sunlight, the straw falling and lifting in the high winds. Lines of mud and wattle chimneys stood guardian above them, their smoke churned to a frenzy of spitting sparks.

Below she saw Ian and his fellows working at the edge of the trench Gregory called his "brother's folly." In her five months here, she'd somehow managed to alienate almost every resident of Lochlorraine with behavior Gregory deemed brash and impulsive. Ian, alone, remained her friend. He, too, followed the call of his own heart, and was ever curious, ever exploring, ever stretching his laird brother's goodwill. They even shared the same birthday, which the realm would celebrate that evening.

Ian looked up by chance and noticed her presence. He waved, shouting something she couldn't make out. Ignoring the obvious danger, she leaned out over the battlement.

"What?" she called.

"We did it, Caryn!" Ian hollered back. "We did it!"

She cupped her hands around her mouth. "Did what?"

He pointed to Wizard's Spire, a lofty rock protu-

berance that broke the rolling hills of heather surrounding the castle. His finger fixed upon a thick
cable that stretched from his grandfather's windmill
and ran toward the main tower behind her. Turning,
she followed the cable's path and saw that it was
affixed to a gargantuan metal hoop that Ian had
mounted on the tower some weeks earlier.

Since then, he'd attached a long rod to the hoop,
and it now whirled high above her head at a dizzying speed. At the end of this rod hung a second
one, which dropped toward the ground some twenty
meters from the castle wall. Quickly the rods whirred
out of sight, only to return almost as soon as they
vanished. The wind had gained force since Caryn
had stepped onto the roof and now threatened to
dislodge her cap. Holding on to it, she leaned farther
over the battlement wall and saw the vertical rod
descended into the trench.

She felt a surge of joy for Ian. From the moment
she'd arrived in Lochlorraine, he had talked excitedly
about his method for creating the legendary philosopher's stone, the key to alchemy that transformed
base metal into gold.

This was it. The culmination of his work. If his
theory proved true, they'd have something more to
celebrate tonight than their birthday. How grand.
With Ian's success taking the spotlight, she might be
better able to endure her newly imposed gentility.

Ian was nodding excitedly, shouting, trying to be
heard, but the deafening hum of the spinning rods
drowned him out. He gave up, and she could see
him laughing. Around him, the other men laughed

and danced. Ignoring the fierce wind, Caryn stretched precariously over the wall, clinging to her cap, laughing too, loudly, from nothing but sheer delight at the merriment of Ian and his men.

As another laugh left her mouth, she swayed, finding it oddly difficult to stay afoot. The very floor quaked beneath her, while below Ian and his fellows jerked about like marionettes. Suddenly the sky boomed, a horrendous sound that pounded Caryn's eardrums. Her world tilted, propelling her forward, and she grabbed for the wall. Pushing back, sliding down, holding the stone so tightly it scraped skin off her hands, she fell to the floor.

There came a flash of blue-white light that turned the sky as flat as slate. Next came tremors that pasted her against the wall. A hideous screech followed, then total darkness. Though it seemed a lifetime, the blackness lasted mere seconds. When it eased, the sun had all but disappeared, leaving the day in the grips of dusk though the chapel chimes had not yet struck three.

Climbing to her feet, Caryn raced down the castle stairs, through the great hall, and out the door. Others were running too. Somewhere she saw Gregory, heard him call for her. But she ignored him and raced toward Ian and his men, who were at the heart of the terrible explosion. Surely they were injured, even dead. As she ran, she saw the aged village healer stumbling away from the trench toward the dwellings.

"Hurry, Bessy," she urged. "Get your medicines. Sir Ian, his men, they need us."

"Nay." The woman stopped and gripped Caryn's hands. "My medicine will not help. They are all gone quite mad."

Caryn quite agreed. In the midst of all the destruction, Ian laughed and danced, gleefully displaying an object high in the air. Some of his fellows slapped him on the back. Others roared in delight. When Ian saw her, he let out a raucous cheer. "The philosopher's stone!" he declared.

"The philo—"

Her response was cut off by an enormous shadow that completely blackened the slate-grey sky. Caryn looked up, then looked away, not believing her eyes. Bessy let out a horrified gasp.

By the time Caryn looked back, small explosions were erupting in the village. Fires scurried across the cottage roofs. Men and women screamed and ran, carrying buckets of water, shouting directions, calling for their children. Someone was weeping.

"Ormeskirk," Bessy intoned dully, squeezing Caryn's hand ever tighter. "Ormeskirk has returned to plague us once more."

Chapter One

"No more arguments. The kid isn't going to be part of an armored car robbery." Fixing Vinnie and Don with a challenging stare, Luke Slade gestured toward Plotkin's Bank, then placed his hand protectively on his cousin's shoulder.

"Golly, Luke!" Randy scrunched up his face as he shrugged off Luke's touch. "Why're you tryin' to ruin it for me?"

"You end up in prison, Randy, you'll really know ruin." The kid had a puppylike face that guaranteed him unwelcome attention. Big, almost round, hazel eyes. A button-type nose, smooth unblemished skin, and white even teeth that had somehow survived lousy prenatal care. Even now, looking hound-dog sad and sporting a fading black eye, he made you want to smile when you looked at him.

At this moment, however, Luke didn't much feel like smiling, and Vinnie's superconfident grin soured his disposition even more. "Why the hell did you get Randy's hopes up like this?"

"He'll only be driving, Luke. Sure, he's a bit slow, but he handles a car like a pro. You treat him like he's a half-wit."

"Yeah!" Randy interjected. "You act like I don't got no brains. Least Vinnie thinks I can add two and two."

Don elbowed Randy as he lazily flicked his gaze toward the people rushing past them. "Keep it down."

Luke had to agree. Quarreling on a street corner at the edge of Central Park was a damned sure way to get unwelcome attention. He paused, trying to reassess the situation. He'd grown up with Vinnie Carbello and Don Wicorowitz, but it'd been a long time since they'd played kickball in the alleys and dreamed of growing up to be rich. None of them were squeaky-clean these days, but what Vinnie and Don were planning? It was nuts, no other word for it.

"It's not like we're stealing from a church, bro," Vinnie said. "These guys are terrorists."

Luke laughed mockingly. "Whatever. But I sure know they're not Sunday school teachers. Aside from the chances of getting caught, you could get killed."

Vinnie shook his head with his usual confidence. Don looked off into the distance, his customary low-key self. Only Randy's behavior was out of character, and Luke would never learn the reason while Vinnie and Don were looking on. But he might as well try.

"What happened to your eye?" Luke asked, only now picking up on that possible clue.

Randy looked down at his shoes. "Nothin' much. I ran into a door."

"Marv been beating up on you again?"

"I tole you." Reddening, the kid slanted his eyes toward Vinnie and Don. "I ran into a door."

"Look, Randy, let's you and me take a walk."

"Go ahead," Vinnie said. "Have a heart-to-heart. Keep me waiting. I just love to wait. But Randy's in, you like it or not."

Luke ignored the remark. He walked alongside Randy in silence, letting the boy pout until they were well out of Don's and Vinnie's hearing range. "What happened this time?"

"Nothin'. I already tole you it was nothin'."

Yeah, and like Luke believed him. It really ticked Luke off the way people abused and exploited his cousin. Bad enough the boy's pa used him as a punching bag; Vinnie didn't have to manipulate him into risking his freedom and life in a robbery.

Stopping beside a high hedge in a heavily wooded area, Luke turned toward Randy. "What say I give you the hundred thousand? Will you back out then?"

"No!" Randy whirled and slapped at the shrubs, then circled back with his hands fisted. "That's money you're saving for your Mercedes dealership! How would I ever pay you back? You already give me everything. Weren't for you, I wouldn't have no job. And I know you pay the rent when Pa don't. Even my car belongs to you."

"You're family, Randy."

"Can't ya see I'm tired of owing you? Besides, we

ain't gonna get caught. Vinnie don't do nothing that ain't a sure thing."

"He's only done petty stuff, kid. This is an armored car heist."

"But the money belongs to terrorists. Vinnie says that makes it okay."

Luke blew out his breath. "Get real, Randy. Vinnie's saying that to get you to go along."

"No, he ain't. Vinnie don't lie." Randy rocked back and forth on his feet, absently plucking leaves off the hedge and shredding them one by one. He was clearly distressed and Luke suspected the reasons went well beyond this disagreement. "What's going on, kid?"

"I gotta make changes, Luke. I can't take it no more. Pa gets meaner and meaner, and he's hardly ever sober anymore."

"You're bigger than he is. Why don't you just deck him?"

Randy's eyes widened in honest shock. "The Bible say to honor your mother and father."

Christ, the kid sounded like Luke's mother. Even as she lay dying, she'd beseeched Luke to promise he'd forgive his father for what he'd done to him and his little brother. Luke hadn't argued with her, but he hadn't promised either.

Kevin. He'd never forgive his father for Kevin.

"Okay, I'll tell your dad to lay off—"

"No! Don't! Pa . . . Pa told me if I . . ." Randy kicked at the shrubbery before continuing. "If I ever said somethin' to you again, he'd kill me." Randy met Luke's gaze with sorrowful eyes. "What's wrong with him, Luke? Aren't fathers supposed to be nice to their kids?"

Luke hesitated. Yeah, in the bigger scheme of things. But not in the world the Slades came from. Knowing that, Luke tried hard to make things better for Randy. Without question he often fell short.

Just as he had with Kevin.

"Hey, what's that?" Randy abruptly asked, interrupting Luke's train of thought.

Before Luke could respond Randy bounded along the line of the hedge, coming to a stop at a dip in the otherwise unbroken foliage.

Startled but not surprised by this mercurial change in the boy's mood, Luke walked down to join Randy. As he approached, the kid bent over, coming up with an object that glinted dully in the dappled sun. "Look. Ain't this ring pretty?"

It was okay, Luke thought. Wide, flat-edged, and crudely etched with runelike symbols, the ring looked like one of the New Age trinkets so prevalent in cheap jewelry stores. Valueless, he was sure, but not to Randy, who was now sliding it down his finger.

"And didja see this?" Randy disappeared into the brush, then immediately reappeared. "There's a regular room inside here."

Luke peered over Randy's shoulder, mildly amazed at this discovery. The hedge was growing in a semicircle that backed up against a stand of tall trees, and what Luke had thought was a break in the foliage was actually an overlap of bushes that created an almost-invisible entrance.

"Half a dozen people could sleep in there, don'ja think, Luke?"

"Yeah, I'm surprised the homeless haven't found this place."

"Maybe cops scared 'em off." His interest clearly waning, Randy idly twirled the ring. "If I ever get married, I'm gonna give this to my wife."

Suddenly a stark flash of pulsing light filled the alcove, casting Randy in such extreme shadow that he looked like a film negative. Head spinning, Luke jerked away, struggling to fight off memories.

"Don't do it, Kev. He's not worth it," an inner voice cried. *His* voice, echoing words from the past.

"I have to. He's our pa."

The vibrating white flashes made Luke's head spin. His connection to the present faded.

"Don't, Kev!" he implored repeatedly, holding Kevin's arm, trying to drag him away from danger. "Don't!"

As quickly as it had come, the light vanished, abruptly returning Luke to reality

"Let go, Luke! That hurts!" Randy was insisting. "And you're calling me Kev. Why're you calling me Kev?"

Taken aback to find his hand brutally encircling Randy's lower arm, Luke released the limb as if it were a burning poker.

"Sorry," he mumbled. "Strobe lights always freak me out."

Randy rubbed his manhandled arm and looked at Luke warily. "Yeah, I guess so. You okay now?"

Luke nodded, then turned for the street. "Come on, let's head back."

"Did you see that stuff?" Randy asked, looking back as he walked. "How do you think it got there?"

Luke shrugged. "Maybe someone with a camcorder was standing behind the trees." He didn't actually know, and cared less. He still trembled inside and was filled with a protective tenderness that had him yearning to reach out, touch Randy, make sure he was okay.

"Not the light, Luke, the lake. And there was a castle, too. High up on a hill."

"Must've been an optical illusion."

"No it weren't. It was really real, really, really real. I saw it. You think the ring I found is magic? I bet it really is. I bet that's why . . ."

Luke *really* wished Randy would stop talking. The kid's childlike wonder, the way he jumped from subject to subject, the constant questions, grated on Luke's raw nerves right now, so he tuned out the chatter. This was all plain weird. Not that he hadn't experienced replays of that unwelcome memory before. He had. Especially when subjected to flashing light. But never so vividly that he'd spoken and acted as if he were in the past.

A shiver crept up his back.

Luke scorned superstitions. He didn't believe in angels or spirit guides. He'd never seen a ghost or talked to a channeled entity. But the chill coursing along his spinal column was familiar. It usually came just before a tragedy, and its presence now made him wonder if his hallucination was actually a premonition that Randy would be harmed during the robbery?

"Hurry, Randy," he said, quickening his pace. When they reached the street, encountering a very annoyed and impatient-looking Vinnie, Luke told Randy to wait near the edge of the park.

"Okay, Vinnie," Luke said when he knew his cousin was out of earshot. "Give Randy his share. But I'll drive in his place."

Luke wouldn't exactly say he was in good spirits as he approached the appointed midnight meeting spot, but knowing Randy wouldn't be involved had lifted a burden from his soul. So it was with a modicum of peace that he opened the minivan door and climbed into the backseat.

"Hi, Luke."

He jumped, nearly banging his head against the top of the van before he whirled toward Vinnie, who sat in the front passenger seat. "What the hell is Randy doing here?"

"Driving the van. What's it look like?"

"You told me you'd cut him out."

"Geez, Luke," Randy wailed, looking back. "Why do you keep trying to screw things up? Vinnie said he'd give you a hundred grand too. Now you can get that dealership."

"Think of it, Luke," Vinnie said smoothly. "No more busting your butt, no more waiting. You can buy all them Mercedes right away."

Luke glared furiously. "What the hell goes through

your mind? I said I'd take the kid's place. I didn't ask for a share. Wasn't that enough for you?"

"Ain't that sweet?" Don piped up from his spot beside Luke. "He don't want his little cousin to get hurt."

"Shove it, Don." Luke grabbed for the door handle. He'd damn well drag Randy from behind that wheel if he had to.

"Don't even think about it, bro." Vinnie wearily reached back and pushed down the lock button. "Read my lips, and read 'em good. The heist is in an hour. I got thirteen million on the line. And I'm not risking having the cops called because you and Randy got in a scuffle."

"We made a deal, you and me."

"Yeah, but you forgot to tell your cousin."

"That's right," Randy said. "And I don't care what you say. I'm gonna do it!"

Vinnie shrugged helplessly. "Same thing he told me. What's a man to do?"

Vinnie's calm response made Luke realize he'd been blind. "You counted on that, didn't you? Which means you must want me along, too. Why?"

"I made the mistake of telling you about the heist, thinking you'd jump at the chance so you could buy your dealership. Who'd figure you'd turn me down? So even after you agreed to take Randy's place, what's to stop you from changing your mind and leaving me without a driver? Besides, it ain't healthy having someone with nothing to lose knowing secrets we don't want out."

Don nodded. "Vinnie's right. It ain't healthy."

"And the insurance that you'll keep your lips zipped is worth a hundred thousand to me, especially when Don and I get millions. You want to make sure your cuz doesn't get hurt, then do your part. Anyway, think of it like this. We're stopping terrorist activities. Makes us some kind of heroes, don't you figure?"

Luke studied Vinnie for a long moment. The guy acted as if he believed his own hype. Well maybe he did, maybe it was even true, but just because the money was dirty didn't make it right. Robbery was robbery, a line Luke had never crossed before.

Neither had Randy, and someone had to watch out for him.

"The deal is foolproof," Don said.

Vinnie was already smiling in confident anticipation. "What could go wrong?"

Randy leaned forward to turn the key, and Luke was tempted to stop him, but the set of the boy's face revealed an irrevocably made-up mind. Clearly Randy wanted independence, not only from his father, but from Luke.

"Okay," Luke said gruffly. "But stay in the van no matter what happens. You understand me, kid?"

"Okey-doke."

"Good. It's a done deal then," Vinnie said. "Put your foot to the pedal, Randy, and let's get on with it. We can go over the details again on the way."

Don groaned, cluing Luke that Vinnie had already covered this ground dozens of times. But looking after details was what made Vinnie effective, so Luke was interested. If he and Randy were going to do this, he'd damned well make sure they didn't get caught. Besides, much as he hated to admit it, getting a share of the money wasn't hard to take. He'd worked hard toward buying that Mercedes dealership, saving diligently, investing wisely, but it was still a good five years down the road. A hundred thousand would make it happen overnight.

Despite Vinnie's slippery ways, Luke didn't doubt the guy would make good on his promise to pay. In Carmine Bescallia's organization, guys didn't welsh on these kinds of agreements—a twisted form of morality Luke currently found reassuring.

Realizing his mind had drifted, he asked Vinnie to repeat his instructions. Don groaned again, but Vinnie gladly complied.

The funds were being transferred to Plotkin's Bank by common armored car, and only two rent-a-cops for security. Luke saw the wisdom behind that decision. Although it was unproven, the bank was still suspected of money laundering and was well watched. A sizeable convoy in the middle of the night would draw unwanted attention. A single car would draw little.

"You know how to use a hypodermic needle, Luke?" Vinnie interrupted himself to ask.

Luke shook his head. "Only in theory."

"Well, let Don give you a crash course while we drive. If the man waiting to let in the drivers comes out of the bank ahead of schedule, you can send him nighty-night."

Don feigned an evil glint as he thumbed down the plunger of an empty hypo, then handed it over, forc-

ing Luke to split his attention between simultaneously delivered instructions.

It was now a quarter past midnight. They'd reach
the park in about fifteen minutes. After Randy
dropped them off, he'd circle the block, returning
at approximately one twenty. The armored car was
scheduled to arrive between one and one fifteen.

Vinnie and Don were dressed in security guard
uniforms. As soon as the armored car drivers opened
the back doors to expose the cash, Vinnie and Don
would descend and inject them with a fast-acting
sedative. The guards would be unconscious before
they knew what happened. By this time, Randy
would have returned to double-park beside the armored car while Don and Vinnie transferred the
cash. The theft would take just minutes, and by one-
twenty-five, they'd be driving away with fistful of
dollars, so to speak.

"The money isn't marked," Vinnie concluded.
"The terrorists can't report it stolen and neither can
the bank, since they're aiding money laundering. All
we gotta do is not flash too much, too soon, and
we're set for life."

"Like I said," Don added. "It's foolproof."

"I hope so," Luke said, dubious without real reason. Get over it, he told himself. Other than turning
him into a bona fide felon, what could possibly go
wrong tonight?

Chapter Two

-

Clutching Randy tight against his chest, Luke barreled through the park like a hunted animal, weaving right, veering left, slamming into branches and bushes, and desperately trying to convince himself that the sticky fluid seeping through his jacket wasn't really blood.

Don't die, Kev. Please don't die.

The boy squirmed, unsettling Luke's precarious balance. "Be still," he grunted.

"B-but . . . you called . . . you called me Kev again," Randy wheezed.

"I-I didn't . . . say anything." Speaking was a labor and Luke could barely get out the words.

"Y-you did. Am I gonna d-die . . . like K-Kevin? Don't let me die, Luke."

"You're fine!" Which Luke didn't believe for a minute, but he said it anyway. "Now save your breath."

The park was eerily silent. If not for his and Randy's voices, the only sounds would be Luke's rasping breath and the slap of his shoes against the pavement. Were the others dead? The last thing Luke had seen as he crawled beneath the gunfire toward Randy's fallen body was Don lying glassy-eyed on the sidewalk, blood trickling from his mouth. And he'd left Vinnie inside the armored car, hiding behind a door and spitting bullets from a gun Luke hadn't even known he had.

Where had it gone wrong?

It began so perfectly. The armored car had arrived shortly after one. Don's sedative knocked out the drivers immediately, and he and Vinnie had tossed the unconscious men in back, then climbed in themselves to get the money. Don had thrown out yet another canvas bag when a dark sedan pulled up. Two men jumped out. One carried a machine gun, the other had a huge pistol.

At that very moment Randy drove around the corner. Heart jack-hammering, Luke waved him on. Instead, Randy brought the minivan to a squealing stop and leaped out, shouting, "Get in!" as he aimed a gun at the gunmen.

How had Randy gotten a weapon? "You were supposed to stay in the van," he now accused.

"Th-they was g-gonna kill you guys."

And they still might, Luke thought as a rush of pounding footsteps broke the stillness, followed by thuds that could easily be silenced bullets.

When Luke had snatched Randy from the ground, his first and only thought had been to run far and fast, get his cousin to safety. The full moon aided their escape, but now he realized it also made them easy targets.

They needed to hide. But where?

Just then they passed through an area free of overhead branches, and moonlight reflected off the ring Randy had found that afternoon, reminding Luke of the alcove. He veered off the main path and headed for it.

He hoped the idea hadn't come too late.

Uneven footfalls sounded behind him. Though his overtaxed muscles screamed, and stiffened even further in anticipation of a bullet in the back, he looked over his shoulder to gauge how much time they had.

Instead of the terrorists he'd expected, he saw Vinnie lumbering toward them under the weight of three large money bags. Their pursuers must have had a bead on Vinnie for a while, but they'd clearly lost him, because the gunfire had stopped. But Luke could still hear fragments of conversation. Was Vinnie crazy or something, lugging those bags with armed men hot on his tail?

"This way," he hissed, then forged onward, letting Vinnie fend for himself. If the guy valued money more than his own life, let him live with the consequences.

What seemed a lifetime later, Luke skidded through the narrow entrance to the alcove. Vinnie darted in behind him.

If all went well, they could hide here until the threat passed.

This place had been practically invisible in daylight, Luke thought. At night it would be impossible to find.

He clung to that thought.

Vinnie dropped the money sacks as carefully as if they were as precious as the cargo Luke carried. "What is this place?" He leaned forward, pausing until his breathing eased, then added, "We're like fish in a barrel here. You think this is smart?"

"Look, you got a better idea?"

Vinnie shook his head.

"Over there!" a man called out, his voice so clear it sounded as if he were standing right next to them. "I heard somethin'."

Luke eased to the ground. His arms and legs sighed as they were relieved of Randy's weight, but he barely noticed. The kid had grown quiet, too quiet. Blood covered the front of his white polo shirt, looking almost black in the moon's muted light.

Footsteps neared. Words came in unintelligible snatches, then grew clearer.

"I know I heard someone, Hub."

Hub? There was someone on the hit squad named Hub. Who were these guys? Luke pulled Randy closer to him, then watched in disgust as Vinnie pulled a gun from the pants pocket of his bogus uniform. Damn Vinnie! The son of a bitch had promised no weapons.

"I don't see anything," said a gravelly voice outside. Christ, you could pick that voice out of a crowd at the Met. Marco Gann! These _were_ Carmine Bescallia's hit men. Vinnie had stolen from the mob.

There was discussion, scuffling footsteps, but soon the voices grew more distant. When Luke could no longer hear anyone talking, he pointed to the money bags. "What were you thinking, pulling a heist on the mob?" he asked coldly. "That Carmine would let us get away with it? And what were you doing giving Randy a gun?"

"Kid needed to be able to defend himself," Vinnie muttered, shoving his weapon back into his pocket.

"And now he's shot. We wouldn't be in this mess if not for your bullshit."

"Least Randy's alive! Don's dead, and weren't for the kid the rest of us would be too."

"Thanks, Vinnie," Randy murmured.

"You okay?" Luke asked.

"Hanging . . ."

"Yeah, I see that." Luke looked at Vinnie. "He needs a doctor, man. Leave the money. It's all Marco wants."

"And our hides," Vinnie argued, appearing just as confused as Luke. Flaky even, which wasn't like him. The man had a cunning mind and always planned ahead. He'd have made it big in Carmine's organization if not for his reputation for backing down from a fight. "You think Carmine will forgive us for this? He'll never forgive us. Without this cash we got no chance."

"You got us into it!" Still, Vinnie's convoluted logic held a grain of truth, but Luke was more interested in an explanation. "You knew that was mob money. How come you don't have a contingency plan?"

"I didn't—Don said it was . . . Oh, Jesus, Luke. This is a friggin' mess."

A gurgling laugh left Luke's throat. "A *mess*? It's sure as hell more than a mess."

"I didn't know."

Luke waved his hands in disgust. "Sure you didn't."

A spasm shook Randy's body, so strong Luke felt it in his own gut.

"Luke . . ." The voice was reedy, frightening. "I want you . . . I want you to . . ."

Randy was pressing his hands together, squirming, trying to do something Luke didn't understand. Abruptly, the boy stopped fidgeting, and the next thing Luke knew a hard, cold object was sliding down his right-hand ring finger.

"I-I want you to have the ring," Randy said. "I'm g-gonna die, I kin feel it . . ."

"You're not going to die," Luke replied harshly, grabbing for the ring and trying to pull it off.

"Yeah, I might . . . You . . . you want me to s-say hello to Kevin when I get to heaven? You th-think I'll go to heaven, Luke, af-after what I done?"

"Dammit, Randy, you're not going to die! So take your ring back!" But the ring hung up on Luke's knuckle, and he twisted it furiously, trying to pull it free.

A crash shook the night air. The alcove turned as bright as day.

"God Almighty," Vinnie sputtered, pointing toward the space where the trees stood. "There's an opening outta here!"

"An angel's comin'," Randy said.

Although Randy's weight on his knees held him down, Luke struggled to turn away from the light and its accompanying ugly images and sounds.

Whirling lights—red, blue, and white. Sirens.
Squealing tires of cruisers slamming to a halt.
Shouting voices. His voice, yelling through the din.
"He's just a kid! Don't shoot!"

"Come on, Luke! Let's go!" Vinnie commanded, jumping to his feet and picking up his payload.

An instant later, though his eyes were still averted, Luke sensed that Vinnie was gone. He forced himself to turn, saw an arch of vibrating light silhouetting a landscape of lush green foliage and shimmering water. Vinnie stood on the other side, his movements urgent, his mouth uttering soundless words.

"It's true," Randy whispered. "They d-do come in light."

Dazed, barely able to keep his memories at bay, Luke picked up Randy. That familiar shiver skittered down his spine, a sudden knowing that by stepping through that arch he would unalterably change his life.

"There! Over there!" boomed Marco's deep voice from somewhere beyond the alcove.

Randy let out an anguished moan.

"You okay?" Luke asked softly.

Randy didn't answer.

"Noooooo!" cried his voice from the past.

Luke's shiver became a shudder. The hair on his body stood on end. That long-ago cry had done no good and would do no good now.

Ignoring all his inner signals, Luke shifted Randy over his shoulder and stepped through the pulsing gate.

*   *   *

Alarm horns woke Caryn from a dreamless sleep, and she shot straight up in her feather bed, dimly aware of the boom that always preceded the sentry's warning. The portal had opened. Travelers had breeched the forest wall. Repetitive blares of the horns informed her that there were three this time.

Flying out of bed, she raced to her wardrobe and pulled out a healer's skirt—one with deep pockets that would hold bandages and medicines—and slipped it over her shift. Forgoing a bodice because it would take too long to lace, she pulled on a tunic, belted it, then gathered her plaid and clipped it in place.

This done, she sat on the bench at the end of her bed and put on her boots, which were better for riding astride. As she tied up the lacings, her eyes grazed a tapestry mounted on her far bedchamber wall.

Woven with threads of brilliant color, it depicted the half-kneeling image of a man in full kilt. Supporting the limp figure of a wounded comrade, the warrior held a bloodied sword aloft and fiercely tilted his head to the sky. Above him hovered an injured dragon, its mouth open as if uttering a tortured scream.

Dark locks clung wetly to the man's square jaw, partially concealing a gash on his face. His wide brow shadowed dark, intense eyes that held no triumph. Instead, they seemed to bleed with an anguish matching that of the creature he'd so mortally wounded.

Beneath was a threaded inscription.

Sir Lucas, The Last Dragon Slayer.

Would this be the time? Would Sir Lucas return to save Lochlorraine as the legends foretold? Caryn's heart quickened at the prospect, just as it had on the day she'd found the work in a storage room.

Sir Lucas had slain Ormeskirk, the last of the dragons, ridding the world of this menace forevermore, but had lost his valued and unnamed comrade in the battle. Although the event happened before the world's years had even reached twelve hundred, minstrels had sang of it well into the last century.

Caryn's discovery of the tapestry revived the legend. If Ormeskirk had returned, the people concluded, then so would his slayer. The entire kingdom put their hopes on the hero's eventual appearance. An artist had even painted a fresco replica on the wall at the back of the great hall. But now, after twenty years in the bubble, with nearly a like number of travelers entering the realm and none of them the dragon slayer, most had given up hope.

Except Caryn. Each time the portal opened, she expected to see the heroic face of the man in the tapestry.

In little over a week, she and Ian would be feted for their joint birth dates, marking twenty years since Ian's experiment had torn them from their time and brought the monster to plague them. Soon after, Gregory died in a quest to kill the beast.

She'd had no wish to see her husband dead, but to Caryn's eternal shame, she grieved less than she did for the loss of her youthful freedom. Ian had no desire to rule Lochlorraine—the laboratory was his mistress and he labored day and night to reverse the damage he had done. He had named Caryn chamberlain of the castle and made her his ambassador to the tacksmen and clan chiefs who so despised her.

Undisciplined, headstrong, and prone to unwise speech, she had been ill-suited to the task. Had her concern for the servants and laborers—whom the lesser lairds were inclined to mistreat—not overridden her unbridled disposition, she would have quickly abdicated the duties.

Through hard lessons she'd changed. She'd learned to uphold the arrogant expectations of the chieftains while giving those of lesser station the kinder, more respectful treatment she'd observed at her father's knee in Invergair. By adding wisdom and restraint to her natural Campbell courage, she'd won the leaders over. Her rulings at a council were hailed as wisely. New methods of farming and animal husbandry, which she'd harassed Ian into developing, had brought prosperity to Lochlorraine.

As much, that is, as could be expected when living under the shadow of a dragon.

Giving her boot laces a final tug, she tied them, then gave one last look at the man who would come to redeem them. Color rose in her cheeks as she recalled her girlish fantasies. Sir Lucas would ride up Wizard's Spire on a great black stallion, cut off the monster's head, then return to lay it at her feet.

His declarations of love would cause her to swoon, and soon they'd adjourn to their marriage bed where he'd show her the delights bards sang of.

Even now, in the maturity of her years, passion

rose within her. She immediately chided herself for impure thoughts, then hurried to the chest where she kept her medicine pouch. Securing the pouch to her belt, she told herself that her foolish yearnings did not improve her husbandless state. As long as she dreamed about an immortal hero, she'd never accept an ordinary man as her mate. Moreover, she'd squandered time, and she was undoubtedly needed at the loch.

She hurried from her room and toward the stairs. At the main floor, she encountered Ian, who was ascending from the lower regions.

"Caryn," he called. "That blasted fool Chisholm gathered his soldiers and rode off without waiting for my instructions."

The Earl of Lochlorraine hurried toward her, his plaid in complete disarray. Tufts of his tawny hair sprouted from his head. Even now, as he skidded to a stop in front of her, he ran his fingers through the strands, creating more untidy cowlicks. But Caryn was accustomed to his lack of concern about personal appearance, and barely noticed his dishevelment. "These men have come from a future time." He paused to rub his chin and Caryn waited patiently for him to continue. "One or more may hold the knowledge that I need."

"The needle of your time compass rests on the future?"

"Aye. The years have reached two thousand. Can you imagine? But what excites me more is that finally we've lured a future-dweller into the realm. Surely they can impart wonders I have never dreamed about."

Ian continued speculating about the knowledge so near at hand, but Caryn barely heard him over her disappointment. So this wasn't the moment of the hero's return, after all. Sir Lucas would come from the past, not the future.

"Caryn!"

Several seconds passed before Caryn became aware that Ian knew she wasn't listening. With a mumbled apology, she gave back her attention.

"This knowledge must not be lost. The success of our mission depends on it. The travelers will be frightened and possibly hostile. Go. Keep Chisholm at bay."

" 'Tis where I was going," Caryn said.

And she could tarry no longer. Chisholm's rashness in battle was well known. More than one traveler had died under his sword.

A new alarm came from the tower. Three again.

"Six travelers!" Caryn exclaimed. "Never have we had so many."

"A rare opportunity," Ian agreed. "And I must speak to each of them."

Caryn gathered up her skirts. "I must hurry."

"Tell the captain that none of the travelers are to be harmed," Ian called as Caryn turned and rushed toward the great hall. "Inform him that it is my command."

Only with Chisholm would she need the power of Ian's authority, but Caryn was glad enough to have it as she pushed through the heavy castle doors and dashed to the stable. She'd ride her stallion without saddle, saving time, for she feared she'd be too late.

Even as she ran, her mind returned to the dragon slayer and her moment of unseemly lust. A useless fantasy, she thought. A folly, in fact. She'd never accept a man into her bed again. They had such a tiresome way of trying to rule a woman's life.

Chapter Three

"What the hell is this?" Vinnie asked in a hushed tone.

Luke only got blurred images—moonlight flickering inside rising waves, thatched roofs spilling smoke, a castle rising from rolling hills. Then a raspy voice intruded.

"Drop the money, Vinnie."

Vinnie spun around. Weighed down by Randy's limp body, Luke turned more slowly.

Marco stood in front of the quivering gateway with his two men. Although he was unarmed, his companions weren't. One man held a machine gun. The other, who made the small-of-stature Marco look like a pigmy, held a revolver of enormous proportions.

"You sonuvabitch," Vinnie snarled. "One of your flunkies killed Don!"

"The money, Vinnie."

"No way!"

"Ralph." Marco's tone was deadly soft.

The machine gun rose. Ralph fingered the trigger.

"Give him the money, Vinnie," Luke said.

"Hell, no. It's ours."

"Look, man," Marco said. "I'd kill you in a heartbeat, except I don't want to explain to Carmine how you turned up dead. But you don't hand over those bags, I'll sure think of something."

A rustling sound from a cluster of nearby cottages momentarily caught Marco's attention. He glanced in that direction, then returned his gaze to Vinnie.

"So what's it going to be, man?"

"*Tàbhachd!*"

The unintelligible cry arose from behind the nearest cottage. Hordes of men and women in tattered clothing streamed out, repeating the word at the top of their lungs. A few had ancient-looking guns, others swords, but most held axes, hoes, or pitchforks.

Luke hit the ground, bending to shelter Randy. Vinnie landed not far away and hunkered over the money bags in a manner that almost mocked Luke's protectiveness. Ralph seemed stunned. His machine gun hung loosely in his hands and his jaw went slack.

"Shoot, dammit!" When Ralph didn't respond to his shout, Marco grabbed the machine gun. It jammed on the first shot.

Apparently regaining his bearings, Ralph snatched the gun back from Marco, cleared the jam, then peppered the ground in front of the charging mob.

A man at the front fell. His companions retreated, and Ralph stopped shooting.

For a moment the night was still again.

The thunder of hooves broke the silence. From the hill above a troop of kilted men barreled down on them. Their mounts' swift legs ate up the distance, moving them closer and leaving behind the silhouetted castle. His mind whirling with astonishment, Luke stared at them blankly and tried to make sense of it all.

Then a woman rounded the curve of the castle wall. Red hair streaming behind her head like flames, aristocratic features sculpted by the moonlight, she wore a look of fierce determination that took away Luke's breath. So singularly intense was his reaction that for an instant, amid all the craziness, he failed to register anything else around him.

Then new sounds broke the spell.

Emboldened by the approach of the troops, members of the horde emerged again, clearly intent on rescuing their fallen friend. Ralph unleashed another volley of bullets. An explosive sound followed. Thick smoke clouded Luke's view. Burning chemicals assaulted his air passages. Coughing, he covered Randy's face to protect him from the fouled air.

At the same moment, Ralph roared in pain. "Shit! I'm hit."

Before anyone could react, a barn-sized man darted to Ralph's side and put a small knife to his throat. "Give it over," he growled, nodding at the machine gun. Another man disarmed Marco's second thug, and the rest of the tattered crowd surrounded them all. A skinny woman, who carried a torch in one hand and a pitchfork in the other, stood over Randy and Luke, appearing ready to jab at the smallest hint of rebellion.

Luke curved his shoulders to better shield his

cousin. Was the kid even breathing? There was so much noise he couldn't tell.

"Hang on," he whispered, then looked up at his captor. "He's hurt bad."

"Lady Caryn will tend to him in due time," the woman replied tersely. "Do not be makin' any trouble till then." She looked over at the man who'd captured Marco. "Bernie, what's we to do with these villains?"

"Hold 'em for the captain is the earl's standin' order."

"The earl's daft," said a second man. "Let's kill 'em and be done with it."

"None of that talk about our laird, hear me? It ain't fitting."

They argued among themselves in brogues so thick Luke could barely understand them, though the language was clearly English. Where had this band come from? They didn't even appear to be of this century. Their weapons were antiques, and by comparison to this horde, street people wore designer clothing.

He turned his eyes toward the flashing gate. On the other side was the world he understood. He had no idea what waited there. Cops. Carmine's hit men. Even prison. But it had to be better than this. Whoever these people were, he doubted they had a sterile bed sheet or skilled surgeon among them. No, this wasn't a hard choice. No matter what he'd face in New York City, passing back through the quivering gate was his only option. Since the woman was aiming a pitchfork at his head, the question was how.

Luke decided to wait for the next diversion. Judging by what had happened already, one would come in good time. He slid an arm under Randy's shoulders, then the other under his knees, readying himself for the first opportunity to escape.

At that moment a rider broke from the approaching troops.

"*Tàbhachd!*"

"Chisholm!" The call came from the redhead, who had easily caught up with the regiment and now rode at the front of the line. It was a clear demand to stop, but the man paid no attention. His kilt flapped and his tam rippled from the force of the wind, but he nonetheless managed to draw a sword even as he urged his animal on.

The time for escape had come. Luke rose onto his knees with Randy in his arms, preparing to stand.

"Dinna move!"

Sharp tines pressed against his chest. He froze, waiting for them to puncture his skin. The woman relaxed the pressure, but did not remove the pitchfork.

The horse skidded to a halt just feet away from Luke and Randy, spraying grass and dirt in every direction. The woman jumped away, taking her weapon with her. In the meantime, the fierce rider vaulted to the ground and bellowed, "Apprehend these scoundrels!"

The barn-sized villager stepped forward. "Beggin' your pardon, Captain Chisholm, but we already done it." He nodded toward Ralph. "Her lady's shot clipped this'n right good, giving us our chance."

Chisholm grunted in displeasure, then reached over his shoulder and stuck his sword in a scabbard. "Come close to missing him, she did. 'Twere me, I wouldna have missed. Just dumb luck she hit him at all."

The remaining troops reined in behind Chisholm's, with the redhead right behind. A torch sparkled within her catlike green eyes as she gazed down from atop her gigantic horse, and smoke still drifted from the small pistol in her hand.

"Nay, not luck, Captain. Practice." Her lilt was softer than that of the others, Luke noticed. Her pronunciation more precise. And, damn, close up she was even more magnificent. "I *meant* to hit his arm."

"That may be," the captain mumbled sullenly.

"It is. And do not again take it upon yourself to ignore my orders. I had my reasons, and they were not for ye to question."

"I didna hear you, Countess."

"Your deaf ear turns to me at most opportune times, is that not so?"

The captain returned her remark with a sour grunt, then moved off toward his horse. The lady gave his attitude no apparent notice as she directed her attention to the villager. "Well done, Bernie."

The big man flushed. " 'Twas only my duty, milady."

"Nonetheless, well done. Are any injured beyond the man I shot?"

"Arnie got hit by the spitting weapon. And methinks one of the travelers is hurt." Bernie frowned.

"What manner of weapons do these men carry, milady?"

"Wondrous and terrible creations from a time yet to come, which is why the earl wishes to speak with them."

The archaic phrases swirled around Luke's head, and he again found it hard to breathe, although he knew it wasn't only from the dust and disorientation. The redhead's proximity made his heart pound and he had no idea why. In her loose clothing she differed very little from the peasant-type women who milled around him. But there was power and contrast in her personality, and those green eyes blazed with vitality. What kind of woman was hard enough to shoot one man and chastise another, yet soft enough to praise a villager and ask about the injured? None in his experience.

His thoughts were interrupted by a high-pitched screech that came from the distance. He looked around him, trying to figure out where it had come from. He saw nothing, and when he turned back, he noticed several people looking toward the castle but none seemed startled by the sound.

Before he could speculate further, the skinny woman with the pitchfork suddenly shrieked, "Arnie! My Arnie is dead!"

She threw herself on the man who'd been hit by Ralph's gunfire, crying out in a guttural foreign language.

The redhead shoved her weapon somewhere deep in her skirts and leaped off her mount. She ran toward the wailing woman, gently pried her off the man's motionless body, then knelt to examine him.

"Can ye save him, Lady Caryn?" The woman twisted her apron anxiously, her face revealing to Luke that she already knew the answer. "Please save my husband. We got three wee bairns to feed."

Sadly, Caryn shook her head. "He's gone to God."

For a moment Arnie's wife was deathly still, then she lifted her head and emitted a keening cry. As the grief-wracked sound died on the wind, she whirled and pointed an accusing finger at Marco. "On the head of a *Daoine Shi'* I shall see this devil's spawn thrown in Lucifer's Window to be eaten by selkies."

One by one, like a row of falling dominoes, the members of the horde hushed. Ralph, however, merely clutched his wounded arm.

"What a da-ween shis?" he asked of no one in particular.

"Don't know," Marco replied disinterestedly.

"Hush!" a man commanded. Then he turned on the grieving widow. "What think ye, Naomi, to speak so heedlessly? 'Tis folly to call a Man of Peace by his true name."

"Go to the devil," Naomi spat back. Dismissing their censure, she turned from the crowd and sank down beside her husband. "I will prepare him for his rites, milady. Ye have other work to do."

Her soft sobs tore at Luke's heart, renewing his own fear for Randy. Already bent over, he turned his head and listened for breathing. There. Soft and irregular, but still there.

"Get your fucking hands off me!" Marco suddenly

growled, throwing off a man who held a long, thick staff. The staff came alive, twirling in the man's grip like a baton. The edge clipped Marco's chin and he staggered back.

Luke's diversion. He had to act quickly. Just as he reached his feet, Vinnie bolted for the gateway, dragging the three money bags behind him.

"Stop!" Chisholm ordered.

With all eyes on Vinnie, Luke wasn't even noticed as he made his own move toward the gate. He'd barely gone ten feet when Vinnie screamed.

Sparking pinpoints of light filled the arch. Vinnie threw himself at them, then ricocheted off the substance that now blocked their exit.

"No, no," Vinnie intoned leadenly. "No." Still clinging to the money bags, he pounded at the field with his fisted free hand. It penetrated, bounced back. Again he tried, with the same result.

And again.

For some reason the gate was closing.

"Oh, God," Luke whispered, filled with so much dread he almost doubled over.

Vinnie continued to pummel the force field, but each blow grew weaker. Chisholm was now nearby. Several soldiers had joined him. But apparently no one saw any reason to take action. With a final flare, the gate vanished and Vinnie's last blow struck the branch of a tree.

"Let me out," he babbled. "Let me out. Oh, God, please get me outta here. Please, please."

Off to the side, Marco and his men exchanged agitated words. Ralph tried to break away from the villager who was guarding him. Even as an ax handle struck his head, he struggled to escape.

Luke could barely accept what he saw. Vinnie never lost control, but clearly he was undone. And Marco's band was on the verge of losing it too. Luke couldn't let that happen to him. Randy—hurt, unconscious Randy—still hung on by a thread and someone had to take care of him. Which Luke would do. Somehow, some way, he'd keep himself together. It had to be done.

Vinnie pulled out his gun. "There's a way outta here!" he screeched, pointing the gun at Chisholm and the soldiers. "Show me where it is! Now!"

"There is no other," one of the soldiers said.

"Aye," said a villager.

"Lies!" Half-crazed, Vinnie waved his gun around. "You're all lying."

Aiming the gun at Chisholm's feet, he pulled the trigger. The man lurched backward as dirt and grass spit around him.

"Tell me," Vinnie demanded.

"There is naught to tell."

With that answer, Vinnie swung his gun from side to side, firing randomly, at no one, at nothing. Just firing.

"Don't, Vinnie!" Luke shouted.

Luke's words went unheeded. Lost in frustration and panic, Vinnie emptied his weapon into the ground. The crack of gunfire died, replaced by futile clicks.

Luke saw the exact moment that this fact registered

in Chisholm's mind. The man reached into the crook of his left arm and pulled out a small knife.

Torn between Randy's need for him and Vinnie's certain doom, Luke hesitated only a second. Letting Randy slide gently onto the ground, he leaped up and elbowed through the people in his way. None tried to stop him.

"Don't!" he shouted. "He doesn't know what he's doing!"

But with a few ground-eating steps, Chisholm was already there.

"Stop!" Caryn cried sharply. "The earl wants none of them harmed! He commanded it!"

Even as Caryn's warning left her mouth, a knife streaked across Vinnie's neck. A fountain of blood spurted from the cut.

When Luke got there, Vinnie was still standing, weaving back and forth, wearing a puzzled expression as he held his hand against the wound.

"Lay down," Luke instructed. Jesus, Jesus, Jesus. He'd known this guy since before he could remember. Their moms used to push their strollers in the park together. Sure, he'd purposely drifted away over the last decade or so, and he'd been mad enough to kill when he learned Vinnie had lied about whose money they were stealing. But this? No, never this.

"L-Luke?" Vinnie eyed him blankly. "I-I think . . . I think I bit it, man."

Luke knelt and pressed his hand against Vinnie's throat, trying to stop the blood, but, oh, Jesus, it just kept gushing out. Then Caryn was next to him, placing a pad over the wound, intoning something in that odd language Naomi had used.

A throb arose above one of Luke's eyes. His stomach churned. A whine assaulted his ears. His unseeing eyes saw images of flashing red, flashing blue, flashing white.

"Kevin . . ."

Caryn stopped her intonation and looked at him. "Is your kinsman not called Vinnie?"

"Vinnie, yes. And save him, please."

Caryn looked at the fallen man, then reached down and closed his eyes.

"What was that you were saying to him?" he asked.

She hesitated a second. "A Celtic prayer of deliverance. He's gone to God."

The man took a gulp of air, then pressed his stomach. A shiver overtook his body, although the night was comfortably warm.

He turned to meet her eyes. His were large and dark, set deep in the head. Soulful. And at this moment filled with great pain. Caryn's heart went out to him. "God?" he finally asked, his voice choking. "No God I'd ever go to would let something like this happen."

Someone behind them gasped, and meaning to comfort as well as chide, Caryn put a hand on his arm. "Sir, ye must not speak heresy even in such difficult moments."

He swung his head around, stared at the shocked and gaping faces, then returned his gaze to her. When he spoke, his voice was thick and hushed. "What is this place?"

The question always came, Caryn thought. She doubted this one was ready for the truth, but he'd already seen most of it for himself. "In Lochlorraine by the sea," she finally said. "On the western shore of Scotland."

Before he responded, two soldiers walked up. One bent to take Vinnie away, but Caryn's eyes remained on the dead man's kinsman. She could almost see the struggle within him, and suspected she knew that he would rebel with force even before he did.

"Don't touch him, you bastard!" he roared, dragging his friend's lifeless body into his arms.

A soldier drew his sword.

"Stop!" Caryn said. "As chamberlain for your laird I command you. The travelers must not be harmed."

Even as she spoke, the traveler rose on a single leg, then swung an elbow that struck the soldier directly behind the knees. The man's legs buckled and he tumbled, letting loose of his sword. Although the weapon grazed the traveler's cheek as it fell, he swung around without faltering, catching the other soldier mid-stomach. Then he swept up the sword.

The first soldier scrambled to his feet and drew a *sgian dubh* from its place beneath his arm. Waving the small knife, he said, "I dinna want to hurt you, man, but ye must give back the sword."

"Stay back!" Precariously poised on one bent leg, the traveler held his kinsman protectively in one arm. His damp, dark hair stuck to his skin and partially concealed the beads of blood seeping from the shallow cut on his cheek. Then he raised the sword.

Caryn gasped.

She wasn't given to swooning, in fact she never swooned, but suddenly her head felt light. The tapestry in her bedchamber had come to life before her eyes. Why hadn't she seen it before?

"What is your name, sir?" she asked in a voice close to a whisper.

The traveler regarded her as if he couldn't fathom the reason she had asked. Nor, apparently, could the onlookers, because their chatter instantly subsided.

"Luke," he replied. "Luke Slade."

Luke . . . Luke. Lucas!

"By the saints," Caryn said. "He is the dragon slayer."

Chapter Four

Luke's blood pounded in his temples. He had no idea why he'd committed this suicidal act. Vinnie was already gone. Nothing would change that. But Randy still needed him, and that alone was reason enough to survive.

The moment stretched. Around him, hushed voices mingled into a wordless hum. After Caryn had asked his name, people began staring at him and he didn't know why. Then the soldier lowered his knife and backed away. Luke let down the sword, prepared to lift it again if necessary.

To his astonishment, the soldier bowed. "Welcome, Slayer."

At that, the onlookers fell to their knees. "Sir Lucas. Sir Lucas. Sir Lucas," they chanted. "Hail to the dragon slayer come to save us!"

Marco, Ralph, and the big man with them remained standing. So did Chisholm, who'd been securing the locks on their chains. Caryn glanced disapprovingly at the captain, and taking note of it, he cuffed Marco in the head. "Kneel, knaves," he commanded loudly. "Pay homage to the dragon slayer."

Grunting, Marco sullenly sank to his knees, gesturing to the others to do the same.

"Christ, Marco," Ralph grumbled. "My arm'll hurt like hell when I try to get up."

"Just do it!"

"Dragon slayer!" The crowd broke into cheers upon cheers.

This was crazy. Luke was on the ground with his murdered friend in his arms, and these people were celebrating as if the whole bloody thing hadn't happened. Sadly, he lowered Vinnie onto the grass, then climbed to his feet and walked over to Caryn.

"My friend is dead, but my cousin still needs help. Can't you get them to stop this nonsense?"

Without agreeing or disagreeing, Caryn stood up and moved to the front of the crowd, where she raised her arms and asked the people to depart.

The cheering continued. If anything it got louder.

"Stop!" Luke finally demanded. "I'm not your dragon slayer. I don't belong here. I just want to take my cousin home."

His pleas had no effect.

Through gaps in the huddled crowd, he saw Randy stir. Dozens of kneeling people surrounded the boy, but no one noticed his suffering. What kind of skewed value system gave more importance to empty praise than to the pain-filled moans of a bleeding, half-conscious boy? Luke wondered as he shoved people aside to get to his cousin. Hands reached out as he passed, touching his cuffs, the hem of his jacket, impeding his progress. Repulsed and impatient, he shrugged them off.

Still standing in front of the throng, Caryn repeatedly asked for silence, but her influence, whatever it might be, seemed useless against this giddy hysteria.

Finally, Luke reached Randy.

As he crouched beside the kid, a few nearby chanters noticed and stilled their voices. Caryn's pleas grew more insistent, catching a greater number of ears. Soon the roar ebbed, leaving only the occasional cry. Eventually even these remaining celebrants lapsed into silence.

"Thank you for welcoming the dragon slayer so warmly," Caryn said. "But Sir Lucas is weary and his kinsman unwell. Please go back to your homes."

"Aye, we must give the man some peace," Bernie affirmed, rising from his knees. With unyielding insistence, he then started clearing the area of villagers. Soon, only Chisholm lingered, along with his soldiers and his prisoners. Caryn walked over and engaged him in muted conversation, and when she finally turned away, the captain ordered soldiers to lash Vinnie's and Arnie's bodies onto horses. When this was done, the column departed, but two soldiers stayed behind, although at a discreet distance.

"Bessy will see to your Vinnie's preparations," Caryn solemnly told Luke as she leaned over Randy and lifted his polo shirt.

Though he had no idea who Bessy was Luke nodded numbly. "Can you help Randy?"

Caryn examined the wound, then took a bandage out of her voluminous skirt and pressed down to stop the blood. Luke waited nervously, afraid to question too much, afraid to hear the answer. Finally, she stood. "Aye, I can help, but we must take him to the castle."

She walked over to get her horse. "We'll mount him on Neptune, for he has a most even gait."

Luke glanced at the monstrous animal.

"Thanks," he said as evenly as he could muster, then bent to pick up Randy. "I'll carry him."

"Ye'll carry him? Up the hill?" Her eyes widened in amazement. "I see I was not mistaken. Ye are the people's hero."

Luke had gotten his fill of this unwarranted adoration and the time it had consumed. While people were bowing to him like some pagan god, Randy had lost more blood.

"Don't count on me to slay any dragons," he said. "I watch out for myself, that's all. Just myself and nobody else."

"Bring hot water to the surgery," Caryn instructed the scullery maid who'd been waiting at the door. The girl nodded, handed Caryn a flickering lamp, then hurried away.

"This way," Caryn said to Luke, turning into a nearby hallway.

"Okay."

She had no idea what that meant, but since he followed her, she assumed it was an agreement. The two soldiers—assigned to her for life by Chisholm's orders, or so it seemed—fell in behind them as they headed for the apothecary.

She glanced briefly over her shoulder at the dragon slayer. He'd carried his kinsman all the way up the steep hill, and even now, as they made the twisting climb up the steep, narrow stairs, he refused assistance. As she observed the effort that carrying his kinsman cost him, she recalled what he'd said about watching out only for himself, and believed his words not at all.

By the saints, he was fine-looking. Tall, very tall. Of course, excepting the one with the gruff voice, his clansmen were all of uncommon height. But Luke was taller than the rest and glowed with the health of a well-bred stallion. Especially now, when his smooth skin glistened like morning dew beneath the flickering candlelight.

At the top of the stairs she paused and waited, then led him down a long hallway to the apothecary. The candles were guttering here, and she was glad she'd remembered to ask for the lantern.

As they walked, Luke studied the myriad artwork that hung on the walls. The faces of stern-looking, helmeted warriors and dour women in costumes of lace and velvet glared down at him. Nooks abounded, many guarded by full suits of armor. One held a vase that, if genuine, was most likely priceless.

"Here," Caryn said as they rounded the corner. She turned into a door, then moved aside to let him enter.

He dipped his head to keep from colliding with the lower than normal crossbeams, and when he looked up he felt like he'd entered King Arthur's realm. Logs blazed in a fireplace that occupied the entire far wall, and a long narrow table piled high with linens occupied the adjacent wall. Nearby sat a waist-high recliner carved in roughly the shape of a man. A hole had been cut in the headrest.

A row of cabinets covered the wall opposite the fireplace, some with doors of rippling, opaque glass that revealed bottles within. Lanterns sputtered on either side of the cabinets. In the center of the room sat another table, on which rested a mortar and pestle. Several ragged-edged books were piled beside them, and countless bottles occupied the far side.

As he took in the surroundings, Caryn sent the soldiers for buckets of hot coals.

"The apothecary and surgery," she then said to him, as if noticing his disorientation. "Bring your kinsman here." She picked up a linen sheet from the table near the fireplace and spread it across the wooden recliner.

Luke settled Randy gently into the chair, then stepped back while Caryn draped a rough wool blanket over the boy.

She forced a smile that Luke suspected was supposed to reassure him, but failed completely. The disinfectant smell that filled the room assaulted his senses, making him fuzzy-headed. Everything about this place was off—the dark, smoky patches on the walls, the unevenly cut beams traversing the ceiling, the slightly rancid odor of the burning candles—and contradicted his known reality. He felt as if he were trying to assemble a jigsaw puzzle with only half the pieces at hand.

"Now what?" he asked, a profound condensation of all his questions.

"My maid went to fetch old Bessy," Caryn said. "Both ladies will assist in the surgery, and we'll begin as soon as they arrive. Your friend is lucky to have a healer such as Bessy by his side. It bodes well for his recovery."

Luke glanced quickly around. "Surgery? You have only candlelight. What happened to your electricity?"

She looked at him blankly.

"You don't understand, do you?"

"Lord Ian has spoken of this electricity, aye, but none have it here, sir. Such modern accoutrements remain far in the future." She turned away, moving toward the row of cabinets, but kept him in her sight. "Although if he put his mind on it, I am quite sure our laird could conjure it up. How I wish he'd turn his attention to such matters, but—"

"Far in the future?" She'd touched on the conclusion Luke had been sidestepping. Part of his mind screamed to reject her words. What she was suggesting wasn't possible. But another part told him there wasn't any other answer. So he asked, dear God he asked, although he really didn't want to know. "What the hell is going on, Caryn?"

She flinched, broke eye contact, and opened a cabinet door. After lifting out a metal box, she moved to the table next to Randy's chair. "Your language is not fitting for decent company, sir." She hesitated, then added, "Furthermore, it isn't proper to address a lady by her given name on such short acquaintance, and even after time, not those of greater station."

Luke blinked, futilely wishing that when he opened his eyes he'd discover this had all gone away. There had to be an explanation. "Oh, I get it. You belong to one of the sects that rejects progress, like Quakers . . . or the Amish."

She gave a puzzled frown as hurried footsteps echoed in the hallway outside, growing nearer. He had little time to get his answers.

Randy groaned. Caryn put down the box and grabbed a linen.

"He's bleeding again." She removed the old cloth from Randy's wound and handed it to him. "Drop this in the bucket," she said as she pressed the fresh linen in place.

Luke saw the bucket, which rested under the head of the recliner, and let the bloodied bandage fall. It was red, fresh, and his head again spun with images of the past.

"Your answers will have to wait, sir," Caryn informed him, bringing him back to the moment. "We must do surgery immediately."

The soldiers returned with buckets of red-hot coals. Behind them were two women. One was old, small, and bent, and carried a bowl of eggs. The headpiece that concealed most of her face would have resembled a nun's wimple except for the color, which was bright blue. Dark, birdlike eyes scanned the room as she nodded to the other woman whose youth was made more apparent by the contrast.

The younger woman—undoubtedly the maid Caryn had mentioned—carried a kettle that billowed steam, and both women hurried to the narrow table and put down their burdens. Meanwhile, the soldiers arranged the coal buckets around the chair, leaving a wide span that permitted free access to Randy.

All of this was done without instructions.

"Did you treat the wounded prisoner's arm?" Caryn asked the older woman, who was gently easing Randy out of his shirt.

"Aye. 'Twas only bruised." The old woman chuckled. "That one has a mouth on him, he does, but he will live to do the devil's work again."

Caryn laughed, and inclined her head toward Luke. "As does our dragon slayer. Seems the language of their time is quite colorful indeed."

"Aye," said one of the soldiers with a smirk. "They could teach the rest of us a thing or two."

Bessy and Caryn laughed again, this time joined by the maid, who'd gone to the cupboards for additional items.

Okay, Luke thought. Let them laugh at his expense. His aim was Randy's welfare, not their undying adoration.

"Are you a doctor?" he asked.

Caryn shook her head as she replaced the blanket over Randy's still form.

"A nurse?"

"I am a healer." She plucked a woven cap from the table of linens. "Albeit it is not the most fitting skill for a lady, I was trained by Bessy, who is a master of the craft."

Bessy took no notice of the compliment as she methodically folded Randy's shirt and placed it on the table.

Luke frowned. "You're a New Ager?"

"I do not know of these New Agers, but I can assure you I am not of their clan." She folded her hair into the cap, then tied the strings beneath her chin. After tucking in the stray strands of her admittedly gorgeous red locks, she spoke again. "Perhaps we can talk of this later, when your kinsman is in better health?"

With that gentle rebuke, she turned away and opened the box. Candle and lantern light gleamed demonically off the variously shaped knives inside.

"You're planning to cut on him with those?" Luke took a step forward, reaching to still her hand. "I can't let you do that. You'll kill him!"

Her eyes flashed with sympathy, then hardened with resolve. "And should I not operate immediately, he will surely die. He cannot suffer further loss of humors."

Humors?

Blood, he quickly translated, remembering the soaked rag he'd just disposed of. Shit. What were his options? She was right. Randy wouldn't survive the night if he kept bleeding like that. Despite his misgivings—a word that didn't begin to describe what he felt about letting three women with questionable credentials operate in these unsanitary quarters—he remembered horror stories about guys having bullets dug out by back-alley doctors. Could this be any worse? At least the "doctors" seemed to care about the patient.

"All right," he said reluctantly. "Do it. But I'll be watching you."

"Ye will feel better about your choice later, sir, I assure you." She smiled confidently, then looked at the soldiers. "Gentlemen, lead Sir Lucas to his quarters."

Luke widened his stance as he turned toward the soldiers. "I'm not going anywhere, fellas. So stay where you are."

The men moved forward anyway. Luke looked at Caryn. "You want me out of here, then tell your men to kill me, because that's the only way I'm leaving Randy."

There was a long silence. The soldiers looked eager to answer his challenge. The old woman gazed at him with sharp piercing eyes as if she already knew the outcome. The maid gnawed on a knuckle.

A candle sputtered. One of the men coughed.

Caryn sighed heavily. "Very well, you may stay."

She came around to stand in front of him, her eyes filled with green fire. Close, very close. The scent of lavender tickled his nose. He could see each strand of hair that had already escaped her cap.

"But hear me, and hear me well. Do not interfere with this surgery. If ye utter so much as a word, I shall have the men drag you away and tie you to your bedposts. Do you understand me, sir?"

Chapter Five

"This place stinks!" Hub Barcowski complained as he stalked up and down the long room. "What the fuck is it?"

"Well, geez, Hub, I don't know," Ralph remarked. "Maybe a castle?"

"A new tourist attraction, you think?"

"Tourist attraction! For crissakes, Hub! You had any brains, you'd see we're not in Kansas anymore."

Hub took a menacing step forward. "Let me snuff him, boss."

Ralph shrugged his uninjured shoulder, giving Marco a he's-so-stupid look. The man's eye was beginning to swell and blacken from the blow to the head he'd taken from the ax handle, making him none too pretty.

Ugly sons of bitches, Marco thought, telling them both to shut up. "And stop pacing, Hub. You're getting on my nerves."

Hub obediently sank onto a mat. Half-disgusted, Marco watched the man pluck a piece of straw from the coarse fabric, then examine it as if he didn't know what to make of it.

"What a mess," Hub finally said. "Cops are probably everywhere. Money's gone. When Carmine finds out what we done, we're dead meat. And what that guy in the fairy skirt did—"

"The muscles that guy's got, I wouldn't say that to his face," Ralph interjected.

"He slit Vinnie's throat like it was nothin'."

"You done worse, Hub."

"Yeah . . ."

Marco stared at Hub, wishing he'd been the one hit instead of Vinnie. Vinnie had smarts, at least, while Hub's brains fairly well resembled the straw in his hand. Ralph was better, but when he got with Hub it was as if stupidity was contagious.

Their bickering annoyed Marco. He was trying to work out what to do next and was already distracted by his throbbing jaw, which felt like a little man inside was pounding to get out.

The room they were in was long and narrow with lumpy, soot-blackened pads scattered throughout. With a shudder of revulsion, Marco collapsed on one that looked cleaner than most. The filthy thing reminded him of the unwashed sheets in the hovel where he'd grown up. The shadowy light of the smelly candles on the wall brought to mind hallways filled with broken and burned-out lightbulbs. So did the smells that crawled along this mausoleum's cold stone floor.

He struggled to block his surroundings out, a skill he'd developed to the nth degree. Unfortunately it was failing him when he needed it the most.

Marco had always lived by the slogan "Never let

'em see you sweat." But he sure wasn't living it now. He was dripping with the stuff in this airless room. Just as he had done during the ass-chewing he'd received from Carmine Bescallia, an event that now seemed a lifetime away, although it had actually taken place just that afternoon.

When Marco had realized the don was on to him— knew about the skimming of drug and prostitution money—his armpits had flooded with sweat. Heat had flushed his face. He'd been put on the list, he'd known it then, and thought he'd be leaving the old man's mansion in a vertical position.

But Carmine had let him go. At least for the time being, which was all Marco had needed. His scheme, long in the planning, would hatch that night.

God, the deal had been sweet. Feed a couple of patsies false information. Let them carry out a major theft of Carmine's treasure chest, then use those funds to topple that dinosaur.

Marco had planned it down to the second, covered all the details. Vinnie, Don, and the others would rob the armored car while Marco waited not far away with Ralph and Hub, moving in to take it only after the bags were unloaded. What could they do? Complain to the cops? To Carmine? If everything had turned out the way it was supposed to, Marco would be laughing even now. A few weeks up the road, he'd be running old Bescallia's empire.

So how had they landed in a castle hidden inside Central Park?

Marco briefly reviewed it all, hoping to discover where it turned bad. But he fell into a series of if onlys. If only that kid hadn't jumped out, firing a peashooter of a twenty-two that couldn't harm a flea. If only Hub hadn't fired back. If only Vinnie hadn't also had a gun and been filled with life-risking determination to keep the money. And where had Luke Slade come from? He wasn't part of the original plan. The guy wasn't in the same league as Vinnie and Don. Slade almost worked *inside* the law. You wouldn't figure him to be part of a robbery.

Hell, he thought, this is doing no good. The past wouldn't change, no matter how much Marco wanted it to. For once in his life, straw-brained Hub was right. They were in deep shit. Unless the armored car drivers just got up and drove away, the police would be called. Either way, Carmine would learn that his funds had been hit, and Marco's sudden absence would instantly put him on the suspect list. The old don wouldn't even think about Vinnie or Don. Those guys were small-time, just tiny cogs in Carmine's immense organization.

But Marco had been the don's right hand, one that had come damned close to being cut off.

A shrill scream made him jump, another sign he was losing his edge. Collecting himself, he settled back onto the pad. "What the hell was that?"

Hub was already at one of the high windows, trying to reach up and see outside. "I dunno. Sounds like something dying." He turned back to Marco. "I heard the same noise down below. Didn't you hear it?"

Marco nodded. None of the residents had seemed

to think the cry was unusual so he'd forgotten about it. "Probably some wild animal."

"In Central Park? We're a long way from the zoo."

Thinking that was a matter of opinion, Marco laughed bitterly.

"What's that, boss?" Hub asked.

"Nothing."

The men resumed their nitwit conversation, with Hub trying to talk Ralph into lifting him up so he could pull aside the filthy canvas window covers and look out. Ralph whined about his arm and said Hub's weight would break his back.

What difference did it make if they looked out? They were trapped in a stinking ward. Their escape totally depended on the goodwill of the people who'd put them here.

Marco couldn't wrap his mind around their situation. As a kid, he'd loved Sherlock Holmes books and had poured over them by flashlight under his covers. Now he recalled a line about eliminating the impossible. If you did that, Holmes said, whatever remained, no matter how improbable, must be the truth.

He swallowed the scoffing sound that immediately rushed to his mouth. Christ, in this instance the improbable *was* the impossible. No way they could have traveled in time and space.

But those people. Their clothes. Their weapons. Even the way they talked. Crazy as it seemed, it was as if this were Scotland. But he'd been to Scotland,

and kilts aside, the average guy didn't dress or act like that.

The possibility boggled his mind and he let it go, turning his thoughts to the problem of getting free.

Slade. He was the key. Marco had met Luke at one of Carmine's many command performances—a wedding, maybe, or possibly the christening of a new great-grandbaby—Carmine was big on family. All he'd heard before then was that the guy ran Gaskin's Garage and the high-end chop shop in the catacombs beneath it. Did a fine job, too, according to Carmine. Top-notch work. And he also managed to turn a profit with the legit streetside shop.

Until that meeting Marco always figured Slade as a grunt ex-con—greasy fingernails, Bronx accent, the whole works—so he'd been surprised to discover an educated, well-groomed man who knew how to say the right things at weddings and christenings.

What's more, those moves Luke had pulled on the soldiers had been slick. Stupid—after all, he could've been killed for a guy who was already dead—but still slick. Yet as much as that impressed Marco, it was the following event that sparked his interest.

Those people got on their knees and worshiped Slade.

Dragon slayer, Dragon slayer.

Did these folks really believe in dragons? Although the memory of those eerie wails provoked a moment of uneasiness, he threw that question in the trash along with the one about where he was. They'd gotten into this place, there had to be a way out. And

Slade had somehow earned a status that might be
the ticket.

Marco had to win Slade over.

Considering he'd been party to shooting at the
man, it wouldn't be easy, but the details would come
to him. All he had to do was sleep on it. Something
he planned to do right now.

"You guys wanna talk, fine," he said, softly rubbing his aching jaw. "But keep it down and blow out
all but one of those candles so I can sleep." He
started to roll on his stomach, but the smell of the
mat made him stop. "Tomorrow's gonna be hell."

"Tonight already is, boss," Hub replied.

The second smart thing Hub had said that night.
Maybe it was an omen.

"The ball is deep," Caryn murmured as she spread
Randy's ragged flesh in search of the bullet.

"Aye," replied Bessy, who swabbed away Randy's
blood as Caryn worked. "We must hurry lest he
bleeds to death."

Luke's overworked muscles complained, and he
shifted his weight to ease his soreness. Between the
blazing fire and buckets of hot coal, the room had
become too warm for his sports coat, so he'd taken
it off and hung it on a peg near the door, trying to
ignore the dense, dark stains of Randy's blood.

It was on his hands, too, embedded in the creases,
under the nails. He wanted to wash it off, but he
saw no signs of running water, and Randy's care
totally occupied these women.

He paced the floor, unable to ignore the conclusions that leaped to his mind from observing the lack of modern conveniences. Going back in time only happened in the dreams of quantum physicists or in the fertile imaginations of science fiction writers. There had to be another explanation, but now wasn't the time to ask.

He found their methods fascinating. While Bessy and the maid had washed Randy's wound with a soap that reeked of lye, Caryn had sharpened one of the razors, then poured wine over it, doing the same with a set of tongs that had also come from the box. When she then poured more of the liquid on Randy's shoulder, Luke realized it was a crude form of sterilization.

Caryn inserted the tongs into Randy's wound, starting a fresh gush of blood. Although he had no doubt Caryn would keep her word to eject him if he protested, Luke could barely restrain himself. Randy, didn't react, however, and Luke relaxed, comfortable that the kid wasn't feeling any pain.

In instant contradiction, Randy moaned and stirred. The young maid immediately stepped forward and placed a wet sponge over his face. Soon Randy returned to slumber.

Luke wondered what was on the sponge. Opium, perhaps, and it did the job, which gratified Luke. This was one of the few times the poor kid ever had a break. Brain-damaged at birth, motherless before he could talk, and raised by a bastard who loved his bottle more than his son, Randy's life had been hard. Now, not even twenty-four years old, he was in a candlelit room being cut on by a woman who behaved as if she lived several centuries in the past.

Still, it couldn't hurt that Bessy crooned over Randy in their foreign language, which he was beginning to think was Gaelic. Prayers, he supposed, something you wouldn't see in any operating room in New York or Jersey.

Soon Caryn had the bullet out. Holding it in the jaws of the tongs, she studied it for a moment.

"How could a thing so small cause so much damage?" she asked of Bessy. The old woman shrugged and Caryn let her question drop, disposing of the bullet in a pan provided by the maid.

He resisted the urge to explain about the power of velocity, forgetting he'd even wanted to when Caryn started threading a needle. By God, she was going to stitch Randy up!

She worked for nearly half an hour, and Luke wondered how she endured standing on the hard floor, bent over, making impossibly small stitches in scant light.

At one point, Bessy said, " 'Tis remarkable, milady, that you stitch the wound so cunningly when even wee Sally McCullough surpasses ye in needlework."

Caryn only smiled and snipped yet another thread. As she worked, the young maid broke the eggs Bessy had carried in. Separating them, she dropped the whites in a bowl, then whipped them into a froth. Finally the wound was closed, and the maid handed the bowl to Caryn, along with a small brush that she'd dipped in a cup of wine. Caryn lathered Randy's wound with the mixture.

When she then turned away from Randy, the young woman held out a bowl of hot water so Caryn could wash up. As her hands emerged, a towel was provided. "Thank you, Nancy," she said, then turned toward Luke. "The surgery was a success. By dawn he should be taking fluids. He will mend well unless a fever comes."

She dried off with the towel, gave it back to Nancy, then walked toward Luke. "Come," she said. "Bessy and Nancy will dress your kinsman's wound and see him put to bed."

"Randy," Luke said.

"Pardon?"

"Randy. That's his name."

She glanced back at the sleeping patient. "A fine name for a hearty lad. He is most hale of body. For which we must be grateful, taking into account the graveness of his injury."

"But he'll be okay?"

"It's in God's hands."

"God," he repeated dully. "Sure. I'd still feel better if he had a good dose of antibiotics in him."

"Antibiotics? Another of your curious words. At least this one is fit for a lady's ears." She regarded him with those green eyes. They were soft now and almost Kelly green, where in anger they became the color of jade. He smiled at her. She smiled in return. "Come. 'Tis almost dawn, but surely you still have questions. Lord Ian can answer them better than I. He is up and about at all hours—none can ascertain his schedule—but methinks we'll find him in his laboratory."

* * *

They traveled down the twisting stairwell deep into the castle. Although Luke saw lanterns here and there, they had been snuffed, and the only light came from candles mounted in sconces on the wall. Gone were the portraits, the pretty vases, and the statues. The walls seeped brown dew and smelled of raw earth.

"In here," Caryn said, walking through a high door-way.

Luke followed, then stopped to look around. From this vantage, the ceiling went up farther than his eyes could see, and he tilted back his head to take it all in.

He'd thought he'd already lost the ability to be amazed, but the pulleys, boxes, gears, and dials that occupied the room caused him to gape. Cables ran everywhere, converging on a sunken area that contained an enormous centrifuge. What purpose the centrifuge served, Luke could only guess, but judging by the enclosing rail that discouraged casual touching, its inventor valued it highly.

"What did you say this Ian does?" he asked.

" 'Tis awe-inspiring, is it not?" Caryn's smile held fondness. "The earl is an alchemist, a man of science, and I do not pretend to understand what he does in these nether regions."

Luke was about to ask more question, but just then he noticed a man working under lantern light at a tall book stand. Hands outstretched, the man turned away from the volume he'd clearly been studying and walked toward Luke. "Ah, our guest."

This wasn't a tall man—he probably topped Caryn

by only a couple of inches—but he exuded a presence that filled the cavernous room. He smiled in welcome, his hazel eyes twinkling, and looked no less delighted to see Luke than if he'd been a beloved son who'd returned from a war. Luke shook his hand.

"It's a pleasure to meet you, Ian."

Caryn gently jabbed him. "*Lord* Ian. And you're obliged to bow."

"Nonsense, Caryn," Ian responded. "This man is a peer and may address me informally."

Caryn raised her eyebrows, then said, "Then please allow me to present Sir Luke Slade."

"We have much to talk about, Luke Slade." He glanced at Luke's left hand, then lifted it and examined the ring Randy had put there earlier. "An interesting piece."

"Aye," said Caryn, her voice sounding strained. "Most interesting."

"Thanks, but it's really not much." Luke glanced around, fascinated by the contraptions that filled this enormous room. "Interesting work, you must do."

Ian beamed. "Allow me to show you, sir."

He steered Luke to the centrifuge, which he called a gyroscope, and explained how magnets sped its rotation. Next, he showed Luke a compasslike gauge, which he said measured time. Fascinated, Luke's fatigue lifted, and he asked a number of questions that led to the final obvious one. "What are you trying to accomplish?"

"Accomplish? Why, man, I thought you understood. I'm trying to control movement through time."

Time travel? Luke's interest vanished. "Look," he

said, as courteously as he could muster, "I'm tired, but I have lots of questions about how I got here. Could we sit somewhere and talk?"

"Certainly," Ian replied. "Forgive me. I should have thought."

Caryn steered them to a sitting area off to the side, which had a fireplace bigger than Luke's apartment back home, and offered him a high-backed chair. Although the fabric was damp and hadn't been improved on by its exposure to sooty candles and lamps, Luke took the seat without a second thought. Ian and Caryn went to the facing settee.

As soon as Luke sat, weariness overcame him. He leaned back. The fire snapped, spilling warmth his way, and he almost succumbed to the urge to close his eyes.

"Ye seem very tired, Sir Luke," Caryn said, looking concerned. "Could this conversation not wait until the morrow?"

"I'm okay." Luke straightened up and rubbed his neck. "I have a million questions, but the first ones are where are we and how do we get out of here?"

Ian and Caryn exchanged glances.

"Perhaps after ye rest," the earl offered.

"No," Luke said, more harshly than he'd intended. Another look passed between the pair.

"Ye are in Lochlorraine," Caryn finally replied.

"So you told me. Forgetting how crazy I'd be to believe I walked out of a park in New York and into Scotland, let me . . . let me rephrase . . ." Suddenly he couldn't find the words. If he let them out, what then? Would that make him certifiable? He leaned forward urgently. "What I'm trying . . . What I'm—oh, hell, am I still in the twentieth century?"

Caryn leaned forward and took his hands. She stroked the ring on his finger, then lifted her head. " 'Tis the twelfth of May, sir, in the year of our Lord sixteen hundred and ninety-two. And we *are* in Lochlorraine." She hesitated, as if searching for words. "But we are not in Scotland."

"We're adrift, if you will," Ian continued, "in a bubble of time and place that floats through the eons and makes chance stops at this port and that."

Luke tried hard to reject this news, but in his heart he knew it was true. Extracting his hands from Caryn's loose grip, he massaged the spot between his eyebrows. The fire snapped again; a log crashed through the slats of the grate. But not even the renewed warmth could take away the chill in Luke's body.

"Sixteen ninety-two," he repeated dully. "Okay, okay." He leaned back in the chair again, his weariness painful. "So how do we get back?"

Ian shifted position, provoking a rustle of fabric. Caryn stared at Luke, a shimmer in her eyes.

"Ye cannot, sir," she answered. "Once a traveler passes through the portal, there is no return."

Chapter Six

Luke shook his head, his dark eyes blazing.

"Look," he ground out. "I've been chased and shot at. I saw my friend murdered; saw my cousin operated on under conditions that made me sick. Everything that's happened in the last hours defies belief, but don't expect me to buy this bullshit." He stood up, rubbing his forearms, which Caryn noticed were covered with gooseflesh. "I'm tired," he said. "I need to sleep. And when I wake up tomorrow I want real answers."

"Sir," Ian exclaimed. "Your statements alarm me. Surely the learned men of your century have solved the riddle of time."

"No, they haven't."

Ian's shoulders sagged under the blow of Luke's answer. He opened his mouth as if to speak, but seemed unable to find the words. Caryn's heart went out to him, and she took his hand in hers, hoping to ease his pain.

"Leave him be, Ian," she said. "He is weary to his soul. We all are."

Aye, it was true, for both men were pliant and willing, permitting Caryn to whisk Luke from the laboratory and leave poor Ian to his grief. She summoned Nancy, asked that she fetch a manservant, then gave instructions on an urgent task that the man must carry out before leaving Luke's room. 'Twould be easy enough to accomplish, Caryn felt, considering Luke's battered emotional and physical state.

Then she led Luke to a guest bedchamber, asking if he wanted something to eat. He shook his head and told her he just needed rest.

Caryn was also tired. First light was already filling the windows, leaving scant few hours to sleep before it was time to check on Randy's welfare. The hours following surgery were always the most dangerous, and she dared not stay away too long. But as badly as she yearned for bed, she still waited until the servant emerged from the room.

"The slayer seemed none too pleased with my presence," the man said, handing Caryn the ring. "Indeed, he appeared most unfamiliar with our nightly routines."

"Not uncommon with travelers," Caryn replied distractedly, staring down at the trinket in her hand. Such mischief it caused, and she was tempted to throw it in the garderobe. If the act wouldn't cause Ian such distress, she would do it in the blink of an eye.

The man waited expectantly, Luke's bloodied clothing draped over his arm. Caryn told him to take them to the washerwomen, and when he'd scurried out of sight she put the ring in her pocket, then headed for the stairs.

She descended with leaden steps, feeling careworn and faintly dishonorable. Though it no doubt came to less than an ounce, the object in her pocket weighed her down. Heavier still must weigh the dragon slayer's cares. One of his clansmen lay dead, the other hovered very close. And he had yet to accept his fate.

She'd always pitied these travelers. It had been dreadful, being unmoored from time, but the original inhabitants of Lochlorraine had at least remained with their people. These others were torn from their homes, dropped in a far-off land in a far-off time. It always took weeks, sometimes months, for them to grow accustomed to their new surroundings.

In many ways Luke Slade was different from previous travelers, but in this respect he was the same.

After briefly dozing off, Luke woke up with Caryn's and Ian's words parading through his head, and found himself unable to fall back asleep despite his intense fatigue.

He'd used the last of his energy fighting off the blasted manservant, who'd been intent on undressing and redressing him as if it was a duty. Eventually he'd kept the man at bay by obediently removing his jewelry and stripping down to his skivvies. He then donned a long flowing shirt to "protect" him from the night air and climbed into the high soft bed.

This seemed to satisfy the servant, who then busied himself with some unseen tasks before finally leaving. When the door clicked shut, Luke removed his briefs, but having no idea who might creep into his room while he slept, he left on the shirt. He'd fallen off immediately, only to be awakened by this troubling replay of his conversation in the laboratory.

A person should be able to trust his five senses, but Luke's were continually affirming Ian's and Caryn's assertions, even as his mind cried out that their claims were impossible. Furthermore, he refused to accept that there was no way out of this place.

But what if they were right? What if this world was his future? Luke unconsciously shook his head. He didn't believe in divine retribution, but if it existed he'd brought it on by agreeing to an act that violated all of his values.

Which was a bitter pill to swallow. Although nobody would believe it, he'd never committed a crime until after he'd been released from prison. Part of him believed he still hadn't. True, running a chop shop was as illegal as it got, but he didn't steal the cars, he just rebuilt them. He did it well, too, made sure all his employees did the same, and because of his reputation for fine craftsmanship most of the vehicles that came his way were high-powered high-dollar sports models.

Honest work that he enjoyed, and it gave him an illusion of respectability that he sometimes bought into himself.

Well, he thought, giving out a bitter laugh, there'd be no further worries about self-deception. If any of it was going around, it came from the inhabitants of this scrambled, cockeyed land. It was just him and

Randy now. For the time being he'd concentrate on keeping the kid safe and finding a way back to New York. In fact, he'd go right now to check on Randy's condition, then start hunting for a way out.

He'd get up in a minute. Just as soon as his limbs stopped aching. This decided, he shifted on the pliant, yielding bed and adjusted his nightshirt. Just another minute. One minute more, then he'd get up.

Before even a second had passed, he drifted off again.

Ian was still on the settee when Caryn entered the laboratory. Elbows on his knees, head in his hands, he stared into the flames, waiting a long time before he looked up. "Ye retrieved the ring?"

"Aye." Caryn removed it from her pocket, glad to be relieved of the burden.

"Place it with the philosopher's stone, if you would." She walked to the book stand, glancing at the drawings resting on its slanted top before opening the drawer beneath. The tangle of lines, circles, and numbers that Ian recorded on his parchments never failed to befuddle her, and she frequently wondered how he managed to turn his lofty thoughts into these symbols. But not this night. Her thoughts remained occupied with Ian's obvious disheartenment. The traveler's words had punctured his hopes.

She dropped the ring beside the innocuous stone that had brought them all to ruin, thinking that this, too, had been a disappointment to Ian. He'd originally embarked on his search because he believed the stone would turn base metal into gold. Its only magic, it seemed, was to open the portal to other times, an end that Ian hadn't intended. Nor had God, at least in Caryn's estimation.

Closing the drawer, she returned to the fireplace and sat in the chair. "Each time you leave the ring out there"—she moved her arm in an arc meant to encompass the bubble—"I fear it will be lost to us."

"No matter. We'll make another."

"Aye, but Bessy grows older with each passing day, and she alone inscribed the runes and gave the blessing. How does the ring do its work? Is it science or Bessy's magic?"

Ian gave a bitter laugh. "I know only that the portal opened after she wrought her craft. Her method, as ye well know, is unknown to me."

Caryn leaned forward and took his hands in hers. "I plead with ye, Ian, do not bring more travelers into the realm. It does no seeming good."

Ian shook his head. "We cannot stop just because we haven't met with success so far. All great achievement is preceded by many failures. But I well understand how heavy it weighs on you. Each time I hear the portal crash open, my heart leaps. Finally, I think, at long last, *this* traveler will hold the secret to our return."

"But if the ring is lost, we'll be unable to leave the bubble when you discover the means of our return to Scotland."

"A more unlikely occurrence every day," he replied harshly, his gaze drifting back to the fire. "Luke Slade's report is the heaviest I've had to bear. If men three hundred years ahead have not unraveled this problem, what hope is there for me?"

"But he's the dragon slayer. Finally the realm will be freed of Ormeskirk. That alone is cause for rejoicing."

"Men of science have little faith in legends, my dear."

"Ye are not alone in your lack of faith. Until this evening, it appeared that only I held fast to the legend's promise. And if he is not the one . . ." She let her gaze follow Ian's and come to rest on the flames. "From the depths of my heart, I wish we could send the travelers back when we learn they can't provide what we need. Their pain and confusion are so great. 'Tis so cruel to keep them here."

A look of irritation flashed across Ian's face. He leaned against the back of the settee, pulling his hands from Caryn's hold. "Send them back, aye," he said sardonically. "Let them tell their stories and be thought mad, or worse, believed. Can ye not see what damage this knowledge could do to all of time, Caryn? Can you not see? I meddled enough during my search for the stone. I will not let my work interfere with the greater scheme of things again."

Caryn nodded. She understood her brother-in-law's remorse. She herself felt some of it. For even as she pled, she was willing to sacrifice a fine man— one who cared so deeply for his kinsmen that he'd risk his life to protect them—to the better good of the kingdom. What hypocrisy. Yet it could not be helped.

She allowed the silence to stretch for a time, then

introduced the matter of Chisholm. She told Ian of the death of Luke's comrade.

"Ye relayed my command that none be harmed?"

"Nay, not at the time," Caryn said, swinging her head. "All appeared under control, so the man's outburst surprised us."

"But the traveler fired his weapon?"

" 'Twas only his frustration. He aimed the gun at no one."

"Still, the captain did his duty." Ian looked as though this last burden would bring about his end. "Chisholm is a buffoon, 'tis true, but his loyalty is beyond question, and no others have the skills to keep the warriors in hand."

She'd lost. Chisholm would go without reprimand. Accepting this, Caryn stood. She leaned over and kissed Ian's forehead. "Sleep," she urged. "All things look better when ye've rested well."

"The night is gone." His gesture took in the thin streams of light seeping through cracks in the mortar. "You sleep, milady. But I have much to ponder and the day starts anew. I must not let it go unused."

As Caryn walked away she heartily wished Ian would turn from his time mechanism and devise a method of thwarting the beast, then her spirits immediately lifted. Sir Lucas was here. He'd rid the realm of the dragon, bring peace to the land. The golden days of Lochlorraine would begin.

Concealing the means of his escape was a small sin when compared to this larger reward. Truly it was.

*   *   *

Randy! Where was Randy?

Luke's eyes snapped open as he bolted upright, his thoughts consumed with his cousin's welfare. His clothes weren't in plain sight, so he climbed out of bed to search for them. The huge cabinet that overpowered one wall was probably a wardrobe, so he went there first, but found it empty. On the opposite wall was the waist-high stand where the servant had lingered the night before. A large metal bowl and pitcher sat on top, and a chamber pot was tucked into a recessed lower shelf, leaving no room for additional storage. Next to the stand was a chest of drawers.

It was between these two items that Luke found his shoes and socks. Further searching revealed that his jacket, slacks, and shirt were not in the room, but finding them would have to wait. He'd have no peace of mind until he made sure Randy was all right.

After making hasty use of the chamber pot, he slid his bare feet into his shoes and hurried out the door. Soldiers stood on either side of it.

"Where's my cousin?" he demanded of the man to his left.

The man looked at Luke, then at his companion, an odd expression on his face. The other man's gaze flickered over Luke's body, then quickly moved away.

"Well, where is he? My kinsman," he added, thinking the men might not understand.

"The Lady Caryn kept him in the apothecary." A gesture to the right accompanied this information.

Luke rushed off in that direction.

"Sir," one soldier said. "You mustna roam the halls dressed in only your shirt."

Luke hesitated, looking down. His shirt was longer than their kilts and he'd worn bathing suits that showed more than this, so he shrugged off the warning and hurried on.

Unclear about how to find the apothecary, he tried every door he passed. Some were locked, others held odd bits of furniture, while others appeared to be bedrooms.

Finally he found it.

He stormed through the door, clearly startling Caryn, who was sitting on a low stool beside a narrow bed. Vaguely registering her presence, he rushed to Randy's motionless form.

"Sir," Caryn said, her voice slightly alarmed. "You canna be here wearing only your nightshirt."

Her words seemed little more than meaningless sounds to Luke. Randy was still, too still, and his thick blanket so closely resembled a shroud that Luke felt compelled to pull it back.

He let out a strangled cry.

Dozens of long, dark shapes pulsed on Randy's unbandaged shoulder. Luke stifled a gag and forced himself to pluck one off. Turning, he hurled it toward the wall, then reached for another.

Caryn flew off her stool and rushed toward the fallen abomination.

"Stop," she commanded. "Stop immediately."

Her voice held such authority Luke hesitated.

"Sir Luke," she said sternly. "Ye must not pull the leeches off, for they are most difficult to get in

Lochlorraine. Your kinsman's wound is grievous, and his recovery depends on the proper cleansing of the blood."

"But bloodletting's barbaric!"

"Barbaric, nay. Some speak against it, but none have found better ways to ward off fever." She bent over and deftly lifted the fallen insect off the stone floor, leaving behind a streak of bright red blood.

Luke's stomach rolled. Again, he reached for Randy's shoulder. It made his skin crawl, but he'd get those things off no matter what it took.

"I said stop!" A basin sat on a nearby stand, and Caryn dropped the leech into it, then squeezed between Luke and the bed. "The ball severely injured Sir Randy's shoulder and his health hangs by a thread. I see you are worried, but I am a trained healer and know what must be done." She half turned to pull Randy's covers back in place. "He must not take a chill. In his frail state, it can be very dangerous. This is partly your doing," she added, moving back to face him. "Had ye not failed to protect the boy, he would not require my services."

"Failed to . . . Failed to protect him?" Her accusation hit him like a slap in the face, and brought to mind his mother's constant expression while he was waiting for trial. Although she didn't say the words, he'd heard them clearly: *You didn't watch out for your little brother.*

Lights flashed in his head—blue, red, white.

"Well, I'll protect him now," he said harshly, pushing the memories away. "I'll start by making you tell me how we can get out of here."

He took a threatening step, narrowing the small space between them. She backed up, bumping into the bed frame, and although she showed no trace of fear her eyes widened in surprise.

"I do not know how," she said sadly. "There is no way."

No, she wasn't scared. Even though he towered over her with a face filled with wrath, she wasn't scared. Her courage made him feel ashamed.

What was he planning to do? Hit her? He'd never struck a woman in his life. Not after the many times he'd seen his own mother cower under his father's beatings. He must be out of his mind to even come this close.

His shoulders sagged; he averted his eyes.

"If it makes you feel better, I'll remove the leeches at sundown. Their work will be done by then."

Nodding, he edged away, then slumped down on the stool. Propping his elbows on his spread knees, he rested his head in his hands. He dimly registered a low gasp coming from Caryn's vicinity, but it was drowned out by his chaotic thoughts. She was right. He *had* failed to protect Randy. In fact, every decision he'd made the day before had led to this morning. Trapped in a bubble of time, in a foreign land, with well-meaning people who bled his cousin with leeches.

Leeches, for God's sake!

"Sir Luke."

Luke glanced at Caryn, then returned to his thoughts.

But what waited outside? Cops? Carmine and his

hit men? Vinnie had lied about where the money came from, put them all in the gravest danger, then got himself killed before he could fix the mess. No matter where Luke turned the answers came up the same. His life as he knew it was over. Nothing would ever be the same.

"Sir Luke," Caryn implored again.

A burst of hope leaped inside him. This was a nightmare, that must be it. He'd wake up soon and it would all be over.

But the stool pressed hard against his buttocks. The stone floor seeped cold through the thin soles of his loafers. And Randy looked nearer to death than anyone he'd seen.

Except Vinnie.

Except Kevin.

"I just want to keep Randy safe," he whispered into his hands.

"I know," she said, "but you must—"

The door crashed open. Captain Chisholm burst through, his face a mask of stunned fury. "Mother of God. 'Tis true what the soldiers said. Where is this man's clothing! Look how he exposes himself! This is an outrage, Lady Caryn!"

Luke glanced down, then snapped his legs together. His slumped position had hiked his nightshirt well above his knees, and by spreading his legs to support his elbows he'd revealed himself. He yanked the shirt down over his knees and shot to his feet.

"Sorry, I didn't realize."

Chisholm glowered at him, one massive fist clasping the handle of his sword. Behind him, the two soldiers who'd guarded Luke's room darted their eyes around the room as if unsure of where to let them rest.

Caryn stood by the bed with her head bent, one hand covering her face. A faint tremor shook her shoulders. He'd caused her to cry, Luke realized, unsettled by how much that distressed him.

"Seize this man," Chisholm ordered. "Lock him in his quarters!"

The soldiers hurried to obey.

"No!" Caryn commanded in a choked voice, her head snapping up. "He meant no harm."

"How can you defend him?" Chisholm cried. "His behavior is vile, beyond contempt. No decent man parades around in his bed clothing, nor shows himself to a lady." The man's outrage vanished abruptly. A cruel smile crept across his face. "Unless, of course, the lady—"

Caryn met Chisholm's lewd gaze with a cold stare. "Captain! You forget yourself!"

"My duty as a soldier remains, milady, and this traveler has defied all decency." His hand tightened on the hilt of his sword.

"He is the dragon slayer," she said, in an imperious tone, "and he is under my protection. Furthermore, sir, none are permitted in my sickroom if they have not the patient's welfare in mind. I must ask you and your men to leave."

She walked to the door and pulled it fully open.

"These men come from a time far ahead," she continued, "and while they bring with them the wonders of their century, they do not understand our ways. We must show leniency in these matters."

The soldiers dashed out without remark, but Chisholm remained put and met Caryn's stare with one of his own. Luke watched the exchange with the same fascination he'd experienced the first time he'd seen the lady. Her eyes flashed with outrage, her shoulders were squared, her carriage uncompromising. She held herself with a pride he'd only seen in women who were far out of the reach of an ex-con like himself, and he didn't wonder that her bearing offended the captain.

"Very well, Countess," Chisholm said sullenly. "But do not think I won't speak to the earl of this." He spun smartly on his heels and left.

Caryn closed the door behind him, then leaned against it. Small mewling sounds escaped her mouth, and her shoulders again trembled. His fault, Luke thought. He'd unwittingly disgraced her by his behavior. He'd studied the past enough to know a woman's reputation hung on her sexual virtue. This incident could ruin her. No doubt the castle would be buzzing about it before supper.

"Caryn . . ." He walked over to her, placed a contrite hand on her shoulder. "I'm sorry. I should have thought."

Slowly, she turned to face him. Tears streaked her face, but the door no longer muffled her tinkling bubbles of sound. "Chisholm . . . Did ye see . . . Did ye see his face?"

Her laughter was contagious. A matching chuckle

rose in Luke's throat. He threw back his head and let it out, enjoying the release. And despite his injured cousin and his irreconcilable predicament, he found he badly wanted to kiss the Lady Caryn.

Chapter Seven

As Caryn watched his pupils dilate, her laughter subsided. His eyes were the color of the tasty chocolate
morsels nobles served at court. Aye, and just as
tempting.

He met her gaze with breath-catching intensity.
His mouth opened slightly, revealing perfect white
teeth like none she'd ever seen. Involuntarily, she
licked her upper lip. He made a sharp, hissing sound
and his hold on her shoulder tightened ever so
faintly.

He wanted to kiss her. That she comprehended
without difficulty. But she did not as easily understand the sudden quickening of her heart and
lightness of her head. Nor what to do about them.
Married at fourteen, widowed fewer than two years
later, and cast into the untouchable role of the lady
of the castle, she was unschooled in matters of the
heart. She sensed, though, that to invite his kiss, she
need only sway subtly forward.

It took all her will not to make that move, which
evoked a rush of shame. She'd forgotten herself, for-

gotten her duty. She moved away, letting his hand slip off her shoulder.

"Forgive my outburst, sir. 'Twas unseemly of me." She spoke more stiffly than she'd intended. "Chisholm is correct. We must get you proper clothing."

Her abrupt movement appeared to jolt Luke, for he dropped his arm and took a quick step back, bringing a sudden ache to Caryn's heart. Ignoring the throb, she hurried to the bedside table to get the bell.

Nancy appeared in short order. A smile tugged at the corners of her mouth as she caught sight of Luke.

"Please find proper attire for our gentleman and take them to his chamber," Caryn instructed. She gave Luke's body a goodly inspection that, judging by the way he shifted back and forth, made him uncomfortable. "Fetch the largest size you can find."

"Where are the clothes I wore in here?" Luke asked.

Caryn frowned in mild distress. "They were badly bloodied. I fear our washerwomen will fail to remove the stains, but they will try."

"Oh. That was nice of you."

" 'Twas the manservant's duty," she informed him, then returned her attention to the maid. "Swiftly now, Nancy. Tongues are already wagging."

"Aye, Countess." Nancy gave a perfunctory curtsy and started off.

As she reached the door, Caryn added, "Do not be gossiping in the kitchen about Sir Luke's garb . . . or lack thereof."

"Never, milady." She hurried away with a familiar

mischievous glint in her eyes, the smile still pulling at her lips.

"How long do you think she'll keep that promise?"

"Till death."

"Then why could she barely keep from laughing?"

Caryn's own smile broke free. "For the same reason as I. 'Tisn't often we see a man in nothing but his shift outside the sickroom or marriage bed."

"I don't get you. If everything you and Ian—"

"*Sir* Ian."

"If what you and Sir Ian told me last night is true, being caught with a half-undressed man has ruined your reputation."

"Do not concern yourself with that. I am ever a source of gossip. Noblewomen do not engage in the healing arts, and I have seen much more of the male body than anyone deems proper. Some even believe I'm a witch."

A circumstance Chisholm would do his best to inflame. She wasn't troubled by his threat to talk to Ian. As soon as he recovered from the traveler's shocking news, the earl would find the situation as amusing as she had. But she would have preferred that the captain hadn't seen Luke's unseemly attire with his own eyes. He'd tell all who would listen, and the incident put the dragon slayer in an unfavorable light. She suspected this would please Chisholm, who put even less faith in the legend than Ian. Moreover, Luke's presence threatened his status among the clan chiefs and villagers.

To think the pompous fool had once proposed they marry. If she had her way, Ian would dismiss him and command the guard himself, but after last night's discussion she knew that wouldn't happen. It was up to her to make the captain remember his place.

She might even enjoy such a cat-and-mouse game were Sir Luke not the target. If Lochlorraine was to survive, Ormeskirk must be stopped. God had sent them the dragon slayer; she must assure he did his work.

She became aware of Luke's intense regard. A flutter arose in her chest. She'd interrupted a question when she'd corrected his use of Ian's given name, but it took no great intellect to discern what he'd been about to ask. Eager to escape the discomfort his gaze provoked, she renewed the subject.

"Regarding the information Sir Ian and I imparted, let me assure you it is all true." She moved to the windows. "Is it also true what you said, that your scientific men have not mastered time?"

She opened the shutters as she talked, letting in the late morning sunlight. "No."

"You mean they have?" Excitement shivered in her voice.

"No, yes. No, I mean it's true that they haven't. No one really understands time."

"Aye, it is as I thought." Filled with a nervous kind of energy, she picked up the snuffing rod and moved along the wall, extinguishing the candles. "This is a mystery God does not want us to solve. He is a brilliant man, my brother-in-law, but I fear he meddles where man should not."

"Seems more like the mystery got dropped in his lap, the way I see it."

Although Luke's phrasing was odd, Caryn understood his meaning. "True, the earl did not aim to interfere with time, but his grandiose dream of turning metal to gold set these events in motion. Had the Provider wanted us to do such things, surely the means would have been given."

Luke hesitated, running his hands through his tousled hair, which was the color of rich, oiled wood. "In my time . . ." He said the words as if they pained him. "Scientists have discovered marvelous things that weren't readily apparent. And while the philosopher's stone proved to be a myth, men in your century were only beginning to learn that." He took a step toward her, stepped back, and moved toward Randy's bed. "If men didn't investigate the unknown, Caryn, we'd have made no progress at all."

· With this he bent over Randy. Gazing down in rapt devotion, concern etching his face, he drew a finger along a scratch on the young man's face. "He been awake since the operation?"

"His eyelids flutter now and again, and sometimes he calls out a word."

"What is that?"

"Your name, Sir Luke. He calls your name. Ye must be a hero to him, as ye are to be in Lochlorraine."

"No way. Like I said, I'm nobody's hero."

"But you are," Caryn countered fervently. "All in Lochlorraine hail you as one. You've been sent to save us."

His frown deepened. "Tell me about this legend, Duchess."

"Countess," she corrected absently, already trying to find the words required to do justice to the story.

"Countess," he echoed, straightening up. "So what's it about?"

Caryn assumed a storytelling stance and spread her arms dramatically. "Ormeskirk," she began, "was a fierce dragon, the last of his kind. Ever did he terrorize the people of the lands, swooping down to snatch up small children, setting structures afire with his foul breath. Distraught, the king summoned the kingdom's remaining dragon slayer. Sir Lucas, the bold, the brave, the mag—"

"Look," Luke said wearily, "I'm not trying to be rude, but I don't need a performance, just information."

My, these future dwellers were impatient people, Caryn thought, somewhat taken aback by the interruption. "Very well," she said self-consciously. "The king sent Sir Lucas out to rid the land of the menace. Boldly, bravely, with his faithful companion, he ascended . . ."

Luke shifted his weight from foot to foot. Aye, his tolerance was low. Best that old Chief Storyteller Edgar didn't catch up with this man in the bailey.

"He went to the top of the mountain with a page whose name was never known. The page died in the battle, but Sir Lucas prevailed. Thereafter, dragons no longer existed." Momentarily, she cast her eyes downward, flooded with memories of the harm Ormeskirk had wrought since his return. "Until now, that is, and presumably only in Lochlorraine."

Luke's eyebrows rose. "A dragon," he replied flatly, gesturing toward the window.

"Aye, a monstrous beast. 'Ormeskirk' we call him."

"Of course. Why else would you need a dragon *slayer*?"

He was mocking her, an act she should have found annoying, but didn't. After all, his attitude came from ignorance. He'd soon have reason enough to change it.

"So what happened to Lucas?"

"Happened?" The question startled Caryn. "Why, I don't know."

"You mean no one ever heard of the guy again?"

"Nothing that the bards wrote about."

"Quite a reward, don't you think?" He turned back toward Randy, caressed the pale, sleeping face. "Look, if I keep hanging around, someone else might come in. I think I'll go back to my room and wait for Nancy to bring the clothing."

"A wise decision." But one that caused a prick Caryn didn't quite understand.

"Hang in there, kid," he whispered to his kinsman, then walked toward the door. Halfway there, he turned. "It's only a story," he said. "It never happened. Dragons don't exist. They never have."

He walked out of the room before Caryn could tell him he was wrong. Well, she thought, he'd soon see that for himself. When he had, they'd talk again.

"Arise, curs!"

Something crashed into Marco's ribs, and he came up off his bed with fists curled.

"What the fuck?" he heard Hub exclaim, a sentiment he was about to echo until a sharp blade caught him under the chin.

The dark room came alive with sunlight. Through a slanted glance he saw soldiers tearing down the canvas window coverings, felt blessed cool air filtering through the open slits. A pair of thick legs covered with stockings filled his line of vision.

"We will talk," a harsh voice said. "You will tell me what I need to know."

"Not easy to do when you've got a meat cleaver against my throat." As the sarcastic words left his mouth, he had a flash of recognition and instantly regretted them. But he leaned back a fraction of an inch, testing the extent of the danger. The blade didn't follow, so he figured the man wasn't planning to use it. At least not immediately.

He raised his head to meet the scowling face. This Chisholm guy was formidable. Not much taller than Marco—who was admittedly shorter than he'd prefer—this fact was offset by massive shoulders. His arms looked hard as steel. Each time he moved, muscles undulated beneath his embroidered shirt. Square of face, hard of jaw, a nose flattened as if it had once been broken—all combined, this added up to one scary son of a bitch.

But Marco still dared a look around. The long room was filled with the skirted soldiers, two of them holding swords at Hub's and Ralph's necks. "You mind asking your goons to back off?"

"Ye speak strange words."

"Yeah?" He almost made another sarcastic remark,

but the sudden throb in his bruised jaw made him think better of it. "Let me put it to you straight. Ask your men to put away their swords."

Chisholm gave a curt nod, then made a gesture. Immediately the soldiers sheathed their blades.

Marco suppressed a satisfied smile. The act confirmed his suspicion that he had something the man wanted. What that was could be anybody's guess, but it gave him some measure of power.

This wasn't the first visitor to their room. Late the night before a man whose hair looked like a rat's nest had come in, accompanied by several armed guards. He'd asked questions, lots of questions. While Hub and Ralph stared blankly at the walls through the entire interview, Marco had tried to keep up his end. He'd soon begun to feel like someone was reading to him out of a Stephen Hawking's book. Eventually, the man cut him off midsentence, thanked him and left, muttering something about lack of knowledge.

At least Chisholm talked straight, and maybe Marco would ask some questions of his own. "What's so important you needed to wake us up?"

"Your weapons. What manner of firearms are they?"

The guy towered over him menacingly, so Marco was cautious as he moved to stand. The soldiers' hands went to their hilts, but Chisholm remained calm.

"The cur is unarmed," he said. "He can do no harm."

"You their leader?" Marco asked, now meeting the man's eyes.

"Aye. I am captain of the castle guard."

"Pleased to meet you, Captain. Name's Marco Gann." He stuck out his hand.

The captain put away his sword and accepted the handshake. "Robert Chisholm," he grunted.

"Well, Captain Chisholm. Exactly what do you want to know about the guns?"

"We have never seen the likes of them in Lochlorraine, and I am eager to know how they were contrived."

"What?"

"Surely such devilment is the work of infidels. They come from the East, these weapons? Tell me true."

"If you call New York east."

"New York?" Chisholm frowned again, an act that didn't make his face any prettier. "In the New World?"

Now Marco frowned. "New World? You mean America?"

"Aye."

"We're in America."

"Nay."

"Then where the fuck are we?"

The sword came up in a flash and again pressed just beneath his chin. "Mind your manners, sir! I will ask the questions."

"Sure, sure." Marco stumbled back. The sword returned to its sheath. Except for knowing he was unpredictable, Marco couldn't figure Chisholm out. Not surprising. He couldn't figure anything out. Men with swords running around in kilts. Women wearing long gowns. Candles and open windows covered only with shutters and blinds. Not to mention the filth and stink. He needed to take it easy on the questions, though. Knowledge was power, and at the moment Chisholm held all the cards.

"Tell me of the weapons."

"Sure, sure," he said in a placating voice. "Mine's a Walther 38PPK, Ralph there uses an old Colt forty-five when he's not flashing the Uzi. Think he keeps a twenty-two in an ankle holster too. The guy's a regular arsenal." He glanced at the boys, who were sitting on their respective mats with glum expressions on their faces. "Hey, Hub. What kinda gun do you use?"

"I got me a Remington Magnum."

Marco looked back at Chisholm. "He's got a Remington."

"Walther. Uzi. Remington. And hosts of numbers," Chisholm responded. "Ye speak gibberish."

Yeah? Join the club. "They're the names of the companies who manufactured them, okay?" Marco kept his voice even, much as he might with a child.

Chisholm took no notice of the tone. "The big gun. Tell me of the big spitting gun."

"The Uzi?" When Chisholm nodded uncertainly, Marco continued. "It's a submachine gun. Shoots one bullet after the other." He put his elbow to his hip, pointed his finger, and made a rat-a-tat-tat sound.

" 'Rat-a-tat-tat,' " Chisholm repeated.

"Rat-a-tat-tat. You hit, you go boom." Marco listed sideways in a parody of falling down.

Chisholm smiled widely. " 'You hit, you go boom.' I like that."

Marco was tempted to dismiss this parrot as an idiot, but something told him there was more to the guy. He decided to test his theory.

"You need our weapons for something?"

The man regarded him suspiciously, confirming that this was no dummy. " 'Tis a possibility. First I must know their uses."

"I'll tell you what. Why don't we get rid of our boys? Let's me and you talk one on one."

"I have many ways to make you talk," Chisholm replied.

"Sure you do. But that won't help you use the guns, will it?"

The captain fixed him with a hard stare that would cause a lesser man to flinch. Marco held his eyes, boring into them with an intensity that he hoped proved he'd never talk no matter how bad he was tortured. Eventually Chisholm looked away, moving his gaze to Ralph and Hub. Marco could almost see the wheels turning.

"I am *their* leader," he said. "They obey without question." He snapped his fingers. "Hub, break the neck of that goon next to you."

Hub gave him an are-you-nuts-boss look, but started to rise anyway. The soldiers all pulled swords, but as six-foot-five of flabby body emerged from the mat, their eyes widened.

"He is a monster of a man," Chisholm intoned.

"That he is. He'll probably take down five of your men before you kill him."

"Aye, I can see that."

Chisholm repeated his earlier gesture. The soldiers eagerly complied, pulling away from Hub and putting space between them.

"Relax," Marco said, and Hub bounced back down on the mat. Marco met Chisholm's eyes again. "Well? I've got something to offer you. What do you have to offer me?"

"The respect of one leader to another." Chisholm bowed quickly, then looked at his men. "Find these two prisoners something to eat, then instruct a scullery maid to bring food for their captain. We have much to speak about."

Chapter Eight

When Luke returned to his room he found the feather bed made up and covered by a stack of clothing he could only call costumes. He rummaged through the pile, looking for something he could actually wear. The first item he picked up was a length of plaid fabric from which he assumed he was supposed to make a kilt.

Forget that.

He found vests and jackets, some with buttons, some without. Tunics. Several swashbuckler-type shirts with drawstring necklines. Long tubes of knitted material that he assumed were socks, although some had straps at the bottom instead of toes. There was also an odd assortment of belts, clasps, buckles, and garters, and he found himself wondering how anyone in this place got work done considering the inconvenience of just getting dressed.

Some old clean blue jeans and a work shirt would have made him happy, but he finally settled on an odd-looking pair of trousers. Not trousers, exactly. More like knickers, but they had legs attached that narrowed down to—

Dammit, with that stirrup thing spanning the bottom of the foot, they resembled women's tights. But they were the best of the lot, so after yanking on his briefs he pulled them on.

A rap sounded on the door and he threw a swashbuckler shirt over his head. After the scene by Randy's sickbed, he didn't want to offend anyone else's sensibilities.

Nancy stood at the door with a tray in her hand.

"To break your fast." She whisked in, headed toward a small table in one corner, and set down her tray. Plucking off a large container, she then buzzed toward the washstand where she poured its steaming contents into the metal pitcher. "Scented water," she explained when she saw his confused frown. "For your toilet. I see the clothing fits you fine. Aye, I thought they might. They belonged to Chisholm's da, who was a right big man, not only in body but in heart. Much bigger than the priggish son he begot." Her hand flew to her mouth. "I forget meself to go running off at the mouth like that. Saints be praised, the countess is forgiving, else I'd be in the stocks day and night."

With that, she swung her free hand down to the lower shelf of the washstand to pick up the chamber pot. "The garderobe be down the hallway to yer left, should ye be needing it. But it truly ain't fitting for men of station like yerself." She wrinkled her nose in distaste, then headed for the door. As she started to exit, she looked over her shoulder. "Dear sweet Mary, I almost forgot. Lady Caryn asked me to say that she sent the soldiers away and gives ye free run of the realm. Is there aught else I need to tell?"

Luke was beginning to feel like a dervish had just whirled through the room, but he did need to know one thing. "How do I get outside?"

Nancy gave him instructions in her perpetually breezy manner, then swept out the door like the north wind, leaving the room smelling of steaming food and scented water. Luke couldn't decide which to use first.

His growling stomach cast the deciding vote. Moving to the chair, he sat and lifted off a silver cover. Oatmeal and cream. Brown sugar. Sliced pears. Even a cup of brewing tea. Luke preferred coffee, but he doubted there'd be a Starbucks in the lobby downstairs, so he was grateful enough for what he had.

After wolfing down the breakfast, doing his best not to notice the suspicious speck here and there, he went to the washstand to clean up. He lifted the pitcher, ready to pour, when he saw his belongings in the basin: his watch and college ring, his keys and penknife, a collection of loose change and his wallet. After checking on his cash and finding it still in the wallet, he set the items aside and washed up, cringing when the bowl turned red from all the blood. Afterward, he sat on a chair that resembled one in his late Aunt Vi's parlor and cleaned his nails with the penknife.

He then threw a tunic over his flimsy excuse for pants and shirt, and since the pants were held up by only a thin drawstring, he secured the whole mess with a thick belt. Last, he reached for his jewelry, slipping on the watch and the Penn State ring imprinted with the date he should have graduated. He'd picked up the ring at a pawnshop. Although wearing it was a form of cheating, he always felt good having it on, like he was holding his dream.

A heavy cloud came over him. His dream? What dream? It was gone. No Mercedes dealership. No white house in upstate New York. No respectability. Even if—even *when* he took Randy back home, he'd encounter more heat than he'd ever known. Being chased by the mob had never been his nightmare— no one went after a guy who just ran a chop shop. But it was now harsh reality.

Or was he exaggerating the danger? If it weren't for his mysterious disappearance, no one would connect him to the heist. He could always claim he'd gone off on a bender. Carmine would be pissed, but others had done it and forgiveness had always been granted.

He discarded that idea. He'd be continually looking over his shoulder, and with the taste of his dream still in his mouth he doubted he could return to his old life anyway. And he had funds in the bank. Enough to give him and Randy a new start. Maybe in San Francisco. Not a bad idea, one that would give Luke a chance to make it up for all Randy had endured during his sad life.

This was hardly the time for making life choice decisions. It would be more productive to go out in search of the portal. At moments, talking to Caryn, he almost believed he'd traveled through time. Of course, he also wanted to kiss her more than he'd ever wanted to kiss a woman before, which increased her credibility.

But dragons, crissakes. She believed in dragons. As did many or perhaps all of this place's inhabitants. How could Luke trust the perceptions of people who were so deluded? True, Lochlorraine appeared to be a far cry from New York City, but this gave him reason to believe that inmates were running the asylum.

As he reached for the door latch, he noticed he'd left Randy's ring behind. It had no true value, but . . . He tried not to think about it, but if the boy died, the ring would be all he'd have left of him.

He returned to the washstand, lifted the wash basin and pitcher, then checked the floor and behind the stand. It wasn't in any of those places, and he finally gave up.

With a feeling of loss, he headed out, keeping Nancy's directions firmly in mind. Soon he walked through a chaotic courtyard, and fearing an uprising of admirers, he marched straight through and out the gate without looking to either side. He had an uneasy moment as he crossed a bridge made of nothing but loose planks, and when he safely arrived on the other side, he looked into the deep trench below. A moat, he assumed, but he'd always thought moats were filled with water.

Another mystery. One that would go unsolved for now.

From there, he walked down the hill. Another bridge appeared, this one spanning a winding stream that separated the crop fields from the castle.

Men, women, and children tilled the soil. As he neared, they all stopped working to look at him.

"Dragon slayer! Dragon slayer! Dragon slayer!"

Luke groaned. He hadn't realized he'd have to pass people to reach the lake. But there they were, lined up along tidy rows of crops, cheering him as if he were a football star. Luke gave a small obligatory wave.

The cheering increased. Some of the villagers beat on the handles of their hoes with trowels. Others whistled. His stomach flipped over. He didn't need this, and he felt phonier now than he'd ever felt wearing the Penn State ring.

With another wave, he increased his pace. When he was out of sight they'd surely settle down.

Dragon slayer. Ridiculous.

Clearly some animal was terrorizing these inhabitants, but what made them think it was a dragon? He thought people stopped believing in mythical creatures long before the seventeenth century.

The smell of salt water diverted his thoughts, and he kept walking until the lake came into view. Daylight allowed him to see that it was actually an inlet from the sea. Shaped somewhat like the body of a bass fiddle, it ended in a round pool not far from the forest. Off to his right the stream circled the cottages to pour into the sea as a miniature waterfall. He paused a moment, caught up in the view. The most scenic spot in Lochlorraine, he thought, although the four nearby cottages appeared abandoned.

So maybe this location wasn't as perfect in winter, but right now he was glad enough to be here. Kelp littered the beach and lapping waves created a gentle white noise. Gulls cooed overhead. Soothing sounds and scents, especially after the chaos and odors of the castle.

A man could make a home here, a good one, a thought that turned his mind to Caryn. During his year at Penn State he'd often dreamed of marrying a woman with her strength of character and purpose. A doctor, a lawyer, or possibly a thriving entrepreneur. Not only smart and ambitious but beautiful. A woman who turned heads.

Now, nearly forty and looking back, he recognized he'd been seeking a trophy wife. Achievable for a young college student on the rise, but very unlikely for a hood with a prison record. Since his parole, he'd never tried to find out. If he'd ever found and won such a prize, he wouldn't have married her. He could think of nothing worse than humiliating a woman he loved by being arrested for his work. Besides, he'd never even seen a woman who'd measured up before, and found it ironic that the one to attract him this powerfully was in many respects his jailor.

Several nearby seagulls quarreled over a piece of kelp and their angry sounds pulled Luke from his reverie. He'd wasted enough time, and he hadn't come here to moon about a woman he'd soon never see again.

He turned toward the thicket of trees. Somewhere in there was the place where the portal had closed. His job was to find it. A breeze blew through the leaves, swaying them softly, but as he got closer he saw the forest wasn't as pastoral as it first seemed. Thick and crowded with undergrowth, it was pitch-black inside, and unsavory rustles came from the thick piles of fallen leaves and branches.

He stepped back. Judging by the sun's position, the trees were east of the village and castle, while the inlet was south. The forest appeared as an unbroken line. Moving south, it passed the lake to disappear over the southern horizon. To the north, it grew along the eastern edge of the fields, then sloped up the hills to the rocky terrain higher up. Here it curved west toward the open sea, blocking the view farther north.

But this was where the portal had vanished. And since things didn't appear and disappear except in subatomic physics, it had to be there somewhere.

Holding on to that certainty, Luke elbowed through a tangle of limbs and leaves to search the forest.

It didn't take Marco long to peg Chisholm as a number-one A-hole. After providing some rancid stew and a chunk of bread with a rock so big Marco had almost broken a tooth on it, the man had asked— no, commanded—that Marco go with him.

As they crossed a courtyard crammed with milling people, and made their way through hordes of chickens and dogs, a girl stepped in their way.

"Good morning to you, Captain." She curtsied prettily, but her tone was openly mocking.

"Watch your tongue, wench." Chisholm swung an arm to brush her from his path, but she twirled out of reach with a giggle and ran toward the castle steps. "Women today are far too bold," he said, as though it were an explanation.

Marco committed the girl's face to memory. If, as he hoped, this excursion with Chisholm earned his freedom, he'd look her up and find out what she knew.

"Where are we going?" he asked.

"Ye'll see."

They walked in total silence, passing over an unsteady bridge, down a rocky trail, then over another bridge, where they veered off to a path that twisted through the village. Now and then Marco saw wagons and wheelbarrows heading toward the rear of the castle, but except for the occasional woman with a baby and a few old people rocking outside their cottages, the village itself was empty. Finally they arrived at a place Marco recognized.

Divots of dying grass lay upon the ground, undoubtedly uprooted by machine-gun bullets. Two indentations in the overgrowth vaguely resembled bodies. Puzzled, Marco looked at Chisholm. "Why did you bring me here?"

"In due time ye'd have come on your own," the man replied. "All travelers do, thinking to escape."

"All travelers?" He'd heard that word several times the night before and knew it referred to him and the others. "There are more?"

"Aye. Over a baker's dozen, I'd wager. From all lands and eras. Most still live among us, though some were lost trying to escape, and a dark-skinned man, who dressed most peculiarly, hung himself soon after entering the realm. The earl told us he was from a land called Egypt, but I've heard naught of such a kingdom."

Chisholm's words made sense, the way they were put together was clear, but the content buzzed in Marco's ears like a swarm of bees. He stared at the deliverer of this incredible information a long moment, at a rare loss for an answer.

"Uh, you're . . ." He looked away, took in the solid mass of trees, where only the evening before he'd seen an incredible arch of light. "Are you telling me—Are you saying I'm in a different time?"

The captain's mouth again formed words. A year— 1692. A place—Lochlorraine in Scotland. Something about being lost in time. More bees swarmed in Marco's ears.

"I see ye dinna believe me," Chisholm said. "None do at first, so there is something I must show you."

Chisholm proceeded toward the lake, which Marco soon saw wasn't a lake at all, but a bay that led to the ocean. At the water's edge, the captain stripped off his boots and stockings, motioning for Marco to do the same.

When Chisholm waded in, Marco stopped to roll up his pants, then went after him. The water felt like ice, rocks jabbed at his bare feet, and he felt somewhat sick, which wasn't helped by the rushing waves.

Finally Chisholm stopped. "Here. Lucifer's Window. Gaze upon your home, but go no farther. The water sinks to a deadly depth beyond this spot."

The water itself caught Marco's attention. Swirling

over a deep tunnellike sinkhole, it was as clear as liquid crystal. Images floated inside, reminding him of the snowy glass balls so popular at Christmastime. He caught a glimpse of the Marriott Marquis, then the discount show ticket booth came into view. People stood in line around it. Men and women panhandled the waiting crowd.

Times Square. Home.

So this was where the portal went.

Mesmerized, it was all Marco could do not to jump in. He'd heard the captain's warning, but, Lord, home was just a swim away. His mind raced. He had no compunctions about abandoning Ralph and Hub. But the money. He needed the money, and those bastards had hidden it somewhere. Without it, he had no chance of surviving.

Still . . .

He could test the depths, see if he could make it, see if it was possible. Then he'd worm the location of the cash from Chisholm. One bag would be enough to give him a new start. Maybe he'd go to Paris.

Taking several deep breaths to fill his lungs, he dove into the pool.

"Don't!" Chisholm roared as Marco's body broke the water. But he was swimming now, swimming deep, holding his breath, moving his arms and legs to reach the images. There. Within the reach of his hand. There. He could almost touch them. And while a saner part of his mind wondered if he'd tumble to his death if he reached his destination, another part said that everything was skewed here, nothing made sense, and he'd simply float to the ground as if the air back home was also like water.

He stretched out his arm, trying to touch the bill-board that overlooked the square and struck something soft and resilient.

He pushed hard.

Before he could register what happened, he was propelled backward like he'd been snapped from a rubber band. He spun, tumbled, lost control of his breath. Bubbles of precious oxygen drifted before his eyes. An undertow nipped at his body, threatening to drag him back under. Flailing, kicking, struggling to hold on to his remaining air, he strained to reach the surface.

Suddenly someone grabbed his collar. Seconds later he broke through the water. Gasping for air, he allowed himself to be hauled to his feet.

"Fool!" Chisholm growled. "Did I not warn of the danger? Many a traveler has gone into those depths, only to be spit back out by the sea. Most lost their lives in the attempt." Abruptly Chisholm's tone took on a rare edge of compassion. "Yet I understand. Aye, I do. 'Tis torture for travelers to gaze through the window. Many stand for hours, weeping for their homeland. Even as our own laird did when Lochlorraine was first torn from our times."

Marco bent over, his hands on his knees, gulping for air. When finally he could breathe again, he looked up at Chisholm.

"You mean the earl?" he asked numbly, vaguely wondering why that was the first question out of his mouth.

Chisholm shot a disparaging look at the castle. "The daft wizard? Nay. I speak of his brother, Sir Gregory, who was the true laird of the realm. Now there was a man warriors would gladly follow to the death. But this *pretender*? Bah! He takes after his grandda, who was every bit as daft, and assigns a lass to rule in his stead."

His voice hard again, the captain spewed criticisms of the current earl's regime, and Marco let him blather on while he recovered from his near drowning. Finally he'd had enough. He was half-freezing, what with the cold water, his wet clothes, and the ceaseless wind that swept over them.

He straightened, smoothed back his soaked hair, then asked, "Why did you bring me here?"

Interrupted midsentence, the captain looked floored, but he quickly hid his reaction. "Should be plain as the nose on your face. Had I merely spoken of your new circumstances, ye'd not have accepted it, and would be forever planning an escape. I wanted you to know there was none. Your fate rests in my hands, man, and it will benefit you to see that my will be done."

Tremors shook Marco's body. The cold, he told himself, but he knew it wasn't. He'd just witnessed, he'd just experienced, something beyond the fantastic. Although everything in him railed against what he'd seen, he had no choice but to accept his own senses.

"I want to go back to land," he choked out.

Chisholm complied without argument. Soon, Marco was trudging alongside him toward the castle, gusty breezes biting at his wet hair and clothing. They'd taken a different route this time and the captain appeared compelled to point out each sight along the way. Now they were crossing tilled farmland, with Chisholm kicking up dirt and seeds with each step.

"Hey, Robert," one of the workers called out. "Take heed of the seedlings."

"A troublemaker," Chisholm confided to Marco, while he nevertheless turned onto one of the many paths that bisected the field. "Considers himself of some import 'cause of being chief of the wee Clan MacNab. Got himself elected Lord Mayor on account of it." Although Marco showed no interest, Chisholm droned on. "Yet the man does have Lord Ian's ear and his voice carries a measure of weight. He'll be a foe when we take over."

Marco slanted the captain a wary glance. His mental agility had returned to normal during the hike, and he now automatically assessed how to make use of this information. He'd been right in not dismissing Chisholm as dimwitted out of hand, but now he wondered if he wasn't still underestimating the man—or at least the extent of his ambition.

"You're planning an insurrection?"

Chisholm's eyes narrowed. " 'Tis the right of all free men under the crown to remove tyrants and buffoons. To all of reason, the earl is the latter."

"I see." Marco bobbed his head sagely. "And how do I fit in?"

"Why, ye'll be by my side when I claim the realm." Chisholm looked off in the distance momentarily.

"As will the countess, who undoubtedly refused my offer for her hand on account of my lower station."

So he was hot for the redhead who'd shot Ralph. Interesting, Marco thought, stuffing that item away for later use. "I agreed to teach your men how to use the guns, not to help you take over. Show me the way out, and I'll give you everything you want."

"Ye deny the sights of your own eyes?"

"How do I know it wasn't a trick?"

Chisholm burst into derisive laughter. "Ye wish to delude yourself, man, but ye cannot. We are trapped inside Lochlorraine, every man, woman, child, and other poor creatures as got caught up that terrible night. Do not fight it. Work with me to topple our lairdship's reign. 'Twill be to your benefit. Moreover, ye're not exactly in a place to bargain."

"You got a point," Marco replied, telling himself to take it one step at a time. Getting out of that stinking prison would be the first. "Tell you what. It's hard to think straight when I'm locked up. Free me, and then we'll talk."

The captain hesitated. In the resulting lull Marco became vaguely aware of a stirring among the field workers, but he was too intent on Chisholm's answer to give it more than passing notice.

"Had Arnie Miller not been killed, this would be no difficult task. However . . ." Chisholm lapsed into another silence, and Marco kept his tongue, giving the man room to think. Off to the side, he noticed workers leaving their hoeing sites. "If we found another to blame for the deed, your freedom would be assured."

Hand over one of his men, the captain meant. As Marco pondered that sideways suggestion, a horn blew from the castle tower. A spooky wail immediately followed. People scattered in the fields, calling out, running in all directions.

Abruptly he and Chisholm were in total shade. Cold again, Marco shivered and looked up to see what had cast such an enormous shadow.

"Holy shit," he whispered, incapable of speaking any louder.

Chapter Nine

The light was ghostly gray, the sounds muted and slithery, and the portal hadn't appeared. Dispirited, Luke turned back, suddenly unsure about how to get out. As his journey lengthened and escape became more uncertain, he found himself speeding up, tearing through the dim leafy passageways, slapping away brush, swerving between trees. Finally, he spied light, and he lunged through the final branches that blocked his path and stepped into the meadow.

Almost pathetically grateful for sunlight on his face, he stopped a moment and took in the view. The day seemed very normal; the sun-splashed land felt almost like home.

But his relief quickly faded. This wasn't home, and he still had work to do. They'd gotten in, which meant they could get out. The portal had to be there somewhere. Still breathing heavily from exertion, he scanned the timberline. Despite the spooky atmosphere inside those woods, he'd search every inch of it if that's what it took.

This prompted him to look down at his feet. No

way he could hike that forest in his loafers. Besides, even with boots, it would take weeks to cover that much ground on foot.

Discouraged, he started back for the castle, hunting for an alternative. Caryn would gladly give him a tour, but the second she realized he was searching for the portal, she'd begin reminding him of there being no way out. He was in no mood to deal with naysayers. Maybe Ian would take him, but the earl had the look of a man who seldom left his laboratory.

Lord, Luke wished he had a Jeep. Since he wasn't given to dwelling on useless fantasies, he returned to sifting through his options. As he passed back through the castle gate, he considered asking for a wagon.

Inside the courtyard, people went about their business and gave him little notice. Somewhat surprising considering his reception in the fields, but he counted his blessings.

Various buildings lined the walls, most housing animals. Smoke curled from the chimney of a brick structure not far from the castle stairs, carrying the scent of baking bread. Beside the cookhouse were covered pens, where several hounds snoozed in a pile.

Nice proximity for a kennel, Luke thought, hitching to his left to avoid a goose that had flown from the ground. Animals abounded, many with free rein of the yard. Horses, sheep, even a lone goat. Dogs of all sizes, chasing and playing, or lying under tables. Hens strutted through with chicks in tow, and one now clucked angrily as she chased a small boy who'd run off with one of her young.

"Put the wee chick down, laddie!" a woman hollered.

The boy did as told and the hen shuffled her baby back in line with the rest.

Despite the chaos, everyone seemed purposefully occupied.

Everyone but him.

This was how he'd felt in prison, where the inactivity had been as unsettling as being imprisoned in the first place. There wasn't enough work to go around, so even though he'd managed to snag three days a week in the body shop the rest of his time had been empty.

As early as he could remember, Luke had worked hard, both physically and mentally. He'd studied diligently, excelled at sports, and held part-time jobs on top of it. In college, between football, studies, and work, he'd been so busy he hardly found time to sleep. Even recently, Gaskin's Garage had filled all his days and many of his nights.

Idleness didn't sit well with him, and this he realized was part of his problem. At least the prison had a library, and he'd killed a lot of time by reading everything he could get his hands on. He'd absorbed so much information on such a variety of subjects, in fact, that some of the other prisoners had started calling him Renaissance Man.

He wondered if the castle had a library.

Deciding to find out, he started up the stairs, then paused as he caught sight of his shoes. A leafed twig clung to one vamp, decayed foliage sprouted from the soles. A damned ugly thing to do to fine Italian leather, he groused to himself. Looking for a place to scrape the mess off, he saw a row of stone blocks beside the steps. Judging by the clumps of dried and half-dry mud clinging to them, muddy feet must be a constant problem in the castle. He had no wish to add to it.

He was just starting on his second shoe when he noticed a good-sized creature regarding him with more than mild interest. Creature was a good word, too, because it sure was one sorry rheumy-eyed, scrawny, mud-spattered excuse for a horse. Luke hadn't known the species *had* hair, but this one did, and it hung in long ragged strands all the way down to the knobby knees.

When Luke returned the stare, the horse lowered its head to chomp on a wildflower sprouting from the foundation, then closed its eyes. Until the night before, his experience with horses had been limited to watching them race at the track or trot through Central Park. This pathetic specimen didn't begin to match the size of Caryn's beast, but neither did it have much in common with the sleek, beribboned animals back home.

He moved in for a closer look, jumping back when the creature snorted and raised its head.

"You a good horse?"

It continued chomping and showed no further interest. Luke studied it for a while, an idea forming in his mind. Although the reins were tied loosely to a log, the horse appeared abandoned, and so far no one had objected to his nearness.

The animal was calm enough, lazy even, and probably tame as a kitten. Moreover, Luke would lay book it could climb the rocky hills outside like a mountain goat. What if he borrowed it? Would anyone even realize it was gone? The opportunity was too promising to overlook.

Trying to forget he'd never even touched a horse, let alone ridden one, he bent and untied the reins. The animal ignored his movement.

"Nice horse," he crooned, pulling the reins over a high protuberance at the front of the saddle that was duplicated by one at the back. Made of wood, but padded in the center with leather, the thing looked alarmingly like an instrument of torture.

The horse's lazy eyes opened. Leaf tips protruded from the chewing mouth, wiggling like captive insects. Otherwise, it didn't move.

So far, so good.

Standing on the right side of the animal, Luke put a foot in the leather stirrup and gingerly applied weight. Still no reaction. Now the hard part. He straightened his leg, quickly swinging his opposite one over the saddle like he'd seen in Westerns. Although he'd tried his best not to slam down on the animal's back, he hadn't been very successful. Luckily it didn't seem to mind. In fact, if not for the sound of grinding teeth, he could easily believe the animal was dead, which suited him just fine.

But he couldn't say he was comfortable. Putting his feet in the stirrups had raised his knees almost to his waist. Since he'd seen jockeys ride that way he figured it was normal.

He tugged on the reins.

With a whinny, the formerly placid creature tossed its head like a prize Arabian, fairly well scaring the shit out of Luke. But at least he wasn't on one of those flimsy scraps of leather he'd seen in the park. This saddle was big, with lots of places to grab, a serendipity he took full advantage of.

Following this display of independence, the horse returned to its fine dining experience. Luke tugged on the reins, earning another head toss that discouraged him making a third try. He had no idea what to do next, and he cast furtive glances around the courtyard. They hung horse thieves in the Old West, and he wasn't too sure what the policy was here in Lochlorraine.

"Okay," he growled. "No more Mr. Nice Guy."

He kicked, gently actually, but the horse whirled around like Luke had slammed it with a two-by-four, giving him another opportunity to practice grabbing the saddle. They headed toward the gate at a rocky jog that was only marginally unbearable, and Luke gave one last wary glance around the courtyard, relieved to find that no one took exception to his impending departure.

"Hey, you! Where're ye takin' my Toby?"

Luke looked back and saw a boy of maybe eight or nine staring after him with an outraged expression.

"I'm just borrowing him," Luke said.

The boy whistled shrilly.

Toby whirled again and trotted toward the sound.

By this time, Luke knew what to do, and he had a hand firmly on the front of the saddle by the time he reached the boy.

"That's my horse!" The boy's face and voice were filled with fury.

"I'm sorry. I didn't know it was your pony."

"Don't be calling Toby a pony! He's a horse!"

Just as the words flew out, the boy's expression changed. A second later he was kneeling with his head bowed.

"Dragon slayer," he said contritely. "Forgive me. Keep me Toby as long as ye want."

"Get up," Luke said gruffly. "The ground's covered with crap. It's getting all over your knees."

The boy shot to his feet. He was small, wiry, and suntanned, with sandy brown hair, and he twisted a tam in his hands.

"What's your name?"

"Tom, Sir Dragon Slayer," he said earnestly, his round gray eyes widening. "Tom, the stable master's son."

"Okay, Tom. May I borrow your horse for the day?"

"Aye, sir. Keep Toby as long as you like."

"Just for the day, that's all. Now do me a favor, will you?"

"Anything, sir."

"Stop kneeling or bowing when you see me. Tell everyone you know to stop doing it, too."

"Aye, sir." Tom bowed again, then stepped back. "Ye be wanting me to give Toby a nudge?"

Luke gave a nod that took more courage than he

wanted to reveal. To his relief, the horse responded to Tom's slap by moving into a gentle walk. Luke circled him toward the gate, then gave a quick look back. The boy was already gone, and Luke had little hope he would keep his promise.

Rather than risk more adulation from the workers in the field, he chose to begin with the northern leg of the forest, so he aimed Toby toward the high ground on the west side of the castle. Although the ride up the steep incline was bumpy, Toby climbed it easily, and Luke found it preferable to walking.

The timberline was his destination, but when he saw a rock spire that seemed completely out of place in this land of rolling hills, he decided to give it a better look.

The thing was five hundred feet tall at least, and an enormous windmill sat on the top. But Luke's interest lay more with the ribbon of a road carved into it. A twisting, irregular spiral that undoubtedly made the trip over a mile long, it must have taken decades to build.

Toby stirred restlessly, and Luke gave him a steadying pat as he leaned into the front of the saddle and stared up. The windmill puzzled him. It was at last fifty feet high and had clearly been abandoned long ago. One of the sails was missing, while another hung only by its supporting brace.

Even at this distance, he could see it employed a fantail that automatically turned the sails into the wind whenever it changed. An advanced design, one he would swear hadn't surfaced until the eighteenth century. Moreover, the amount of power it could deliver was far greater than required for the simple grinding of grain.

So why build it in the first place? Especially when it required a road? What purpose could a windmill serve so far from the fields? Surely people hadn't carried grain all that distance in order to mill it. Besides, there was a much smaller water-powered mill by the stream. He was suddenly eager for another meeting with Ian, sure the man could provide those answers.

He was tempted to dismount and climb up for a closer look, but Toby snorted uneasily and tossed his head. Reluctantly, Luke released his hold on the reins. The animal bolted forward just as a shadow darkened the sails of the windmill, then slid along the side to disappear at the structure's base.

Abruptly Luke found his attention taken up by Toby, who was leaping up the rock-strewn hill in panic. A long, undulating wail came from the top of the spire. The sorrowful lament pierced Luke's heart and he became almost unbearably sad.

Although Toby was already climbing at a dangerous pace, Luke grabbed the saddle and gave him an urgent kick. Suddenly he wanted out of there, too, but it had nothing to do with fear for his life.

Caryn hiked up her petticoats and skirted the animals and objects in the bailey, stopping everyone she came across. After receiving more than a dozen shakes of the head, she stuck her head in the bake house. "Have you seen Sir Luke?" she asked of a woman who was sliding loaves into an oven.

She received a quick, puzzled frown, then a spark of recognition. "Oh, the dragon slayer. Aye, I've heard folks buzzing about him, but I been so busy readying for the feast I've not laid me eyes upon him."

"Feast? What feast?"

"Why, for ye and the lairdship's birthday, of course."

"Carry on, then." Caryn withdrew her head, beginning to wonder if it was totally empty. She'd forgotten her own birthday and its traditional celebration, which was now little more than a fortnight away. Moreover, she'd misjudged the dragon slayer. After his harrowing experiences, she'd expected him to stay close to the castle.

She continued questioning people, but no one recalled seeing him. How could that be? The man had gained considerable repute overnight. Then she remembered that except for the field workers, only a handful of soldiers and servants had actually seen his face.

Had he gone down to the loch, hoping to find the way out? And if he had, could he have waded in and encountered Lucifer's Window? Been lost at sea like so many before him? She thought not. He was too devoted to his kinsman to dive in alone and abandon him, but the possibility still sent shivers through her body.

Deciding to ride to the loch, she headed toward the stable. As she reached the door, someone tugged at her sleeve. She turned. "Have ye something to tell, young Tom?"

The boy twisted his cap and cast his eyes down, shuffling between his feet before he got the nerve to speak.

"Th-the d-dragon slayer done borrowed my Toby and ride him clean out of the b-bailey." After this inauspicious start, the boy's confession flooded out. "I run after him a wee distance, then seen him go into the hills. I shoulda tole someone, but I didna know who. Pa woulda whupped me, and Lord Ian were busy with the work of gettin' us back to Scotland. I saw Captain Chisholm coming from the castle with one of the clan what some with the dragon slayer, and I thought—" The boy shuddered visibly. "Maybe I shoulda told *him*, but . . ."

"It's fine, Tom. You were a brave lad to come forward. Thank you. I'll take care of it now." Caryn patted his shoulder. "Now would you kindly saddle my stallion so I can ride after Sir Luke?"

"Aye, milady." With a shy, relieved smile, Tom ran off.

Caryn sighed. Without realizing it, Tom had told her more than she wanted to know. That his father was still beating him after being told scores of times to stop, and that Chisholm had let at least one of Luke's ruffian companions free.

But first she had to find Luke. He must not be lost. His value to Lochlorraine was inestimable. Surely, that was the only reason her heart pounded so badly.

Chapter Ten

Luke's anxiety subsided quickly. By the time he was halfway up the mountain, he almost forgot about his reaction to the cry. He did wonder what kind of animal had uttered it, and assumed it was the creature that frightened the villagers so, but he didn't dwell on his questions overlong.

The trip was peaceful. Although noises abounded here—the clip-clop of Toby's hoofs, the chippering of birds in the brush, the hiss of grass rustling in the wind—it was another welcome break from the bustling noises that filled the castle and its courtyard. Settling back against the saddle's rear support, he loosely guided Toby up the hill. For the most part he let the animal choose his own path and soon they reached the top.

Luke gazed down on the ocean. Waves crashed against huge rocks, rolling up on the stony rubble before retreating. The shoreline sloped inland to the mouth of the inlet. At times the beach was sandy, and in these places sat neat rows of cottages where people were busy at work.

Squinting into the reflection off the dark blue waters, he looked farther out to sea. Small boats bobbed in the waves, filled with fishermen casting their nets. Flocks of gulls and sea ducks dotted the clear sky.

Eventually the glare forced Luke to look away, and he turned Toby inland. The land grew steeper and wilder. A hare darted through the low grasses. Below, in the meadows to the west of the stream, he saw short-horned beasts with hair down to their hoofs. Judging by the occasional lowing sound, they were cattle.

A true child of the city, Luke had no experience with animals other than cats and dogs, and the ones he'd seen at the zoo, so these sights fascinated him. When a deer suddenly appeared at the top of the hill, he stared, transfixed. It was only when the animal bolted away that he realized he'd reached the forest.

Oak, alder, birch, and conifers of all kinds huddled together in thick masses just as they did down below. But the undergrowth appeared thinner, and the trees were dwarfed and twisted from beatings by the ocean breezes.

Luke's spirits lifted. All along, he'd figured he'd have to explore the forest on foot, but the memory of his previous excursion had spooked him a bit. Knowing he could ride in on horseback took his edge off.

"Okay, Toby," he said. "Here's where you earn your keep."

He gave a flick of the reins and squeezed with

his legs. Toby stayed put. His head turned toward the castle.

"Ah, ah. None of that."

Luke applied the heels of his shoes.

After a couple of defiant snorts, the horse put a reluctant foot forward. A gull cried out mournfully. Toby let out an answering whinny. Then they entered the shadowy forest, leaving the fullness of the sun behind.

After providing some dry clothes, Chisholm put Marco back in the stinking hole he shared with the other guys.

"Whadya see out there?" Hub asked as soon as they were alone, then hesitated as he saw Marco's condition. "You went for a swim? Why didn't you take your clothes off?"

"Later," he replied irritably. He still had goose bumps, but he didn't kid himself that they came from the cold.

He stripped off his wet things, then pulled on the pants Chisholm had given him. Ralph snorted. Marco gave him a quick hard look, then gazed back down at his legs. Christ, if he wore these pants back home he'd be arrested for indecent exposure. There was also a loose shirt with full sleeves that reminded him of the seventies, and a vest with clasps, which fell just above his knees.

After he dressed, Marco flopped down on the pad, not giving a rat's ass about the fleas—or whatever else might be crawling in there.

Luckily, he'd left his cigarettes behind. If they'd

been soaked, he didn't know how he'd make it. His hand shook as he lit up, and his body trembled when he fell onto his back.

What the fuck was that flying monster? For the first time in Marco's life he understood what people meant when they said their minds were boggled. He'd already had enough on his plate before the creature showed up, and he was beginning to wonder what other surprises were in store.

Smoke drifted toward the ceiling and he watched it spiral, trying to calm his nerves. Time to regroup. Again he saw Slade as the key. Chisholm's conspiracy could easily earn him a head on the chopping block, and judging by what he'd already seen, he didn't doubt these people had one. But right now the captain was his only connection to freedom. He couldn't reach Slade until he got out of lockup.

Gradually, he became aware that someone was snoring. Hub, on his filthy mat, and the guy probably never gave a thought about what he was sleeping on. He glanced over scornfully, catching Ralph's eye, which prompted the guy to walk over and crouch beside Marco's mat. "So what *did* happen out there?" he asked softly, pulling a cigarette from his pocket.

"You wouldn't believe it."

Ralph glanced at the open slits near the ceiling. "I'm not sure what to believe anymore. Those screams—they ain't like nothing I ever heard before. Did you see what made them?"

"Yeah, I saw."

Agitated, he rocked to a sitting position and snuffed his cigarette out in the heap of butts already on the floor. He gazed at the pile in disgust. Only yesterday, his vision of running the organization had been hours from his hands. Now here he was living in squalor, just like in the projects.

"So what did you see, Marco?"

"It flies like a dragon and screams like a dragon, so it probably is a dragon." He grinned sarcastically. "Oh, wait, isn't that saying about a duck?"

Ralph chuckled dryly, then drew on his smoke. On the exhale, he asked, "So are we gonna get out of here?"

Marco felt a flash of appreciation. With Hub briefly out of the picture, Marco again saw the levelheadedness he'd relied on so often. Reaching for his lighter and another cigarette, he glanced over at Hub, back at Ralph, then again at Hub. "Yeah," he said, flicking the lighter. "I believe we are."

They were now well inside the forest canopy, traveling down what must have once been a well-used trail. Here and there, patches of thriving brush blocked their way, and at one point Luke had been forced to dismount and lead Toby over a fallen log. But they'd apparently passed the worst of it.

The woods were as dark as a smoky bar. Visibility was limited. His transportation was poky at best, and he found himself restless. A bit scared, too, if he wanted to be honest with himself, which at the moment he preferred not to be. Then he caught a spot of light. His heart thrummed with anticipation, but he forced himself to keep his expectations under control. They were probably reaching the far side of the forest. That didn't mean the portal would be there. Nevertheless, he gave Toby an insistent kick. It produced no response. If anything, the horse slowed down.

The farther they went, the more mule-headed Toby became. He tossed his head, snorted repeatedly, and frequently stopped to paw the ground. With dogged persistence, Luke kept him moving.

Then he saw the torch, backlit against a glaring field of blue. The upheld arm of the Statue of Liberty! His hands began shaking so violently he almost lost the reins, and he could no longer deny how frightened he'd been since the moment gunfire broke out. Frightened of dying, frightened for Randy, horrified by Vinnie's murder. But what had terrified him the most was the possibility that Caryn was right.

But there it was, proof that she was wrong. That was New York City, home. So sometimes it wasn't so great, it was the world he knew and understood, and he hadn't expected it to be so easy to find. Too easy, niggled an internal voice, but in his excitement he pushed it away.

Without warning, Toby shuddered. His head went down, yanking the reins from Luke's still trembling hands. The next thing Luke knew he was on the ground, listening to the deflating thuds of Toby's retreating hoofbeats. When he finally climbed to his feet, he took a few cautious steps to prove he could still walk, then broke into a run.

Home. He forced every ounce of speed from his worn-out legs.

Home.

He stretched out his arms. It was close, so close. He could almost touch it now.

Home.

Suddenly he reeled. He fell back, hitting the ground with brutal force. His ears rang, his vision blurred. For one hideous second, he thought he might lose consciousness.

His dizziness passed. He got up on quivering legs and moved cautiously toward the image. Reaching forward, he tested the air. Something hard yet pliant contacted his fingers. Reflexively, he jerked back.

Taking a moment to rebuild his courage, he tried again. The invisible barrier had a consistency that made his skin crawl. Like touching moss on the dark side of a tree or picking up something you thought was dry and discovering it was actually wet and slimy.

He forced himself to push against it firmly. The surface stretched, then snapped, and he jumped back again. Finally, he got as close to the barrier as he could and stared out at Ellis Island. He saw the mottled green surface of Liberty's crown, the people lining up to tour her, the kids running around her base.

He could see it, dammit! Why couldn't he reach it? There had to be something that would puncture that wall!

He spun around in search of a tool, unwilling to examine the wisdom of what he was planning. Spotting a fallen tree limb, he snatched it from the ground. With an involuntary howl, he braced the branch against his body and charged the barrier.

The rebound hurled him through the air.

Time stood still. His senses heightened. He saw each twisting vein of each leaf he passed, heard each subtle crack of each dislodged branch, and though bark and thorns mauled his skin and tore at his clothing, he didn't feel their bites.

Then he landed. The impact coursed through him like an electric shock. Time returned to normal, bringing with it waves of pain. Fighting for his breath, he lay motionless on a carpet of dead leaves for what seemed an eternity. Finally, he rocked onto his knees and stared through the transparent wall.

Jesus, he was in prison again. It was like looking out through a chain-link fence topped with razor wire. Although his physical pain was ebbing, it was minuscule compared to the loss that tore into his gut. Unable to bear the sight of what he'd lost one more second, he turned his head away and bent over.

A sob held fast in his throat, then escaped on a moan of despair.

The surefooted stallion galloped fearlessly up the hills, covering ground quickly. About halfway to the top, Caryn found young Tom's horse grazing amid the heather. Pulling Neptune in, she grabbed the smaller animal's reins and headed into the steeper mountains.

When she found Luke, he was making his way through a particularly rocky patch, stepping gingerly, as though his feet hurt. Small wonder, she thought, hiking through the hills in those wee slips of shoes. It looked as if there were also other ways his travels had done him no good. His shirt and trews had gaping holes, and a foot strap had slipped off, allowing the leg to ride up well above his dark stocking. An angry welt streaked his forehead and he had several scratches on his cheeks that showed beads of blood.

"Ye're a man who uses his clothing hard, Sir Luke Slade." She knew she sounded churlish, but her relief at finding him safe was so great she dared not reveal it. "And your steeds as well. It appears you lost yours."

"I—I was . . . It was—" He took a half step toward the forest—"It was right there. I saw it"—a step back toward her—"New York, Caryn. My home"—yet another toward the forest. His voice was hoarse, impassioned. "I could almost touch it, smell the smells, hear the sounds."

Caryn dismounted and moved to Luke's side.

"We can't go back, Randy and I, can we?"

She put a steadying hand on his shoulder and shook her head.

"Nay, Luke, you cannot." She'd suffered just as he now did, had also seen sights that wrenched her apart. Home. They called it by different names, he and she, but the anguish of being torn away pierced their hearts the same. She felt his loss as keenly as if it had been her own, and tears suddenly rushed to her eyes. Of pity? Aye, but also of remorse. She had the power to free him, yet the needs of the realm must come first. " 'Tis cruel and unjust, I know, but 'tis also the way of things in Lochlorraine. Naught you do will change it."

Her tears were for him, Luke dimly realized, suddenly caught up in her eyes. The sheen made them glow like emeralds, and he could almost see himself reflected there. He couldn't remember the last time someone shared his happiness, much less his sorrow, and something hard and brittle cracked inside him.

"Caryn," he murmured. Turning into the arm that rested on his shoulder, he ran his hand along the curve of her jaw, caught up by the tears that splashed over her lashes and streaked toward his fingers.

"Caryn," he said again as moisture contacted his skin.

Below them, cattle lowed in the meadow. Above, a bird called out to its flock. The afternoon breeze whispered in the brush. But all that filled Luke's mind was that this woman had wept for him, and he had no idea why she cared.

Toby snorted loudly, breaking the spell.

"We'd better get back," he said gruffly, turning to mount.

"Aye. Already we've missed the midday meal."

With that, she vaulted onto her horse.

He glanced at her in astonishment. Feeling self-conscious, and more than a little edgy after getting thrown, he put his foot in the stirrup and climbed into the saddle. The horse seemed his placid self again, so Luke picked up the reins, then shoved his remaining foot in the other stirrup. When his knees were again level with his waist, he gave a nudge and Toby broke into a misery-creating jog.

"Sir Luke," Caryn offered tentatively.

Luke turned and saw that Caryn hadn't moved, so he pulled on Toby's reins.

"Perhaps we could lower your stirrups. 'Twould make your ride more palatable."

It was then he noticed that though she sat on a horse half again the size of his, her feet reached the animal's underbelly. Not surprising, since that's where the stirrups were.

So why were Toby's so short?

"Of course," he said. "This is a kid's horse."

"Kid?" Caryn frowned prettily. "Sir, I have no wish to offend ye, but that makes no sense. Do horses run with goats in your time?"

The laughter that erupted from Luke's belly caught him by such surprise he couldn't hold it back. He collapsed onto the saddle and rode the wave of what he recognized was maniacal glee. When it finally subsided, he looked back at Caryn.

"Was there something amusing about my question?" A faint chuckle accompanied her inquiry.

"I was referring to Tom. Kid is a word for child. And since this is a kid's saddle, it makes sense the stirrups are so high."

"He is a stout-hearted animal. One suitable for many riders, I am sure."

"Old ladies, maybe, and short, fat men." He climbed off Toby and began fiddling with the gear. There were so many straps and buckles he didn't know where to begin. "Would you give me a clue?"

Luke's good-natured request startled Caryn. Most men would be full of cranky bluster under these circumstances. He was quite unlike the men she had known, and not only in this way. From the first she'd noticed it, but hadn't been able to grasp its full nature. Now she did.

He regarded her as a peer.

The men of her acquaintance treated women as possessions, or annoying encumbrances to be herded like a sow or a ewe. To give Ian his fair due—although she sometimes thought he did it only to avoid all the mundane details—he allowed her to deal with the daily life in Lochlorraine without interfering. And during the few times he separated himself from his work, which wasn't often, he solicited her opinions. But Ian also recognized that his unconventional behavior drew criticism so he seldom demonstrated this trust in public.

She wondered if Luke's century was that much different. If women there were finally celebrated for their deeds, not just for beauty or station. Or perhaps Luke was simply an unusual man, one who respected and treated all equally well. A most refreshing thought. How happy she could be in the company of such a man.

Suddenly aware he'd been waiting expectantly while she wool-gathered, she jumped to the ground and walked over to help. She lowered the stirrups one step at a time, giving Luke instructions as she worked.

"I believe your ride will be more comfortable now."

She straightened up and found herself fairly well pressed against his muscular chest. His dark eyes smoldered for an instant, then he uttered a soft apology and stepped away.

"Thank you," he said, again moving to Toby's right side.

"My pleasure," she murmured uncertainly, unable to fathom the rush of pleasure she'd felt at that one brief moment of eye contact. Then she cleared her throat and assumed a brisk manner. "This time, perhaps, you might mount on the left side, as is commonly done."

He gave her a crooked grin as he rounded the animal's head, coming close to her again. "I applaud your tact, Duchess."

"Countess," she corrected with a smile, knowing he'd used the wrong title deliberately. Simultaneously, he reached out and pushed a flyaway strand of hair under her cap. At this simple touch, his smile faded. So did hers. A burst of heat flooded her body, bringing back memories of her impure thoughts that morning. She lowered her head, fearing he might think her wanton, fearing even more that it might be true, knowing that were she ever to have an indiscretion, the dragon slayer was the worst possible choice.

"Come," she said, turning toward her horse and away from the man she would send to possible death. "I know your experience was most trying, but there is a place I want to show you."

Chapter Eleven

She'd warned him, and Luke thought he'd been prepared, but staring through that crystalline pool onto Times Square, he'd felt the same powerful yearning he'd had on the mountains. Caryn had virtually dragged him from the water.

Now, sitting on a flat rock, replacing his shoes and socks, he struggled to pull himself together. He'd already humiliated himself enough by falling off his horse and babbling up on the hill; he didn't have to make it worse.

"There was much Ian meant to tell you last eve," Caryn said softly, standing not far away. "Of matters far beyond my comprehension, but which he felt certain you would understand. This much I can say: The bubble we spoke of is like a membrane surrounding the realm. None can penetrate it until the portal opens." She glanced toward the castle. "We do not know what causes the openings. They happen as if by magic."

"So why don't you just leave?"

"To where? Another time, another land, where

manners and customs differ from our own? How would we live? How would we survive? None in here wish to find out."

"Which is why I want to go back. Can't you understand?"

She turned her head toward Lucifer's Window. The water was choppy now, and Luke wondered if the window itself was still crystal clear. He still ached to wade back in, to find out for himself if what she said was true. He knew it was, of course. His experiences on the mountain had proven it. But one more try. What could it hurt?

His aching scrapes and bruises answered that question. The next try could cost him his life. But what about the ocean? Couldn't they set sail until they reached the bubble's edge? Puncture it with cannons or bombs? He looked out to sea. The sun had started to set. A swath of hazy red and yellow filled the far-off sky. "What's out there?"

"Our men sailed that way when we were first separated from Scotland. Though we once held the hope I see in your eyes, it offers none. The ship nearly perished on the rocks." From the corner of his eye, he saw her smile sadly. "We are enclosed, Luke, completely enclosed."

"Yet you knew we were coming, you must have. So many people couldn't have shown up so fast without prior warning."

"Ian has a compass of sorts that tells him when the portal opens and what year we've encountered. 'Tis why he was stimulated by your arrival. Ye are our first visitors from a time yet to come."

"Your first . . . ?" Twisting on the rock, Luke looked toward the spire. "But . . . Up there . . . That windmill has features that shouldn't exist yet."

When he looked back, he saw that Caryn's face was puzzled. "I know little about the windmill's construction. Ian's grandfather devised and built it. He was a man of uncommon genius, I'm told, and he, too, sought the philosopher's stone. His guidance excited Ian to delve into matters beyond our ken."

Uncommon genius? Luke supposed so. Part of him wished he could have met that old gentleman and found out what else he'd known, but the larger part just wanted to go home.

"The realm moves on, Luke. As days pass, we will drift farther from your homeland. The bubble does not remain still."

Luke stared at her in shock. Of all the information she'd given him, this piece caused the most misery. His spirits sank.

"The views through Lucifer's Window are forever changing," she continued. "This is why Ian so feverishly toils to control the bubble's movements."

"How long do we have?"

"Till the next full moon, perhaps longer, perhaps not. There is no way out, Luke. Accept it. Ye'll have no peace until you do."

Luke heard Caryn's words, didn't doubt she offered them sincerely, but he wasn't as sure she was right. An entire colony had been snared in the bubble. Six more people had gotten in, breaking the barriers of space and time. Where there was an entrance, there was also an exit. So what if no one had found it yet? That proved nothing.

He needed to put his head together with Ian's. The man must have records of his work. With the more advanced knowledge of his century, Luke might be able to see where the experiments had gone wrong. But he had to hurry. Time wasn't on his side.

Just as he was about to stand, a bugle blared.

"Ormeskirk!" Caryn cried.

Seconds later, a shriek shattered the peaceful twilight. Luke recognized the sound, and he tilted his head back to find the source.

Sailing on the air currents was the biggest bird he'd had ever seen.

"Hurry, Luke." Caryn tugged at his ripped sleeve. "We have tarried here too long. The dragon hour is upon us."

Caryn rushed to the castle roof, and Luke suspected she was barely aware he was behind her. The area swirled with activity. Men scurried about shoving powder into massive cannons. Others supplied arrows to archers who ceaselessly fired at the gliding bird. Their shouting voices were muffled by the cannon booms and the bird's shrieks. The twang of departing arrows couldn't be heard at all. To Luke, these frantic efforts seemed futile. The heavy cannonballs lost velocity almost as soon as they left their chambers, and even when an arrow hit its mark, it glanced off and fell to earth.

Twilight limited visibility, but Luke could see why these people thought the animal was a dragon. An elongated snout held rows of jagged teeth designed for eating flesh, and a crest streaked with brilliant green rose from the crown of its head. Its grey-green skin looked as thick as a rhinoceros hide and had no feathers.

He knew there were featherless birds, but he didn't think they could fly. Most certainly they weren't gliders like this one, who traveled hundreds of feet on a single flap of its long, jointed wings. He could smell fear all around him. But beyond the inexplicable ache that arose in his heart when the creature cried, his only emotions were admiration and curiosity.

Suddenly the bird dove toward the ground.

"Hold yer fire lest you strike a villager!" shouted Chisholm, his voice thin and strained.

From below came the panicked cries of people. Animals chattered in alarm. Somewhere a dog barked frantically.

A pig's squeal rose above the rest.

Luke ran to the battlement just as the bird swooped down to snare a massive hog. With the fluid motion of a fighter jet doing maneuvers, it then swerved and shot straight up.

It leveled out at an astonishing height, the squirming animal dangling from its claws. Compared to its captor, the pig looked like a small stuffed toy, and its piteous squalls brought a hush to those on the roof.

"God was with us," Caryn said when the squeals were finally muted by distance. "The monster set no roofs afire tonight."

Puffs of cannon smoke floated in the dusky sky, and the archers remained standing half at ready.

Luke looked around, thinking these people were lucky the bird had done no worse than stealing a pig. They'd put the poor thing under siege. What did they expect? But Caryn's face was filled with impassioned fear and loathing, her eyes burned jade and her chest rose and fell erratically. At a time like this, he doubted she'd listen to environmentalist tripe about saving a species.

As he caught one last glimpse of the magnificent creature gliding off to the west, he couldn't help thinking it was one of a kind.

"Luke," Caryn said, suddenly and breathlessly. "I did not realize you were here."

No surprise to him, and he was too caught up with the departing bird to respond. She stood beside him, also watching.

"Since ye have now seen the cruelties the dragon performs, do you understand our joy at your arrival?"

The bird had taken a pig. He found nothing particularly cruel about that. "It's not a dragon," he said. "I don't know what it is or how it got here, but it's not a dragon."

"Not a dragon? Did you not see with your own eyes how he swoops down to terrorize the land? Had ye also seen him ignite a roof, ye'd be thinking differently. None but a dragon could wrought such damage."

"There must be an explanation," he said, although he didn't have one. "It's only an animal. There's a way to live with it in peace. You only have to find it."

Caryn made a scoffing sound. "Ormeskirk steals our animals and sets our villages to ruin. Many a man has been killed or injured during his attacks. We cannot seek peace with such a monster. Killing him is our only salvation." Suddenly her heated voice softened. "This is why you were sent to us, Luke. To free us from Ormeskirk's reign."

"Caryn . . ."

She put a finger to his lips, a gesture much more personal than he thought she realized. "Do not protest," she said. "On the morrow I will take you around the realm. Perhaps then ye'll see what we are trying to save."

When Nancy brought Luke's breakfast again the next morning he asked about his original clothing.

"The washerwomen did manage to save yer trousers, sir, but the shirt and jacket were beyond their skills."

"How soon can I get them back?"

"Since we've been having such bonny spring weather, I'd say most likely on the morrow."

"I see," he said, feeling grateful it wasn't winter. "Can you stand another silly question?"

"Most certainly, sir." Nancy's hand flew to her mouth as she realized the implication of her answer. When Luke simply smiled, she giggled. "And what might it be? Your question, that is."

"Where can I get a bath?" He supposed a shower was out of the question.

"I will arrange it, sir."

With a curtsy, she breezed from the room, leaving

behind the already familiar scent of brown sugar and rose water. Soon there was a rap on his door. Luke opened it on two men bearing a large porcelain tub. With them were women, carrying buckets of hot water. After the men set the contraption in the only open space in the room, the women filled it.

"We'll stay to scrub your back, if it pleases ye," one woman said.

Luke declined as graciously as possible, and when the entourage left, he returned to his breakfast. Being waited on so thoroughly made him extremely uncomfortable. Although he'd mange to dispense with the manservant, he didn't know how to make the others stop offering these constant ministrations. Like most people back home, he'd always thought it would be great to have people respond to his every whim. Now he knew how intrusive such attention could be.

The women had left soft linen towels and washcloths. There was also a fresh bar of translucent Castile soap. He turned it over, watching the light catch on small imperfect bubbles inside. More confirmation that he truly was in a different era.

He finished eating, then stripped down and climbed into the tub. The water soothed his ragged nerves, and he soaked awhile, reviewing the events of the previous day. Although he was somewhat annoyed that he'd agreed to ride with Caryn that morning, when he really wanted to go to the laboratory to confer with Ian, he'd awakened in surprisingly good spirits.

This he attributed to seeing the anomalous bird.

The creature had struck a chord of sympathy in him, and he felt some regret that he'd never have a chance to learn more about it.

Impossible, of course.

He leaned back in the tub, deciding to stay in until the water grew cool. He ached from head to toe and had learned that horseback riding required muscles he had never used. Massaging his inner thigh, he thought about the day ahead. He'd stop by to see Randy first, make sure Caryn had removed the leeches, then he'd go on her tour to keep her happy. As a secondary benefit—although he didn't hold much hope for it—he'd keep an eye out for signs of an overlooked portal. After that, he'd go see Ian.

The water was getting chilly, so he grabbed for a towel, stepped out of the tub, and began briskly drying off.

Going riding with Caryn wasn't an unpleasant prospect. In fact, he looked forward to it more than was healthy. He needed a focused mind to devise an escape, and she was a distraction if ever there was one. Besides, she was taking him out for a reason, and one reason only. To convince him to slay her dragon. Well, he hated to disappoint her, but . . .

Kill that astonishing animal?

Right.

Randy was propped up on bed pillows when Luke arrived. Nancy sat at his side, holding his hand and beaming like a naked hundred-watt bulb. Luke wanted to demand an explanation for why he hadn't been informed of Randy's recovery, but the couple glowed so brightly, he held his tongue. "Look at this, Sir Luke. Our Sir Randy is awake."

"Aw, you don't hafta call me sir," Randy objected, but he was clearly basking in the girl's attention. "How come everyone here calls everybody sir, Luke? Huh? How come?"

Luke moved closer to the bed. "They don't. For instance, I've never heard anyone call Nancy that."

Nancy and Randy shared a laugh that made Luke feel excluded.

"They treating you okay, kid?"

"Huh? What? Oh, sure. Real okay." Randy was distracted by something in Nancy's face. "Don't she got pretty eyes, Luke? Don't she?"

"Very pretty. You sure you're doing okay?"

With visible reluctance, Randy turned his eyes on Luke. "Well . . ."

"What?" Luke reached for Randy's blanket.

"Lady Caryn said I couldn't have no coffee yet."

"They have coffee here?"

"Aye, sir," Nancy responded. "And quite good it is I'm told. Meself, I prefer me tea."

"Lady Caryn is pretty, ain't she? And nice, too. I was only kidding about the coffee." Randy looked at Nancy again. "Nancy's prettier, though. You ever seen such eyes?"

"They're both good-looking." Luke's curt tone surprised even him, and when Nancy's and Randy's expressions turned suddenly wary he knew he'd been painfully obvious.

"When did he wake up?" he asked Nancy, forcing more warmth into his voice.

"I came in after I ordered your bath, sir. When I saw Sir Randy awake, I rushed fast as I could and fetched the countess. She come down and examined him."

"She said my recovery was remarkable!" Randy added with childlike pleasure. "Ain't that great, Luke? I'm remarkable."

Luke had never seen Randy so . . .

So happy. This was something that would normally please him, but for crissakes they weren't in a New York hospital, they were in—

"Anyone tell you where we are, kid?"

"Huh?" Randy was gazing at Nancy again. "Oh, yeah, sort of. Nancy explained we're in Lochlorraine, floating in something bubbly. It don't make much sense to me, but you understand it, don't ya, Luke? You understand everything."

"I have a feel for it."

"See, Nancy? I tole you. Luke knows everything. He's smart. Real smart."

Nancy picked up his hand and beamed again. "So's our Sir Randy," she said to Luke. "He knows how to read and do his sums, and he promised to teach me."

"Very nice." Luke drifted to the opposite side of the bed from where Nancy sat, and stood behind his cousin, furtively plucking at the edge of the blanket. "You been telling her about our home?"

"Aye, he has. The Americas! 'Tis so exciting!"

"Yes, exciting." He could have been spouting gibberish for all Nancy cared, and since neither paid him much notice he managed to lift the blanket just enough to peek underneath.

No pulsing slugs. Caryn had kept her promise.

"Hey, I'll tell you what, kid," Luke said, letting go of the bedcovers. "I'm going out now to make arrangements to leave. I'll stop by again this afternoon. Maybe we can have dinner together."

"Sure, Luke. That's be real good. Nancy's gonna eat with us too, ain't you, Nancy?"

The girl nodded eagerly.

"Great!" Luke replied with forced heartiness.

As he reached the door, he looked back. The couple was again gazing into each other's eyes.

"You get better now, Randy," he said. "Soon as you're well I'm going to take you home."

"Huh?" Randy turned unfocused eyes in Luke's direction. "Oh, yeah, okay." Then moved them back to Nancy. "But don't hurry none on my account."

Chapter Twelve

Luke borrowed Tom's horse again. The boy possessed a winning charm that reminded Luke of Kevin when he was young. He even sported the same perpetual bruise on his face. Although Luke liked the idea of talking to the boy while he waited for Caryn, what did you ask a kid of his time? *What do you want to be when you grow up?* He was a stable master's son; he'd grow up to be a stable master, too. *How do you like school?* He probably didn't go to school. *How'd you get that bruise?* Yeah, Kevin and Luke had always liked that question.

Not that the bruises were sufficient reason to think the boy was being beaten. This was a hard land, and most of the residents displayed some sort of wound. But just the thought of it made Luke sympathetic, and it didn't hurt that the boy's constant chatter made it easy to avoid stupid questions.

"We all been so happy since you come," Tom now said, "knowing Ormeskirk won't be plaguin' us no more."

"Oh, yes, the dragon," Luke replied noncommittally, holding on to Toby's reins and suddenly wishing Caryn would hurry up.

"How will ye be slaying him, sir? With your claymore? Surely ye won't be using your dirk." He eyed Luke up and down. "Hey, where are your weapons?"

"I'm going on a friendly ride, Tom. No need for weapons."

"But a warrior . . ." Tom looked away, shifted his weight a time or two, then appeared very grateful when Caryn walked up.

"Milady," he said. "I got Neptune all saddled. I'll be getting him now."

He scurried off, relieving Luke of the need to answer his insightful questions.

"Was young Tom chattering off your ears?" Caryn asked with some amusement.

"He's a good kid, but I haven't called him that to his face."

Caryn laughed. "Aye, he would not take kindly to it."

When Tom returned with the white stallion, Luke and Caryn headed out for the hills, with Caryn pointing out various features of the land. They watched fishermen haul out their nets, and she told him the many uses they had for fish, not the least among them as fuel for the lanterns. The timber, she told him, was not only used for lumber and fires, its ash was turned into soap and lye.

Now they were stopped on a ridge near a cluster of boulders, gazing down on the village and the castle. From this view, Luke saw that the courtyard extended to the rear of the castle, forming cloverleafs on the sides. Vegetation filled these private areas. The left cloverleaf housed a greenhouse and small patches of greens. The right one was a profusion of blooms.

"We grow herbs and vegetables too delicate to be fare in the fields," she told him. "The greenhouse contains fruit trees of many varieties." Which explained the pears, Luke thought. "And the other is our private garden where I like to take tea in mild weather.

"The rear bailey is where most of our commerce takes place," she went on, pointing toward a cluster of buildings. Two of them emitted billows of smoke from tall brick chimneys.

"The smokehouse and the main kitchen," Caryn explained. "Next to them are the weaving house, and the wee cottage beside is where the seamstress crafts the cloth." Her finger moved. "Off there is the cobbler's shop. And the small shed to the left of the gate sells such sundries as may bring comfort to daily life."

"What do you use for money?" Luke asked.

"Money?" Caryn's smile implied he'd asked a childlike question. "We have none, much to the sorrow of those whose pockets were once lined with the gold of commerce. Each family tills their plot or plies their craft, then trades what they have for what they have not. All pledge a percent in support of the castle."

Luke nodded. "Seems you've built a slice of paradise."

"Aye, paradise it could be." At this, her expression turned sad. "If not for Ormeskirk."

Luke felt a flash of anger. "Oh, the ubiquitous dragon."

She turned toward him so abruptly her horse started, which sparked a jump from Toby. "You sound bitter, sir."

Settling his horse down, Luke then leaned against the front of his saddle. His legs were aching and the cuts on his face stung, something he hadn't noticed before. Their shared moment of normalcy had lulled him into believing that life really was normal. But that feeling was gone now.

"Look," he said. "Two mornings ago I woke up in my apartment. I like that apartment, okay? I like brewing my coffee when I get up, hearing it percolate, breathing the smell. I have a radio that plays music. Now I have this." He arced his arm to encompass the valley. "While it's beautiful it's no substitute for home. To top it off, you folks think I should gladly risk my life to kill a creature that just wants to survive. Bitter? No, I'm disgusted. That animal isn't a dragon. They don't exist, Caryn. Not here. Not in my time. Not ever. But no matter how often I tell you, you don't seem to hear."

"But ye saw him, Luke."

"There's a logical explanation," he answered stubbornly.

"And what could be more logical than one's own eyes? How can such proof be denied?"

"It's a bird, for crissake!"

She cringed, and he realized he'd once again committed blasphemy. He thought of apologizing, but what was the use?

"And ye have birds of his proportion in your time?"

Luke shook his head.

"Then what matters it if Ormeskirk is a dragon or a bird? The monster still thrusts himself on us, stealing our lambs and our calves. More than one man has died by his cruel beak and talons. My own husband perished during a crusade to vanquish him."

Clearly upset, she nudged her big horse forward. Toby fell into line behind the stallion with no urging. As they rode slowly down the hill, the silence stretched.

In the tense stillness, Luke's despair returned, bringing a sinking feeling that they'd never get out. If that were true, how would he cope? He was a street kid turned mob entrepreneur. He knew nothing of these people's ways. Furthermore, many of them repelled him.

They lived a filthy life. No running hot water, no flushing toilets. Who knew what manner of bacteria thrived in that indoor privy? He'd probably die of blood poisoning or a simple flu before the year was out. And Randy? Already weak from loss of blood and the trauma of his gunshot wound, he was a sitting duck for every microscopic bug that ever was.

Not that Randy seemed to care. His infatuation with his nurse had seen to that. For some reason, the memory of the besotted couple provoked Luke to glance at Caryn. He'd expected her face to be hard and grim, but instead he found sadness. Moments before she'd been smiling with pride over her small kingdom. He'd been the one to take that away.

The depth of his regret surprised him, and he had a momentary glimpse of what Randy felt. With a woman like Caryn by his side—and in his bed, he couldn't deny he felt that need—life in Lochlorraine might be bearable.

Maybe more than bearable. Maybe rich. Maybe complete. All his years of seemingly useless study would come in handy here. He could join Ian in his work, bring modern advancements to the land.

Just then, Caryn's horse let out a jittery whinny and jumped sideways, catching Toby on the snout. Toby skittered, giving out a whinny of his own. As Caryn effortlessly reined in her uneasy horse, Luke struggled with his. Not a simple task, and it occupied his attention completely.

"What is it?" Caryn asked, her voice heavy with apprehension.

At Caryn's question, Luke turned his eyes to the valley. Cattle bawled in the meadows. Newly shorn sheep scattered in all directions, some barreling across fields of sprouts. Workers shouted, trying to head off the marauding animals.

A shadow flew over them, then was gone.

"Something has changed," Caryn said. "Ormeskirk appears only at the dragon hour. He has never come early before."

A horn sounded below, loud and long. The field workers abandoned their attempts to save their crops and ran toward the cottages. People streamed out of the castle compound, across the bridge, and toward the village. Women and children emerged from doors, some carrying baskets of belongings.

Dozens of people clustered around a platform that supported a large cistern. Others unwound a thick coil that lay beside it. As the coil unfurled, several more strained to attach it to the cistern.

"What are they doing?" Luke asked.

"Preparing for Ormeskirk."

"So why the water?"

"Clearly you know naught of dragons, sir."

Her tone annoyed him. "Only what I've read in fairy tales."

His sarcasm was lost. "Then you must have read of their fiery breath. And if you know that, then you must also know that it sets the roofs afire."

"Of course. How could I have forgotten?" With the amount of sparks that flew from the chimneys, Luke found it miraculous that the straw roofs didn't routinely burst into flames.

The horn blew again.

Ormeskirk swooped low over the village. Not a volley had been fired at his approach. His unexpected appearance had apparently caught the castle sentry off guard. Now, with the bird so close to the ground, the soldiers wouldn't shoot for fear of hitting one of their own.

Most of the previous night Luke had stood too far behind the battlement to see events on the ground, but now he had a clear view. Despite the danger, he found himself cheering for the creature and glad the soldiers couldn't shoot at it. Not that the villagers were completely unprepared. As the bird glided low, they rushed forward with pitchforks and axes. A man leaped up on the dip of a wing and caught it with the tine of his weapon.

Ormeskirk faltered, a sight that evoked a prayer of thanks from Caryn's lips. But Luke's heart twisted at the ensuing scream. As the bird struggled to stay aloft, his injured wing struck a cottage. Straw flew into the wind. A rafter collapsed, pulling in a stretch of roof. With another scream, the bird rose and turned, his open beak poised just above the crumbling roof. The cottage instantly burst into flames.

"Jesus!" Luke exclaimed, snapping his head toward Caryn.

She gave him a censuring look. "So, Sir Luke Slade, do ye still affirm that dragons do not exist? Or do birds of your time breathe fire and smoke as this one does?"

Luke shook his head in bewilderment. He hadn't actually seen the dragon breathe fire, only the roof igniting, but . . .

He couldn't believe his eyes.

"Now the poor McCormick family will have to rebuild their home. Do ye see why we must slay this creature? Peace shall never come to Lochlorraine until Ormeskirk lies dead."

Luke didn't know how to respond. Still confused, he watched as the group at the cistern came forward, holding the hose as they might a rope during a game of tug-of-war. Someone behind must have opened a ballcock, because the hose rippled like a snake, then spewed water on the burning roof.

Another horn sounded. Luke searched for Ormeskirk, coming upon him just as he'd snatched up a full-grown sheep. A wail of pain escaped as the bird flapped his wings to rise, and he listed toward his injured side. The sheep, even bigger than the pig of the night before, struggled mightily in the predator's grasp. This was more than the bird could bear. He lost hold of his quarry, which plummeted to the ground, and landed just yards from Luke and Caryn, where it bleated weakly, but otherwise it didn't move. The bird rose in the air, then circled the spot where he'd lost his prey.

Luke wasn't sure what to do next. They had to leave immediately, but barreling down the mountain didn't seem a hot idea. He knew what dogs did to fleeing rabbits.

Caryn leaped off her horse and snatched a bow and quiver from her saddle. Holding her skittish animal's reins, she walked over to Luke and gave him instructions. He was having his own troubles with Toby, and at first he wasn't sure he heard her right.

"You're going to do what?"

"Send Neptune back to the castle. Your mount will follow if you give him his head. Go with him. Go now!"

She slapped her horse's flank. He sprang into a gallop, spurring Toby into a jog. Making a split-second decision, Luke jumped off. He stumbled as he landed, and rocks bruised his feet through the soft soles of his loafers, but he managed to stay afoot.

Caryn slanted him an inscrutable look. "Have you decided to stay and fight, Dragon Slayer, or were you merely too clumsy to remain on your mount?"

"Just take it that I'm clumsy," he replied. "Now what?"

Before she could answer, Ormeskirk gave another cry and sped toward the ground. Grabbing Caryn's hand, Luke dashed for the nearest boulder. As they crouched low, Caryn pulled an arrow from her quiver.

"What are you doing?"

"Preparing for an attack."

"Your archers can't hit him, for God's sake, what makes you think you can?"

Just then, an immense shadow fell over their hiding place. Luke pulled a protesting Caryn under the protection of his arm, then looked up. Ormeskirk stood above them, looming a good twenty feet high. Even at that distance, his hot breath fanned Luke's hair against his face. The touch was almost more than his suddenly sensitized skin could bear, but he couldn't find it within him to brush away the strands. Frozen, he awaited the fate of the pig and the sheep.

Chapter Thirteen

A long time elapsed and nothing happened. Slowly, Luke gazed up to see the creature looking down on them.

What kind of bird was this? He cocked his head on his long neck much like a vulture. But the narrow bony crest on top of his head was nothing like the vulture's feather-rimmed dome. In fact, beyond his wings and body shape, he looked like no bird Luke had ever seen. His swordlike snout appeared less rigid than a beak, and the smooth skin covering his skeletal body conformed to the contours of his frame like a membrane.

As Luke watched the bird, he appeared to watch back. Rather than moving smoothly, his head jerked from spot to spot, and his eyes blinked mechanically. Could he see them? Luke wasn't so sure, and he struggled to categorize the creature. Something clicked, and when it did, he knew exactly what the animal was.

His fear instantly vanished.

Caryn stirred beside him. He turned and saw her

trying to notch an arrow into her bowstring. The bird's head snapped in her direction.

"Be still," he hissed. "Be totally still."

But already a leathery snout lowered over the top of the boulder. Caryn shuddered and dropped her bow. "Be still," he repeated, pulling her closer, waiting, testing, willing himself to be right.

After an endless moment, the snout retreated. Soon even the shadow withdrew. Luke heard scuffling sounds, the clatter of dislodged rocks rolling along the ground. He let go of Caryn and crawled to the edge of the boulder.

With a waddling gait, the creature walked bow-legged toward the sheep. From here Luke could clearly see the wings, which were drawn up against the body, causing his taloned appendages to jut out like grasping hands. Fibers ran beneath the wings' translucent covering, and the myriad bones that formed them protruded like the collarbone of someone near starvation.

But he doubted this animal was starving, for its elongated trunk and femurs didn't appear emaciated, and it moved with vigor, though it had been wounded just a short time ago. When it reached the softly bleating sheep, it lowered its head and gave a nudge with its snout.

Caryn scooted in beside Luke. "What is Ormeskirk doing?"

Luke shook his head and continued to observe. Chirping, the bird nudged the sheep again. Then a third time. On this last nudge, the sheep let out an audible sigh, but didn't lift its head.

The bird gave the sheep several more prods, then suddenly scuttled back. Spreading his wings, he let out a keening wail.

A moment later, he rose into the air and flew off into the echo of his cry.

Luke watched until he disappeared. Convinced he'd arrived at the right conclusion about the animal's origins, he turned to tell Caryn.

She was huddled against the boulder, quivering from head to toe. Luke took her in his arms and stroked her hair. She trembled, her lavender scent rising from her heated body. "I . . . I—Oh, dear heaven, I was deathly afraid."

"Of course you were." He kissed her forehead and murmured soothing words that had no real meaning.

Abruptly she pulled away, clearly embarrassed. "I mustn't succumb to—" She shook her head. Tears brimmed in her eyes, and she gnawed at her lower lip, a weak attempt to hold them back. " 'Tis nothing. A mere . . . That is—I've never seen Ormeskirk so near. He is more fearsome than ever I imagined."

Gripping the boulder, she pulled herself to her feet, but her legs still quivered. Luke put out a steadying hand.

"Nay," she said. "I have let weakness have its way with me too long. 'Twas unseemly of me. Especially when work must be done."

At this, she marched shakily toward the sheep, but Luke stayed where he was. The breeze fluttered through the curls that had escaped her braid, and she squared her shoulders in a way that revealed her determined spirit. This was a woman any man would cherish.

He wanted to be that man. All his concerns paled when compared to his fortune in finding her. He couldn't leave. He'd work diligently with Caryn to restore Randy's health. He and Ian would find ways to improve conditions in the kingdom. But he'd stay. He'd accept his fate. And he'd win this woman as his own.

When Caryn reached the sheep, she bent toward her ankle, coming out with a flash of metal. Wondering what she was doing, Luke started to rise. Then she knelt, and in one quick movement slit the sheep's throat.

As blood poured from the open wound, seeping away the last of the unconscious animal's life, she sliced its belly. Luke's stomach roiled as if struck with a sucker punch. Images whirred through his mind. Vinnie, weaving against the backdrop of trees, trying to stanch his flowing blood. Kevin, pouring his life's essence onto black asphalt. Lights, red, white, blue, whirling, swirling, twirling, making him dizzy.

Why're you so stupid, Kevin? Stupid. So stupid.

Pa wasn't worth it.

Sickened, terrified of getting caught in his waking nightmare, Luke sprang to his feet. He covered the ground in just a few strides. "What the hell are you doing?"

She jerked around and met his eyes. "Gutting the sheep so the meat will not sour."

"But, you're a countess, not a butcher."

She paused, and he forced himself to avert his eyes from the coil of entrails spilling from the animal's wound.

"I do not understand," she said, clearly puzzled by his turmoil. "Don't your people slaughter animals for food?"

As hard as he tried, he couldn't keep his eyes from that gaping hole. Again, lights whirled in his head. Sirens blared. "We don't . . . we don't kill them ourselves."

"I do what I must," she said evenly. "The wool from this sheep would feed the owner's family for a month. The least the realm can offer in recompense is unfouled mutton."

No longer able to bear the sight, Luke glanced away. This was a different era, a harder time, he told himself. These people lived closer to the earth and regarded animals as food or beasts of burden. But his revulsion overpowered him. In his experience, only twisted people killed animals. He couldn't make his home in a place like this, or care for a woman who was capable of such an act.

"How do you expect to get it down there?" His voice sounded hard, but he didn't care. "You sent the horses back."

"A wagon is coming." Her face filled with sadness, she gestured behind him with the dripping red knife in her hand.

Looking back, he saw a line of troops coming their way. An alarm must have gone out when their horses had arrived without them. He anxiously awaited their arrival, praying they had a blanket to cover the slaughtered beast so he wouldn't have to look at it.

It wasn't until sometime later, back in his room and immersed in another bath, that he remembered he hadn't told Caryn what he knew about the bird.

Forget it, Slade. It would be a waste of breath. She was too busy hating Ormeskirk to listen.

The services for Vinnie and the villager shot by Ralph were held in a large chapel just outside the commerce bailey. Afterward, the bodies were wrapped in wool shrouds and placed on litters, revealing a familiarity with death that Luke found as unsettling as seeing Caryn slaughter the sheep.

In a ritualistic procession, the mourners walked to the sea, where the litters were set on individual rafts that Luke later learned had been rigged with explosives. With words of blessing, Ian lit each fuse, then gave the rafts a shove. The ebb tide quickly swept them toward the horizon.

As Vinnie's craft burst into flame, he thought of the man's mother. A warm and loving woman, she'd forever ache to know what became of her son. Even when Luke returned, he wouldn't be able to tell her. His fantastic tale would sound like a cruel joke.

Arnie's widow, Naomi, had stood beside Luke during the entire procedure, staring out in stony silence, but when the flames on the horizon began to fade, she turned to Luke.

"No selkies shall defile their bodies now, but yer other clansman has a curse on his head. Remind him I have not lifted it."

"He's not my clansman," Luke replied. "And I'm sorry for your loss."

"Tell him," Naomi said, her eyes hard and cold.

Afterward, Luke chose to eat in the big hall, hoping to find another traveler. More than ever, he yearned to leave Lochlorraine, but time was against him.

He entered the hall, bypassing a line that was waiting to wash up in a murky tank of water mounted on the wall. People surreptitiously glanced at him as he walked by. Servants paused in their duties. Ignoring the attention, Luke approached one of the long tables. The occupants deferentially lowered their gazes. "Dragon slayer," one man murmured, glancing at a giant mural on the wall of a man and a dragon. Both bleeding, but what would he expect. This was Lochlorraine.

"Luke," he corrected, but not a soul called him that during the brief conversation. He asked if other travelers were there, and a man guided him to a table near the back entrance.

Now he sat next to Jose Vasquez, who'd come from "the year of our Lord twelve hundred and thirty-seven," and had been in the time bubble for nearly ten years. Jose was cheerfully talkative, and apparently not easily intimidated. Upon questioning, he told Luke that he had farmed a small plot in the hills outside Málaga and had gone into the higher mountains in search of fresh game for his wife and children.

"When in front of my eyes, the light comes," he

said, in clear but fractured English, "I think God, he has come to smote me for breaking the king's laws."

"Did you ever try to escape?"

"Oh, sí. Every meter of this land I search, and—" He looked away nervously, drew a chunk of bread through the gravy on his plate, then took a bite before continuing. "The Lucifer's Window, I swim to it."

"You got through?" Luke asked excitedly, then shook his head at his own stupidity.

"No. The skin of the bubble, it throws me back to the beach." Jose crossed himself. "The angels, they smiled on me that day. Many others did not have such blessings and so go the way of Arnie and your friend."

Luke had barely touched his food, and he prodded a chunk of mutton with his two-tined fork. Just smelling it reminded him of Caryn bending over the butchered sheep and made his stomach lurch. He pushed it aside in favor of a small, stuffed bird. "How long before you gave up?"

Jose fiddled with a pouch belted at his waist and pulled out a pipe, then went on to fill it from a second, smaller pouch.

The incongruity escaped Luke only a second. "Where'd you get tobacco, Jose?"

"Chisholm's sundry shop. The cost it is dear, but my pleasure is much so I pay the price." He tamped down the tobacco with great concentration that took a painful amount of time. Meanwhile Luke waited for the answer to his original question.

"Five seasons, I search," Jose finally said, "and never did I find a way. I learn to make a home in

Lochlorraine. You will also learn." He put away the tobacco bag, made a move to rise, then hesitated. When he spoke again his voice held sorrow. "But my Maria, I still miss her. It pains my heart that she I will never see again."

"Get your hands the fuck off me!" Hub barked, elbowing a soldier in the gut. The man let out a grunt and staggered away. Another took his place, but this one held a musket aimed at Hub's chest. The big man gave it a stare, then lifted his eyes to angrily meet those of the soldier's.

"I canna miss at this range, man. And I will shoot if you dinna come peaceably."

"What's going on, boss?" Ralph asked.

Marco shook his head. He knew, of course. Chisholm now had a killer to placate Maclachlan.

He stepped toward the soldiers, keeping his head imperiously high. "What is the meaning of this?"

A soldier, who displayed several emblems on his tam that indicated rank, held a scroll in his hand. He unfurled it, then began reading. " 'By command of Sir Ian Maclachlan, Fifth Earl of Lochlorraine, Hub Barcowski shall be turned over to the court to stand trial for the murder of Arnold Miller.' "

The man droned on about the trial being held at council on such and such a date, with the Lady Caryn Maclachlan sitting in judgment, et cetera, et cetera.

"You're not gonna let them get away with this, are you, Marco?" Hub asked in panic.

"There is naught he can do," said the soldier with the gun.

"Talk to that Chisholm guy, boss. Pull some strings."

" 'Twas Chisholm who presented the evidence to his lairdship," said the reader of the scroll.

"What? No!" Hub swung his head back and forth, as if hunting for someone to help him. "Boss?"

"Where are you taking him?" Marco asked.

"To the tower, where he shall await trial, then be summarily beheaded if convicted."

"Jesus, I didn't kill that man! Ralph—"

Hub's abrupt end to that sentence told Marco he would keep the vow of silence. He wouldn't snitch. Good.

Marco gave the man in charge a questioning glance, and when he got a nod of permission, he walked over to Hub. "It's a misunderstanding," he assured. "We'll get you out of this. Stay cool."

Hub's big shoulders sagged, his eyes took on a tormented cast. "Okay, okay. Just don't forget me."

"Never," Marco vowed.

The soldiers then marched Hub from the room, leaving only the scroll reader behind.

"Our laird also instructed me to show you and your companion to new quarters," the man informed Marco, not unexpectedly. "Ye shall be housed on the garrison floor, and hereafter be free to go where you will."

"Hot dog!" Ralph exclaimed, kicking the filthy mat he'd claimed as his bed. "Can't wait to leave *that* behind."

Marco smiled, trying to look happily surprised. After gathering the pipe and tobacco Chisholm had given him the day before—a puny reward for betraying a friend—he followed the soldier.

They traveled through long halls lit only with candles and lanterns, but the unsteady light didn't hide the treasures in the alcoves along their way. Holy shit, there was a fortune in gold and jewels, right here for the taking.

And no place to fence it, he reminded himself glumly. As they walked, Ralph asked the soldier about the screeching and commotion the previous afternoon. " 'Twere Ormeskirk, the dragon," replied the man. Marco ignored Ralph's questioning glance, and tuned both of them out.

When their escort showed them into a small cheerless room, his spirits took a further nosedive. At least there were beds of sorts, if that's what he cared to call those Spartan-looking cots. "Where will Ralph be staying?"

The soldier looked at him blankly. "With you, sir, of course."

"There's some mis—" Marco caught himself, realizing he was about to reveal too much. "This'll do for now."

"It sure beats the dungeon," Ralph said as soon as the soldier left.

Refraining from saying that dungeons were normally underground, Marco simply nodded.

Ralph flopped onto a bed. "What're we gonna do about Hub— Hey, what do you know?" He flicked a flowery container sitting on the bottom shelf of the washstand that separated the beds. "This piss pot's made of china instead of tin. So what about Hub?"

"Funny question," Marco replied. "Since you're the one who actually shot that guy."

"Yeah . . ." Ralph leaned forward. "Yeah." Propping his arms on his knees, he rested his head on a fisted hand and stared at his feet. "Poor Hub."

Leaving Ralph to his microscopic moment of grief, Marco reclined on his bed. At least this one didn't stink, and he couldn't hear anything crawling inside. But he was damned sick of living this way. He'd had enough of those scraps of food that weren't fit for dogs. Furthermore, he hadn't had a shower in days. His skin was starting to crawl.

He let his eyes roam the cramped room, which was meagerly furnished. Other than the beds and washstand, the only other piece of furniture was a tall cabinet that probably served as a closet. It beat that long, dank prison of a room, but it still wasn't good enough. If Chisholm wanted his help with the Uzi, things had damned well get better than this.

Marco wondered, though, how far the man's influence actually went. Look at what freedom had cost. While Hub wasn't any Einstein, he'd been loyal, and someone his size frequently came in handy for a short guy like Marco. It hadn't felt all that good handing him over.

Abruptly Marco sat up and pulled his pipe out of his pocket, irritated by the inconvenience. Loose tobacco lined his pocket now. And what had Chisholm been thinking, anyway, giving him this pittance of an offering like he was some goddamn peasant?

He wanted riches and comfort, servants waiting on him hand and foot. This sure as hell wasn't it.

Dumping the half-burned tobacco into the piss pot, he brought out a pouch and began pouring fresh.

"You get that lit," Ralph said, "give me a few puffs. I haven't had a smoke all day."

"Fuck off," Marco snapped. "It's mine."

When he finally had the stubborn pipe glowing, he leaned back on his bed. It was time to start scheming again.

Chapter Fourteen

Jose got up to smoke outside and Luke returned to his meal, but the man's discouraging information had reduced his slim appetite to zero. He considered seeking out other travelers—he'd learned from questioning the servants and guards that there were nearly a dozen more—but he suspected their stories would all end with the words "no way out."

Perhaps they were right. Perhaps he did need to accept it. At least, unlike Jose, he hadn't left loved ones behind. While Carmine and the organization would be steamed about his abrupt disappearance, few beyond his employees at Gaskin's Garage would even notice he was gone.

This wasn't something he'd reflected on before, and it hit him like a hammer blow. It was true, he realized. He'd dropped off the face of the earth, but no one back home would really care. What a lousy testament to his life.

Feeling half ill, Luke excused himself from the table and returned to his room. For the next several days, he took most of his meals there. Each morning, after eating and taking a bath—a habit that had the servants lifting their eyebrows—he went to see Randy. Nancy was always with him, so he seldom stayed long. In the afternoons he borrowed Toby and rode down to the loch to stare out over Lucifer's Window, aching to swim home.

On the fourth morning, Luke found Randy alone, dozing. He took the chair next to the bed and waited. Not like he had tons of other stuff to do.

Soon Randy opened his eyes. "Hi, Luke."

"How you feeling, kid?"

"Good, I'm good." He tried to sit and winced. "I'm still not so hot at sitting up."

Luke stood and supported Randy as he straightened, then arranged the pillows behind his back. Although the kid had come through the primitive surgery with flying colors, he didn't look well this morning. His skin was flushed and his eyes red-rimmed.

Luke put his hand on Randy's head. "Feels like you have a fever."

"Aye, aye." Randy smiled when Luke responded with a questioning look. "Just tryin' to fit in, is all."

"You sound like a pirate."

"Cool, huh?"

"Maybe you're getting an infection," Luke said distractedly, reaching for the shoulder of Randy's nightshirt.

"Lady Caryn says the same thing. She gives me some icky-tasting stuff to drink every morning, so it must be medicine. She's real smart, the smartest person I ever met." Randy immediately looked contrite. "Course you're smart too."

"Don't worry about it." Luke lifted the cloth and found the bandages fresh, which was reassuring, but he decided to peek underneath them.

"Hey!" Randy protested. "Nancy'll throw a fit, you mess up them bandages."

"She'll never know."

But, she would, of course. No way Luke could duplicate that intricate winding, though he tried his best.

"Your wound's a little red. Not too bad. You'll be fine." He sat back down in the chair, only mildly worried. It was probably normal body defenses, and the kid had been healthy until now. If only they had antibiotics.

"Look," he said, not actually believing his words, "I'm working on a way to get us home, so you just hang on, hear me?"

"Home? New York, you mean?"

"New York, yeah. You need a doctor."

Alarm flooded Randy's face. "Lady Caryn's a doctor and she takes real good care of me. I don't want no one else."

"Randy, this isn't a good place for us."

"Yes it is, yes it is! This is a real good place, Luke. They treat me real nice, an' the food's real good, an' they bring it to me and everything."

Luke reached for Randy's hand. "It'll be okay, kid."

Randy jerked the hand back, wincing afterward. "No! No, it won't! I don't wanna go back." He tried to lean forward, winced again, and fell back. "They think I'm smart here, Luke, you know that? In New York, Pa just beats on me, and everyone else makes fun 'cause I'm dumb." He shook his head with more energy than his peaked body should have contained. "New York ain't home, Luke, and I ain't going back!"

Luke jumped to his feet. "Take it easy, kid." He eased Randy back onto his pillows. "I'm sorry I upset you. We won't talk about it anymore, okay?"

"Okay," Randy replied sullenly. He turned his head toward the window, stared at nothing in particular. "I'm tired. I'm gonna sleep now."

"Sure, anything you need."

When Randy's breathing grew shallow and regular, Luke left, feeling hollow, like part of him was half dead. Randy had found Nancy, who gave him admiration like he'd never known, and even Caryn seemed to provide him a measure of heightened security.

Luke's earlier thought had been spot on. He could disappear without leaving a hole in anyone's life. Jose might grieve for his wife, but at least he'd known love. The last person who'd cared for Luke had died, brokenhearted over Kevin's death.

Since he'd arrived in Lochlorraine, he'd ridden a roller coaster of shock and emotion. During those fleeting hours on the mountain with Caryn, he'd felt himself being born anew. But he couldn't live here, not amid this barbarity and filth. But Randy could. If Luke found a way out, the kid wouldn't go with him.

From the moment Randy had gone down from the

bullet, Luke had been driven by his need to protect him. But Randy didn't need or want his protection anymore.

Having lost that, he wondered if anything would ever fill up the empty space inside him.

Caryn tore into the disorderly apothecary cabinet with a fury. Herb jars were tipped over, rolling among untidily folded bandages that belonged in the other cabinet. The laudanum bottles had been separated, some placed on the upper shelf, others on the lower. She must speak to Bessy and Nancy. Such disarray was an impediment to treating patients efficiently.

Over the last few days, she'd tended most of the illness and injuries herself even though Bessy normally handled routine treatments. She told herself it was because Bessy was overworked, but she hadn't been all that convincing, especially since her thoughts continually returned to Luke Slade.

He'd been in a dark mood ever since their close encounter with Ormeskirk and now scarcely left his room. On one occasion, when they'd passed in the hallway to Randy's sickroom, he had given her the barest hint of a nod before hurrying on. His behavior puzzled her. After his first explosive burst when she'd killed and disemboweled the sheep, he'd done his best to hide his tumult, but had failed to explain the reasons behind it. The animal had been dying. What else was she to do?

His judgment of her hurt. Why it should, she had no idea. He wasn't the first person to protest her behavior. Gregory had done so without surcease. No matter that her father had applauded her skill, a lady of her station should not ride astride, aim an arrow, wield a sword, or partake in animal husbandry.

After Gregory's death, Chisholm took up the mission, and had berated her constantly for those activities until she bade Ian to make him stop. Even to this day, the man never failed to raise a disapproving eyebrow whenever he saw her swing a leg over Neptune's back.

But Luke Slade? She'd thought him different, disinclined to scorn a woman because she engaged in supposedly male endeavors.

Her mood hadn't been helped any by her encounter with Gann that morning. She'd been hurrying to her chambers, hoping to get a moment's respite between scratched arms and sore throats, when he'd stopped her in the hall and introduced himself.

"Your reputation precedes you," he'd said, shaking her hand, which was odd behavior toward a woman. "But it doesn't exceed your beauty."

What a gnomish dissembling bootlicker, she'd immediately thought, withdrawing her hand as quickly as possible. Thank the virgin, he hadn't tried to kiss it. She'd disentangled herself with as much haste as courtesy allowed, but the encounter had left her with a bad taste in her mouth.

She'd been enraged when Ian told her the man was free. One of Arnie Miller's murderers? Nay, it should not be so. Although it might not have been he who'd pulled the trigger—in all the confusion, no one was quite sure—the other men clearly regarded him as their leader. Had he not fired the shot, he surely ordered it. But, as usual, Ian let Chisholm have his head.

Dandelion leaves were scattered all over the top shelf of the cabinet, distracting Caryn from the unpleasant memories. She irritably brushed the scraps into a dustbin. This carelessness could not be tolerated. She righted the jar, then replaced the stopper. Having done this, she decided to store the jars in the order of the alphabet, and was busy doing so when she heard Bessy's irregular footsteps behind her.

"I am putting this cabinet to rights," she said, not bothering to turn, and failing to hide the short edge in her voice. "Heretofore, we shall keep the herbs in order of the first letter of their names."

"A clever design, milady." The old woman paused overlong, alerting Caryn to expect some unwanted advice. "Though, since I know my letters poorly, and Nancy knows them not at all, ye might think about putting them up by the shapes of the leaves on the labels."

Caryn let out a long sigh.

"Ye are weary," Bessy said. "Let me prepare a wee cup of tea."

Caryn rubbed the back of her neck. Aye, she was weary, both in body and in heart.

Soon she and Bessy sat in rocking chairs in front of the hearth, Caryn cradling a warm cup between her hands.

"Are ye now ready to reveal what weighs so heavy on your heart, milady?" Bessy asked after a time.

Caryn took a sip of tea. What weighed so heavy?

An excellent question, and one she couldn't readily answer. But if anyone could help her work the problem out it was Bessy, who'd been her teacher and adviser for most of these twenty years.

" 'Tis Sir Luke," she finally said, putting her near-empty cup on the small table that sat between their chairs. She spoke of what transpired between Luke and her the first day Ormeskirk appeared in the afternoon. "He was so distraught," Caryn finished. "I cannot understand the reason. Had he been another man, I would not have wondered, but his sensibilities appeared to lack the ordinary man's harsh judgment of our gender."

"He comes from a time far ahead," Bessy offered. "Perhaps they do not eat the flesh of beasts in his world."

"Nancy says he eats all she brings him."

"A puzzle, to be sure." Bessy picked up her tea, slurping as she drained the cup. Putting it down, she turned sharp eyes on Caryn. "Ye find him comely, do you not?"

Caryn laughed. "Aye, both in body and demeanor. He is a fine figure of a man—" Caryn breathed out another sigh, and leaned forward, the darker truth in her disquiet finally coming to her. "I fear he is not the true dragon slayer. He cannot sit a horse, knows naught of swords, and he—this I find most hard to accept—he views the dragon as a pitiful creature, not the monster we know him to be."

"Yet Ormeskirk now comes at irregular hours," Bessy replied softly.

"Indeed, twice again since the day he stole the sheep."

"Some event has wrought this change, and it comes on the heels of the dragon slayer's arrival."

When Bessy picked up Caryn's teacup she wasn't surprised. The woman often had mystic insights, earning her the wary respect of the villagers. Now she handed the almost empty cup to Caryn. "Ye know what is to be done." Her voice sounded far away.

Caryn twirled the remaining liquid three times in the direction the clock runs, then inverted it into her saucer. A few seconds later, she righted the cup, then handed it to Bessy.

"Well . . . ?" Caryn said when Bessy studied the leaves for an excessive amount of time.

"Aye, change is speeding forward. Already, the dagger and cat are upon ye. Beware of treachery and false friends." Bessy paused again, making Caryn squirm with impatience. "Yet the signs be mixed. The blessed seed of the oak lies atop the doleful omens, and below, coming to pass behind the danger, be the fruit of success. The spider of reward crawls across it."

Bessy lifted her head and set the cup down, signaling the reading was over.

"Nay." Caryn reached for the cup and offered it back to Bessy. "What of the dragon slayer? What does it say of him?"

Bessy shook her head. "The leaves are silent on that matter. Naught do I see of Sir Luke."

"Read them again."

"Will do no good, milady. What secrets the leaves do not tell, they willna give up until another day." She eased her way out of the chair. "I shall excuse me old bones now and let you get back to your tidying."

"He's not the dragon slayer." Caryn sank back into her chair dispiritedly.

"The cup didna reveal that, yea or nay."

Caryn looked into Bessy's dark eyes, feeling her warm compassion flooding over her. "But it did. Were he our true slayer, the dagger would be in the dragon."

"Ye must follow your own heart, milady."

With that, Bessy shuffled out of the room, and Caryn didn't try to stop her. As always, the old woman's advice was sound, but Caryn's heart wasn't telling her what to do.

Perhaps it was time to hear from the intellect. With the Lord's help she might possibly pry Ian from his work.

Despite all evidence to the contrary, the voice in Luke's head still insisted there was a way out. Now, as he tied Toby to a rail in front of one of the abandoned cottages, he decided this delusion explained his daily visits to Lucifer's Window.

After taking off his shoes—along with the knitted socks he'd been forced to wear after he'd washed his and realized they didn't dry overnight—he rolled up his trews and waded in the chilly water.

The pool was like a regular tourist's video promoting the city, shifting vistas each time he came. Today's view included the tower of the Empire State Building.

It hadn't been so great back there, he reminded himself. He'd been close to no one, and generally uneasy about the way he made his living. But memories of the good times flooded his mind—beers and laughs with the guys at The Greeley Factory sports bar after work, seeing the first run of *Phantom of the Opera*, running through the park on warm summer mornings.

Bittersweet feelings coursed through him, bringing a longing so intense he fought to keep from doubling over.

He leaned and put his hand in the water, aching to touch the place he'd once so dubiously called home. All he got for his effort was a wet sleeve.

The bubble was too far away.

Not that far. All it would take was a few more steps and he'd sink into the deep pool. If he swam down, maybe he'd see women in business suits racing to work in tennis shoes or glimpse the stubble on the faces of panhandlers. Small details of his former life he hadn't known he'd held so precious.

And also encounter the elastic membrane, only to be dashed back against the rocks. Or so he'd been told.

What if this truly was a portal? Maybe Caryn and Jose were mistaken. There could be an opening no one had found before. He'd wondered this all along, but the lure of finding out hadn't been so strong. If he'd lost his life in the attempt, Randy would have been alone. If he'd survived and actually found the portal, the logistics of getting Randy through were insurmountable.

But this was a different morning. Randy wasn't going back with him no matter the state of his health. He couldn't blame the kid. Luke had his own dissatisfactions with their former life, but his cousin's were greater. He truly had nothing to return to.

Neither did Luke, most likely, but there was still a chance of making one. He wasn't a young man anymore, but he wasn't old either. A screwed-up life might wait for him there, but, dammit, he'd at least have running water.

He moved one foot forward, then another. One more and he'd fall into the sinkhole.

Steeling himself, he lifted his foot, prepared to take that final step.

Chapter Fifteen

"Slade! Slade! Don't do it!"

Marco stood at the tip of the loch, close to apoplexy. His pigeon was about to drown himself.

Slade lowered his foot beside his other and looked back, his face filled with weary resignation. "What's it to you what I do?"

"You'll drown for sure, man."

"How do you know?"

"These people have been here twenty years. You think someone wouldn't have found a way out if it was down there?"

With a bob of his head, Luke mercifully acknowledged Marco's logic. He turned for shore.

"Why do you care?" he asked as he splashed out of the water. "Unless my memory fails me, last I recall you were trying to kill me."

Marco waved his hand, sending sparks flying from the pipe, a frequent and annoying occurrence. "Business, man, just business. Nothing personal."

"Sure, I understand." Luke's reply carried sarcasm. With no more words, Slade rolled up his trews, then reached for his shoes and socks.

"Hey, what's your hurry?"

"Don't want to miss dinner."

"You already did." Marco pointed at a large flat-topped rock. "How about we shoot the shit for a while. I come here a lot and the seating's not too bad."

Actually, Marco never came here unless Robert Chisholm dragged him. Luckily, he'd been crossing the stream toward the village and he'd spotted Luke in the water.

Unlike Luke, who folks claimed never socialized, Marco used his freedom wisely. He ate all meals in the great hall and had talked to dozens of people, many who were travelers themselves. He understood Luke's refusal to accept his fate—he often felt it himself—but he'd never been one to chase lost causes. By his way of thinking, escape fell into that category.

What wasn't nailed down was why this guy didn't know he had it made. If Marco had been in his position, he'd be milking it for all it was worth.

He took a place on the rock, leaving plenty of room for Luke. "Looks like we'll be staying in Lochlorraine a spell. Sit down and let's get to know each other."

"Spell?" Luke stopped, pulling on his sock just long enough to direct a pointed look Marco's way. "Kind of an understatement isn't it? And since when are you from the South?"

Guessed he'd erred on the side of folksy. "Cut the attitude. I'm just trying to be friendly." He inhaled from the pipe, "I'll share my smoke."

"I don't smoke."

But Slade moved closer, an encouraging sign.

Thinking the man needed space, Marco moved over further. Luke took the bait.

After settling in place, Luke looked out over the loch. "It looks so close, you know. Like you could reach out and touch it."

"Were you really going to jump in?"

"Yeah, I think I was."

Marco was tempted to tell him about his own experience, then realized he'd also have to describe how Chisholm had pulled him out, and saved his life, which wasn't a fact he wanted going around.

"Haven't you heard—"

"Of course I heard. I just thought maybe I'd—"

"Succeed where everyone else failed."

"Yeah."

"Then you owe me, man."

A half smile curled Luke's lips. "*Owe* you? Exactly how do you figure? Way I see it, you probably stopped me from escaping."

"If you're crazy enough to think drowning is an escape, I give you that one."

"Jose didn't drown."

"Maybe so, but five others did."

"Who told you that?"

"I've been talking to other travelers. They sure have stories."

"I bet they do. Regardless, don't wait for my thank-you note."

Marco hunkered forward over his knees to give his back end a rest. The rock was a damned hard easy chair. "You have a sweet deal going, know that?"

Luke raised his eyebrows.

"They treat you like royalty. Meals and baths sent to your room. Bet you even have a feather bed like that babe of a countess."

A blaze flashed in Luke's eyes, quickly disappeared, alerting Marco to tread carefully where the Lady Caryn was concerned. He briefly wondered if anything had developed between her and Luke. Remembering his unfruitful meeting with her that morning, he felt another surge of bitterness, and he quickly dismissed his speculation in favor of the opportunity at hand.

"You could live like a king, people waiting on you hand and foot. And look at this day . . . this place. No smog, no traffic noises, no crowds."

"You been in the castle lately?"

"Yeah, well, so it's a beehive. But the people are nice. When's the last time you had a cab ride where the driver treated you good?"

"Last week."

"Tell me another lie."

"Okay, you made your point. But how can you stand the smell? And don't tell me you actually use that communal mud bath in the mess hall."

"It's called a great hall."

"Whatever, the washbasin still looks like a watering trough for pigs."

"You can change all that. The people think you can slay their dragon," Marco continued. "They think you're sent from God. Anything you ask they'll give you."

Luke let out a scoffing sound.

"No, it's true." He'd heard Carmine sing praises

about how Luke could fix anything with wire and chewing gum. "Think about it. You could maybe rig up running water. Hell, I heard they had it in Rome, so why not? And all it'd take to sweeten up the latrine is a way to drain the shit."

"Yeah, digging a pipe would be fun, if you had a gas mask, that is."

"Don't toss the idea away without thinking on it. Look at it this way, Slade. You have a chance to build something here, bring some modern-day comforts, shape attitudes. Hey, man, you could actually be a king."

He was laying it on pretty thick, but he wanted Luke's goodwill. If the man did even half the things they were talking about, he might remember that Marco had suggested them. And this last one had caught Luke's attention. Hey, maybe he did want to be king. Not too bad, especially if he took Marco in his confidence. "You kill that dragon, Slade, you'll be made king for sure."

Luke snapped his head toward Marco. "Dragon? It's not a dragon, and I have no intentions of killing it. But I do have some thoughts on how to deal with him, and most of what you say makes sense. It's time I make the best of what's happened to us." Luke levered to his feet and extended a hand. "Much as I hate it, I guess you do deserve my thanks."

Marco shook Luke's hand like they'd met at a wedding, then watched in dismay as Luke walked over to his horse and climbed on.

"Where you going?"

"Back to the castle to have a long talk with the

laird." He gave a disgustingly jaunty wave as he nudged the horse into action.

Shit, Marco thought as he watched Luke ride off, this hadn't turned out like he wanted. True, it had been nothing but luck he'd found the guy here in the first place. But after laying the groundwork, he'd expected to be asked for his help so he could reluctantly agree, thus earning a measure of gratitude.

Instead, he'd sent Slade on a quest.

He gnawed on the stem of the pipe and slumped forward.

Well, this was only the first try. He'd give it another. Luke was a lamb among wolves where self-interest was concerned, always looking out for someone else and wanting to do good. If anyone could exploit such a weakness, it was Marco Gann.

Caryn's heart skipped a beat when Luke burst into the laboratory as if he were about to be late for his own wake, and fairly well skidded to a stop between her and Ian. They'd been discussing his new drawing of changes to the time mechanism, an undertaking that never failed to give Caryn a headache. Under these circumstances she would have welcomed any interruption, but her sudden happiness had nothing to do with this need for a respite. Luke looked vital again, animated and full of life, which lifted her heart.

"What brings you here?" Ian asked pleasantly.

"I have things to tell you about Ormeskirk." As Luke spoke, his gaze idly moved to the drawing.

"You still working on that?" He picked up the

parchment and flapped it in the air. "Forgive my bluntness, Sir Ian, but you're wasting your time. Whatever happened to you was a cosmic accident. You'll never figure it out."

This undid Ian. He squared his shoulders and regarded Luke sternly. "Sir, I have asked for your presence in this laboratory countless times over these last days. Yet only now do you appear. From your own mouth we heard that the men of your century have not mastered time, so how do ye think to understand the work to which I have devoted twenty years of my life?"

"Sorry, Your Eminence, but—"

"Milord," Caryn corrected. "He's an earl, not a cardinal."

Luke shook his head. "I'll never get the hang of titles. Look, we got off on the wrong foot, milord, but back to Ormeskirk—"

"Again, sir. Ye have seen the creature scant times compared to our own experience." Ian's unnatural stiffness made Caryn squirm. Her brother-in-law wasn't prone to pride, but Luke's careless words scraped the raw spot of his failure to return them to Scotland.

"Please, milord," she implored, as eager as Luke to talk about the dragon. "Listen to Sir Luke. There is little that has more importance than defeating Ormeskirk."

"Defeating him? No, that's not what I'm saying. Let's sit down and talk about it." Luke returned the parchment to the stand, then cupped Caryn's elbow, and gently nudged her toward the seating area.

"Very well," Ian grunted. He followed them and took the chair, leaving Luke and Caryn to share the settee.

"Milord." Luke cast a sideways glance at Caryn as if seeking confirmation that he'd used the right title. She nodded. "Milord Ian, Lady Caryn, Ormeskirk is not a dragon, he's a dinosaur."

Caryn frowned. "A dino . . . ?"

"Dinosaur. Ormeskirk is a flying dinosaur known as a pterosaur. An extraordinarily big one."

"I have not heard of such creatures." Ian cupped his chin in his hand, his snit already forgotten in light of this new information. "Are these animals that live in the future? If so, how did it get here? What do you know of them?" A stream of further questions spilled from his mouth, with no pause that allowed Luke to answer.

Finally, smiling at the man's obvious excitement, Luke raised his hand. "Whoa, one at a time. No. Pterosaurs don't come from the future. They're almost two hundred million years old, and they vanished from the earth over sixty million years ago."

"Two hundred million years. I had no idea . . . Is our earth truly that old?"

"Much older than that, probably billions of years. No one knows exactly, but they keep trying to find out."

The information, so like heresy, troubled Caryn. "How can this be? Everything our Bible tells us suggests the world has existed only thousands of years."

"And some said it was flat, but you now know it

isn't." He looked troubled by this path of the conversation.

"How could a beast from such a distance past have entered Lochlorraine?" asked Ian, giving Luke the opportunity to avoid her questions, which pleased Caryn not at all.

Luke turned his attention to Ian. "Tell me what happened the day of the accident. Maybe we can figure it out."

"There was a great cracking sound . . ." Caryn offered.

" 'Twas the day I hoped to find the philosopher's stone," Ian said simultaneously.

"You first." Luke gestured to Ian.

Ian imparted that he'd started the quickening device. "The wind was high that day, exceedingly high, increasing the promise of success. The bang astounded my colleagues and I, as we had no understanding of why it occurred. When the glowing stone appeared, I believed we had won our quest. Then I saw the fire and the rubble. Many died that day. Cottages burned and crumbled. Aye, even one wing of the castle had to be rebuilt." Ian's square-jawed face turned sorrowful.

"The men who helped him with the experiment turned away, believing they had earned God's wrath," Caryn interjected. "So Ian persists alone." And how she wished he wouldn't.

"About the pterosaur," Luke said, bringing them back to their original subject. "Although there is some question about it, dinosaurs are believed to be reptiles. Since cold-blooded animals eat infrequently, couldn't you spare a sheep or a cow, say once a month or so, to keep him happy?"

"Once a month?" His suggestion shocked Caryn. "Nay, sir. Ormeskirk comes upon us daily. Ever he feeds. Naught can satisfy his prodigious appetite."

Luke blew out his breath. "Guess the guys who vote for warm-blooded must be right."

"I know nothing of warm or cold blood," Caryn said, "I only know he consumes our stock at an alarming rate." She looked away, gnawing at her lower lip. "Before ye entered Lochlorraine, Ormeskirk arrived only on the dragon hour, permitting us to house our beasts and keep them from harm's way. Now he comes at times we cannot predict."

"You think that's my fault?" Luke asked, a clear edge of anger in his tone. "Why? I didn't ask to come here."

" 'Tis an omen. Providence has sent you, don't you see? And if the dragon stirs in daylight, will that not increase your chance for success?"

Luke's brown eyes flashed. "That's superstition, Caryn. Providence has nothing to do with Ormeskirk and me being here. From what you've both said, the bubble most likely bounced around in time and drew the creature in . . . just like I was, and all the others. You cannot put faith in legends, or place blame where none exists."

Ian got up. With a hand in his wheat-toned hair, he paced in front of the fire. Were her hair not braided and capped, Caryn would have buried her hands as he always did.

With that choice denied her, she tossed her head.

"Do not tempt the fates with blasphemous words, Luke."

"The traveler is right, Caryn," Ian said abruptly, interrupting his pacing. "He didn't ask to come, but it may bode well for us that he did. Perhaps his scheme to placate the beast is sound."

"Sweet Mary! Had ye two seen John Carbuckle's shredded arm last winter, ye'd be of a different mind. I used remedy after remedy, yet naught I did reduced his fever and I was forced to amputate. Now his wife must till the soil while he looks after the wee ones. Ask John if we should give his sheep to Ormeskirk. I think he would say not."

"I guess you're right."

Luke's ready agreement startled Caryn, but she didn't know why. The man had already proven himself to be a Pandora's box of surprises.

"I didn't mean to upset you," Luke continued. "It's just that I wanted—"

"Ye wanted what? To pamper this monster all of his days? Precisely how long do these pterosaurs of yours live, might I ask?"

Now Luke wore the startled face. He looked down uncomfortably at his insubstantial shoes. When he looked up, he breathed out a sigh. "Some say as long as a hundred years."

"What?" exploded Ian, prompted into another round of pacing by this news. "Man, we canna feed the beast for nigh on four score years. Our people would soon have naught to eat."

Luke spread his arms helplessly, evoking a pang of sympathy from Caryn. He meant well, she could

see that. Yet this man from a world of untold knowledge was an innocent in the ways of their land.

"Sir Luke cannot even bear to see a dying sheep
slaughtered," she offered in his defense. "Although
it exceeds my understanding, he pities our monster."
She inched around on the settee to eye Luke directly.
"But we cannot employ your scheme. If, as you say,
the creature does not live eternally, that is a blessing.
But his life is still too long to suffer his presence
among us."

Resting her chin on steepled hands, she gave more
thought to a plot she'd considered while on her way
to see Ian. "The fearsome gun your fellow travelers
brought. Would it not pierce the beast's thick hide?"

"What gun?" Ian asked.

"It's called a submachine gun," Luke replied. "It
shoots bullets in rapid fire."

"Aye, Ian," Caryn concurred. "Very rapid. One
upon the other."

"And, as the lady asks, will such a weapon destroy Ormeskirk?"

"A gun with that much power?" Luke answered.
"It would probably blast him to hel—I mean Hades."

Ian again stopped. One hand went into his hair,
the other to his chin. "Then our course is clear, sir.
Ye must take the fearsome gun to Ormeskirk's lair
and blast him to hell, as ye were about to say." A
small grin played around Ian's lips, but he was only
mildly amused. His words, Caryn knew, were not a
request, but an order.

No, that's not what she had in mind. She'd wanted
Luke to show the soldiers how to use the weapon. It

wasn't fair. If Ian wouldn't send their own men on such duty, why would he send Luke?

"Milord," she began, "could he not work with our warriors—"

Luke's laugh cut her off. "Like I could do that."

"Surely, you could," Ian countered. "Even as monstrous a creature as Ormeskirk couldn't survive an assault from a weapon such as you described."

"Except for one thing."

"And that is?"

Luke hesitated. The silence stretched. The tap-tap-tapping of Ian's spinning machine filled the quiet space.

"I don't know how to shoot a gun. In fact, I've never even touched one."

Chapter Sixteen

Every Sunday after chapel Caryn held council in the great hall. Over the last several years, the residents had become uninterested, and few attended council anymore except to present mundane requests. McDougal's sheep wandered onto the Miller's plot of land. Will there be recompense? Sally McCollough wanted to marry James Callahan. Will permission be granted?

This morning the great hall was crowded. Another sign that things had changed with the coming of the dragon slayer. First on the docket was Naomi Miller, with yet another plea to arrest Marco Gann for murdering her husband, this time formally, so it would be recorded in the castle records.

Regretfully, Caryn told her that testimony from Gann's other companion, a man called Ralph Gianni, was to the contrary, and several soldiers had confirmed that Hub Barcowski acted alone, undoubtedly provoked by the heat of the moment.

"That will not protect Gann from the *Daoine Shi'*," Naomi replied bitterly. "Were Arnie not murdered by his hand, he ordered the deed."

A murmur ran through the crowd, and Caryn felt it her duty to correct the woman.

"Naomi, do not tempt the Men of Peace by calling them by their true name. Ye bring danger not only to yourself, but to all around you."

While Caryn did not completely believe in these shadow beings who reportedly lived beneath the ground, there had been times when others had openly used their name and later come to great harm.

"I have no wish to offend you, milady." This was said politely, but without contrition, as Naomi turned her head to glare at Gann. "I want justice, 'tis all, and will not rest until I get it."

To Gann's credit—and she'd been startled to see him there—he didn't smirk at Caryn's decision. Instead he looked concerned, and he tried to approach Naomi as she backed away from the dais. She whirled on him and made a hex sign, then melded into the crowd. Appearing distraught, Marco returned to his companions, an unlikely crew that included MacNab, the village mayor.

A few more supplicants came forward: another request for marriage banns; a matter of encroachment on a plot of land; a disagreement about a child's welfare.

After that, the hall grew quiet. Myriad pairs of eyes gazed on the dais. Caryn heard shuffling feet, muted conversations in every corner. Something was occurring, but what she did not know.

Then MacNab stepped forward. "Milady, what of the dragon slayer? When will he be seeking out the beast?"

MacNab's request was a reasonable one, but she had no ready answers. The discussion between her, Luke, and Ian had been only four days earlier, and she'd left the laboratory more befuddled than when she'd entered. But she did know that Luke would meet certain death if he wasn't the chosen one. Moreover, a man had little chance of survival if he couldn't sit a horse, wield a sword, or even fire weapons from his own time.

She believed in her heart that God had sent Sir Lucas in the form of Luke Slade. But why hadn't He also provided the skills to do the deed? Was Ormeskirk's death to come about by His magic? Was she to trust, was that the test?

"Milady?" MacNab said imploringly. "How do ye answer?"

Just then, Luke stepped from the shadows of the entrance to the great hall. "Let me answer that, Lady Caryn."

Caryn felt surprise flash on her face, but she quickly hid it with a look of intense interest. Her chest tightened. Why was Luke stepping forward now? This was a crowd on the verge of anger. One misstep and he would earn their dangerous wrath.

"The dragon slayer," murmured several people as Luke made his way to the dais.

"Look," he said, after he'd stepped up on the platform and turned to face the group, "to help protect you from Ormeskirk, I've been studying his habits." He explained that the creature didn't fly in the dark, and that he thought the villagers' routine of lighting fires at twilight was what drew him. "Now this is more complicated," he went on. "I believe the creature emits"—he struggled for the word—"well, ethers from his digestive track, which the flames ignite, then sets your roofs on fire."

"Are ye saying that Ormeskirk's belches and farts are what's causin' the fires?" a man catcalled from the audience.

This provoked a number of amused hoots.

"Hear the man out," Gann shouted from the back of the room.

Several others echoed his opinion, and the uproar soon ceased.

Luke displayed surprise at Gann's show of support, and caught the man's eyes. Gann nodded in acknowledgment, then said something to the man beside him. Luke's attention went back to the audience.

"That's it exactly," he said, referring back to the remarks about Ormeskirk's bodily functions. "Although I was trying not to put it quite that way. It's called methane gas and it explodes like gunpowder. So, here's what I suggest."

Luke had discussed this matter at length with Ian, but Caryn hadn't been privy to their talks, so she listened with great interest. He told the people that their household fires were drawing Ormeskirk to the village. If they delayed lighting them until after sunset, they could prevent him from coming. Even if he did appear, without the fires there'd be nothing to ignite the methane.

"But Ormeskirk now comes at irregular hours," said Tom the Elder, stepping forth with his cap in his hand.

"I believe that's because he's trying to avoid your attacks. If you stop, then so will he."

Caryn doubted that assertion, but many in the audience were nodding.

"Even if your scheme works," a woman threw out. "His nighttime screams still curdles the milk of our cows."

"Aye, and he still will eat our sheep and swine."

"And swallow the fish in the loch."

Despite the loud objections, many discussed the suggestion among themselves with expressions of approval.

MacNab stepped to Luke's side. " 'Tis a clever idea. One we should put to the test." After this seeming agreement, he glanced at Luke. "But when will ye kill the beast, Sir Dragon Slayer?"

Luke visibly cringed at the title. "As soon as I'm sure everyone will survive the attempt."

"Everyone?" MacNab echoed uncertainly.

"You don't expect me to face the beast alone, do you?"

Shocked faces followed his answer. Another rush of individual discussion followed.

"Yeah," Marco called out. "He can't do it alone."

"No one can."

"Who could ask him to go it alone?"

"Aye," MacNab said, apparently going with the mood of the crowd. "We must plot well before any ascend Wizard's Spire."

A chorus of agreement swept through the room.

"*Tàbhachd!*" a woman roared.

"Tàbhachd!" echoed the high, sweet voice of a child.

The cheer filled the room, music to Caryn's ears. She gazed down at Luke, swelling up with pride. This man was a natural leader. Perhaps he could best the beast without losing the blood of a single man. Perhaps God truly was guiding his way. Her innate trust in divine guidance returned.

" 'Tis settled, then," MacNab roared, his voice carrying over the chant. With that he strode forward and made his way through the group. People fell in behind him, some chattering among themselves, others continuing to shout the battle cry. Soon the hall was almost empty.

Luke stared after them for a time, then angled his face toward her. "What does *tàbhachd* mean?" he asked.

Caryn smiled. "It means success. Success in your endeavor."

"Then they bought it." He grinned with pleasure.

"Yes, they did." She wasn't at all certain what he meant by that, but could see he regarded it as good. "There is one thing, however."

He cocked his head in question.

"Do not tell anyone that you don't know how to use your powerful weapons."

His grin widened. "Absolutely, Countess. Absolutely. In the meantime, there are other things I want to talk about."

Puffing on his pipe, Marco stared up at the unfinished wood ceiling. Ralph had met a chick and had gone into the village to sweeten her up, giving Marco time to reflect on the meeting.

It went well, he thought. He'd achieved his aim. Folks had gotten stirred up by Luke's inaction, then he had been the one to come to his defense. Clearly he'd built goodwill that he could expect to cash in on later.

His attempted apology to the widow had been a nice touch. No question that the woman would reject it, but he'd been trying to impress the onlookers. It worked. But what really blew him away was that the Lady Caryn had approached him afterward, thanking him for his support of Luke and for his gesture toward Naomi.

He'd kissed her hand—after a few bumbling hand-shakes, he'd learned it was the customary greeting for women in Lochlorraine—and she'd smiled with a warmth he hadn't seen in her eyes before. That smile. God, it had taken his breath away. From that moment on, he was lost. He had to make this woman his, and she clearly favored Luke. The only way to change that was to grab for the power.

He'd always thought she was a babe. But even without those startling good looks, she was the target of every man in the land. She was the countess, after all. Any man of ambition would aim for her title. He hadn't cared to jump into that pool of suitors without sufficient status to be considered. But now he had to get it, which meant usurping Chisholm's revolt and claiming the kingdom as his own.

When he took over, when he explained that the earl was destroying the realm, Caryn would understand. She'd fall all over him to become his wife. She'd cater to his every whim.

The door rattled, and Ralph came in, looking pleased with himself. Marco felt a flash of irritation at being torn from his thoughts. "You get some?" he asked, although he really wasn't interested.

"Nah, but I will. Things move a little slower here than in the city."

They sure did. But Marco was a patient man. He'd guide this little kingdom behind the scenes just as he had the organization. And when the takeover was accomplished, he'd dispose of Chisholm and move to the top. With one incredible woman at his side.

He sighed, then sat up and tamped out his pipe. Time to call it a night.

"Put out the candles, Ralph."

Ralph grunted a response, but Marco paid it no attention. He hoped he had good dreams. Far too often lately, his sleep had ended with him in the clutches of the dragon. But that wouldn't happen tonight, he told himself. Not when he was nodding off with such pleasant memories. Tonight, he'd dream of the Lady Caryn.

"Lady Caryn, may I have a word?"

"Certainly, Bessy. Just let me finish with Tom." Caryn reached for the tin of sweets she stored in the back of a cabinet and opened it, taking out a candy.

"Here ye are, lad. Chew carefully so as not to harm your lip." She handed the boy the treat, trying not to frown over his split lip. Although he claimed he'd failed to duck when a horse swung its head around, she believed his father had inflicted the injury. The ban on interfering with family matters prevented her from doing any more than talk to the boy's father, something she'd done time and again with no results.

"Wash that cut every day until it closes, hear me, Tom?"

"Aye, milady. Thank you, milady." Tom jumped down from the table, gave a courtly bow, then scampered out of the apothecary.

Caryn watched until he disappeared, wanting a solution for Tom's situation, but she'd have to think upon it another time. Judging by her old friend's worried face, other matters awaited. "What is the problem, Bessy? I can see you're a wee bit distressed."

" 'Tis the dragon slayer. He is driving the servants mad. He makes them wash their hands every time they use the privy. Moreover, he insists they replace the water in the lavabo every morn."

Caryn raised her eyebrows in interest. She'd long thought the communal washbasin was an invitation to disease, and wondered if this had been confirmed in Luke's century.

"Now the man has gone too far!" Bessy's voice took on an uncharacteristic ring of hysteria. "He's ordered lye poured into the privy once a week. This is preposterous, Lady Caryn! He'll use so much ash that none will remain to make soap. The lassies are all in a twit." Bessy stopped, caught her breath. "Please do not misunderstand me. The lassies feel affection for Sir Luke. Aye, who cannot? But his unreasonable demands have them running in circles. Why, do ye know he bathes each and every day?

"And others are asking for the same privilege. Just this morn, I heard that ye . . ." Bessy's trailing voice suggested she thought she'd gone too far, a rarity for the healer, who was not one to keep her peace.

Caryn smiled. " 'Tis a pleasant habit," she replied. "Already, I have grown fond of it."

"Ye do not worry that such frequent soaking will sap your strength?"

"Up to this time, I've seen no reason for fear."

"I suppose." This was said doubtfully. "Still, the lassies canna keep up, and the lads are grumbling louder, for they don't as easily fall under the spell of Sir Luke's charms. If his requests continue, we shall have to bring in folks from the fields just to haul the tubs up and down." Bessy's bent shoulders straightened purposefully. "Can you not speak with him?"

Caryn put a hand on Bessy's bowed shoulders. "He merely wants the best for Lochlorraine, but clearly his pace is dizzying. I'll be eating the noon meal with him, I'll bring up these matters then."

Bessy looked greatly relieved. "Thank you, Lady Caryn. Now if ye will excuse me, Nancy is dithering about his frequent laundering requests. I shall hurry to reassure her." Before turning, she gave Caryn one of her piercing glances. "I may reassure her, may I not?"

Caryn suppressed a smile. "You may."

After Bessy left, Caryn put away her supplies, took a sweet herself before closing the tin, then tidied up the apothecary, smiling all the time. On the day of the council, she'd given Luke permission to modern-

ize the fief. She'd been so delighted that he was settling in, she'd not given a second thought to what
havoc he might wreak. Well, she would talk to him
soon.

Her smile widened in anticipation. So Luke
thought the great hall font spread disease too? Intri-
guing. She was eager to discuss it, as all matters of
health engaged her interest.

Pleased by that prospect, she walked to Randy's
sickbed. The boy had slept through all the commotion. His state of health was still unsteady, but with
such sound rest, improvement would surely come.

After readjusting the bedclothes, she went to the
table by the surgery chair and picked up a freshly
laundered bandage from a pile that needed folding.

She couldn't keep from humming as she worked.

Chapter Seventeen

"Don't you look pretty?" Luke said, joining Caryn at a stone table in the middle of the flowering courtyard. She'd removed her cap and loosened her braid, and now her hair fell down her back, a cascade of sparkling red sunshine.

She smiled and gave a shy nod of her head, a pink blush rising to her cheeks.

"Tea?" she asked, reaching for a bone china pot that sat on a silver tray in the middle of the table.

"Thanks." Luke took a seat at a chair opposite her. He still hadn't adjusted to the combination of luxury and squalor in Lochlorraine, and he couldn't keep from tapping the tray. "Nice."

She glanced at it indifferently. " 'Twas part of my dowry, but it isn't an important piece. The teapot is lesser still, but it belonged to my mother, so it does have meaning to me."

She had no idea how important those pieces were in his time, and probably wouldn't care, so he dropped the subject.

"I've been thinking about moving the garbage pit farther from the castle."

"Interesting idea. What purpose would moving the pit serve?" She handed him his cup, then reached for silver tongs. "Sugar?"

Luke shook his head. "It's a breeding ground for germs," he said. "Actually we should bury the stuff, if possible."

"Then how would the farmers slop their swine or mulch their gardens?"

"They feed that stuff to the hogs?"

Caryn tilted her head and regarded him intently.

"What?" he asked.

"Do they not feed slop to hogs in your century?"

"Beats me. I never thought about it."

"Then how do you get meat?"

Luke laughed. "I buy it in a grocery store. But how it gets there is beyond me. Someone grows the animals, someone else kills them, another someone packages them, and then, miracle upon miracle, I find it in the meat case."

"Aye, it does seem a miracle. Do ye pickle and salt all your meat then, so it does not go foul during the wagon's journey to these grocery stores?"

"Modern transportation and refrigeration, Countess, but those are different stories."

"Of which I have much curiosity, but we must speak about the compost heap . . . and your— But first I must know. Is it true that ye make the servants empty and refill the lavabo each morn?"

"I asked 'em to, yeah. Why?"

"It's your reason that excites my interest. What purpose does this serve?"

Luke tried to couch his words carefully. He'd been questioned on this issue by Bessy several times and couldn't figure out why anyone would object to throwing out disgusting, mucky water. "It's unsanitary," he finally said.

"And the meaning of unsanitary?"

"If someone is ill and washes their hands there, the following people are exposed to the disease."

"As I thought. The lavabo was not used in Invergair, where I grew up. We had closer ties to England and thus their modern methods. When first I saw the tank I feared people here still ate from trenchers." She paused reflectively. "Perhaps we should remove it and have the servers bring washing bowls for each person. Surely this would be easier than asking the scullery staff to empty and refill it each morning."

Luke grinned. "You've had complaints?"

Caryn smiled so charmingly Luke could barely restrain himself from tapping her nose. Back in the city, he wouldn't have hesitated, but he guessed such familiarity wasn't greeted warmly in Caryn Maclachlan's world.

She nodded her head. "Not only about the lavabo, but of your many baths, the lye in the privy, and making the scullery servants wash their hands each time they use it." She blushed at this last statement, charming Luke even further.

"Hey, you gave me a free hand," Luke said good-naturedly, enjoying the conversation too much to be defensive. "Now you want me to stop?"

"Perhaps you might use a more leisurely pace."
She picked up the teapot. "More?"

"Sure," Luke said. There was grace in the way she
lifted the saucer and cup, then slowly filled it, as
though the act of pouring tea were an art instead of
a task. When he took the cup from her hand, she
refilled her own with similar elegance, then took an
unhurried sip before setting it on the table.

"Do all people of your century rush through their
duties as if their houses were aflame?"

"Where I come from, yeah, but I've heard other
parts of the country aren't so single-minded."

The doors to the courtyard opened with a squeak.
A girl carried in another silver tray, this one laden
with domed silver covers. She was small and young,
barely twelve if Luke was any judge, and clearly
overtaxed by her burden.

"Let me help you," he said, standing up.

"Luke . . ." Caryn's mild warning barely registered
as he grabbed one edge of the tray.

"Nay, sir," the girl said. " 'Tis my duty to serve
the food."

"It's too heavy for you."

The girl pulled back, trying to gently dislodge
Luke's hand, and the tray became unbalanced. Her
eyes widened in dismay as she attempted to right it.
Still holding on, Luke took a circular step, intending to relieve her of the weight and place the
tray on the table, but the girl caught his meaning too
late. The tray tipped. A dome slid off its plate and
clanged onto the table.

A crash followed.

"Oh, milady," the girl gasped, "I've broken your mother's wee teapot."

"It's all right, Jenny," Caryn said. "Do not be troubled. Continue serving the meal, and when that's done you can clean up the broken pot."

"That's okay. I'll do it." Luke reached for a fragment of broken china, feeling sick at heart. It wasn't Jenny's fault. He'd broken the teapot, not her.

"Please, Sir Luke," Caryn said authoritatively. "Do not interfere with Jenny's duties."

"But it wasn't her fault," he protested.

"Nevertheless, it is for her to pick up the pieces."

Jenny kept her head down as she arranged platters on the table, but Luke could see her lower lip trembling. When the meal was laid out, the girl knelt and scooped up the broken china so hastily Luke was sure she must have cut herself, then dropped the pieces on the tray and rushed out of the courtyard.

"She'll cry all the way back to the kitchen," Luke said. "And I'm the reason."

Caryn leaned forward and took his hand. "Luke, you must understand. In Lochlorraine, people all have duties. To do Jenny's work is to rob her of her purpose. Can ye not see that?"

"Sounds like union talk to me." He picked up his fork, wondering crossly why they couldn't have more than two tines, and speared a thick lamb chop. As he dropped it on his plate, an image of the slaughtered sheep flashed through his mind.

"Don't, Kevin. Don't!"

Red, blue, and white whirled in his head.

He pushed the images away by taking a bite of

small potatoes cooked in a creamy sauce. He'd
thought he'd gotten used to the food being no more
than lukewarm, but today it sapped his desire to eat.
Except he'd lost it already. Never in his life had he
felt more like a Saint Bernard in a knickknack shop.
He had no measure to gauge his actions, and nothing
he did here seemed to fit what he'd known before.

The teapot once belonged to Caryn's mother. To
her, it had to be priceless. But he found it hard to
bring up the subject. She should be upset by its loss,
but if he judged her state by her appetite, he'd have
to conclude she wasn't.

Despite his lack of hunger, he forced himself to
eat. Supper wouldn't come until after the dragon
hour, and if he skipped lunch he could hardly raid
the refrigerator later.

"Perhaps we should speak of protocol," Caryn
said, breaking the uneasy silence.

"Perhaps we should not," he replied stiffly. He put
down his fork and stood up. "I'll never get it, Caryn.
You folks have rules for everything, and I don't see
the reason behind them. I was just trying to help
the girl."

Ormeskirk cried in the distance, something he
seemed to do a lot, and the call increased Luke's
angst. He walked to a vine of honeysuckles that
climbed the stone wall. A hummingbird abandoned
its sipping and lifted off, buzzing not far above his
head. Luke bent to smell the vacated flower. Plucking
it from the vine, he turned back, walked over to
Caryn, and placed it behind her ear.

"I'm not good at apologies," he said. "But I'm

sorry about your mother's teapot. My mother is also gone, and I would be—"

"I never knew her, Luke. She died giving birth to me." She took his hand between both of hers. "I don't like to see you distraught over a wee bit of pottery. My father gave me many of her belongings. The teapot is not all I have of her, and while I . . . while it meant . . ."

Suddenly she blinked hard, but not before Luke saw tears collecting in her eyes. She looked away, her lower lip caught between her teeth. "Sweet Mary," she said. "I had not realized its dearness before."

Gently, Luke lifted Caryn to her feet. Turning her to face him, he pressed her against his shoulder. "I wish I could make it right for you," he whispered. "I watch you, you know. I see how much you have on your shoulders, how much others rely on you. I think— I thought . . . Somehow helping your servant girl with the tray, it was like making things . . . like helping you— Geez, I sound like a dimwit."

Caryn lifted her head, then brushed a lock of hair off his forehead. "Luke . . ."

She shivered faintly, her eyes moving to his mouth. Luke parted his lips to speak, but his heart was about to stop. Of its own volition, his head lowered. She moved nearer. Their lips met with an electric spark that coursed through his bones.

Lord, she was sweet, soft, and pliant in his embrace, and her mouth parted slightly, tempting him to run his tongue along its edges, drink of her like the hummingbird had the flower.

He pulled her fiercely close, running his hands over her hair, then skimming her shoulders, her arms.

She stiffened and gasped. A second later she relaxed and fitted her body against his growing erection, clinging as if her knees were weak. Lord, he was hot and hungry for her. His need for her was so strong he thought he might die from it. If he was in New York, he would have read the signals well. But this wasn't New York. He was in a different world where he didn't belong. This was a woman different from any he'd known, but she belonged in his arms.

He didn't fit here.

They fit perfectly.

Stifling an anguished moan, he broke the kiss. He wanted to cup her chin, reclaim her lips, but he couldn't resolve this conflict of realities. If he seduced her, if he took her here in this perfumed flower garden, word would get out somehow, undermining her reputation and authority.

"Caryn," he finally said, gentling his embrace. "We need to talk."

"Talk?" she asked breathlessly, her eyes wide and dazed. She stared at him a second, then abruptly moved out of his light hold.

"I shouldn't have done that." He was talking to her back. Dammit he wanted to see her eyes.

"Y-you . . . regret kissing me?"

"Regret? How could I regret something so wonderful?" A sound, half laugh, half sob, left his mouth. His entire past haunted him now, more than ever before. "It's not fair to you, Caryn. You deserve so much, and . . . There's so much you don't know about me. I didn't come in here with less than admirable characters by accident. Before we . . . before you—" He spun around in frustration. "You have to know more about me. When you do it might change your feelings. Maybe we have a future, but I won't do anything that could hurt you until I'm sure."

She glided toward him. "I know this much. Our affection for one another grows with each passing day, yet much lies before us. I'm unsure of your reasons, but your words steer us well. The beast won't go away until something is done, and I—" She glanced up at the wall in the direction of the unseen spire to the west. "If I give you my heart, dear one, it would shrivel into dust if harm should come your way."

He touched her cheek, guiding her eyes back to meet his. She'd skirted on the edge of declaring her feelings, and he had to search those green pools, read their depths, try to assure himself this wasn't a dream. "Nothing's going to happen to me, Caryn. And I've already begun dealing with Ormeskirk. I can't understand why you think killing him is the only solution."

"Aye." Her voice took on a sad ring. "As little as I know of thee, ye know that much less of us."

Luke chuckled dryly. "I'm aware of that, sweetheart, but I'll learn."

"Learn, you will," she said. "We've given you little choice." She stroked his face tenderly, her expression filled with regret, and he had the feeling she was about to tell him something. He almost groaned. He wanted to give her happiness, not pain.

Just then, the garden door creaked. Luke turned his head to see Nancy's worried face. "Lady Caryn," she said. "Young Tom has had an accident. I fear his leg is broken."

Chapter Eighteen

Tom was sitting in the surgery chair when Caryn and Luke got to the apothecary, with Bessy examining his ankle. Randy, propped up on his bed, looked on with a worried frown.

"Lady Caryn." As soon as he saw her, the boy averted his eyes.

Luke, went to kneel beside the chair. "What happened here?" he asked cheerfully. "Toby give you a kick?"

"Nay, nay. Were my own foolishness." Tom's gaze darted around the room. "I fell from the loft while tossin' hay."

"Nay, hay? That rhymes you know." Luke tousled Tom's hair, then took the crumpled tam from his hands. "You won't need this for a while. Holding on to it won't make your leg feel better. But with Bessy treating you, you'll be up and around in no time."

"Ye are in my way," Bessy grunted, not the least impressed by Luke's flattery.

Luke just grinned, scooted closer to the head of the chair, and gave Tom his hand. "Here, hold on to this." He inclined his head toward the foot. "It hurt?"

"A wee bit." But Tom also grinned, and his posture relaxed. His restless eyes settled on Luke's face. Caryn watched the pair, Luke rising higher in her already lofty estimation. His innate kindness came ever to the forefront. How well he seemed to understand the boy. How tenderly he treated him.

"He gonna be all right?" Randy pleaded to know, looking ready to crawl from his bed.

"Don't be troubled," Caryn said. "I'm certain he will be." She looked down at Bessy. "How *is* the leg?"

"The bones seem sound, but the lad's ankle has taken a terrible wrenching." The older woman wrapped a long bandage around the ankle as she spoke. "He'll be hobbling around on crutches till the equinox."

"Crutches! I canna be on crutches, milady. Me da has work for me to do."

"Perhaps a cane might suffice." Caryn crouched beside the chair. "Tell me again how this happened."

"I were climbing into the loft, and lost me footing."

Luke slanted a quick glance at Caryn. "I thought—" Caryn squeezed Luke's shoulder and he started over. "How it happened doesn't matter," he said. "All we want is for you to get better, okay?"

"What does okay mean?" Tom asked.

As Luke explained, Caryn's thoughts drifted. When they'd been interrupted, she'd been about to tell Luke about the power of the ring. Although the thought of him leaving split her heart in two, she wouldn't have hesitated if not for her duty. He was so miserable in Lochlorraine, so anxious for his kinsman's welfare. He missed his home; he'd told her so.

Even now she was tempted. Take him to the laboratory during one of Ian's rare moments of sleep, hand him the ring, and tell him to flee.

Then what? Let Ormeskirk ravage the land evermore?

She'd handed him over to God, this dragon slayer, allowing Him to guide her dear one's course. But none of Luke's activities were aimed toward the dragon's end. True, delaying the villagers' nightly fires had stopped the burning of the roofs, and the beast no longer foraged by day. But the people's true desire was Ormeskirk's death. If Luke didn't act soon, the danger to him could come from *their* hands.

Could she remain faithful to the kingdom and also preserve Luke's health and happiness? It seemed not so, but this much was true: No matter which course she took, her happiness would be the price.

Ormeskirk's shriek drifted in through the open shutters. Evermore, the beast cried out these days, always reminding her of her duty.

Which, at this time, was to young Tom, who was still protesting that his father needed him in the stables. Brushing her hair behind her ears, Caryn stood up. "Ye will remain in the castle, Tom, until the ankle heals. The realm will pay for a worker to help your father."

Relief flooded the boy's face. Luke caught Caryn's eyes again, and she nodded. "Come," she said. "Let us leave Bessy to her work." She could see the woman was displeased by Luke's presence.

He seemed to sense that, too, because he got up without protest, ruffled Tom's hair again, and said he'd see him soon. "I want to talk to Randy first," he then told Caryn. "He's very worried about Tom."

She agreed, briefly conferring with Bessy about the treatment of Tom's ankle. But all the while she kept Luke in the corner of her eye. He and Randy talked softly, and she heard only snatches of words. But their words did not interest her anyway. Once more Luke had shown the depth of his caring. He cared about Tom, about Randy, about Lochlorraine. And unless she was a poor judge of character, he cared about her. How could she let him leave? How could she risk his life, even for the land?

When he came back to get her, she still had no answer.

They left the apothecary in silence, but Luke stopped soon after they'd left the room.

"Is young Tom's father beating him up?" he asked, his tone filled with the same fury she herself often felt.

"Aye, or so the evidence dictates."

"Why isn't something being done about it?"

She started to explain about the clan's taboo on interfering in family matters, but held back. Like so many of their ways, this one clearly violated the rules of his time. " 'Tis not our way," she finally said.

"Another thing I don't understand." But his fury had faded. Already he was resigning himself, but not easily. Nay, not easily at all.

They walked without talking for quite a while, then Luke said he was going to meet with Ian. As they started to go their divergent ways, he hesitated. "About what happened in the garden. Don't you think we should talk more about it?"

His eyes darkened even further, and he took her shoulders, turning her to face him. "You mean a lot to me, Caryn. I don't want this to come between us."

She shook her head. "It will not. But talk more? What is there to say? A cloud hangs over Lochlorraine. What is in our hearts must remain there until this storm has passed."

"Yeah," he said. "Yeah. I guess it must."

With that he walked away, leaving Caryn no closer to her answers.

Although he was aware that some people grumbled about his inaction, Luke had done his best to forget about his dragon slayer title. Moreover, his fall from grace had brought an unexpected blessing: Each day fewer villagers bowed and chanted when he passed.

Over two weeks had passed since he'd walked through the portal, and he was satisfied with what he'd accomplished. Caryn had carried out her promise to replace the lavabo with individual washing bowls, and despite old Bessy's dour prediction that they'd soon burn every tree in Lochlorraine to fulfill his demands, he'd managed to get lye added weekly to the privy.

Now he was on the roof, working on a pulley system to semi-automate the disposal of wet garbage. It hadn't taken him long to understand how moving the garbage pit would overtax the staff, so now he was working to overcome that objection.

"Hand me that length of rope, would you, Tom?"

The boy lifted his cane off a cannon and limped over. "Right away, sir."

It would be faster to get it himself, but Caryn's lecture about everyone needing a purpose had stuck. While it made him feel bad to watch Tom hobble about on the cane, that feeling was offset by the obvious pleasure the boy took in being useful.

"Thanks." Luke clipped off the frayed end with his penknife, then threaded the rope through a series of pulleys to create a kind of horizontal dumbwaiter that would allow the servants to freewheel garbage buckets to a pit he'd had ordered dug almost a mile away. Luke thought it solved the distance problem rather nicely, although it still required the staff to carry the garbage to the roof. But in time he'd work on a traditional dumbwaiter to get it up here.

Getting the stuff down was the easy part; gravity helped. Bringing back the empty buckets was the problem. Large and fashioned from thick, heavy planks, they required a great deal of effort to get them up the incline. Where was plastic when he needed it?

Maybe if he used double pulleys. As he fiddled with the gears and their placement, his mind wandered to Randy. Nancy bathed his wound with alcohol daily. Bessy had used all the herbs and potions at her disposal. But it had still become infected. A few days ago, Luke concocted a crude form of penicillin by soaking moldy bread. But Randy's improvement was fitful. Better one day, slip-sliding the next.

He'd tried to remember the folk remedies he'd read about, but his self-education, while broad, hadn't been comprehensive or hands-on. Caryn was doing the best she could to help him, but her education was still three hundred years behind his. Bessy's mumbo jumbo appeared to have the most success, which puzzled Luke, but as long as her treatments helped he didn't care.

"Ye think that will work?" Tom asked, looking over Luke's shoulder with curiosity.

"Not sure." Luke threaded the rope Tom had given him through the pulley.

"If ye not be needing me anymore, can I go look in on Toby?"

Luke looked up from his task and noticed the longing in the boy's eyes. Tom was motherless, so it must be his father he missed. At his age, Luke had still adored his own pa, despite the frequent beatings.

"No problem," he said. "Why don't you ride in the hills while you're at it?"

"Or maybe I'll muck some stalls."

"With that leg? How will you hold the rake?"

"I could lean on the wall."

Luke laughed. These Lochlorraine kids. They'd rather work than play. "Whatever you want. Just be back for supper."

And avoid your father.

Tom smiled. "Of that ye can be sure. I never had so much mutton, cream, or butter in me life."

As Tom leaned on his cane to turn around, Ormeskirk wailed. The boy cowered, and a visible shudder coursed through his body.

"It's okay." Luke put a reassuring hand on the boy's shoulder. "He's still off by the spire. Let me show you."

He stood up and carried the boy to the battlement, lifting him so he could see over the saw-toothed edge. The pterosaur glided around the vanes of the windmill, wailing again, a deep, soul-piercing sound that never failed to trouble Luke. But he never experienced the tremors of fear that now rushed through young Tom's body—and every other resident of Lochlorraine no matter the age, if Luke's eyes served him right.

"He's not really a dragon, you know."

Tom twisted his neck to look at Luke. "If he not be a dragon, what else is he?"

"A pterosaur. An ancient creature, long vanished from the earth. He's alone here, separated from his kind, and unhappy. Can't you hear it in his cry?"

Tom's grey eyes darkened. "Nay, Sir Luke. I hear naught but his evil heart calling out our doom. He will not rest till each and every one of us is wiped from the land."

"Did you ever think he believes we feel the same about him?"

"We do." Tom squirmed and Luke lowered him to the ground, supporting him until he'd grabbed his cane. Leaning on it, the boy looked up at Luke in question. "When will ye be going to slay him, Sir Luke? Ever'one is asking. Will it be soon?"

Luke hesitated for a considerable span of time.

"When we've devised the right scheme," he finally said, uncomfortable with the lie, but unwilling to disillusion the boy with the full truth.

A grin nearly split Tom's face. "That's what I been saying."

"Well, good." Luke gave him a pat on the back. "Now go see that horse of yours. Give him a carrot for me."

Luke knelt back down beside his contraption and listened to the scuffling of the boy's cane echo off the stairwell walls. Luke really liked having him around. The castle staff treated him as one of their own, and Caryn's loving attentions did him no harm, a motherless kid like that. The only bad thing that came from the accident was that Caryn never finished whatever it was he'd sensed she'd been about to say.

What she'd said afterward, in the hall—she'd been right. Their feelings for each other were better left unconfessed for now.

Thank God the kiss hadn't left them tongue-tied around each other. They'd fallen back into their easy discussions as though it hadn't happened.

Still, he hadn't forgotten about it, or about his desire to bare his past to Caryn. Another time would come, he supposed, although as each day passed his courage faltered. He wasn't sure he could stand it if she was repelled by what he'd been. An ex-con. A hood, at least by association. Or, in the words of her land, a ruffian.

He worked on the conglomeration of rope and pulleys and gears for another half hour or so, then decided to call it a day.

Tonight was Caryn's birthday celebration—well, Ian's too, but she was foremost in his thoughts—and he'd promised her he'd wear a kilt. Lots of fun, and something he didn't look forward to. But she'd ask it of him when he'd told her he wanted to give her a present. Oh, the things he did for that woman, he thought, rising to his feet.

As he shook out his stiff legs, his thoughts remained on his project. He still needed more leverage to bring back the bucket and wasn't quite sure where to find it.

The problem could wait another day. But as he turned for the stairs, he took notice of the huge metal hoop Ian had mounted on the tower so many years before. When Ian built his quickening device, he'd powered it by connecting the hoop with cable to the windmill on Wizard's spire.

What if Luke gave it a different use? If he threaded a rope through the ring, he'd gain enough leverage to bring back the buckets.

He'd better ask Ian about it. Ormeskirk's presence on the spire rendered the hoop useless, but Luke wasn't so sure the earl would like his invention being used for disposing of garbage.

For the first few days after his decision to make Lochlorraine a better place, Luke spent hours in the lab. But Ian had no idea how he'd created the time warp. He'd backtracked his methods countless times, following the scientific method of recording all his actions, but had been unable to find the variable.

Luke hadn't added much, except to be a sounding board, and his attempts at engaging the man's help with the realm's domestic problems had met little interest. Ian was simply too intent on getting back to Scotland. Finally concluding that the project was hopeless, Luke had turned his attention to improving the standard of living in the castle.

At least that's what he told himself. But he'd also lost his sense of urgency. Life was good here. Despite his detractors, most people respected him. The blacksmith had been quite interested in his information about levers and pulleys, and just that morning the wine steward had asked Luke to invent a device to rotate the bottles without removing them from the racks. If Randy's health weren't an issue, Luke doubted he'd even think about New York.

If only he could walk through the portal and return with antibiotics for Randy, life would be perfect. But he couldn't, and that lay heavy on his mind.

Chapter Nineteen

"No, sir." Young Tom knelt beside an impossibly long stretch of plaid wool, rearranging the folds. "Ye must pleat it in this manner or ye'll not be able to get it around your body."

Luke backed away, giving the boy room.

What had he been thinking when he promised Caryn he'd wear a kilt? He had to admit the boy made the pleating thing look simple enough as he swiftly reduced eight yards of fabric to forty inches or so, but Luke had tried it himself and knew it wasn't so. Moreover, he had no faith that the wide belt now peeking out of each folded side would really keep the kilt up.

"Lie down on it so that your knees are at the bottom part," Tom instructed courteously.

"Sure thing."

Luke felt foolish as Tom wrapped the fabric across his stomach and secured it with the belt, even more so when he stood up and the top half fell to his feet. "Now what?"

"Do not worry, sir." In seconds, Tom had tucked

the ends of the fallen fabric deep inside the belt, which made it bunch around Luke's waist. Before Luke could object, Tom did something mysterious with the pile of plaid, twisting it here, wrapping it there. Finally, he asked Luke to hold the end.

"There," he said proudly. "Ye look ever' inch the noble gentleman that you be."

"I'm just a man, like your dad."

"Nay," Tom said. "Not like my da. Ye are kind and soft with me."

A ball of anger fisted in Luke's stomach, and he forced himself to get it under control. Unwittingly, Tom had given him the opening he needed, and he wanted to make the best use of it. "What do you mean, Tom? Does your father hit you?"

Tom shrugged. "Not much. Only when I be misbe-havin'." He gestured toward Luke's hand, a transparent attempt to change the subject. "Do not let go." He dug into his sporran and came out with a pin. "Her ladyship give me this bonny clasp for your plaid."

Smiling proudly, he displayed a round gold brooch with ornate carvings. In the very center was a dragon, wings spread wide, mouth open as if uttering a menacing cry. Luke scowled, wondering if Caryn would ever give up.

Tom's smile faded. "It displeases you, sir?"

"No, Tom. No. It *is* a bonny pin. Now if you'd fix me up here, we'll almost be done."

The smile returned when Luke bent over to make it easier for the boy to reach his shoulder. After the brooch was affixed, Tom asked him to turn slowly so he could fluff the plaid. Last, he buckled a sporran of thick fur around Luke's waist, then led him to a cheval mirror.

"There," he said, clearly happy with the results. "Ye look grand, do ye not?"

"Grand. Absolutely." His wavering image stared back at him from the mirror, a picture of the perfect clansman. "Now show me what to do with the garters for my socks, then you can go."

"Socks?"

"Hose. My hose."

Tom insisted on putting the hose on Luke's feet, then affixed the garters himself. "Are they too tight?"

"No," Luke said, wondering how long it would take for circulation to return to his feet.

He then slid on a pair of boots Caryn had ordered fitted for him last week—except for being a bit stiff, they reminded him of brogans from Bloomingdale's—and before he could lean over to tie them, Tom did the job.

"Good work, Tom."

Luke expected the kid to bolt, but he stayed put. "Do not forget yer tam."

"I won't. Your work's done, though. Time to go get ready yourself."

"Aye. After I muck the stalls."

"Sure." Luke's heart twisted, and his stomach balled again. This was one fine kid. Smart, eager to work, polite. How could a father hit a son like this one? For that matter, how could a father hit his son at all? Considering the many beatings he and Kevin had taken, the question seemed odd. Fathers hit their kids all the time, he knew that. He'd been unable to do anything about it then, but couldn't he do something about Tom?

He put a hand on Tom's shoulder. "I'll talk to your dad."

"Nay!" Tom's head wagged frantically. "Nay, Sir Luke, you canna say naught to me da!"

"Okay, okay, Tom. I won't. I promise."

"Aye. And you will keep your word." It was a statement of trust not a question. "I thank ye for permitting me to serve you, sir."

With his small head bowed, Tom turned and left the room.

Luke sank onto his bed, the wheels of his mind spinning. No way he could approach Tom the Elder directly, the boy left no question that he'd suffer for it, and Luke pondered the problem until the clock rang. Seven bells. He was late for the celebration.

Picking up his tam, he found he'd sat on the bed so long the feathers had formed a pocket that made it difficult to get up, but with a minor struggle he managed. Feeling heavy, emotions still churning, he walked to the mirror to place the cap on his head.

Damn! In his effort to get up, he'd loosened one end of the plaid. Now the top flap of the kilt hung halfway down his calf. Feeling bad about undoing Tom's careful work, he tugged and pulled, trying to shove the loose end back in. This effort resulted in shifting the material behind his shoulders, and it wasn't long before he felt the brooch nudging his shoulder blade. After more tugging and pulling, he finally re-arranged the fabric until it looked normal again.

He felt self-conscious as hell, and soon he'd have to walk into the great hall dressed like this. Some part of him knew he was making it a big deal to keep from thinking about Tom, but another part did truly dread this first appearance in a kilt.

A rap sounded at the door, probably a summons to the great hall. He opened the door, and a smile instantly split his face.

"Caryn." She took his breath away. Instead of her functional work clothes, she wore a flowing pale blue dress. The skirt was gathered with ribbons and billowed below her waist, revealing a darker blue skirt underneath. Her copper hair, now a mass of curls, was clipped to the top of her head with jewels. Tendrils drifted around her cheeks and neck.

"You look beautiful."

She curtsied. "Ye are fine in my eyes, too. My, my, the kilt does suit you."

She touched his arm, guiding him to turn and give her a better look. A tinkle of a laugh escaped her mouth.

"Goodness, Luke," she said. "Ye do have a leaning for exposing yourself, do ye not?"

"W-what?" He shuffled around, then turned his head to get a glimpse of his back in the mirror.

"Oh, shi—crap—crud! I knew it!" In his efforts to rearrange the kilt, he'd pulled the back up so far his drawers showed. And none too secure they were either. He'd put them on only because his briefs were still wet, though he'd washed them two days ago.

Damn, he missed washing machines and dryers. "I'll never get the hang of this, Caryn. Not if I live to be a hundred."

"In time you will, Luke. In time. But for now, permit me to repair the damage."

She unclasped the pin, retucked the kilt's loose end, then performed the same twisty, winding movement that Tom had used.

"There." She secured the ends on his left shoulder with the pin, then stepped back and looked him over. "As handsome as I knew you would be. Do ye like the brooch I sent?"

Luke touched it, then met her eyes. "It's nice. I'd find it nicer, though, if I didn't take it as a hint. I'm not going to kill your dragon, Caryn."

She smiled confidently. "Aye, you will, one way or another. 'Tis your destiny, Luke. You cannot avoid it."

"Watch me." But he couldn't help smiling back, and taking a cue from movies he'd seen, he extended an arm. "In the meantime, Countess, allow me to escort you to your birthday ball."

"Celebration," she corrected. "A ball is only for—"

"Caryn . . ."

Her smile widened. "Why thank you, Sir Luke. I would be honored."

With that, Luke opened his door and prepared to lead the most beautiful woman in the world to the ball. Never mind that he'd look like a fool beside her wearing this goddamn skirt.

*   *   *

As it turned out, all eyes were upon them, but the reaction was much different than he'd expected.

"Do they not make a bonny pair?" a heavily jeweled woman remarked to her companion.

"They please the eye, to be sure. And he is quite the handsome one."

"Will I be permitted to touch the countess and dragon slayer?" a young girl asked.

"Perhaps," came the answer. "As the festivities go on."

The girl clapped her hands in excited anticipation.

They headed for the dais at the far end of the room, past other tables that had been pushed against the wall, presumably to be pulled out later. The table on the dais had already been laid with crisp white linen. In front of each chair sat a jeweled cup and service plate. Several people were already seated.

The throng parted, forming a living corridor for them, and as Luke and Caryn walked through it, she smiled and nodded, exchanging quick pleasantries with all who spoke to her. When they reached the dais, Luke helped her onto the platform.

Ian occupied the center chair, an ornately carved number that flowed into thick padded arms. On his left was Chisholm. Beside the captain sat a portly woman who was flanked by Fergus MacNab. The two chairs to Ian's right were empty, and Randy sat in the third one.

"Hiya, Luke." Randy waved enthusiastically.

"Glad to see you here, kid." Luke settled Caryn in a stiff, high-backed chair beside the earl. After she was seated, she presented him to MacNab's wife.

Then he moved to his assigned place between Caryn and Randy.

Although he wondered why Randy hadn't mentioned he would be attending the celebration, the anticipation of his company wasn't the only reason Luke was pleased to see him. It proved he was feeling better.

As soon as Luke took his seat, he doubted that conclusion. Unlike everyone but Ian, Randy's chair had arms, and Luke saw he was propped up by pillows. His face looked grey, and his round hazel eyes didn't hold their usual sparkle.

"Nancy fix you up with the pillows?"

"Aye, aye." Randy always grinned when he said those words, and this time was no exception, but his voice sounded reedy. "Just so's my shoulder wouldn't hit hard wood, is all."

"How're you feeling?"

"Feeling?" There was a second of hesitation. "Great. Fine. Real fine. Bonny, methinks."

"You're getting the lingo, hey, kid?"

"Aye. I like the sound of it."

Besides the obvious lack of energy, Luke heard reticence in Randy's voice, as if he feared Luke would make him leave Lochlorraine if he admitted how bad he felt. Well, it was true, but only if there was a way, which there wasn't.

"Don't worry, Randy," he said. "We aren't going anywhere. We're staying put."

Randy's smile and eyes instantly brightened. "Really, Luke? Really, really?"

"Yep, really."

Saying those words sent relief coursing through Luke's veins. Not until they'd left his mouth had he realized how badly he wanted to stay. Which obviously pleased Randy even more than Luke had thought, because he now gazed over the crowd with increased animation.

"Look at all them people."

"Yeah. This is probably the biggest social event of the season." And the dais gave a bird's-eye view.

The huge hall was crammed with people, talking, laughing, grabbing tidbits or glasses from trays borne by servants, who wove among them. A small group of celebrants turned toward the dais and raised their cups. Others cast frequent glances toward the front of the hall.

"Ain't the ladies dresses pretty?" asked Randy.

"Very pretty."

"You look real good in that kilt. Maybe I can wear one, soon as I get better."

"I bet you'd look grand," Luke answered, taking a cue from young Tom.

"There's Nancy!" Randy waved excitedly. Nancy's face lit up as she waved in return.

Such high spirits and goodwill, Luke thought, at least on the surface. But underneath it he sensed a current of intrigue. Several people talked behind their hands. Off to one side he saw Marco offering tobacco to Bernie, the villager who'd threatened to cut Ralph's throat the night they'd arrived. Whatever Marco was saying caused the giant man to nod.

Soon there was a gradual ebbing of voices as if everyone was waiting for something to happen. Then the double doors opened and the guests again moved toward the walls.

In came a parade of servants. The first one held a huge tray above his head that contained a replica of Lochlorraine, complete with tower, battlement, and flags. On the roof were dozens of figures, manning cannons or holding crossbows. The next man carried a replica of a dragon with a long curling tongue and colorful scales. After these men came more servants, all bearing baskets of breads. Last in the line were musicians with bagpipes and flutes, who broke into music upon crossing the threshold.

These folks really know how to throw a party, Luke thought, wondering what would happen next.

Sometime between the procession's entrance and their parade toward the nobles, other servants had dragged a long draped table to the front of the hall. Now the lead servant took the hand of the one who had followed him. Facing the dais, they both bowed.

"Lord Ian, Lady Caryn," the first man cried dramatically, "may we present our humble effort?"

At a nod from Ian, he placed the replica of the castle on the far end of the table. The man behind him put the dragon on the other end. The remaining servants broke bread and began dispersing it through the crowd.

A roar of pleasure arose as Caryn and Ian stood, bowing and giving appreciation. At that, all the lanterns were snuffed, leaving the room only in soft candlelight.

With a dramatic flourish, the two men swooped toward a silver box and brought out short, slim torches. Holding them aloft, they moved to opposite ends of the table. Suddenly, after a small explosive sound, the mouth of the dragon spewed flames. The reach was enormous, and as the smell of burning black powder dissipated, the fire singed the sugary shell of the castle. The second servant lowered his torch, igniting a volley of explosions from the tiny cannons. Small balls nicked the dragon, but a new dip of the torch sent forth another burst of fire from its mouth. Soon, a full-fledged battle took place, with each new touch of a torch escalating the conflict.

People laughed, jumped, and clapped with delight, but Luke had a feeling where this was taking them, and wasn't so sure he liked it. By this time, the dragon was nicked and burned almost beyond recognition.

When the finale came, Luke looked away. A last dip of the lead servant's torch sent dozens of balls soaring toward the dragon. The guests oohed and aahed. At this point, both servants attended the castle, using their torches repeatedly, touching on the tiny arrows in the crossbows, on small muskets in the hands of kilted soldiers. Smoke clouded the confectionary as the arrows and bullets released, one after another.

A new burst of flame came from the dragon, creating more smoke. Accompanied by repeated gasps from the crowd, soaring balls and speeding arrows blasted through the wall of flame, repeatedly striking the dragon. Its head caved in. Pieces of its body crumbled. Finally it collapsed in a broken heap. As the smoke dispersed, the dragon's head snapped forward in a movement too lifelike for Luke's comfort.

When its tongue fell off, dissolving into scorched granules, the guests went wild, jumping, hooting, and applauding. Missiles of torn bread flew from the audience, raining down on the dragon. Laughing, the servants raised their hands to ward off the blows, then scurried to one side as guests reduced the charred dragon to a pile of blackened sugar.

The party on the dais stood up, smiling and clapping their hands. The servants returned to the table, bowed, then backed away again. Belatedly, Luke stood also, realizing it was expected. But the glee in the room grated on him like the roar of heavy traffic. Mingled with these joyous sounds was the stink of malevolence. And of fear so great it could barely be contained.

"Did ye not enjoy the subtlety?" Caryn asked, slanting him a sideways glance as she continued to applaud.

"Nothing subtle about it," he snapped without thinking. Quickly he nodded his head. "No, it was fine. Quite a production."

"You disapprove," she said, her lush lips thinning. "Aye, I should have suspected as much. Ormeskirk is your friend. Never mind that he destroys our people's homes and livelihoods, he must be protected." She tossed her head, sending the copper curls flying. "What sensibilities do you bring from your century that ye favor animals over people?"

"Don't, Caryn, please. It's your birthday. I want this to be a happy night. Let's not argue over this."

She renewed her applause and smiled widely, though Luke could see it was forced. Then she looked at him. "I'll hold you to your word. We will not argue tonight, no matter what the cause."

"Suits me fine."

Soon the applause settled down. The table and mangled sculptures were whisked from view. The other tables were pulled into the center of the room, and people took their seats. Countless servants entered the hall, bringing endless platters of meats, roasted vegetables, sugared fruits, and more.

Before the meal began, Ian rose and announced grace. Heads bowed, conversation ceased. The prayer was long, repetitious, rote, and Luke's mind wandered. Then he felt a nudge from Caryn and realized the blessing had ended. "Rise up," she instructed.

Puzzled, Luke did as she said.

"Now," Ian said, "may I present to ye good folks of Lochlorraine, our savior, Sir Luke Slade the dragon slayer."

"Dragon slayer! Dragon slayer! Dragon slayer!" cheered the crowd with even more enthusiasm than they'd greeted the mock battle. But as Luke gazed over the multitude, he noticed that not all joined in the cheers. Though Chisholm and MacNab stood, their applause was unenthusiastic. Farther out, he saw people exchanging glances. But Marco and Ralph smiled, bringing a tinge of suspicion to Luke's mind for no real reason. Gann had openly supported him of late.

For propriety's sake, he tried to keep a frown off

his face. He looked over at Caryn, who gazed at him expectantly.

"Ye gave your word, sir."

So he had, Luke thought. So he had.

But that didn't mean he'd go out and kill their dragon.

Chapter Twenty

Chisholm leaned against the castle wall, tamping down his pipe. "So, Marco. How're ye doing with winning over Big Bernie?"

Marco took a slow drag from his own pipe, and looked around. Six or seven men were gathered around the great hall door, laughing and talking, and much too close for Marco's comfort. "You think we should talk here?"

"Do not worry. We're just two men sharing a smoke. The others are paying us no mind." His face twisted in scorn. "They're occupied with fawning over the earl and the lady. Now about Bernie."

"He's quite a fan of the Maclachlans, but I've managed to make him wonder if Luke isn't pulling the wool over everyone's eyes. What's happening with MacNab? He's friendly enough, but I don't have him nailed down."

"He's not easy, that one, especially being as there's bad blood between us, but the mayor's been thinking the earl's daft for quite a span. And he's none too fond of having a wench rule the kingdom."

Wench? Marco's blood churned, and he fisted his free hand, pressing it against his leg so as not to use it. How could Robert call a woman like Caryn a wench?

"Hand it over," Chisholm said, referring to Marco's lighter. He did as asked, which gave him the opportunity to cool off. He couldn't afford to blow up. Patience, self-control, those were the keys. He waited for Robert to ignite the pipe, which took a good amount of time, as pipes always did. Finally it flared and Chisholm returned the lighter. "He does like his daily dose of flattery, though."

"Who?" Marco had lost track.

"MacNab. Who else?"

Marco puffed his pipe again, deliberately delaying his response in hopes that Robert would open up. Something in the man's behavior hinted at a holdout. The silence stretched, and he began to understand why Scots had a reputation for being tight-lipped. "You got your hands on those guns yet?"

"Ye know I don't. I spoke with the earl, who says they're being kept safe for the dragon slayer." Chisholm snorted. "Slade busies himself digging holes for garbage, and I hear tell he's planning on piping the refuse out of the garderobes. Some dragon slayer he be."

A sliver of a moon carved Chisholm's square face into dark shadows, making it uglier than usual. Marco had an urge to snuff this guy, one so strong he'd do it in a heartbeat if he didn't need the man. He was developing a full-fledged hate for Slade, too. Not only did Luke rebuff his every effort to cozy up, he got all the goodies this ramshackle kingdom had to offer without even trying—including the Lady Caryn, who still plagued Marco's thoughts like a stubborn rash.

When he ruled Lochlorraine, things would be different. The lady would become his wife. He'd have feather beds and silk robes just like the earl. Pheasant and beef brought to him on silver platters. Maybe he'd even have Luke's and Chisholm's heads carried in on one.

"I have contrived a plot for getting the guns," Chisholm said.

"Yeah?" Marco feigned the mildest of interest, although this was the information he'd been waiting for.

"I think ye might like it." Robert paused to drag on his pipe, and slowly let out the smoke. "Council will be held again tomorrow. If ye offer to slay the dragon—"

"Whoa!"

Robert raised a hand. "Hear me out. This will force Slade's hand. Many believe he is the embodied return of the last dragon slayer, Sir Lucas, and thus have no faith that another could succeed. The lady believes this fervently, and will refuse your offer, mark my word. At any rate, this will provide opportunity to reveal Slade's cowardice, for undoubtedly he will not accept the challenge. When this occurs, some among our number will demand that you go in his place, I have seen to that. The earl and the lady will have no choice but to return the guns."

"Yeah, and I'll have no choice but to go."

Robert cast Marco a sharp glance. "Ye *have* been forthright with me? The Uzi *will* destroy the beast?"

At this question, the dragon shrieked. Like an omen, Marco thought, a chill overtaking him, along with memories of his nightmares. Several of the men standing by the great hall door looked toward the spire, then immediately resumed their conversations, untroubled. The dragon wouldn't attack at this late hour, Marco knew, not with the sun gone.

But he still kept looking at the spire.

That was one big bird. Damned big. But Chisholm had asked a question and he had an answer to give. "If the Uzi doesn't kill him, Robert, nothing will. But I'd sure as hell rather Slade carried it."

"So, do you feel a year older?" Luke and Caryn strolled alongside the loch. Moonlight skipped in her hair, her skirt swayed against his bare legs, and he could barely keep from touching her.

"Only a day," she replied. "What matter are years as long as I am filled with vigor?"

"Healthy attitude. Where I come from, everyone wants to be young."

"Is that a fact? How curious. I could not imagine being young and uncertain again. The wisdom of age is truly a comfort." She turned her eyes on him, giving her full attention. "Tell me more of your time. It appears . . . that is . . ." She laughed uneasily. "Now *this* is being uncertain. But I have noticed, Luke, that you regard me with more . . . I'm not sure how to phrase it. Perhaps the word is respect, or maybe equality, but whatever it's called, you display it in greater measure than the men of Lochlorraine. Is this the manner of your age or simply your own?"

She obviously admired that trait, and Luke was tempted to let her think it was his own special quality. Something he'd probably have done in a New York City bar without a second thought, but didn't feel right with her. "No, it's not just me. Women work alongside men in almost every occupation in my world, or at least in my country. Some even go to war."

"Women fighting wars! 'Tis beyond my imagination."

"No it isn't." He chucked her under the chin, no longer worried about being overfamiliar. "You rule a kingdom, Countess. You've got more going for you than thousands—no millions—of women in my time."

"There are millions of women! Then there must also be millions of men. Oh, my. How do ye feed such a multitude?"

Luke grinned. "It's a long boring story."

"I cannot believe anything you say could be boring."

He gave her an appreciative glance. "Some may argue with you there."

"Tell me about your family," she said quickly, hoping the moon wasn't revealing her face. Luke's warm look had brought on a blush. "I pray you did not leave a wife and children behind."

He shook his head. His thick hair had grown since he'd entered the fief, and it swung about his face. Each day he more resembled the hero in her tapestry.

"Mother, father, sisters, or brothers?" Her curiosity grew strangely intense. She wanted to know everything about him.

"You really want to know?"

"Aye. I know it is taxing to be separated from the life ye knew. At least it was . . ."—A burst of longing caught her by surprise—". . . was for me." Her statements had evoked memories of Invergair, and the family she'd never see again, which hadn't happened in quite some time.

"Are you okay, Caryn?"

She bobbed her head. "I just wonder what they thought, my papa and my brothers, when Lochlorraine simply vanished from their earth."

"Come here. Let's sit down."

He led her to a flat rock. Only then did she notice that they were at Lucifer's Window. "Nay, this place is cursed."

Luke smiled gently. "I come here all the time, and look at me. I'm not wearing horns."

"Only the ones you came in with."

Luke couldn't help but laugh. "Nevertheless, this is just a place. No curses. Trust me."

Hesitantly, she settled on the rock. "It does feel good to be off my feet."

"Which is why I suggested it." Luke took the spot beside her. "Instead of me talking about me, why don't you tell me about Invergair."

She couldn't remember anyone showing interest in the life she'd had before Lochlorraine, and though she deemed it unwise to reveal so much about herself to a man she was fated to send on a perilous quest, she couldn't resist.

" 'Tis a place of rolling hills, green meadows, and winding streams about a hundred kilometers southwest of Dublin. My father, Lord Henry Campbell, was Marquess of Invergair. I was the youngest child, the only girl, my mother having died giving birth to me. Three older brothers did I have, and early on they taught me to sit a horse astride . . ."

Luke listened with fascination as she went on to tell him about racing against her brothers on the heather, swimming in secluded pools, and generally running as free as the boys. Later, they'd taught her how to wield a sword and shoot a gun. "Even a wee bit of falconry." She'd become an avid hunter, who bagged more than her share of deer at an early age.

"Didn't your father object?"

Caryn smiled with obvious fondness. "Papa could deny me nothing. Until I became a woman." Instantly, her lips pursed. "When I was ten and three, he sent me to court to find a husband."

"What happened then?"

Caryn laughed, half in amusement, half in self-deprecation. "I was ill-suited to court. King Charles had reinstated the Church of England, and the mood there was dour. Thousands of my clansmen were persecuted for their Presbyterian faith, and Papa was doing his best to serve both the clans and the crown.

"I was quite the disappointment to him, I fear. Not only did I oft forget to bind my hair as was done in court, more than one dowager chided me for shouting my allegiance by wearing my plaid. 'Twas not my intent, I simply couldn't make my way through their maze of subtle rules."

"Now why can I understand that?"

"I thought you might." She paused to rearrange her skirts, and they again brushed tantalizingly against Luke's leg. "Then I made it worse. At a state dinner I listened to a pompous prelate explain in oh-so-scholarly language why the Scots were necessarily inferior to the Brits. After a tedious amount of time, I spoke up."

Luke laughed at the picture that came to mind. "So what did you say?"

Caryn echoed his laugh, making Luke feel as if they were doing a mental ballroom dance, where one moved and the other followed.

"Much of it should never have come from a lady's lips, but I do believe I compared the prelate to the king's pet macaw. Needless to say, I was banished from court that very night and destroyed my chances of making a good match."

"How did you come to Lochlorraine?"

Her distress returned, making Luke regret his question. " 'Twas a difficult time for Papa. He feared a war was brewing, which required support from all the chieftains." She looked away for a second. "I should not speak this, but truth must be told. There is much I admire about the clan way of life. Their loyalty, the lack of social caste, but we are a prickly people, so quick to take offense, forever warring with one another. 'Tis no surprise that England has so often overran us, when we could not forge allegiance among ourselves."

She paused a moment to readjust her shawl, which had slipped to expose her shoulders to the nip of the breeze. The scent of seaweed drifted in the air, mingling with the lavender fragrance coming from her wrap.

"The Maclachlan clan had n'er been friendly because of a slight some ancient Campbell chief gave a Maclachlan chief. Papa needed Gregory's support, and the man was hard-pressed to find a noble wife because of his distance from court." She ran her tongue along her lower lip. "And for other reasons that have no importance now."

"He traded you? Your father used you as a political tool?"

"I feared ye wouldn't understand, given what you've told me of your century. But this was often done. Two houses bonded by marriage. 'Twas the best my father could do for me given my behavior at court. He blamed himself for allowing me to run so free but was helpless to protect me. He was brave and strong, my papa, yet I saw unshed tears in his eyes the night he sent me to Lochlorraine."

"I understand, Caryn. I've read about your time. It's just—I mean, those were faceless women. But you . . . you're real, you're here."

"Aye, I'm here, but this is not my real time."

Moonlight reflected off her shining eyes, and a tear of her own drifted down her cheek. He reached out and brushed it off, then reluctantly let his hand drop. "I know Papa never dreamed he wouldn't see me again. My disappearance surely must have broken his heart."

"Such a life you've led." Luke put his arm around her. "So much heartbreak."

"And so much privilege," she replied in a far-off tone. Without any urging from him, she let her head rest on his shoulder. " 'Twas my own foolishness that brought me to that far-off realm at the edge of the Scottish kingdom."

"But you admire the clan way of life. You should have been happy here."

"Nothing was as I hoped. Lochlorraine was the worst of the system. Gregory ruled over a half-dozen quarreling clans, and though he himself was a clansman, he was most enamored by his title. I oft believed he encouraged the quarrels to enhance his own station."

Luke's heart jumped at the confession. His feelings for Caryn were growing stronger each day and he couldn't help compare himself to her late husband. Certainly she'd mourned the fearless man who'd marched up Wizard's Spire to face what he thought was a monster.

"Did you love him?" he whispered, fearing to be heard, fearing the answer.

Her silence did nothing to ease his fear. It stretched on for what seemed ages, filled only by the lap of water on the shore and the occasional shout of a reveler returning to the village.

"It shames me to say it but, no, I did not. Gregory was not the most tender of men, and he was unable to deal with the undisciplined girl I was. As time goes by, I wonder if any woman would have suited him unless she'd vanished into the walls."

Luke's sudden exhale surprised him, and obviously Caryn too. She straightened and scanned his face.

"Ye must think ill of me for my terrible confession."

Shaking his head, Luke reached out and stroked her cheek. Her skin was soft, smooth, velvety. "I've never admired a woman more."

She leaned her head into his hand, clasping it with both of hers. "As I've come to admire you."

He'd been wanting to kiss her again since that day in the flower garden, and suddenly he couldn't resist anymore. Slowly he leaned forward, narrowing the distance between their mouths. He felt the pressure of her head against his cradling hand, coming closer, meeting him halfway.

Her lips were as soft and sweet as they'd been that day, and the feel of her was like ice upon fire. Shocking, full of contrast, creating sensations he'd never known before. This time he wouldn't hold back. But his ignorance of their customs made him awkward and he kept the pressure of his mouth soft, barely touching, only brushing. Gently, he skimmed her lips, waiting for a signal.

She gave a small whimper, then lifted her arms and encircled his neck, deepening the kiss. He dared a flick of his tongue. When her mouth opened, he explored the soft inner surface of her plump lower lip. Ah, sweeter than he dared imagine.

"Luke," she murmured into the kiss. "Luke. We should not."

"I know," he said, then deepened the kiss.

*   *   *

"Hey look, boss, ain't that the countess and that Slade character?" asked Ralph as he took a leak on the shore.

"Shut up," Marco hissed. "They'll hear us."

They'd just come from the cottage of Ralph's new girlfriend, who'd conjured up a friend for Marco. For some reason—most likely the free-flowing liquor dispensed at the celebration—the woman had been open to having a good time. Sex without a condom had been terrific, but his woman had sported dirty fingernails and smelled like stale beer. Though it hadn't dampened his sex drive at the time, watching Luke hold the sweetest peach in the land almost made him sick. Damn Slade. Damn him to hell.

"You going to tell Chisholm about this?" Ralph spoke in a discreet whisper, reminding Marco to pull in his emotions. It wasn't like him to be so hotheaded.

"I need to think it over."

As he and Ralph watched, the pair broke their kiss. The moonlight silhouetted them, giving Marco a clear view of the tender way Luke stroked beneath her eyes. Had she been crying? If so, why?

After a short time, the couple stood and headed arm in arm toward the castle. Whatever Caryn cried about, she certainly didn't doubt her affections for the man at her side.

"That Slade's one lucky guy," Ralph remarked.

Marco shot him a dirty look. "Just keep this to yourself, got it?"

Ralph nodded sullenly. "Yep, one lucky guy."

Marco tried not to think about Slade's good luck, and concentrated on his situation. Chisholm was wrong. So what if the countess "fervently" believed Slade was the dragon slayer? She wasn't about to send him into the dragon's claws, not if Marco believed his eyes.

He thought about the plan Chisholm had come up with, and it suddenly looked better to him. The dragon was only a big bird, hard of head and thick of skin, for sure, but just a bird. With the firepower Marco had, no question he could blast it away.

Fragments of his nightmares beat at the edges of his mind, but not hard enough to keep his thoughts off Caryn. She was a lady, a true lady, and he wanted her more than he'd ever wanted a woman. More than money, more than power, more than luxury. He _had_ to have her. And if killing a fucking dragon was what it took, then that's what he'd do.

"Come on, Ralph," he said. "Let's head back."

He needed his rest. The village council met the next morning, and he planned to be on his toes.

Chapter Twenty-one

Luke had been in the second grade the last time a woman cried when he'd kissed her, and he couldn't understand what had brought on Caryn's tears. Why didn't she explain? he asked himself as he walked with her toward her chamber door.

She circled before he could ask the question and opened her door. "Come into my chambers, if you would. I have something to show you."

Slightly bewildered, Luke followed her through a large room filled with luxurious brocades and gleaming wood. Her shutters were still open, allowing moonlight to spill through the windows, and it mingled with the firelight to create a romantic glow. But she didn't stop there. Instead she continued through another door, looking back to make sure he was behind her.

When they stepped into her bedroom, Luke's eyes stopped at the high canopy bed covered with rich fabrics. His first thought was that she was issuing an invitation, but she glided past the bed without a glance, moving to a wall that was covered by a floor-to-ceiling hanging that duplicated the fresco in the great hall.

With a sweep of her arm, she said, "Behold, Sir Lucas, last of the dragon slayers."

Luke had seen ancient tapestries before, but they were always faded and hard to make out. This one was rich with color that revealed every detail. But her reason for pointing it out to him was what interested him the most.

"Yeah, I know. I've seen the picture dozens of times."

"But never when you were in a kilt. Do ye not see the resemblance, Luke?"

"To who? The half-dead guy or the other one?"

She smiled wanly, then took his hand. "Look in the mirror, Luke."

Although the reflected image was as watery as every mirror he'd come across here, he found himself startled by what he saw. He glanced at the tapestry, then back to himself.

The kilted man staring from the mirror stood tall and strong. His dark, shaggy hair fell to his jawline. His eyes contained both caring and purpose. For a moment, Luke could hardly believe it was him. A shiver akin to a premonition raced down his spine.

Troubled, he turned away. "You got me. I look like him. What's the big deal?"

She sat on a bench at the foot of the bed and looked at her hands. "From the day— This is most difficult to confess, but the day I found this tapestry in an old storage room . . . I was young, foolish, and very afraid. My husband had just died, and Ian had named me regent of Lochlorraine. So I told myself Sir Lucas would come as the legends of old promised and save the land. Somewhere, in all those dreams, I gave him my heart." She rubbed the palm of one hand with the thumb of the other. "Then you appeared, holding your kinsman like a child. So fierce ye were in protecting him, I knew the legend had come to life."

Luke crossed the room and knelt in front of her, stilling her restless hands. "Caryn, honey. I'm not a legendary character. I'm just a man from a later time, and not a particularly honorable one. There's so much yet you don't know about me. Who I was. What I did."

"Under the light of the legend your past has no importance." Her words emerged on a thick whisper. "Destiny is bigger than us both."

Luke rocked back on his heels. "So you're saying that in order for us to be together I have to kill the dragon like that guy in the tapestry?"

She shook her head with so much agitation Luke was frightened for her. "I'm telling you that *destiny* says you must. I've tried to convince myself it is not so, that ye are not the dragon slayer, and on this matter, I have gone back and forth. But when you kissed me, I knew ye and Sir Lucas shared the same soul." She shook her head again. "Ye are the dragon slayer, Luke Slade, and destiny will come to find you."

Luke wasn't big on destiny, but he understood that Caryn held her words to be true. Although he couldn't kid himself he wasn't afraid, it wasn't the main reason for his reluctance to go after the ptero-saur. he knew it was more than that. But that after-noon, when he'd seen Tom's bone-deep terror as they'd watched the creature, he'd known that his dream of coexistence was simply that, a dream. The people of Lochlorraine could not live another sixty to eighty years under that kind of fear.

He squeezed her hands. "If killing Ormeskirk is what it takes, I'll do it."

A wracking sob shook her shoulders. Luke slipped onto the bench and took her in his arms. "Hey, hey. That was supposed to make you feel better."

"Don't . . . Don't ye see, Luke? If I . . . if I send you off to battle Ormeskirk, ye may not come back. And yet it is my duty to make you go." Her sobs increased, each shudder sending arrows of pain right through Luke's heart.

He pulled her closer, depositing kisses on her hair and forehead, trying to ease her pain as a parent might.

"I'll come back, Caryn, I promise. I'll go and I'll come back."

"But ye do not even know how to shoot a gun."

"I'll learn."

What had she done?

Caryn tossed under her down coverings, unable to get comfortable. Luke's acceptance of his destiny should have filled her with gladness. Instead she felt every dark and hollow space inside her.

And the heavy weight of guilt.

She hadn't meant to twist Luke to her aim in showing him the tapestry, just to make him understand. But now he'd agreed to go, and had even promised to announce his decision during council the next morning.

What had she done?

Thrashing about had twisted her nightdress. She straightened it and pulled the comforter more fully around her shoulders, trying to warm herself against the cold results of the lies she and Ian had concocted to keep Luke here.

She should tell Luke about the ring. Her heart cried out to do it. But he no longer yearned for home, and she sensed he would refuse her offer now—or turn away, repelled by her deceit.

Surely there was a way to keep him from harm and allow their love to flourish. She needed guidance. Perhaps if she went to the chapel before the others arose, when it was lit only by the morning twilight, God would be near and give her a sign.

The decision to do this allowed her to finally drift into a fitful sleep that was filled with nightmares of Luke being ripped apart by the dragon's claws.

What had she done?

Luke recognized how important spiritual beliefs were to the people of Lochlorraine, but so far he'd manage to avoid attending services. He'd loved his mother deeply, but her habit of attributing their father's beatings to God's will had soured him on religion.

But this Sunday he rose early in order to attend because he knew Caryn would be holding council afterward. He'd be there with her, accompany her to the great hall, then announce his intentions of going after Ormeskirk.

But first he'd go to Ian's laboratory and discuss his strategy for removing the creature. Guns, no matter how powerful, weren't enough. It would take countless rounds to bring down a beast so large, so even the Uzi would have its limits. Armor was the trick, and a method of climbing the spire that would keep them protected from Ormeskirk's attacks.

As he reached the second story of the castle, he thought about Randy. Since he no longer required day and night nursing, he'd been moved to the lower floor to make it easier for him to take the air during daylight. Luke usually found Nancy at his side when he stopped to visit. She probably wouldn't be there this early, however, so he'd poke his head in and see how well the kid was doing.

"Help! Help me!"

At the panicked cry, Luke broke into a run. Rounding a corner, he saw Nancy racing toward him, her face twisted with apprehension.

"Help him, Sir Luke!" she cried. "He canna breathe! He canna breathe at all!"

Luke dashed into the room. Randy was writhing on the bed, clutching his throat and emitting gurgling noises. Red blotches covered his face. In a few long strides, Luke covered the distance to the bed, unsure what to do, but knowing he had to do something.

Eyes bulging, face full of panic, Randy let go of his throat, Lunging, he clawed at Luke's shoulders.

Luke shot a glance at Nancy. "My God, what happened?"

"I gave him that foul liquid ye made for the fever." Her voice held a hint of accusation. "He was breathing easy as a bairn till then."

"And he's got hives. It's anaphylactic shock. Go get Lady Caryn, Nancy. Hurry!"

"She left for the chapel I shall never fetch her in time."

"Then find Bessy! Tell her what's going on!"

Nancy flew from the room.

"Randy," Luke said softly, gently prying his hands loose. "Take it easy, kid. Nancy's gone for help." He urged Randy to lie back down. "I know it's scary, but breathe slow, breathe easy."

Randy fell back on the bed, no longer grasping at Luke or uttering sounds. His eyes rolled back in his head, then snapped open from an obvious act of will. Luke wondered how low his blood pressure had dropped.

If Bessy didn't arrive quickly, he'd lose the kid. It was up to him, and he hoped his constant study served him well right now. Almost as if he were being guided, he tilted Randy's head back, getting a lack of resistance that heightened his anxiety.

"Randy!" Luke shook him, got no response. "Randy!"

He bent over and heard no breath, not the faintest hiss of air coming in and out. "Randy!"

He stood stock-still, hoping to hear the beat of hurrying footsteps in the hall. The room was quiet as a church . . . or a funeral parlor. Bending, he began artificial respiration, but breath after breath, he got no response.

Luke scanned the room. But this was no twentieth-century bedroom with ballpoint pens lying around, and he cursed that fact. And what was he planning to do? Perform a tracheotomy? He couldn't. He had no training. As he bemoaned that fact, he spied a basket filled with objects. A long feather stuck out of the middle.

Luke nearly leaped across the room. Digging into his tunic, he pulled out his penknife. "Hold on, kid," he urged as he cut the quill end off the feather. With no time to waste, he dunked the slender tube into a half-empty glass of wine, counted to ten, then did the same with the blade of his penknife. Trying not to think about the bacteria that may have survived, he quickly returned to Randy's bed.

"If you're really there, God," he said aloud. "Please guide my hand."

With that less than sacred prayer, he braced a hand under Randy's chin, then cut a slit in the hollow of his throat. His hands were steadier and the blood was less than he'd expected. When he felt cartilage, he pressed until it gave away, then pulled the wound open and inserted the quill.

Randy still wasn't breathing. Panicked, Luke shook him, then shook him again. Still no breath. Struggling to keep his wits, he breathed into the tube. Next, despite the danger of opening the half-healed bullet wound, he pressed on Randy's diaphragm. "Breathe," he commanded. "Breathe."

Abruptly he heard a cough. He grabbed for the

quill to keep it from dislodging and crooned, ''That's it, that's it. Breathe.''

When Randy's eyes opened, Luke's whooped with joy.

A rattle issued from the tube.

''Don't talk. Not yet. But you're gonna be just fine.''

Depositing a kiss on the kid's forehead, he said, ''Welcome back,'' doing his best to keep his earlier terror from his voice. His hands started shaking so badly he dropped the knife on the bed. As he reached to pick it up, he heard people approaching.

''Bessy.''

With Nancy in tow, the old woman bustled in the room with a basket of medicinals. ''Move aside.''

Still unnerved, Luke did as he was asked.

Bessy looked down at Randy. She ran a finger over his hives, then lifted his eyelids, and peered intently. Next she opened his mouth and gazed at his tongue.

'' 'Tis sorely coated.'' She shook her head, worrying Luke.

He felt oddly out of place, unneeded and he looked on helplessly while Bessy examined the quill in Randy's trachea, as if he was waiting for a diagnosis from a skilled surgeon. Nancy stood by his side, moving anxiously from foot to foot.

Bessy cast a glance over her shoulder, her lined forehead wrinkling ever deeper. ''Ye did this?''

Luke nodded. Bessy resumed her study of Randy's throat. Moments later, she turned back to Luke, offering him the fallen penknife. ''Seems ye *are* good for something aside from burning trees.''

The wide grin splitting her face was a form of apology for her earlier criticism, Luke knew, but that wasn't what warmed his heart. The healer had affirmed he'd made the right choice. His trembling subsided some, and his blood stopped pounding in his ears.

"MacNab's lad got himself caught in a swarm of bees, had hives like this all over himself, and his breath caught in a fearsome manner."

"Yeah, an allergic reaction."

"Yet this one's been near no bees. What do ye think caused it?"

"The stuff I gave him to drink." Before Bessy could jump in, he went on to tell her that it was actually powerful in fighting off infection. "But some people have a reaction—which is what happened to Randy." He looked away. "I should have thought, but . . ."

"Take heart. I was healing even afore Cromwell overrun the country, yet at times my best medicine has unforeseen and dire results. Do not blame yourself, Sir Luke. Ye did your best, with Sir Randy's good in mind."

She'd been crumbling an odd-shaped brown lump into her other hand as she spoke. Now she turned to Nancy and asked her to fetch a fresh glass of wine. When Nancy left, she looked back at Luke.

"I have much interest in this drink of yours." She grinned again, an act that had a way of taking a decade off her age. "Despite this bad result, I see many uses for it. Tell me"—she gestured toward Randy, who had again closed his eyes, but was breathing regularly and evenly—"is this an oft occurrence?"

"It's not rare, but it isn't usual either. Most people get better when penicillin is used." He frowned. "My problem was I never knew what dose I was giving. It hasn't been manufactured from common bread mold since long before I was born."

Bessy nodded sagely, moved to a table, and pulled a small dish from the basket. Putting the dish down, she dropped in the stuff she'd been crumbling. "And how do your clansmen make it, this penicillin?"

Luke gave a half laugh. "Beats me."

Which earned him a cock of Bessy's head.

"That means I don't know. But I do know they can measure the dose."

"Aye, 'tis always a problem to know how much to give. We must err on the side of too little than too much. This remedy I'm now preparing must be used with great care."

"What is it?"

"The gland of a swine."

Luke's chin lifted in alarm. "Adrenalin?"

Bessy tilted her head. "Beggin' your pardon."

"It's called adrenalin, and the gland you're using is called the adrenal gland."

" 'Tis nice to know the names of things, albeit they work as well even when you don't, is that not so?"

But Luke's attention had gone back to the powder. "You're giving that to Randy? It can cause tachycardia. And how do you know it's sterile?"

"Do I hear this from the mouth of a man who did

surgery on the lad with nothin' but a wee drab of a knife and the quill of a hawk?"

Her response took Luke aback. He hesitated in mild surprise, then let a smile escape. "You've got me there."

"The powder worked its magic well on MacNab's boy, it should do the same for young Randy. Still, I wouldna use it had your medicine not failed. The lad's own strong body would have brought him back to health. But your surgery has opened him up to new attacks. We mustna let the quill remain any longer than needs be."

Luke couldn't quarrel with her reasoning. Besides, he'd watched these women work. They knew their stuff.

Nancy came through the door carrying a glass, which she gave to Bessy.

"I shall begin with half a measure," Bessy told Luke as she took the glass. She poured some wine into the dish, then stirred the powder with a spoon she pulled from the basket. "We shall let it brew for a time, then place a small dab under his tongue. Let's discuss the medicine of your age, while we wait. 'Tis most interesting."

Nancy sat beside Randy and held his hand, rubbing it, crooning to him, as Luke and Bessy talked. Sometime later, the aged healer said the medicine had brewed long enough, and they both went to Randy's bedside.

Luke helped support his cousin's head while Bessy deposited a "wee drop" of the mixture under Randy's tongue, which prompted a repulsed expression that brought a tearful smile to Nancy's face. When both Luke and Bessy chuckled, Randy even smiled. As they reassured him the quill would soon be removed, the chapel bell rang.

Luke sighed wearily. "I told Caryn I'd attend this morning."

"She will understand, Sir Luke," Nancy said.

"I know she will, but it was important."

" 'Twill have to wait another Sabbath. Randy needs us all beside him now."

Luke took Randy's hand, getting a squeeze in return. Yeah, the kid needed him. And he needed the kid. Randy was the only relative he had in the world who was worth a can of beans; and he loved him more than he'd ever known until now.

He loved Caryn too, but their tie was not of blood. He'd made a promise to her, one he'd intended to keep. But now? Without twentieth century medicine, he doubted Randy would make it. Which meant he had to concentrate on helping Ian perfect the time machine.

The chapel bell rang again. Luke looked toward the window, wondering when services would end and council begin. He prayed Caryn wouldn't reveal his promise at that meeting.

It was one he couldn't keep.

Chapter Twenty-two

Caryn gazed down from the dais, taking in the set of the faces, dismayed by what she saw.

And heard.

Lord Mayor Fergus MacNab had the floor. "Folks be wonderin' why the dragon slayer's not done his work yet, Lady Caryn."

"Aye, why?" echoed several in the audience.

"Be he a false dragon slayer?" called out a woman near the rear of the throng.

"Silence!" roared Chisholm. "MacNab is speaking!"

His command was lost in the roar of voices.

Caryn had tried to interrupt several times to tell them of Luke's promise, but she was drowned out at each attempt. The mood of the crowd disturbed her. Her shoulders were tight, and a lump of dread writhed in her stomach. She'd once seen a mob in action at Invergair. Although she'd been very young, the memory had stuck, along with the resolve that it was something she never wanted to witness again.

Where was Luke? He'd promised to come, and she was certain he could explain his plot better than she could. Perhaps he failed to rise on time or forgot the council was held in the great hall. Possibly his kinsman had taken a turn for the worse. He'd given his word and she trusted that, so she decided to wait.

The chaos increased. After more long moments of strident voices, she could bear no more. Rising to her feet, she spread her arms. "Listen," she said softly. "Listen."

At first the jeers got worse, then slowly they began to subside. Soon, save for a few rumblings, the room fell silent.

"Sir Luke has given his word," Caryn said. "Even now he is with our lord devising a scheme to rid us of this scourge."

"Scheme, eh?" cried a loud female voice.

Caryn's head jerked in the woman's direction, and as her eyes crossed the crowd, Gann captured her gaze. Smiling sympathetically, as though they had a special bond, he raised his hand in a small salute. The import of that escaped her, but she had no chance to dwell on it.

"Give us no scheme, give us acts!" the woman screeched. "We want no peace with the monster. Only his death!"

Roars of approval followed.

"Kill the monster!" someone shouted as the cheering ebbed.

"My words be true. Sir Luke is a false dragon slayer!"

"Silence!" Chisholm roared again. He slammed a palm against the hilt of his sword and several of his men stepped closer to the crowd.

"Chisholm," Caryn hissed. "These are free folks with a right to speak their minds."

The captain leaned closer to whisper in her ear. "May I remind milady they are also free to slit our throats should we displease them mightily. The temper of this crowd suggests they may be so inclined."

"They are simply frightened," she said, but her stomach clutched. Complaints about Ian's preoccupation with returning them to Scotland had often run through the village, for the residents believed he should concentrate on Ormeskirk. Luke's appearance had lifted hearts, and his encouraging words of last Sabbath had made them feel they'd regained some control. But something had changed, and they no longer trusted him.

Caryn understood the dashed hopes that raised their ire, but she also knew that understanding alone did not make them less dangerous.

"Your warning has been noted, Captain," she said stiffly. "But tell your men to keep their weapons sheathed, regardless."

She sighed, already weary, though the midday meal was not even upon them. She desperately wanted to bring this council meeting to a close, but had no choice except to allow the crowd's wrath to run its course.

She sat back down in her chair, waiting until it did.

"Go out to slay Ormeskirk: Are ye mad, man?"

Luke gaped in shock as Ian strode across the floor of his huge lab. He'd never guessed the man had such anger in him. Moreover, he had believed that

Ian supported Caryn's desire to have Luke hunt the pterosaur.

"Ye told me yourself you have no acquaintance with guns, and the beast is indomitable by any weapons we have in the realm." Spinning on his heels, Ian headed back in the direction from which he'd come. "I need you here, man, to help me with the time mechanism. If ye should perish, who else has the knowledge to aid me in my work? Nay, you cannot do it. You cannot. That is my final word!"

"Then you'd better go help Caryn," Luke replied. He'd passed through the main floor that housed the great hall and heard the commotion. "She's in real trouble."

"Trouble?" Abruptly Ian halted. Stroking his chin, he eyed Luke speculatively.

"People are demanding that she force me to go after Ormeskirk."

"Will ye agree to that?"

Apparently, the earl had a short-lived temper, because the question was asked quite agreeably.

"I already have," Luke replied. "I promised Caryn last night. But that was before Randy got sick again."

He went on the describe his cousin's reaction, and that as much as he wanted to stay in Lochlorraine, Randy needed medical care that only his century could provide. "So I'm committed to helping you discover how Lochlorraine moved out of time."

"Ye wish to stay then?" Ian asked. "Hmmm. I was unaware of your desire. It does explain a certain lack of eagerness to help me as of late, does it not?"

Under other circumstances Luke might have

laughed. "Your villagers are in an ugly mood." He gestured to the floor above. "Please, Ian, come with me to the great hall and tell them what you just told me. Tell them I can't go."

Having firsthand experience with the way Ian got lost in his thoughts and drifted away from others, Luke half expected the same reaction now. Prepared to apply pressure, he opened his mouth to insist.

Ian surprised him by spinning again, then marching toward the door. Uncertain of the earl's intentions, Luke stayed where he was.

"What are ye waiting for, man?" Ian snapped. "We need to get on with it."

Caryn had endured her fill of shouting, angry people, even though they no longer directed their anger at her. Now they argued among one another, close to blows. She watched with deep suspicion as soldiers drifted through the crowd, stopping at this person and that person to whisper in their ears. Each time they moved on, the one they'd left turned to his neighbor, igniting a new cluster of rage. Like typhoid, their messages raced through the room, rising until she heard them from the dais.

"He canna shoot a musket."

"He knows not how."

"Nor use the broadsword."

Lord Mayor MacNab turned toward Caryn. "What manner of dragon slayer canna wield a weapon, milady?"

Caryn stood up to answer, but was interrupted by

activity at the rear of the room. People backed away, a lass curtsied, several men tipped their hats.

"Sir Ian Maclachlan, Lord of Lochlorraine," a man cried in an officious tone.

"Luke," Caryn whispered under her breath as she spied him following her brother-in-law.

Despite their rage, it was clear none would speak against the earl, not even MacNab, who swiftly removed himself from the dais.

When Ian reached the platform, he leaped up, Luke right behind him.

Luke rushed to her side. "Caryn, I have to tell you something."

Before he could, Ian cried out. "Good people. We canna send the traveler to the Wizard's Spire to battle Ormeskirk. The loss to the kingdom would be too grievous."

Apparently this was too much for MacNab. "Nooooo!" he bellowed. "This must not be! We willna suffer the plague of the dragon another season." He whirled to face the crowd. "Will we, lads and lassies?"

"Nay! Nay!" the mob cried. "Not one more season!"

"Who cares he cannot shoot? Let 'im rot in the dungeon till he does the deed!"

Luke was trying to talk to her, but Caryn couldn't hear him over the din. As she struggled to make out his words, Chisholm inched his way between them.

"I have new information that might ease this troubled crowd, milady," he roared in her ear. "Will ye grant me permission to impart it?"

"Aye, but no threats," she shouted back.

With a curt bob of his head, he turned to face the frenzied gathering. He raised his hand and shouted for quiet.

Shortly, the taunts grew fewer, further between. In a space of relative silence, Chisholm began. "Aye," he said. "Sir Luke is false, but there be one among us who is true."

"Caryn," Luke whispered. "Please understand—"

"Ye know of him, he stands in our midst. Behold, the true dragon slayer. Step forward, Sir Marco Gann, traveler from the future and master of the fierce weapon."

"Wait!" Caryn cried, throwing off Luke's insistent hand.

"Nay, Lady Caryn," Ian said. "Hear Chisholm out."

Heart pounding, Caryn looked at Luke. His face wore shock as he stared disbelievingly at Chisholm. She glanced back at the throng, seeing the avid interest in their faces, their eagerness to believe these words. But she knew it wasn't true. Gann was not the true dragon slayer. He could not succeed.

"Come forward, Dragon Slayer," Chisholm intoned. "Accept your quest."

Gann was always hard to fathom, and at the moment his expression remained so blank Caryn couldn't read it at all. Was he pleased over this announcement or just a man drawn into Chisholm's web of intrigue? She had no fondness for the unsavory traveler, but neither did she wish to send him to his doom. She shook her head, but no one noticed. Her throat would not produce a single sound.

Even as she struggled to carry out her duty, her pulse thrummed with gladness, her heart sang a tune of rejoicing. Luke would be safe, leastwise for now. She would not have to hide her tears and send him off to an uncertain battle. Another would go in his stead.

Now that very man crossed the dais, his heavy footsteps thudding against the wood. In seconds, he would answer Chisholm's challenge, and if he accepted, nothing she said thereafter would ever be heard.

It wasn't too late to stop it. To do what was right. To fulfill her duty to the land. She had to try. She forced herself to rise.

Ian moved forward. Dipping gracefully, he swept his *sgian dubh* from his garter.

"*Tàbhachd*, Dragon Slayer! *Tàbhachd*!" He stood in front of Gann and pressed firmly on his shoulders. The man sank to his knees. A muscle twitched in his jaw, but he still betrayed no feeling as Ian tapped his shoulder with the knife, then did the same to the other. "Take this sign of my goodwill as a symbol of the allegiance of all who live in Lochlorraine," Ian cried dramatically. "*Tàbhachd*!"

Though his kilt had slipped inches below his knees and his plaid was in disarray, Ian had never appeared more noble in Caryn's eyes. And this rare demonstration of his authority apparently had the same affect on the crowd. People sprang to life, dancing, hugging each other.

"*Tàbhachd*, Dragon Slayer! *Tàbhachd*!" they caroled again and again.

Tears rushed to Caryn's eyes. Her hands trembled. She became aware of a weakness in her legs. Putting a hand on Luke's arm to steady herself, she sank into her chair.

Luke looked at her, and through her veil of tears she saw confusion on his face. Her heart ached. How she loved him. More than the land to which she'd devoted her life, and to her eternal shame she'd gladly sacrifice anyone to keep him safe.

Gann had risen and was taking the knife from Ian, bowing artfully. He then moved next to Chisholm and placed a hand on his shoulder. "This man among men has sworn to stay by my side until we free the kingdom."

Several cheered, several didn't, and Chisholm's face went suddenly white. Before he could speak, Gann whirled back to the crowd and raised the knife high. "Death to Ormeskirk!"

"Death, death, death!" echoed the people.

Suddenly a woman elbowed her way forward to stand below the dais. Silhouetted by the dancing figures of her clans people, Naomi tossed her head proudly and stared up at Gann.

"Aye, death!" she said hotly. "Go, false dragon slayer. Go hunt the beast! By his claw and beak, ye shall meet the selkies and I shall have my vengeance!"

"Get her out of here!" Gann spit at Chisholm.

Before Chisholm could react, one of the revelers grabbed Naomi around the waist. "The *Daoine Shi'* promised me ye shall die!" she cried. Then the dancer swept away.

But not before he kills Ormeskirk, Caryn thought as

she watched the woman disappear into the crowd. *And may the good Lord forgive my weakness.*

Surely He would. After all, He'd answered her prayers.

Chapter Twenty-three

"Do not think ye will escape my wrath for your treachery." Chisholm stood rigidly beside Marco at the base of Wizard's Spire, his face passive as he hissed his warning.

"Christ, this from the king of deceit."

"I had no reason to anticipate the laird's impulsiveness."

Marco slammed a magazine of cartridges into the butt of his gun, enjoying the angry snap it made. He'd expected a week or two of adulation—especially from the Lady Caryn—before he set out on this gruesome mission. But the earl had immediately gathered the garrison, and although it was only the morning after the meeting, here they were, preparing to kill a creature three times their size. "And pigs fly. Besides, what are you talking about, the laird's impulsiveness? *You* announced me, and it was your boys who told the people Luke couldn't shoot a gun. Where'd you hear that anyway?"

"The earl admitted it only last week."

"Well, it would have been a lot healthier for both

of us if he hadn't. Don't forget, I'm not one of those lackeys who kiss your skirt hem. If I go down, you're going with me, so if I were you I'd make damn sure you watched my back."

The chime of the chapel clock cut off Chisholm's response. The hour had arrived, and the captain came to attention. Immediately his soldiers lined up in formation. Well-wishers gathered in the heather, waiting to send them off. Baskets of food were being emptied by servants onto well-appointed tables, and the lady and laird had been given front row seats, in chairs brought out for the occasion.

A regular picnic, Marco thought, and the sight of it did nothing to improve his mood. He tilted his head to look at the top of the spire. A long, steep climb, one he dreaded almost more than the battle to come. And their foe was nowhere in sight. Not a good sign.

Chisholm would lead the march, a fact that brought a surreptitious smile to Marco's lips. He, Ralph, and Hub—who he'd managed to get released for this excursion—would travel in the middle of the line, flanked by soldiers with swords hanging down their backs.

The night before, he and the boys had devised a plan. Ralph would pepper the creature with the Uzi until Hub got the right angle with his Magnum—the man was a crack shot with his forty-four. And Marco had his thirty-eight to aim at Ormeskirk's head. Yeah, it could be done, they could snuff the beast. Suddenly his blood boiled for the fight. One thing about war, the winner got the spoils.

"Let's get on with it," he yelled as the tenth clock chime rang. "We got a monster to kill!"

Amid blasting horns and endless cries of *"tàbhachd, tàbhachd,"* the group began the twisting ascent up the narrow spire. The climb was as bad as Marco imagined, and by the halfway point he found it hard to breathe. Beside him, Hub huffed and puffed. Only Ralph seemed unaffected, chewing tobacco and stopping occasionally to spit on the side of the narrow path.

"Jesus, watch out," Hub complained. "You almost hit me."

"Up yours," Ralph said indifferently, sending out another stream of yellow-brown saliva.

"For crissakes, save your energy," Marco ordered. He was getting uneasy. They couldn't see the windmill anymore, meaning Ormeskirk could erupt from it unnoticed. And the column was apathetic. They'd lost formation and some of the men walked perilously close to the drop-off, making easy targets of themselves. Marco yelled a reminder to hug the wall, but his thin voice didn't carry far and many stayed where they were.

How long would they have to climb?

When the high scream came from the ground below, Marco's head snapped up involuntarily, but he saw nothing.

"Ormeskirk!" a soldier cried. The name traveled down the line in ominous tones. Swords were drawn. Ralph slammed the shoulder rest of the Uzi in place. Hub pulled out his Magnum. The chapel bell sounded again. Eleven chimes. They'd been climbing for an hour.

With his Walther in his hand, Marco crept forward. Where the hell was the creature? In his experience, the monster never traveled without a constant screech. But the only sounds he heard were the shouts of warning coming from the people on the ground.

Trigger-finger in place, Ralph pivoted nervously near the drop-off. "You're a fucking target," Marco shouted. "Move to the wall!"

Ralph eased back, swinging the Uzi as he moved. Suddenly he jerked to a stop and let out a strangled grunt. A second later, a long curved object came into view.

Ormeskirk's beak.

"Shoot!" Marco shouted.

Ralph let loose with a round of bullets, then staggered backward under the assault of the dragon's screams. He stumbled, fell. The Uzi clattered as it skittered across the stony trail.

The creature soared toward Ralph. Crouching, Marco fired his gun, but his shaky aim made the shot go wild. Hub threw himself down and got off a shot that missed its mark. Still on the ground, Ralph rolled and grabbed the Uzi. As he propped up on his elbows to get in position a nearby soldier charged and drove a sword into the dragon's neck.

Ormeskirk went crazy. Writhing in the air, he emitted high-pitched earsplitting wails. His flapping wings churned the air into a gale that flattened men against the wall. Others fell, struggling to keep from being blown off the edge.

With a mighty jerk, Ormeskirk ripped free of the sword. His massive jaw opened, clamped around the soldier's waist, then opened again as he tossed his head and sent the man flying. Despite the roaring wind, Marco heard bones snap as the soldier hit the ground just inches away and stared up with lifeless eyes.

A goner. But there was no time to think about it. Ralph opened up with the Uzi again. Marco aimed at the creature's eyes and missed. Hub, now plastered against the spire wall, waited for a ready shot.

Then Ralph stood up.

"Don't!" Marco cried. He could almost read his buddy's mind. The monster was so close. Surely one last volley of bullets would finish him off. But Ormeskirk rose with lightning speed. With a blood-chilling scream the creature made a dive.

Marco leaped up to jerk Ralph back, but it all happened too fast. As he reached out for Ralph, his foot hit a hole and his ankle gave way. Ormeskirk's talons closed around Ralph's body. Just as the beast lifted off, Marco fell. At the same time Ralph's dropped Uzi struck the ground and rebounded to hit Marco's temple.

Meanwhile, Ralph bellowed in terror.

"Jesus!" Hub cried a second later. "The bird let go of him!"

A horrified scream pounded at Marco's throbbing temple, then abruptly stopped.

Poor bastard. Trembling from the knowledge that it

could just as easily have been him, Marco rocked up and grabbed the fallen Uzi. His head throbbed where the gun had banged it and a sharp pain shot through his leg, but Ormeskirk would return, he was sure of it, and they had to be ready.

"Against the wall, men!" Chisholm belatedly shouted.

Soon the entire troop was huddled against the stone, waiting.

Waiting.

Waiting.

When the chapel bells chimed the hour as twelve, Chisholm rose to his feet. "Retreat, men. The cowardly beast has returned to his lair."

Cautiously, his warriors got up, swords drawn, faces tense and alert. One man knelt beside the slaughtered soldier, his expression pained. "Damn the monster to hell," he muttered, then pulled the body over his shoulder. Standing, he said to Chisholm. " 'Tis time to bury our dead."

"Aye." After dismissing the soldier, Chisholm walked to Marco and looked down. "Wondrous weapon, indeed. Your bullets were like gnats nipping at Ormeskirk's skin."

"Beats anything you got." Marco's head still pounded and his ankle hurt like hell. Not sure he could get up alone, he stuck out his hand. "Give me a boost. I wrenched my ankle."

Chisholm gave a rough tug and when Marco hit his feet his ankle gave way. He clutched the wall for support, and carefully put weight on the injured leg. Again, his knee buckled. "Shit, I can't stand."

With a half turn, Chisholm snagged Hub. "Carry your leader. He canna walk."

"You putting me on, man? We'll both be crawling before we go a hundred feet."

Chisholm gave a scornful look that Marco filed away for payback time. "What weaklings you travelers be."

With a grunt of displeasure, he leaned, grabbed Marco's arms, and ungently tossed him over his shoulder. "Do not squirm," he ordered, then broke into a lumbering gait that jarred *Marco's injured head and ankle, but not so much that he forgot the Uzi.

"Grab Ralph's gun, Hub," he said through clenched teeth.

"Aye," Chisholm remarked derisively. "Get your useless gun, for the good it will do in your hands. Ye told me to watch your back, but I should've been keeping my eyes on your feet."

Luke saw hopelessness as he moved through the marketplace in the rear bailey. Shop owners sat in chairs outside their doors instead of taking care of business. The few buyers around searched listlessly for merchandise. And each and every one of them stared at him with censure as he passed. Eager to escape their blame, he hurried to the blacksmith's shop where the parts he'd asked the owner to craft were waiting.

" 'Mornin', Joshua," he said as he approached his anvil.

" 'Mornin', Sir Luke." The Moor looked up from

his work, smiling a greeting. The first friendly face Luke had seen. "I got your gadgets ready." He walked to a low bench and picked up four objects and carried them to Luke. "What are ye going to be doing with these?"

The parts were wheels and axles. The wheels had deep groves perfectly fitted to ride on the main hoop of Ian's gyroscope.

"It's somewhat complicated, but Sir Ian's hoping we'll get more speed from the time machine if we apply force to the central axis of his gyroscope."

"A right smart man is our laird," the man replied, then turned and went back to his anvil. The movement was so abrupt, Luke searched for a reason and he quickly found it. Several villagers had gathered in the center of the marketplace and were pointedly looking into the smithy's lean-to.

Apparently, the shunning was widespread. Even young Tom had deserted him, preferring the uncertain safety of his father's home to the stares he got tagging after a man in such disgrace.

Luke was stung by the loss of their respect. He somehow felt at fault for their unfulfilled expectation, but underneath he knew he didn't deserve what they were dishing out. Ormeskirk had been here long before he'd arrived, and the rout on the spire had been Marco's doing not his.

He placed the wheels in a basket and headed into the square.

"Come again," Joshua said to his retreating back, but Luke knew without looking that the man's eyes were directed at his anvil so as not to betray his words to the onlookers.

He did his best to hide his feelings as he briskly walked back to the castle, but they weighed heavy on him nonetheless. Marco's failure was his failure, at least in the minds of the villagers. Not that he was the only one to pay the price.

After the troops descended the spire, Chisholm dropped Marco at Ian's feet with a remark about "weak constitutions." As a litter bore him to the apothecary, he'd been hissed and booed. They'd taken his guns away again, thrown Hub back in the tower, and shipped Ralph out to sea without ceremony. Luke was certain Marco hadn't anticipated that ungrateful reception.

Although Luke still had no fondness for Gann, he couldn't help admire his "take what life gives you and turn it to your advantage" attitude. If not for the man's advice, it might have taken Luke months to realize the opportunities for fulfillment that Lochlorraine offered. The guy sure didn't deserve the disdain he'd received during the past week.

What right did these people have to ask of them what they would not do themselves? Hadn't Marco at least attempted to destroy the pterosaur? Hadn't Luke made their lives easier?

Still, he saw their side. Each time Ormeskirk snatched up a calf, sheep, or pig, they counted the days until no livestock remained. And Marco's failure had cost them yet another of their own.

He was driving himself crazy with things he couldn't control, so he turned his mind to the problem of the gyroscope. Time and again, he'd made Ian repeat the story of the night Lochlorraine was torn from time, seeking an overlooked point that might bring a solution. Always, it came up the same. A storm had whipped the gyroscope to extraordinary speeds, which Ian believed was the deciding factor. In order to test the theory, they needed to reproduce that speed in the laboratory. Hopefully, applying wheels to the gyroscope would give the needed boost.

Luke had been so engrossed in thought he'd automatically descended the stairs and was surprised to find himself already at the laboratory door. Back to work, he thought, relieved by this means to put the scornful faces of the villagers out of his mind.

"Ye have the wheels?" Ian asked as he entered.

"Yes. Joshua did nice work." He unloaded the parts, and without further words, he and Ian mounted them on either side of the gyroscope. It always surprised Luke how easily they worked together, almost as if reading each other's minds.

Once the wheels were in place, they engaged the axles, then attached highly waxed ropes to the outer ends of each rod. The ropes were then threaded through pulleys Ian had bolted into the floor beneath the gyroscope. The opposite ends of the ropes were already attached to winches that swung free with each revolution only to tighten again and apply force to the axles.

"Splendid!" Ian exclaimed when their work was done. "Let's give it a spin, shall we?"

Luke nodded, his heart pounding with anticipation.

"What happens if we end up in Ormeskirk's era?" he asked, feeling a bit breathless.

Ian shrugged. "Then we try again."

"But Randy . . ."

"We must take the risk. Presently we are at the whims of fate when it comes to the times we hit upon." He stroked his chin. "Do ye have a better thought?"

From anyone else Luke would have interpreted the question as sarcasm, but he'd come to know the scientist well, and understood he was being asked for information.

"No."

"Then try we must." He took his place at one of the winches and nodded for Luke to take the other. In tandem they sent the rope spinning. Ian had built a gauge to measure the gyroscope's speed, and as they strained to get the wheels spinning, they turned eyes toward it. The mechanism hummed, louder, faster. The gauge rose and rose again. And again, reaching speeds it never had before. At Ian's signal, they disengaged the wheels, and the gyroscope jumped to yet greater speeds.

The crude needle continued to rise, reaching the far end of the gauge. Still, the gyro was gaining speed, moving so fast it was a blur to Luke's eyes.

A sharp boom suddenly tore through the room.

"It's working!" Ian cheered, his face lighting up with glee. "I heard that very sound the night of the accident."

Luke was confused. What was that sound? The asking produced the answer as Luke remembered Caryn's remark on the day he'd come to offer help: *There was a great cracking sound.* He'd forgotten it until now, and Ian had never mentioned it again.

The gyroscope had broken the sound barrier.

But that alone wouldn't move them in time. Jet planes did it all the time. He turned his eyes toward the compass that measured their place.

The needle still rested on the twentieth century.

His shoulders slumped; he turned away. Behind him Ian muttered something in his Celtic language. Luke turned to look at him, then caught sight of a cluster of people at the laboratory door.

"What is it?" the wine steward asked breathlessly.

Ian circled slowly, staring at the onlookers as if he'd never seen them before. " 'Tis nothing," he finally said. "Return to your duties."

The group dispersed, and Ian moved to the book table. He lifted the parchments of drawings and equations, then slammed them down.

"We have failed," he shouted, looking toward the ceiling as if cursing God. Next, his tone now defeated, he asked Luke to shut down the gyro.

Luke reversed the winches, an act that took tremendous strength. The gyroscope lost speed. He then turned back to Ian, wanting to talk about what to do next. One look at the earl told him it would be useless.

Ian generally paced the floor when agitated, but this time he moved to the settee, leaning forward to rub his hands in front of the fire. Luke allowed him his peace, knowing how fully he felt the weight of failure.

As did Luke. And his reasons were every bit as pressing. Randy deteriorated daily, and the best of Caryn's medicine had not kept infection from his wound.

Luke walked to the fire. His hands were cold, and stung from his efforts to stop the gyro. Sitting down, he warmed them in front of the flames. What next? He knew the answer, but hesitated to speak it.

" 'Tis as I suspected, Luke. The wind is the variable. We canna solve this riddle until we regain the windmill." He leaned back wearily, let out a deep sigh. "Long have I thought my clansmen mad in their quest to destroy the dragon. Now I see it not as folly, but the only means to our salvation. Clearly Ormeskirk must be defeated if ever we are to escape the bubble."

Luke didn't say a word. He'd already reached the same conclusion.

Chapter Twenty-four

Luke wasn't crazy about asking for Marco's help, but if he didn't learn how to shoot the Uzi he was dead meat. So he headed with this odd partner toward the rocky northeastern edge of Lucifer's Window, where there'd be no risk of shooting passersby.

The path was rugged and uneven, forcing Luke to help Gann make his way on crutches. No easy task, considering Luke was carrying the Uzi and an archery target.

After settling on the flat rock, Marco took the gun from Luke, then pointed to a tree that stood apart from the forest. "Put the target over there."

When Luke had done this to Marco's exacting standards, he went back to the rock, took a seat, and pointed to the Uzi. "Shoot."

Marco's mouth turned up. "Not a good thing to say to a man with a muscle gun."

Luke grinned. "You've got a point. Now show me what you know."

Marco took the weapon apart. As he put it back together, he told Luke how spent shells ejected, showed him the bolt and chamber, then how to set single and rapid-fire. "Ralph modified it to shoot on auto, but that eats up a lot of ammo. Unless you get a clean line to Ormeskirk's belly you're better off firing in bursts."

He then gave the gun back to Luke. "Here, take it apart."

Holding the Uzi as if it were a viper, Luke tried to duplicate Marco's actions. After several tries that evoked the same number of jibes, he finally succeeded.

"Good enough." Marco picked up a long rectangle he'd placed on the ground. "The magazine. This one holds thirty-two rounds." He then took a box of bullets from his pocket. "These are pure gold. Ralph carried three loaded magazines that night, but he only brought two boxes of extra cartridges." Marco grimaced and glanced away. "He didn't expect to be shooting at all, much less meeting up with a dragon."

Luke remained silent, figuring even thugs had a right to their grief. After a couple of seconds, Marco looked back.

"So what do you want me to do now?" Luke asked.

"Load the magazine."

"Right." But after fighting the spring for a while, Luke finally got the hang of it.

Marco then demonstrated how to snap the magazine into the butt of the Uzi. This done, he placed the weapon in Luke's hands.

"Time for target practice."

Gingerly Luke carried the weapon to the target

area, then went back to help the injured man cross the distance.

"Brace the gun against your shoulder, line up your sight," Marco then instructed, so irritably that Luke wondered if the crutches were hurting him. "Then push the bolt release and pull the trigger."

Luke peered down the sight, aligning it with the center of the target. Nervously, he pressed down with his thumb, then pulled back his finger.

A series of rapid explosions kicked him like a mule. Whirling from the impact, he stumbled, totally losing control. Bullets hissed and clanked, bouncing off rocks, going everywhere.

"Let go of the trigger, you idiot!" Marco bellowed, dropping his crutches and diving for the ground.

Still jerked around by the gun, Luke found it remarkably difficult to follow those instructions, but eventually the hail of bullets stopped.

"For crissakes, Slade!" Marco roared. "You have the sucker on automatic! Didn't I tell you to set it for single shot?"

Half-dazed, and with his finger still inside the trigger guard, Luke raised the Uzi to check the settings, having no memory of such an instruction.

"Drop the barrel, drop it!" Marco roared.

At the excited cry, Luke looked down. Marco had rolled into a ball and was clutching his head.

Luke burst into laughter.

"It's not funny, you son of a bitch. Now get over here and help me up."

Still laughing, Luke lowered the Uzi, walked over, and extended a hand.

"That was fun." He wasn't sure he liked the feeling of power that came over him as he held the deadly weapon, but he hadn't minded giving Marco a little tit-for-tat, despite the guy being on crutches. "Let's try it again."

"Just don't get stupid on me again. You wasted near to twenty rounds with that trick. Keep it up and there won't be any ammo left."

Luke looked down. Over a dozen ejected shells were on the ground. He picked one up and examined it, then searched for the bullets themselves. They were blobs of flattened lead, but the cartridge looked almost as good as the ones in the box. "People ever put fresh bullets and powder in these things?"

"All the time." Marco jerked the Uzi from Luke's hands. "Just double-checking the setting," he explained crossly. "Why'd you ask?"

"We could collect the empty shells and take them to the smithy. They have lead and powder in Lochlorraine."

"You crazy, man? Those things are manufactured to tolerances."

"How tight could those be?"

They argued about it for a time, then Marco finally shrugged his shoulders. "Do whatever. If you're lucky the damn thing won't blow up in your face, so I'll show you how to clear a jam."

After that was done, Luke returned to practicing. Marco showed him how to brace his feet and lean forward when he got off a shot. After an hour or so of practice, Luke was hitting the target more than half of the time.

"That'll do it for today." Marco slumped on his crutches, tugging at the rags that padded the tops. "These things are killing my armpits."

With the constant battering from the Uzi, Luke's shoulder wasn't faring so well either, so he didn't complain. Besides, he had more work to do. He slung the strap of the Uzi over his shoulder and collected the spent shells.

He left Marco on the back steps to the castle and hurried to the blacksmith's shop, where he'd left the drawings of mail coats and helmets he and Ian had done. In five days he'd be leading Chisholm and another twenty soldiers—armed with muskets this time as well as swords—to fight the pterosaur. He'd also enlisted Hub, who was hot about Ralph's death, and eager to get revenge.

"Hey, Joshua," he said as he walked into the lean-to. "how're the helmets coming?"

"Other than me needing to rob all the metal in the realm?"

Which wasn't too far wrong. They'd dragged the suits of armor that decorated the castle halls down to the smithy's shop. Then Luke had gathered up every other item of metal, including the copper chamber pots, and added them to Joshua's supply. Bessy had balked, however, when Luke cast a covetous eye on the silver, and he'd backed off, at least for the time being. "You needed supplies, didn't you?"

Joshua grinned and nodded. "I got ever' mother's son who can wield a hammer and bellows workin' on the task, and though I won't be putting me hallmark on 'em, they'll suit. Aye, they'll suit."

He displayed one of the helmets, which resembled those used in World War I. It showed dings from the hammer and Luke had his doubts about the fit, but the leather straps affixed to each side would undoubtedly keep it in place. "Yep. They'll suit."

He dug into his sporran and pulled out a bullet casing. "I've got another job for you."

After he and Joshua talked over what Luke had in mind, with the blacksmith agreeing to try it even though he was skeptical, Luke asked about the mail coats.

"I'm having to do 'em myself," Joshua answered, nodding toward a half-finished suit hanging from a rafter. "All them wee rings are too taxing for the apprentices. But the coats'll be done for the big day, trust me."

"I do."

Luke left the shop, heading for the sundry store, where Chisholm's staff was making an arsenal of Molotov cocktails out of glass bottles filled with fish oil. These were for Luke's backup plan. In case they failed to kill the pterosaur before they reached the windmill, they'd light the crude bombs with torches and throw them into the nest.

The design was simple and the work was going smoothly, so he didn't stay long. The dragon hour was nearing and he wanted to go to the battlement and watch Ormeskirk fly over the fields.

People waved and nodded as he crossed the marketplace. Their earlier ire had vanished when they'd learned he was going to fight the dragon, and young Tom again tagged after him during every free moment.

Luke found himself basking in their admiration, even as he had a cynical thought: All it required to keep their respect was to risk his life . . . and possibly lose it. Would they sing him eulogies if he failed? Or would he receive the same scorn Marco had, then later be dumped in the sea like Ralph?

A chill raced down his spine. Images of red and white and blue. Sounds of spitting bullets and shouting voices momentarily overtook his world, then vanished in an act of his will. A dull headache remained.

He trotted up the castle stairs, hoping exercise would clear his head. As he approached the floor where he had his quarters, he encountered Caryn in the stairwell.

"Where have ye been so long?"

"Learning to shoot the big gun."

Her green eyes darkened. "Is it as fearsome as they say? Will ye truly be able to down the beast?" Her head moved right and left as she spoke, and he wondered if she knew how clearly the gesture revealed her doubts. Or even that she had them.

"With a little bit of help."

Giving an obviously forced laugh, she stepped away and took his hand. "So where are you now going in such a hurry, my brave hero."

Don't, he wanted to say. *Don't pretend you aren't worried.*

He let the urge pass.

"For the roof to catch a look at the pterosaur. Want to come?"

With a smile that was far too bright, she took his arm. He replayed the incident with Marco and the runaway Uzi as they climbed the remaining flights, and by the time they reached the top, Caryn was laughing with true amusement.

Twilight was already falling. He and Caryn walked to the battlement and looked out, watching the men drive livestock in from the fields to the village. A familiar cry arose from Wizard's Spire.

Luke saw a tremor run through Caryn's slight body, and he pushed the Uzi back so he could pull her close. Together they watched the pterosaur fly toward the fields.

Luke took in the creature's every action. He'd come here each night since he'd agreed to mount the assault, believing it wise to know his enemy. He'd observed the flight patterns, tried to figure out what motion warned of a dip or sway. Their hopes, he thought, rested with the animal's tender underbelly. Only there would a bullet easily penetrate.

But Ormeskirk was fast on the glide. On the day of Marco's rout, Luke had been startled to see him hover in the air like a hummingbird. What other unknown skills did he have? How much dexterity did those small digits at the joints of his wings possess? Or, for that matter, the long fingers that formed his feet?

Ormeskirk shrieked again. He sounded angry, hungry.

" 'Twill be wonderful when Lochlorraine is freed of this plague,'' said Caryn with a tremulous voice.

Luke squeezed her shoulder, incapable of speech.

Although he understood the necessity of destroying this unique creature, his throat thickened, his eyes fogged, and an inexplicable sadness hung over him like a shroud.

The soldiers were housed on the floor just below the roof, the better to race to the battlement in case of danger, Marco supposed. Although he usually cursed the fact that his quarters were on the same floor, this evening it suited him just fine. His ankle was healing well, but he didn't yet relish climbing up and down stairs on his poor excuse for crutches, which he seldom risked going without.

He'd seen the couple go up, so engrossed in each other his stomach churned with jealousy, and wanted to find out what they were up to. So he stood in the shelter of the stairwell, feeding his envy.

Luke had landed on his feet again, getting all the respect. But Marco had earned it, dammit! His best man died on that spire, and it could just as easily have been him.

He had to give Slade credit, though, even if grudgingly. For someone who'd never handled a gun before, he had a good eye and a true aim. And the way the guy rode a horse after such a short time, it was like he'd been born in a saddle. This was a foe Marco wouldn't underestimate.

But that didn't stop him from hoping that Ormeskirk would eat Luke alive. He formed a mental picture of Luke caught in that creature's mouth, squirming like a mouse and screaming for his life.

A dark chuckle rumbled in his throat.

"They are a mismatched pair, do ye not think?"

Marco turned to see Chisholm lurking over his shoulder. "What're you doing sneaking up on me?"

"I was not sneaking. I saw you here and came to ask if ye needed my aid." He glanced at the crutches, which lay against the wall. "Your ankle is faring well, I see."

Marco grabbed the crutches and slammed them under his arms, earning a sharp burst of pain when they struck raw skin. "I'm leaning on the wall, in case you hadn't noticed."

"Aye."

The word had a mocking ring that Marco chose to ignore. "So why'd you really come up here?"

Chisholm cleared his throat, hemmed and hawed for a second, then said, "Teach me how to shoot your Uzi."

"You kind of stretched my goodwill thin a week or so back, Robert, in case it slipped your mind. Besides, Slade has it."

"Then perhaps I should ask him. Surely he'd see the wisdom of having two possible assassins for the beast. If he should fall, I could stand the course."

The idea of these two learning from each other brought a small smile to Marco's face, and he was tempted to let them have at it. Then a new idea jumped into his mind.

"Nah. Slade's a numbskull where weapons are concerned. I'll teach you. But you'll have to ask the earl for possession of the gun. I lost that privilege, if you remember."

"Our laird is somewhat tetched and does not think these things through."

"Exactly, but I'm sure you can help him mend his ways."

Chisholm made a few meaningless sounds, then began backing down the stairs. "Tomorrow," he said brusquely. "Lucifer's Window, when the chimes ring three."

"Tomorrow."

He watched Chisholm lope down the stairs, taking them two at a time, and felt another surge of malice. Clearly the captain thought Marco had half a brain. There was only one reason to learn about the Uzi, and it had nothing to do with backing Luke up. No, after the *dragon slayer* did his work, Chisholm planned to use the weapon to overrun the fief—and probably take out him and Hub while he was doing it.

Well, he'd show the man how to shoot the submachine gun, all right, but he'd leave out the most important part—the stance. Put it slightly off skew, train the man on single shots. The first time Robert fired multiple bursts . . . well, at best he'd take out a couple men and get beheaded for the act. At worst, he'd be such a comical sight, he'd lose the respect of his men.

That's when Marco would step in.

This prospect brought a smile to his face that was quickly cut off. Luke had just dipped his head toward Caryn. She laughed and tightened her arm around his waist. Sickened, Marco turned away.

Glancing back only long enough to assure he'd gone unnoticed, he tucked his crutches under his arm.

When he trotted down the single flight of stairs, his injured ankle gave him nothing more than a minor twinge.

Chapter Twenty-five

Till the next full moon, perhaps longer, perhaps not.

Luke walked toward the apothecary to visit his cousin, Caryn's words repeating in his head like a mantra. The moon had been almost full on the night they'd arrived, and only three days remained until the next one appeared. Time was running out.

When the sun rose tomorrow he'd go out to perform an act that his heart wasn't in, one he doubted would do any good. Ian still had to rebuild the windmill and connect it to the ring on the tower. How could they complete this before the bubble moved on? And if it moved on, would they gain control of its destination?

Randy's life hung on the answers to these questions.

The kid had been returned to the apothecary after his reaction to the penicillin, but when Luke entered, the first thing he thought was that Randy looked grey, no other word would describe it. Nancy sat by his bed, her face almost as strained and grey as his. Caryn wasn't there.

"Mind giving us some time alone?" Luke asked

Nancy. It had taken him a while to realize that castle servants took no offense at being asked to leave. "Don't go far. We won't be long."

She smiled wanly, then closed the door behind her.

Luke approached the bed and reached for Randy's bedcovers. "I want to check your wound. Okay?"

"Might as well. Everybody else does." His voice sounded as if he found it hard to breathe. "Lady Caryn. Bessy. Nancy. Course, I don't mind so much when it's her."

"Of course you don't." Luke peeled back the bandages while they talked, and examined the wound. The edges were red and angry. Thick puss oozed from between the stitches. What's more, the puncture wound from the tracheotomy wasn't healing like it should.

"I'm working on getting us outta here, kid."

Randy shook his head weakly. "I wanna stay."

"I know you do, but . . ." A bottle of iodine sat on the washstand and Luke picked it up. "Hold on," he warned, pouring the antiseptic on both wounds. Randy didn't even let out a whimper. Luke supposed he was getting used to the pain.

They'd tried everything, he and Caryn. They had even considered lye, but the pain it would cause made them hold back. For the same reason, Caryn was reluctant to reopen the wound and clean it out. The night of the original surgery, Randy had been half-unconscious from blood loss, so the opium-soaked cloths had easily knocked him out. But now? While probing a raw wound? She thought sheer agony alone might kill him.

"I'm gonna die if we stay, ain't I, Luke?"

"You aren't getting any better."

Randy looked away. Luke replaced the bandages, then drew the blankets up. Still the kid didn't speak.

"Maybe we can come back. I'd like that." Luke knew his tone carried no conviction.

"I ain't stupid, you know!" Randy snapped, with more energy than Luke had thought he possessed. "We got in, we couldn't get out. You think I believe if we get out, we can get back in?"

"It's just a hope. But you need antibiotics, and they don't have any in Lochlorraine." He knelt by Randy's bed and took his hand. "Look, kid. You're all I've got. I'll do anything to keep you safe."

Randy patted his head, a sad movement that tore at Luke's heart. "I know you would, Luke, and I want to go with you. But more of me wants to stay with Nancy." Luke looked up and saw a glow on his cousin's face. "She loves me. She wants to marry me. Think of it. Me, drunk old Marv's half-wit boy, gettin' married to a beautiful woman, maybe havin' kids." A sob caught in his throat. "And I love her, too."

Damn! Luke thought. It wasn't fair. Finally his cousin had found a place where people respected him, where a warm and loving woman wanted to share his life. If anyone belonged in Lochlorraine, it was Randy Slade. Here, even with his limited education and intellect, he'd be respected.

"Besides, Luke. You gotta stay and marry Lady Caryn. I see you laughin' and talkin'. I know you both care. You're in love too."

Throat tightening, Luke got up. He gave the bed-covers one last tuck, then ruffled Randy's hair. "And some people say you don't notice much. A lot they know."

Luke had been dashing around all day, looking after last-minute details. He'd spent the last half hour practicing with the Uzi, knowing he wouldn't get another chance. Afterward, he scrupulously searched for empty cartridges and misshapen bullets, digging out slugs that had hit the target.

Joshua had done a fine job of crafting the bullets and reloading the cartridges. Luke tested the reloads himself, several times. Most had fired perfectly, and when they hadn't he'd discovered he was fast becoming a master at clearing jams.

The arsenal of crude bombs was complete, and soldiers already streamed through Chisholm's store to pick up their supplies. Luke's work was done, at least for today. Dusk would soon arrive, and he wanted to spend this last night with Caryn.

His final stop was the blacksmith's shop. The helmets were finished and so were the coats of mail, a set for every man who would climb the spire. Satisfied, he started to leave. He had no idea why the flash of silver caught his eye, but he moved over to inspect it anyway.

Joshua coughed. "Sir Luke . . ."

By this time, Luke had his hands on a small mail coat. "This looks like it was made for a child. I don't remember any soldiers being this little."

Joshua's face told it all. The coat was for Caryn.

*   *   *

Luke searched everywhere: The apothecary, the great hall, the kitchen. He ducked his head into the lab, waved at Ian. She wasn't in any of those places. Nor was she in the great hall overseeing supper preparations.

In order to avoid gossip, he'd made a point of staying away from her rooms, but as a last resort he knocked on her door. She didn't answer. He knocked again and heard scurrying sounds inside.

"Caryn?"

He lifted the latch and pushed, only to discover the door had been bolted from the inside. "Caryn," he called again.

"Momentarily."

"Hurry," he said through the door. "We have to talk."

He heard the bolt lift. The door opened an inch and her pert nose emerged. "I'm not fit for company. Wait for a moment so I may escape to my bedchamber."

Luke counted to ten, opened the door, then moved in front of the fire, where he tapped a foot.

Dammit, he needed an explanation.

No, he didn't. There was only one.

Yes he did. Maybe, he'd misinterpreted the signals.

But he knew he hadn't, and as the time stretched he thought about breaking into Caryn's bedroom, then discarded the idea. Nevertheless, he glanced that way, coming across a flash of plaid. She'd dropped her shawl, which now rested on the thresh-old, beneath the closed door. Eager for any distraction, he walked over and tugged the loose end, thinking to give her the shawl when she returned.

The door swung open.

Caryn stood in front of her wardrobe, holding a dress that blocked the view of all but her legs. They were covered by a pair of trews.

"It's true!" he said, his tone accusatory.

Still holding the dress, she swung around, her expression startled. Quickly it turned to anger. "How dare you enter my bedchamber without invitation!"

Put on the defensive, Luke started to explain, then caught himself. "You're intending to come with us tomorrow, aren't you?" He crossed the room, tore the dress from her hands and threw it on the bed. "Are you crazy, Caryn? You can't do this."

She gasped. As he clamped his hands on her shoulders, her arms flew to cover her breasts. Not until then did Luke realize she wore no shirt. He felt a visceral throb, an instant erection.

He still held the shawl in his hand, which he belatedly saw was a kilt. Hastily, he bundled it around her shoulders.

She pushed his hands away and clutched the fabric to her body. "How did you find me out?" Her eyes widened suddenly. "Joshua . . ."

"It wasn't his fault. He put the coat aside, but I happened to see it." Luke blew out his breath, shoved a hand in his hair, then decided to say it straight out. "You can't go with us tomorrow, Caryn. I won't let you."

"Ye won't *let* me?" Glaring at him furiously, she gathered the plaid more tightly around her. "Ye think I'm incapable of fighting, don't you? Well, I am capable, Luke Slade, I am. I shoot truer than most of the soldiers you'll take, by half, and I'm a master of both the long and the crossbow."

"Ralph had a submachine gun and that didn't save him!" He started to step forward, but her fury made him hesitate. "You have to stay behind. I need to know you're safe."

She tossed her head derisively. "None are safe as long as Ormeskirk lives. And what am I to do? Sit at the base of the spire, wring my hands, fearing that each fallen man is you? Nay. I will not do it. And ye have no authority to make me."

"You're right. But Ian does." Luke spun for the door.

Caryn grabbed his arm. "Don't! I will never forgive the affront! Never as long—" Her expression abruptly changed. Softening, saddening, draining of fury. ". . . as long as we live. Please . . . Please, Luke. Do not put yourself in harm's way without me by your side."

She relaxed her hold on his arm, moved her hand along the muscles, stroking his biceps. For some odd reason, their quarrel had heightened Luke's desire, and her touch sent an intense shiver through his body.

He turned. Tentatively he cupped her face. The green of her eyes was now smoky, her expression had turned to anticipation. On an anguished sigh, he lowered his head and gently kissed her. Softly, almost reverently, he brushed his lips against her mouth.

For one sweet moment she was all there was, filling his heart, his mind, blocking out everything else. Then the reality of what she was planning came back with a force that nearly staggered him. He broke off their kiss.

"We don't . . . You can't . . ." His voice faltered at the lump in his throat. "It's all so uncertain—Randy—" He needed her safe. If he died on the spire, someone had to care for Randy. But more than anything, he needed her to live a long and happy life, even if he didn't. She couldn't go!

Suddenly he could no longer stand their weeks of restraint. All his love and longing rushed forth. He crushed her to his chest.

She breathed out heavily as if a great weight had lifted from her shoulders. She was his love, he'd known it from the moment he'd first seen her, and his intense hunger for her frightened him beyond belief.

"Don't go . . ." he whispered against her lips.

Then he was scattering kisses on Caryn's face, her hair, her neck, dizzying her with their power. She felt her body weaken with need for him. Her knees sagged. She clutched at his shoulders, caring not that the plaid was slipping away.

He bent his head, ran his tongue along the rise of her collarbone, dipped into the cleft between her breasts. She felt his shudder throughout her own limbs, felt his hard male organ thrusting against the tender, yearning spot she'd guarded so well these many years. She ached so badly she should be crying out from the pain of it, but the whimpers she uttered, despite her efforts to hold them back, were from sheer delight.

"Luke," she murmured on a sigh.

He groaned again, then abruptly let her go. A protest escaped her throat, and she shamelessly groped to pull him back. Resisting, he took one of her hands, lightly placed a kiss on its palm. She shivered, a knee buckled, and he stiffened his arm to support her. "We can't, sweetheart," he whispered. "We can't do this."

She bit her lower lip. "W-why?" She was incapable of anything more.

"You know why. I have to—dammit, Caryn, we can't be together! I have to leave Lochlorraine." He let out a bitter laugh. "If I survive the battle with Ormeskirk, that is.

"Besides . . ." He stroked her cheek with a velvet touch meant to soothe. It had the opposite effect, and she gasped, desire springing anew in her. "You could get pregnant. You'd be disgraced."

Caryn cocked her head. So that was the reason for his refusal. How like Luke to disregard his own desires in favor of her welfare. Her love for him swelled to proportions that overtook the room. No more could she deny it.

Give him the ring.

The inner voice spoke so loudly, for a moment Caryn thought it came from outside. It hadn't. 'Twas love that spoke, warring with duty once more, resurrecting her unanswered question. Suddenly angry at God for failing her during the greatest crisis of her life, she stepped forward.

Quickly she unbuckled Luke's belt. His tunic fell loose. His trews slipped down to hang precariously on his hipbones. She laughed, lightly, devilishly, without regard for propriety. "I am four and thirty years of age. I know the dangers and have suffered the scorn of others many a time. Should ye leave a bairn in my belly, it would be my honor to bring it forth."

She fell to her knees and began loosening the ties of his boots. Her every touch sent discernible shivers through Luke's muscled legs. Off came his boots, off came his hose, then gently she pulled down his trews.

She gasped slightly as his erection was revealed, then looked up at him, meeting adoration in his eyes. With a small hesitation, she took him in hand, felt him stiffen further, though she would have thought that impossible. A hiss of desire emerged from his throat.

"This was something Gregory was wont to ask for," she said, dipping her head toward the V of his thighs. "Although I found it unpleasant then, 'tis something I would gladly do for you."

"Caryn . . ." Bending, he cupped her elbows and lifted her to her feet. "I'll never, ever, ask you to do something you don't like. I want to show you what lovemaking is, not force it on you." He said it fiercely, harshly, and she knew he meant it. He'd risk his life for her. Indeed, he soon would.

"Then lie with me, Luke. Let me feel your trembling body loose itself within me. If we are to part, no matter the reason, let us have this one night together."

Luke could withstand it no longer. He swept her up and carried her to the bed. Brushing her dress to the floor, he put her down and untied the bindings on her trews.

She reached out to him, her lips parted, waiting for his kiss. Her legs separated, an invitation to mount and enter. Instead he reclined beside her, pulled her close, and traced the outline of her figure with his hand.

"Ye do not want . . . Gregory always—"

"Forget Gregory," he growled. "This is us, this is now."

She nestled beside him, shivering as his hand moved over the curve of her inner thigh. Then he claimed her lips in a kiss that held nothing back. Their tongues parried in harmony with his fingers as he entered the smooth, heated surface inside her.

Slowly, gently, he took her to heights of passion, let the passion ebb, then took her to greater heights. When her body trembled with unleashed cravings, he sent her over the edge. Only when she whimpered with fulfillment did he enter her.

She gasped out a cry of renewed pleasure, spread her legs and bucked her hips. Soon, too soon, Luke's body burst into a thousand pinpoints of pleasure. She was right, he thought. They had earned this one night. But even this ecstasy couldn't dim the anguish of knowing they couldn't be together.

He stayed above her for quite a while, taking in her fragrance, listening to the uneven flow of her breath. Finally, she looked up at him, her eyes brimming with joyful tears. "Now I know why bards write and sing of carnal love. But even their fine words have not described the glory of it."

"No," he said, rolling off her and pulling her into the crook of his arms. "But it's not always like this."

"I know."

Wisely, he didn't ask. Instead, his mind whirled with possibilities. As much as he scorned the destiny Caryn so often invoked, it was as if he'd waited for her all his life. He couldn't leave her, not after this.

No more than Randy could leave Nancy.

What if they could return?

He pulled Caryn closer. "Look, we both know I have to take Randy out, but what if we come back?"

"Aye!" she exclaimed, levering up to rest her head on her hand. Her eyes glimmered with excitement. "Come back. Please come back."

The level of her excitement startled Luke. She understood the difficulties as much as he did, but she behaved as if it was a done deal. "I'll have to work out a method first," he said, his attitude considerably more measured.

She flopped back down and stared up at the canopy of her bed. "Aye," she said. "A method."

Her deflated tone tugged at his sympathy, and he stroked her cheek. "I'll think of one. And then I'll come back."

A promise he would keep if he survived the battle with Ormeskirk. And when he did, he'd ask Caryn to be his wife. But first she had a right to know who he'd been. Now was as good an opportunity as any, for he might not get another. If his confession elicited the disdain he feared, well, perhaps that would serve a purpose. If he died on the spire, she would have that much less grief.

He pulled her back down on the bed and wrapped her in his arms. In order to begin, he needed her close to his heart.

Chapter Twenty-six

Luke had won a football scholarship to Penn State. The team had been winning, his grades had been high, and he'd been filled with confidence about his future. If he hadn't forgotten his textbooks that morning, he might never have taken that early morning phone call.

"Luke, h-he's going to b-break him loose," his mother wailed.

"Who?"

"Kevin. Your pa."

She'd been hysterical, and it had been a while before Luke calmed her down enough to understand what she was saying. His pa was being transferred from the city jail to Attica the next evening, and Kevin was going to attempt a breakout.

"Stop him," his mother pleaded.

He'd driven to New York like a demon from hell. Not for his pa. The guy could burn for all he cared. He'd been a thief all his life, and when he'd shot that liquor store owner he'd also become a killer. He deserved whatever he got. But his mother hadn't earned this grief. And Kevin was only seventeen.

Despite Luke's influence, Kevin had drifted into a life of petty crime. He'd taken up with Vinnie and Don, running numbers, peddling a little pot. But so far he'd avoided burglary or robbery, and he'd certainly never kill anyone.

Unfortunately, Kevin loved their pa as deeply as Luke hated him. When Luke arrived home, his attempts to change his brother's mind fell on stubborn ears. He did, however, manage to worm out some information. The car that would transport their pa to Attica routinely stopped at a guarded rest area to use the facilities. This was where Kevin planned to wait. When their pa climbed out, Kevin would throw a Molotov cocktail, providing a smoky cover for escape.

"We'll be gone before those cops can see the hands in front of their faces," Kevin had bragged with a smirk. "Sweet."

"Stupid," Luke responded, getting a sour look in return.

Luke drove to the scene early and waited. When Kevin showed up in a stolen car, they argued bitterly. They were still arguing when the police drove in.

"Get outta here," Kevin ordered. "You're going to screw everything up."

That was the idea. Kevin was still a juvenile, it wouldn't go too hard on him.

With Kevin shouting threats in his ears, Luke walked toward the police car, keeping his hands fully in sight. An officer stepped out, his palm on his weapon.

"Sir," Luke said, preparing to reveal what was about to go down.

"Down!" the officer shouted. Pushing Luke off his feet, he pulled out his gun. As Luke rolled on the blacktop, he heard an explosion. Then several more. Smoke rose all around him; he could barely see. But he could hear the shouts of recognizable voices. Kevin calling to their pa. His pa calling back. The officer who'd pushed Luke over now stood above him, swinging back and forth in a thick cloud. Suddenly Luke's pa appeared. He snatched away the officer's gun, then ran off toward Kevin's call without ever noticing that Luke was lying on the ground beside his feet.

Kevin's expectations from the bomb had been grandiose, because the smoke quickly dissipated.

"Find shelter, boy," the officer above Luke growled, yanking him to his feet, and shoving him toward the municipal building.

But Luke caught his balance and spun around. "Get away from Pa!" he screamed at Kevin's fleeing back.

Behind him, cops poured from everywhere. From the building, from the police car. Weapons were drawn. A siren screamed. Kevin whirled and pulled out another gasoline-filled bottle, stopping just long enough to light the fuse. The fresh explosion created a new cloud of smoke.

The cops shouted warnings, but the two kept running toward the car. Again, the smoke cleared before they'd reached their destination. Their pa spun around, the cop's gun in his hand.

"Noooo!" Luke bellowed, charging forward.

Someone caught his arm, slammed him facedown on the car with a force that sent tremors into the bones of his face. Blood trickled from his nose. "Don't shoot," he cried, just as a shot rang out.

The cop holding Luke's arm jerked like someone had yanked him, then he crashed into the car and toppled to the ground. Straightening and turning, Luke stared numbly at the downed man. Return gunshots cracked around him.

Kevin was in mortal danger. Guns fired like bowling pins crashing in an alley. The air smelled bitter with burning powder. Sirens in the distance signaled more cars were coming. Breaks squealed. Lights flashed in obscenely bright colors.

He saw his pa's head jut out from behind the corner of the car. Then the gun, aimed at the cops.

"Don't, Pa! Kevin will get hurt!" Luke ran, shouting at the top of his lungs.

"Stop!" a cop roared, but Luke paid no attention.

Just then, his pa again leaned out, the barrel of his gun reflecting a funereal light from the overhead halogen lamps. A shotgun blasted. An instant later, his pa rolled out from behind the bumper, coming to a stop by the passenger door. With a hideous shriek, Kevin leaped up and threw himself across the body.

The gunfire stopped. A cop who'd taken shelter behind one of the late-arriving cars stepped out and pointed a rifle directly at Kevin.

"He's just a kid!" Luke bellowed.

Simultaneously, Kevin stood up, the fallen gun dangling from his hand.

"Drop the gun!" an officer shouted.

Luke saw it all in slow motion. A dazed-looking Kevin stumbling in circles, swinging the gun along with him. The mouths of uniformed men opening and closing. A cop's arm rising to take aim.

"He's a kid," Luke said, unaware he was only whispering. "Don't shoot, don't shoot, don't shoot. Dear God, please don't shoot."

A bullet discharged. Even before Kevin jerked from the ground as if tossed by a rodeo bull, Luke was racing across the parking lot.

In the back of his mind he knew he might be shot too, but his thoughts were only of Kevin. Please, God, don't let him die. Please. Then he was on the ground, holding his brother's fallen body.

"Kev. Kev." Blood was everywhere. On the pavement. All over Kevin's clothing. Soaking Luke's pants. Luke tried to pull the wound together, pressed his hand against it to stop blood from spurting.

"Luke . . ." Kevin sputtered.

Luke met tortured eyes and could only guess at how much pain his brother was in.

"You . . . were right . . . bro."

"Hang on Kev," he pleaded. "Hang on. Help's coming."

Lights surrounded them. Spotlights, cruiser lights, flashlights. Swirling, spinning. The siren still wailed. Kevin's head fell to one side. Slack. Lifeless

"Why were you so stupid?" he murmured in Kevin's ear. "Stupid. So stupid. Pa wasn't worth it."

Then hands yanked him to his feet. Kevin's body slid off his lap. Luke tried to stop his brother from falling. The ground was hard. Cold. Kevin was already suffering enough.

"He can't hear you," an icy voice said. The next thing he knew, his wrists were cuffed behind his back.

"You're under arrest," the voice intoned. "You have the right to remain si . . ."

He still heard those words even as he was sentenced to ten years in Attica. He hadn't told his state-appointed attorney the real reason he'd been at the breakout scene. His mother had been ripped apart by Kevin's death, and Luke knew no one would believe his story. He'd go to prison regardless. He figured he might as well save his mother the agony of a trial that would only end up in a conviction. He plea-bargained, and afterward his attorney said he was lucky. If the cop his father had shot had died, Luke would've gotten life.

Lucky? He'd been nineteen years old. Before that night he'd been a college student with a 3.9 average on a football scholarship he'd earned with his own sweat. He'd been planning a dual degree in electrical and mechanical engineering. When the prison door slammed behind him he'd become a con. When he got out, the title would get an ex in front of it, but it would never go away. No, he hadn't been lucky.

His mother visited almost every week, always wearing a mild expression of accusation on her face.

Luke decided she had to blame someone and he forgave her. His pa survived his bullet wound—the bastard was too rotten to die—but as far as Luke was concerned the man could wither away in prison.

They let Luke out just before he turned thirty, a proverbial older and wiser man. And in many ways that was true. With so much free time on his hands in prison, he'd studied everything he could get his hands on—biology, medicine, business management, advanced mathematics, quantum and astrophysics, even a little law. He'd read every tome available, including the daunting *Paradise Lost*.

But that had been of no use when he'd tried to find work. Ex-con. Ex-con. The label haunted him no matter where he applied. He'd ended up working in a run-down garage, repairing cars held together by little but the dirt on their engines.

The first time Vinnie offered him the management of Gaskin's Garage, he'd turned it down. And the second time. But the third offer came on the day his mother's cancer took a turn for the worse. She had to quit her job and needed Luke's support.

"I didn't look back," he now told Caryn. "I loved the job. The cars were sleek, expensive, a joy to work on. The money was very good. I lived well, took care of my mother until she died, and managed to help out Randy. I even saved for a legitimate dealership of my own one day, although that was still a good five years from becoming a reality. Then Vinnie talked Randy into—"

Luke paused before going on. He'd never intended to drag Randy into this. He shook his head. "Never mind. It's enough to say what Vinnie and I did, robbing that armored car, that was wrong. Sure, the people who had the money were going to use it for some pretty nasty purposes, but by agreeing to be a part of it . . . Well, that night I became a thief."

"Ye were a highwayman?" Caryn asked abruptly. He'd leaped into a new incident, leaving out parts that might connect the two stories, but his meaning was coming to her. She sat up and stared at him. "I cannot believe it."

His laugh held no warmth. "They don't call them that anymore, sweetheart, but that's pretty much what I've been saying."

"So the bags of papers locked in our vault were stolen? And ye were part of it. Is that what you're telling me?"

His eyes grew careworn. "Yes."

"Are you contrite? Truly contrite?"

In the silence that followed, she heard Ormeskirk scream.

"I wouldn't put it that strong but, yeah, I feel bad. It's not something I'm proud of."

Caryn sat up. The fire had waned, leaving the bedchamber cold, but that wasn't what chilled her. This man had a heart as big as China was said to be. He stewarded his cousin's welfare. He'd taken young Tom under his wing as a father would a son. She couldn't begin to put a value on his efforts in behalf of the kingdom. Yet here he was telling her he'd been a thief.

"But in Lochlorraine, would you steal in Lochlorraine?"

His burst of laughter startled her. "No, Countess. I would never steal anything in Lochlorraine. There isn't a need."

"Then it's of little consequence, is it not?"

She settled next to him again, stroking the line of his jaw. He took her hand and kissed the palm. "Good," he whispered against her skin, causing her to shiver deliciously. "About tomorrow morning—"

"Ye are worried about me, that I know."

"I couldn't stand for anything to happen to you."

"I feel the same about you," she said. But she knew the beast and he did not. He needed her there.

He levered up and gazed down on her. "I'm not going just to secure the spire so we can leave the bubble. It's also to free Lochlorraine so you'll be safe. What good will that do if you're killed in the process?"

"I understand, Luke. Truly I do." She stroked his face again. "Ye are everything fine and noble to me, and I would do nothing to break your heart."

His brown eyes glistened in the light of a nearby candle. "You call me that even after what I've told you tonight?"

"Aye. Ye might have made some wrong choices, but I see your heart. Ye are a kind and giving man, Luke Slade, and I expect nothing less of you."

"And you see my side? About staying behind, I mean?"

"I do." But she also saw her own, which he did not.

"It's settled then."

Snuggling her head beneath his chin, she wrapped

her arms around him. "Aye," she whispered into the hollow of his throat. " 'Tis settled."

Eager to leave the subject behind and move onto more pleasant activities, she deposited a kiss where her breath had just been, then lifted his shirt to place one on his collarbone. "Ye know that deed ye said I did not have to do before we bedded?"

"Yes. What about it?"

"I think I will not find it so disagreeable now."

Chapter Twenty-seven

There was something about terrific sex that always made a man think he could conquer the world. But true, soul-shattering lovemaking? It made a man *know* he could. Which is exactly how Luke felt the next morning.

He and Caryn had eventually dressed for supper, arriving very late, and drawing more than a few raised eyebrows. Though the glances seemed to roll off Caryn's back, Luke felt uneasy. The fiercest looks had come from Chisholm and Marco, and while the thug's animosity didn't bother him, he knew he couldn't afford the same from the captain.

He'd forgotten it all by the time he'd finished his meal with Caryn, and they'd barely been able to tear themselves apart at her chamber door. But worried about causing more gossip, Luke had insisted on returning to his own room.

He'd fallen into a deep sleep, and woke up well before dawn, feeling refreshed. The coals in the brazier had died during the night and the air nipped at his face, so he'd stayed under the warmth of the down cover for a while, reliving his evening with Caryn.

Later, his mind drifted to the time machine. He reviewed the various methods he and Ian had tried since that day they'd created the sonic boom. So far they'd built a series of fulcrums and levers to relieve all but minimum weight, thus reducing friction. Then, they'd wiped the entire mechanism with graphite. This produced dizzying speeds, and they now routinely broke the sound barrier. The last few days, Luke had worried that the gyro would get out of balance and split the foundation of the castle.

So why hadn't they re-created Ian's accident? Something was missing. He tossed and turned, trying to come up with an answer. Just as the chapel bell chimed five, his thoughts hit the only item they'd never considered—the philosopher's stone.

He jumped out of bed, pulled on his trews and shirt, then shoved his bare feet into his loafers and headed for the laboratory.

Caryn awoke from a restless sleep at five chimes of the chapel clock. Although her body had been sated by the evening of lovemaking, her night had been filled with horrifying images. Luke plummeting from Wizard's Spire. Luke seized by Ormeskirk's massive jaw. Luke ripped apart by the beast's deadly talons.

She bolted upright, clutching her blankets against her chest, perspiration dotting her body, though the fire had long ago died.

Luke had bared his soul along with his heart last

eve, and it shamed her that his revelations had momentarily filled her with misgivings. He'd attempted to steal money from men who appeared very evil, while she . . .

. . . had from the very first deceived the man she now loved. As well as all the travelers before him. Who was she to judge him, she who dealt in schemes that put him so at risk? Her crime was so much the worse. How could she not forgive him?

So she easily had.

But would he forgive? If she revealed the full truth of her machinations, would he forgive her?

Could she, were circumstances reversed? 'Twould be a hard choice, of that she was certain. But how could she cut off her right arm, which would surely be less painful than turning Luke away. She rubbed her chilled arms, still weary after such troubled sleep, but knowing she wouldn't rest even if she lay back down.

Momentarily the servants would stir, climb from their beds to tend the fires. Soon their hushed murmurs and muted footsteps would fill the halls. Right now the castle was still, and in the quiet, Caryn realized the truth.

She loved Luke more than she loved the people she'd sworn to protect. Duty, once the foundation of all she deemed valuable, paled beside the compelling voice inside her that cried out to protect him, no matter the cost. Never, since the day Ian made her chamberlain, had she questioned what was right. Duty had guided her. Duty had been her mentor. Whatever course was right for the greatest number was the course she took. Her own preferences, her own hopes, never entered into it. And so she never doubted the virtue of hiding the ring's power.

But that was before she'd come to know Luke, to experience his devotion, his gentle strength, his respect for her as a woman and a person. Before she'd experienced the passion that now bonded them for eternity.

A shiver swept over her. She pulled her blankets closer, shut her eyes, and cleared her mind, praying for a voice to tell her what to do. But instead of gaining clarity, she was flooded with images from her nightmares.

Her eyes snapped open onto the figures of Sir Lucas and his fallen companion. Dreams of the dragon slayer had given her hope throughout the years. She'd elevated him to a god. Invincible. Unable to fail. But Luke Slade was no collection of colored threads. He was a warm and vital man, more suited to mechanics and science than wielding a sword and a gun. What chance did he have of succeeding where more warlike men had failed?

Agitated, she slipped out of bed into the chill of the dark room and lit a candle. With no idea why—it wasn't her habit to arise before the servants—she drew out serviceable clothing from the wardrobe, placed them on the bed, then went to the washstand and splashed water on her face.

The cold jolted her fully awake, and brought the clarity she'd prayed for. She had a purpose after all: to go to the laboratory. That's where the ring was, and it was the only hope for Luke's salvation.

*   *   *

Luke had always had an avid interest in mechanical and electrical engineering. Physics fascinated him. Biology and botany held his attention. But he'd never much cared for geology. The only time he'd studied it was when he'd exhausted the prison library and was waiting for something new from the library exchange program. So what made him think he'd recognize uranium even if he saw it?

His loafers made little sound as he hurried down the stairwell. The lanterns had been snuffed for the night, and he took care not to miss a step in the dim candlelight. This gave him the opportunity to scour his mind for what he'd read. Uranium didn't exist independently, he remembered that, but he wasn't quite sure what metals accompanied the element. He recalled it was sometimes found with silver and copper, but always in conjunction with something else. Pit, pot, or did the word start with a ''b''?

Whatever it was, he was pretty sure it wasn't native to Scotland. But what did that mean? People traveled, even in the seventeenth century. And the British Isles had been occupied by Europeans time and again.

Ian wasn't in the lab. Luke called out a couple of times, hoping to find him busy in some forgotten corner. Apparently, the man who never slept had chosen this time to indulge in the practice. His bad luck, Luke thought, brushing off a prick of disappointment.

Deciding to give the stone another inspection, Luke opened the drawer of the book stand, which was where Ian had returnd it after the time he had shown it to Luke. Pleased to discover it hadn't been moved, he picked the object up, and turned it in his hand.

Nothing much to look at. Just an irregularly shaped lump of pewter-colored ore about the size of a child's football. Judging by the sheered-off edge that revealed patches of a smoother black mineral, it had been cut from a larger piece. All in all, completely unremarkable. Could something that looked so inert really be radioactive?

Now that he had the stone, Luke didn't know what to do with it. His disappointment at Ian's absence returned. He badly wanted to discuss his theory, although he supposed they could talk about it later, after—

After what?

What made him think there would be an after?

A sharp pain slammed his solar plexus with so much force, Luke almost doubled over. He had so much to live for now. The love he and Caryn shared. His work with Ian. The potential for making this land a paradise. Never had he felt so needed. But in just a few hours, he'd leave on a mission that might end all those possibilities with the flick of a dragon's wing. His stomach lurched, his fists clenched, and he waited motionless for the wave of grief to pass.

Eventually he became aware of another pain, this one physical. He opened his stinging hand, which had been clutching the philosopher's stone so tightly it had gouged his palm. As he transferred the rock to his other hand and flexed his pitted fingers, the name came to him.

Pitchblende. Uranium was found with pitchblende, and if his memory served, the stuff was coal black with a dull luster. Exactly like the particles imbedded in this stone. His spirits soared again. Although he certainly didn't welcome facing death, the prospect no longer sickened him.

With this knowledge, Ian could complete the project without him. But Luke couldn't risk taking the information with him if he died. He had to wake the earl now. Later, he'd also extract a promise from Caryn to take Randy out for medical treatment.

All wasn't lost.

Taking solace in this, he walked back to the book stand to put the stone into the still-open drawer. As he did, it brushed against another smaller object.

A ring. And it looked familiar.

Puzzled, he picked it up.

Silvery. Dull. Thickly and crudely fashioned. With ancient marks carved around the perimeter. The ring he'd lost, it had to be. But why would anyone steal it? As he'd told Caryn just last night, there was no need for theft in Lochlorraine.

Almost immediately, he knew the only answer. Ian had ordered it taken.

Why?

Luke carried the ring to a candle scone and examined it beneath the light. Pewter-colored, yes, but it could also be unpolished silver. He took a closer look and saw tiny flecks. Black flecks.

Like dominoes falling, it came to him: the way light flashed the first time he'd put on the ring; the portal opening when he'd tried to twist it off and give it back to Randy; the sparkles of light that later filled the gate and must have been suabtomic particles. This ring had been cut from the philosopher's stone.

His mind raced with the implications. He'd never been trapped in Lochlorraine at all, but merely deceived into believing he was. All the work on the time mechanism had been a ruse to make Luke think they were making progress, while Ian had possessed the answers all along.

And Caryn? Suddenly the inconsequential hesitations she frequently made took on an ominous shade. The confident way she'd expressed her delight when he'd told her he wanted to return to Lochlorraine. It all made sense. Ian hadn't worked alone, Caryn had been in it with him.

"Luke! What are you doing here?"

A rush of conflicting emotions overtook Luke. Joy, sorrow, anger. Love and hate. Then they vanished, leaving him oddly calm. "I might ask you the same question."

"What does . . ." Her eyes drifted to his hand, coming to rest on the ring, and gradually filled with comprehension.

"Yes, I found out. It came as quite a surprise, let me tell you."

"Please, it's not what ye . . . I was coming—" She stopped a moment, unable to find her voice. How could he take her at her word after what she had done? "I came down here to get the ring," she began again, more certain now of what she must say. "To tell you about it, to give it to you." She rushed to his side. "Ye must leave Lochlorraine, Luke. Now, before the garrison gathers beneath the spire."

"You want me to leave before I've killed your dragon?" His voice was hard, almost cruel.

"Aye, before ye put yourself in danger. Go! Go now! Gather your possessions. I've already told Nancy to fetch a bag of money. Get it from her, get Randy, take him to the portal where ye entered. The ring will open the gateway."

Luke stared at her wordlessly. His face held no softness now, none of the tenderness she'd so frequently seen.

"Why are you telling me this?" he finally asked, suspicion heavy in his tone.

Anger helped her blink away her tears. In a tone as harsh as his, she replied, "Because I want you to live to a ripe old age more than I want Lochlorraine freed from Ormeskirk."

He hesitated briefly, the hard set of his jaw relaxing. For just that moment Caryn thought they might make peace between them before he left.

"As if you'd ever want anything more than that." His face resumed its stony mask. "You lied to me, Caryn. You and Ian manipulated me into agreeing to kill an animal that doesn't deserve to die. But worse—so much worse—you put Randy's life on the line for your selfish purpose. I can't forgive that."

Had he exaggerated, had he added one untruth, his accusations would not have stung so badly. He was right, and there could be no peace between them.

Because of her deception, he would leave now and

never return. What would Lochlorraine do without him? What would she?

"Where will you go?" she asked tremulously.

"To the nearest hospital, what did you think?"

"No, I meant afterward? Will ye return to your old life?"

He stared at her, his dark eyes like blazing coals. "Caryn," he said. "That's none of your business."

With those words, he strode toward the door. But when he reached the threshold, he paused to look back.

Caryn's heart leaped. Anticipating, hoping, she waited for him to speak.

"By the way," he finally said. "Tell Ian the philosopher's stone is the key. But, then he knew that, didn't he?"

Chapter Twenty-eight

"I don' wanna leave, Luke! I won't."

Randy flailed as he shouted his protest, but Luke held on easily, disturbed by this confirmation of how much weight the kid had lost. Hell, the money bag hanging over Luke's shoulder seemed to weigh more than Randy. They weren't leaving any too soon, it seemed, which, he supposed, meant something good had come from his discovery of Caryn's deception. "We'll come back, kid. Soon as you get fixed up."

"You think I'm so dumb I believe anything."

"I don't think you're dumb."

"Do too!"

With that defiant statement, Randy stopped fighting. Luke had no illusion that the kid had changed his mind. He'd just run out of steam. They were now passing Lucifer's Window, and Luke was tiring himself. Stones slid under his heavy footsteps, clattering in the heavy silence that always cloaked this part of the loch. A crow cawed, and the sound scraped his raw nerves.

Caryn . . .

He shook his head.

"Why're you shaking your head, Luke?"

"A fly was bugging me."

"I didn't see a fly."

Randy! he wanted to shout. "You must've missed it."

"Did not."

Luke let out an exasperated breath. Randy always got combative when he felt overpowered, so what had Luke expected?

This was right, he told himself. This was good.

His goddamn chest ached.

Caryn . . .

He was only winded, as soon as he caught his breath, he'd stop thinking about her. But his denial mechanism was getting weaker with every step he took.

Finally, he arrived at the forest. He eased Randy onto the ground and helped him sit up against a tree trunk. As soon as he turned away, Randy began struggling to get to his feet. Luke watched in pity, forcing himself to remain silent. Finally, with a despairing moan, Randy leaned back. "I was gonna run away," he said weakly.

"I know."

"Nancy and I was gonna get married."

Caryn . . .

Luke tried not to feel Randy's pain. His own was so great he couldn't deal with the extra burden. But the obvious agony on the boy's face pierced his brittle emotional shell. His throat thickened.

"You'll die if I don't get you help!" His cruel words were intended to shock the kid into facing reality. Or were they? "Can't you get that through your thick head?"

"I'd rather die with Nancy than live a long life with Pa!"

Randy burst into tears. Sobs shook his wasted torso. Filled with remorse, Luke knelt beside him. "Soon as you're better, I'll do my best to bring you back."

Randy hiccuped several times, wiped a fisted hand across his cheekbones. "You mean it?"

Luke hesitated. The needle on the time compass had been bouncing around for several days. A sign the bubble would soon move on, at least according to Ian. Trying to assess Randy's ability to handle the truth, Luke studied his face. He decided to go with it. "I do mean it, Randy, but I can't guarantee Lochlorraine will still be here when we're ready. What I do know is you'll die if you don't get help. Argue with me all you want, but I won't let that happen."

Randy nodded solemnly. "But you'll try to get back, you'll really try."

"I said I would."

"Will you come back too?"

"Maybe." But he wouldn't, of course. There was nothing here for him anymore.

Randy nodded again, relaxing.

Luke stood up. It was time. They were at the portal. He had the ring. All he had to do was twist it. He glanced over his shoulder at the land he was about to leave behind. Water lapped at the stony shore of Lucifer's Window. Scudding clouds cast shadows on the waves, and overhead a sea gull cried. Another perfect day in Lochlorraine.

Hardening himself against a storm of regret, he raised his hands and twisted the ring.

Caryn had been standing on the bridge that spanned the stream, watching Luke, hoping, praying, that he'd change his mind. Then the boom sounded, and he ran through the opening as if the devil of the loch were chasing him.

Unable to bear it, Caryn swept up her skirts, dashed across the bridge, and flew down the hill. It wasn't too late. She could follow him, tell him how much she loved him, make him understand that she'd never meant to harm Randy.

Her heart pounded with fear as her feet sailed over the rocky earth. It would all be over when the portal closed. Luke had the only ring and he wouldn't return, no matter how eloquently Randy might plead his case. By the time Bessy made another ring, Lochlorraine would have moved to a distant time.

Luke was already on the other side of the gate, out of her sight. How would she find him? But did he not say he would go to a nearby hospital? Surely the city of New York had only one or two.

As she reached the curve of the loch, her footsteps faltered. What would he say when she found him? What made her think he would forgive her?

The portal sputtered and vanished, then reappeared, vibrating at an alarming rate that made Caryn's decision for her. Drawing the last ounce of energy from her tiring legs, she sped toward the opening.

Nurses and orderlies hurried through the emergency waiting room, eyes ahead, ignoring the crowd. A child wailed. A man demanded to know what was happening with his wife. An old woman sneezed and coughed, so badly that Luke feared she might choke to death before she got treatment.

But Randy's condition concerned him more. The kid leaned back in the torn synthetic leather chair, eyes half-closed, his breathing shallow and irregular. Despite his condition, he occasionally lifted his head to remind Luke that if they waited too long Lochlorraine could move away.

Hospital employees sped through the waiting room, some wearing green, some in white, others in brighter colors. At one point, Luke felt he was being watched, and he looked around. A nurse in blue rushed by, glanced his way, then quickly moved on. A man in green scrubs stood just inside the entrance to the treatment rooms, his face obscured. As Luke's eyes grazed the door, the man stepped into the shadows, then walked away. Most likely looking for a patient, Luke thought, tapping his foot again.

The clock hands inched forward. Slowly, very slowly.

Luke had decided to keep his promise to Randy. The kid belonged in Lochlorraine, where he'd live the kind of life he deserved. But if it were also to be a long one, he'd need more antibiotics than a single prescription provided.

Which had brought Luke to another decision. Patting the twenty-two he'd collected when he'd changed into the pants he'd worn into the bubble, he thought about what he was about to do. Caryn had asked if he'd return to his old life, and now it seemed he would. In spades. After this, there'd be no way he could stay in the city.

Mouth dry and cottony, he tapped his foot a little faster. All he'd ever wanted was respectability; the only place he'd ever found it was Lochlorraine. Now he'd have to start again.

But not until he'd committed the last crime of his life.

Caryn absently caressed the leaf of a tree that now stood where the portal once had been. She had no idea how long she'd been here, only that the sun had moved a considerable distance since she'd last noticed it.

She turned away, and found her legs unsteady. Tears brimmed behind her eyes, but couldn't break through the thickness of her sorrow. Inhaling sharply, she attempted to bind herself together. There were people to notify about Luke's departure. Chisholm and his regiment. The ruffian Hub. Ian. She dreaded each encounter, but her duty was clear.

Damn them! What right did these people have to ask so much of her? Of Luke? Not one man among them dared venture up that spire on their own. *Cowards! Damn them all to hell!*

The explosive burst died almost as quickly as it came, leaving her cold. Leadenly, she wrapped her shawl around her. Ian first, she supposed. Chisholm would be the most unpleasant, which would normally cause her to deal with him first. But the earl had the right to know. She would carry out her duties in the prescribed order. It was all she had known and all she had left. And when she was very old and without love, perhaps she'd take solace in fhat fact.

Wearily, Caryn started back for the castle. What she'd do there, she didn't know. The people would be outraged by Luke's disappearance and she could even now hear them cry out: *Coward, deceiver, deserter.* But she was the one who deserved the scorn, not Luke.

Ormeskirk cried out in the distance, but she gave the sound little heed. She couldn't return to the castle just yet. She was too bruised, too raw. She needed time to think.

She was still sitting on the rock that looked over Lucifer's Window when the clock rang five. With an uncharacteristic lack of alarm, she realized she no longer had duties. Luke's failure to appear at the spire had already delivered her message. Moreover, servants must have been sent to search for her. Of course, none would dare to look in this cursed spot.

"Lady Caryn!"

Except Bessy, who feared nothing.

The woman hurried along the shore, carrying a plate and a small bag. As she approached, she shoved the plate toward Caryn. "Eat, milady," she directed. "Ye haven't touched a morsel yet, though the day is almost gone."

The plate reeked of mutton and Caryn's stomach turned. "I'm not hungry."

Bessy scowled as she hadn't done since Caryn was a girl. "Lift the napkin, miss. As your teacher of old I command it."

Startled, Caryn complied. Slices of mutton and potatoes were arranged on the plate, flanked by a halved pear. In the center of one half sat a round silvery object.

Caryn stared at it briefly, then looked up. "There are *two* rings?"

Bessy grinned. "How do ye think the realm has offered the simple vices all these years?"

"You are the one who has been bringing in the coffee, tobacco, and whiskey? All this time, I thought Ian . . . or even Chisholm. His sundry shop always offers an ample supply."

"The laird's head be in the clouds. He thinks not of these comforts." Bessy's smile faded slightly. "And the threat of losing the tobacco has kept Chisholm's cruel tongue from wagging overmuch during these worrisome years."

Bessy crouched down with more agility than her aged body should have allowed and lightly touched Caryn's arm. "Go after your love, Lady Caryn."

Caryn's heart leaped, then quickly fell to earth again, tugged by the war between duty and love. "Who shall guide Lochlorraine if I cannot return?"

"Lord Ian is up to the task should the worst come to pass, but the dragon slayer is in dire trouble and needs your help."

Caryn's pulse started hammering. "Ye've had a vision?"

"Aye, though 'twas not clear. But ye must hurry, milady. Time is not on your side." She thrust out the bag she'd been holding. "I packed ye some scant belongings. A clean skirt and shift, and a tunic as well . . . Also the fine silver brush that belonged to your mama."

This last item made Caryn look at Bessy in question. A shimmer of tears in her teacher's eyes provided the answer: Bessy thought Caryn wouldn't return. Heart aching at the possibility of losing her adviser and best friend, Caryn hugged Bessy tightly, not wanting to let go.

Bessy gave Caryn's waist a fierce squeeze, then pulled away. "None of that now. Ye'll provoke the Men of Peace into a fierce bout of jealousy." Rubbing her hands together as if dusting off a nasty substance, she rose to her feet. "Ye must have your full strength for this journey, so eat well and hearty, then be on your way."

Startled to discover her appetite had returned, Caryn devoured the food. When she finished, Bessy took the plate, moved toward the castle, then hesitated and leaned over to stroke Caryn's hair. "Godspeed to ye, lassie," she said sadly. "It has been a blessing and honor to serve you."

Luke nudged his sleeping cousin. "Come on, kid. We're up."

With Luke's assistance, Randy drowsily eased to his feet. The short, stout woman who'd called for

them introduced herself with a take-charge attitude
as a nurse-practitioner, then guided them into a treatment room. After helping Randy onto the examining
table and removing his shirt and bandage, the nurse
studied his wound. "You treat this yourself?" she
suspiciously asked of Luke.

"A friend did."

"The sutures, too?"

Although her questions weren't unexpected, Luke
nodded uneasily.

"Who did the tracheotomy?"

He hesitated. But what could the truth hurt? "I
did. It was, uh, an emergency."

"Looks like the entire treatment was an emergency," the nurse shot back. "Lucky you came when
you did. Septicemia is about to set in. People die of
it, you know."

"Yes, I know," Luke snapped. "Why the hell do
you think we're here? Just treat him, will you?"

The nurse's expression turned to poorly concealed
alarm. She inched away from Randy.

"Look," he lied, trying to allay her fears. "We just
got back in the country. We were deep in Mexico.
Good medical care's hard to find down there."

"I see." She moved slowly toward the door. "Wait
right here. I need to get a cart. It'll only take a few
minutes."

To call the cops she meant. Oh, hell, there was no
way around it. Luke dipped into his pocket and
came out with the twenty-two. "I'll go with you,
ma'am," he said politely. "Not a peep to anyone.
You understand?"

She responded with a panicked nod.

"We'll be right back," Luke told Randy as he opened the examining-room door.

"Hurry. Nancy . . . we gotta . . ."

"Yeah, I know."

He ushered the nurse into the hallway, gave her precise instructions on how to make sure no one got hurt, then asked what Randy needed to get better.

"He needs to be hospitalized." Her voice quivered.

"Not an option, but what would they give him if he were?"

"Broad-spectrum antibiotics. Saline, maybe even some plasma."

"Get them for me. Clean out the storage cabinet. Antibiotics, both pills and serums. Syringes, antiseptics. Everything you got." Hell, as long as he was doing this, he might as well get enough for all of Lochlorraine. He guessed he owed them that much.

The nurse looked at the gun. Her hands shook, her lip trembled. "I-I c-can't. The s-staff . . . They'll see me, ask q-questions."

"Look," he said. "I know how it seems, but I'm not a thief. Just a man who wants to help a friend." He pulled a wad of bills from his pocket and shoved it at her. "I'll pay for everything. Just tell me what it comes to."

The nurse let out a half-hysterical laugh. "You've got a gun aimed at my ribs."

Luke stared down at the twenty-two feeling ashamed. He hadn't meant to terrorize this woman, just make sure Randy got well.

"Please," he said, lowering the gun and shoving

the cash back in his pocket. "Help him. He's got an important appointment to keep."

She looked at him for a long time, then finally asked, "It's a gunshot wound, isn't it?"

"Yeah, an old one."

"Well, I could see that." She lapsed into silence again, keeping her eyes on the gun.

"All right, I'll help him. He'll die if I don't." She sighed heavily. "Just don't point that thing at me again, okay?"

"Anything you want, ma'am," Luke answered, echoing her sigh with his own.

Chapter Twenty-nine

The nurse pulled the IV out of Randy's arm, then turned for a Band-Aid. While Luke waited, he dug for the cash in his pocket, keeping back a few to pay for the cab ride to the park. "This should take care of the medicine and the hospital bill."

"Who are you guys?" the nurse said, looking down at the wad of money. "There must be almost fifty thousand here. You sure you're not Robin Hood and one of his merry men?"

Luke laughed, helping Randy off the table. "You don't know the half of it."

"I don't think I want to," she replied, laughing too.

To Luke's gratification, Randy slipped his shirt back on without breaking a sweat, and color was already returning to his face. Moreover, the prospect of returning to Nancy put him in high spirits.

"Give us fifteen minutes," he reminded the nurse. He picked up a pillowcase, which contained the medical supplies, and slipped in a pen and notepad he'd later requested.

Soon, they were headed for the exit as fast as

Randy's legs would allow. Thanks to Don Wicorowitz's hasty lesson in the minivan the night of the
heist, Luke knew how to use a syringe. After they
found a taxi, Luke would write a note telling Caryn
how to inject the medicine.

He keenly felt her absence but refused to dwell on
it. His future in the twentieth century was fuzzy at
best, and he needed to give it some thought. Although he knew the nurse wouldn't wait fifteen minutes before reporting the theft, he suspected she'd be
a bit hazy about the details. Which meant he could
still get to his bank accounts. Maybe he'd head out
to New Mexico, or even Wyoming. Start fresh, open
his own garage and lead a simple life, earn the respect he'd always wanted.

Without Caryn. Which seemed like no life at all.

"You okay, Luke?"

Luke glanced at Randy, surprised to see they'd already gone through the outside door and were on
the sidewalk.

"What? Oh, yeah, fine. Just thinking, that's all."

"You sure you don't want to go? Everyone'll miss
you back home."

"Not everyone." Besides, Lochlorraine was home
only to Randy. "So how're you doing? Getting
tired?"

"Not yet." Randy's steps were noticeably steadier,
undoubtedly because of the plasma and painkillers
he'd been given, but his breath appeared somewhat
labored.

Telling Randy to stay put, Luke headed for the
curb, determined to elbow out anyone who tried

beating him to a ride. The sooner he returned Randy to the portal, the better. Damn, it would hurt to send the kid through the gate. He couldn't yet imagine a life without him hanging around.

Or Caryn.

Avoiding that stray thought, he concentrated on snagging a cab. Several passed him by, but finally one pulled toward the curb. As Luke turned to call Randy, he felt something pressing on his back. A hand appeared in his peripheral vison and waved the cabby off.

"The taxi was mine," Luke growled, whirling to see who'd done it.

His jaw dropped. "I thought you were dead!"

Don Wicorowitz smiled grimly. Randy stood next to him, looking pale as he cocked his head toward the long bulge underneath the shirt of Don's green scrubs.

"So that was you watching us in the waiting room," Luke said.

"Yeah, I work here. I'm a paramedic, remember? When I seen you guys I was just as surprised, so don't feel dumb." Don wiggled the gun, creating ripples in his shirt. "Where's the money, Slade? And where're the other guys? They cut me out, didn't they? I knew it! I knew Marco'd cut me out!"

Luke had no idea what Don was talking about. Furthermore, the man was acting half-crazed, a complete reversal of the phlegmatic personality Luke remembered. Then, almost as mercurially as Randy, Don directed his accusations toward Luke. "Or did you, Vinnie, and the half-wit get away with it all?"

"Who're you calling a half-wit?" Randy asked in challenge.

Luke nudged Randy, and thinking it wise to calm Don down, he cheerily said, "Hey, you got it all wrong. Geez, we thought you'd been killed. It's great to see you alive."

"Yeah, sure. You guys probably cheered yourself silly about only havin' to split three ways. Man, you're all crooks!"

A businessman stopped in his tracks and looked back. Other people had started to stare. Don gave the gun another twitch. "Walk toward the alley. Pretend we're best buds. Say something nice, why don't you?"

Luke complied without question and gestured at Randy to do the same. Nothing made sense. Last time he'd seen Don—hell, no one lost that much blood and lived. And the guy was asking about Marco and his boys even though he'd been Vinnie's partner.

Don herded them into the alley, then backed them against a wall. By this time, the unanswered questions were driving Luke nuts. "Why do you say Marco cut you out? As I recall, he was on the other side."

Don laughed bitterly. "I was working with Marco. He's the one who gave me the info about the money transfer and I passed it on to Vinnie. It was a sweet deal. I'd help you guys do the heist, letting you think the money belonged to terrorists when it was really Carmine's illegal weapons haul. Then they'd show up and pretend they shot me. We even used fake blood. Marco was gonna take over Carmine's organization, and he promised to take me along. Where the hell is he, anyway?"

"Dead," he lied. "They're all dead."

"So you two are the only ones left." Don's amusement turned ugly again. "The money, Slade."

"Tell him the truth, Luke," Randy said. "The money's all gone, Don. Luke gived some of it to a nice nurse. The rest's in Lochlorraine."

Don scowled. "Where's that? Upstate?"

"You'd never believe it," Luke said.

"Try me." The gun whipped from beneath Don's shirt and came to rest under Luke's chin. It had a tube around the barrel that Luke assumed was a silencer, meaning Don wouldn't hesitate to use it. Exactly how was he supposed to respond, anyway? *Hey, Don, we went through a time warp three hundred years into the past.*

"Don't shoot him, Don!" Randy wailed. "I'll tell you what you gots to know."

"Randy . . ."

But Randy was already blubbering about Scotland and Lady Caryn, and that Vinnie was killed by a guy in a kilt. When he started going on about Lord Ian, the time bubble, and the dragon, Don whirled and turned the gun on him.

"The kid's nuttier than ever," he said. "Maybe I should put him out of his misery."

"No!" Luke returned heatedly. "The money's hidden in Central Park near Plotkin's Bank." He gave Randy a hard look that demanded he shut his mouth.

"That's where we were headed when you caught up with us."

"Well, I got me a car in the hospital parking garage. Why don't me and you guys take a little trip?"

Luke nodded, having no idea what they'd do once they got to Central Park. Randy had no hope of outrunning Don. But the closer they were to the portal, the better their chances.

His gaze drifted toward the entrance to the alley. Maybe when they reached the street, Luke could trip, drawing enough attention to force Don to back off. As he turned this possibility over, he saw a movement at the corner.

Next he saw plaid, then a mass of red curls. Caryn?

It was. His heart exploded in a burst of joy that had nothing to do with knowing rescue was near. She crept forward, a knife in one hand, a finger to her lips. Keeping his expression impassive, Luke forced his eyes back on Don. "You'll have to bring the car around. Randy can't walk that far."

Don made a scoffing sound. "Sure, right. Like you'd wait here until I got back. Be better for me if I just took the kid out."

Randy cowered against the wall, his eyes flickering toward Caryn.

Luke stepped in front of him. "You shoot, you can forget about the money."

"Always the hero, ain't you Slade?" Don shook the gun. "Move outta the way."

"I wouldna pull that trigger were I you. This wee knife I hold to your back can slice your innards as well as any."

The sudden flash of fear on Don's face was almost comical, but Luke had no urge to laugh.

"What took you so long?" he asked shakily, using the edge of the pillowcase to relieve Don of the gun.

Randy rocked happily from foot to foot. "You saved us, Lady Caryn!"

She smiled quickly, then looked at Don, who was now face-first against the wall. "Getting *him* out of the way was easy. Finding ye two was the difficult part."

Luke hated to break up the party, but . . . "We have to disable this guy somehow."

"Use these." Leather thongs emerged from Caryn's pocket. While Randy stood by, she and Luke quickly tied Don's hands and feet. When that was done, Caryn stopped Don's steady stream of curses with a linen bandage.

Luke then put Don's gun on the ground where the cops could easily find it. To a chorus of incoherent grunts, they left the alley.

Soon they were at the curb, waiting for a taxi. Luke stood next to Randy, trembling internally. Caryn was on Randy's other side, but Luke kept his eyes from roaming in her direction. Caryn hadn't spoken since they left the alley, and by the way she stared blankly into the street, she was unlikely to do so. Randy continually shifted his gaze between them, but Luke ignored his pleading glances.

"Ain't you guys gonna talk to each other?" Randy abruptly blurted out.

This forced Luke to look at Caryn and he asked

what he'd wanted to know since she'd appeared. "How did you find us?"

Caryn returned his gaze, her eyes excessively bright. "Ye said you'd go to the nearest hospital. I merely asked someone on the street where to find it. I did not dream there were so many. 'Twas most surprising." She gave a puzzled frown. "Also, I expected those in your realm to find my attire odd, but none seemed to notice."

"Welcome to New York City where anything goes," Luke replied dryly.

"Indeed it does," she went on gaily, though Luke heard an undertone of agitation. "Why, many of your women wear naught but their shifts and others expose most of their stomachs. Is this common?"

"Sure is."

He then swallowed a groan. These were the kinds of comments that always made him want to reach out and hug her. Fortunately, a cab pulled up just then. As they climbed in, Luke gave the driver the address of Plotkin's Bank. Traffic moved in fits and starts, so the going was slow. Randy nodded off against one window, while Caryn stared out the other one, voicing amazement.

" 'Tis a wondrous place, this realm of yours. How do ye make your buildings so high? They dwarf the great cathedrals and castles of even Edinburgh and London." She bounced up and down in her place. "So firm and full of comfort," she remarked, words Luke never expected to hear about the seats in a taxi. "How do these carriages roll without horses? And those boxes with moving images, what use do ye have for those?"

Her questions spilled out so rapidly Luke had no time to answer, for which he was grateful. He wasn't sure he could speak fluently anyway, or keep his anguish out of his voice if he managed. After discovering the hidden ring, Luke tried to convince himself Caryn feigned her affections just to manipulate him. He'd had no success. After witnessing her devotion to the kingdom, even admiring it, he had to conclude she'd been torn between its welfare and his. By leaving Lochlorraine to come after him, she'd made a clear choice. She loved him. He couldn't doubt that anymore. And Lord knew he loved her. Enduring relationships had been formed on weaker bonds than that, and he was tempted to jump back in without further examination.

But what made him think love was enough? Caryn's culture was different from his. In her world, everyone knew everyone's business. Approval turned to scorn in the blink of an eye. Morever, how many times would duty and love tear at her loyalties? Often, he thought. Too often.

He had a chance to rebuild in his world. Better he take it than try to repair what he'd left in Lochlorraine. No, he couldn't return, even if Caryn asked him. Which she hadn't.

Caryn was still talking nonstop, and she turned to him now. "My," she said, "I can't wait to tell Bessy and Nancy about your wondrous century."

"Obviously, the portal is still working," Luke said.

"Aye. But it is quite unstable."

An oblique way of saying she wasn't sure it would open again.

"I see." Luke had taken for granted it would, and the news unsettled him.

As Caryn went back to viewing the sights, he looked over at Randy. Luke couldn't help but thrill to the possibility that Caryn might stay in his century, but it would break the kid's heart. For Randy's sake, he should hope the portal was still there.

The cab eased onto Park Avenue, and Luke remembered he hadn't written instructions for Caryn. He would prefer actually demonstrating how syringes worked, but he didn't think a city cab was a good place to do that. He scribbled furiously through the rest of the ride, and when Caryn asked what he was doing, he told her about the medicine, then returned to his note. By the time they reached the park, the sun was hanging low. Luke paid the cabby, tempted to tell Caryn and Randy to go without him. Randy, however, was looking wan and needed his support.

Although Randy tried his best to maintain the pace, he required several stops. When they finally reached the alcove, Luke embraced him hard and wished him well. Then, recalling the manners of Lochlorraine, he bowed toward Caryn. "It was a pleasure knowing you, Countess."

He couldn't endure hanging around, so he turned to leave.

"Will ye not be needing your currency?" Caryn asked.

Luke had forgotten about the money, but he figured he might as well keep it. As he moved to get the bag, he noticed a smaller one beside it. "What's that?"

"Nothing of import," Caryn said, the forced cheerfulness returning to her voice. "Just some wee items I brought in the event I couldn't get back."

"But we will," Randy said. "And Luke don't need the money. He's gonna come with us."

Caryn's eyes flared like burning candles. "Are ye?"

"I never said that, Randy," Luke countered simultaneously.

Caryn's hands flew to her heart, then she abruptly dropped her arms. Unwilling to acknowledge what her gesture revealed, Luke reached for the money. That's when he noticed the ring.

Straightening, he moved to take it off. "This belongs in Lochlorraine."

He twisted it, forgetting what the act would evoke. Suddenly, the light flashed in his face. Luke instinctively covered his eyes, steeling himself for a flashback.

Nothing happened. No disembodied words running through his head. No twirling lights of red, blue, and white. Somehow, some way—possibly because he'd shared the horror with Caryn—the expected reaction didn't come. Luke let his arms fall, and dared a straight-on look at the portal. Incredible sparkles of light danced and spun, leaving an ever widening circle that framed the fief. Summer days were long in Lochlorraine, and the sun still spilled its light on the trees, the loch, the castle that sat high above a swath of green, making them appear richer than he remembered.

He ached to return.

Caryn moved to pick up her small bag.

"Come with us, Luke," Randy pleaded. "Please."

At Randy's words, Caryn whirled to face Luke. "Return to Lochlorraine," she feverishly urged. "Share our lives. I cannot face mine without you."

Luke's heart split open, but he knew when the portal closed without him, it would heal. Twice before he'd had it all, had his dream, only to have it torn away: once when Kevin died, taking Luke's education with him. Again, when he'd discovered that Caryn had concealed the purpose of the ring.

His heart wouldn't survive a third loss.

No, better to live in a grey world than to risk losing the sunlight after basking in its warmth.

But Caryn waited expectantly, as did Randy.

"I can't," Luke said. "I don't belong there."

He saw Caryn blink back tears. Her breathing became uneven. Randy wiped his eyes.

"Go!" he said, over his own pain. "Nancy's waiting. And the kingdom will suffer without its leader. Go, before the portal closes."

Caryn nodded, touched Randy's shoulder. "Come," she said. "Luke has given his answer."

She swept her bag from the ground and marched regally through the portal. Randy started to follow. He hesitated at the threshold and looked back at Luke, a question in his eyes.

Luke shook his head. Randy crossed into the fief.

Ormeskirk screeched.

"The dragon is early," Randy said. "It's not twilight yet."

Luke stepped up to the opening and looked toward the sky. The pterosaur's dark shape glided toward the village. Unusual. Since the Villagers began delaying their fires, Ormeskirk never came this close before twilight. He must be very hungry. Without the fires to guide him, he couldn't raid the pens, and animals were always removed from the pastures before the dragon hour. His remaining food source, the fish in the ocean, would hardly sustain an animal as large as he.

This was Luke's fault. He'd done good things for these people, but he wouldn't be around long enough to see any disasters he might have also created.

Steeling himself, he stepped back. Lochlorraine had lived with the dragon twenty years before he arrived. They'd manage without him.

As he turned away, a woman cried out in the village. Screams followed. But these weren't the normal warnings that the dragon was coming. These were cries of terror and despair.

Small pinpricks of light danced across the gate. They would multiply, closing it off soon. " 'Tis, now or never, Luke," she said, open yearning in her eyes. "The gate will close, perhaps for good. My life is here. Where is yours?"

Almost of its own volition, his hand reached out. Back away, he told himself, back away. But Caryn was reaching out, too. Their hands touched in the middle of the portal, fingers to fingers, palm to palm. Subatomic particles bounced against his skin, evoking fluttering sensations in his body. Caryn closed her eyes and shuddered against his hand.

"A lad!" the woman in the village keened. "The dragon has snared a lad!"

Caryn gasped. Luke looked toward the hills. Oh, God . . .

A small brown horse barreled toward the castle, running for its life. Above coasted Ormeskirk, a small squirming form in his claws.

Tom!

More voices joined the keening woman's. The wails rose in volume, mingling with Ormeskirk's screeches. Myriad images of Tom marched through Luke's mind, evoking a swell of rage. As he hesitated, the dancing lights continued to cohere, becoming denser, less fluid, transforming to a field that soon could not be crossed. He had to decide.

Lord, everything in Lochlorraine was black and white, life and death, and he hated that aspect with all his heart.

But he loved all the rest—Caryn, Randy . . . Tom. Even Toby, whose piteous whinnies mingled with the voices in the village.

Caryn and Randy looked at him, waiting, their now hazy features wearing expectant expressions. "Tom . . ." Caryn said, directing her gaze to the sky.

"Help them, Luke," Randy implored.

Forever on his conscience, Luke thought, then stepped through the thickening gate.

Chapter Thirty

The soldiers marching in front and behind wore expressions of scorn, but that was to be expected, given Luke's failure to show up the previous morning. But if his techniques for surviving the trek without loss of limb or life did the trick, the men's attitudes would shift just as rapidly to adulation. It was always so in Lochlorraine. He'd better get used to it.

Luke was left with only Hub to talk to, which was actually worse than no one at all. After shrugging off one of the man's idiotically confident remarks about snuffing the pterosaur, Luke stopped to stare up at the windmill. He'd probably lost his last chance for freedom by returning to rescue Tom, and deep down he found it hard to believe the boy had survived the night. He tried not to think about it, though. Keeping the faith was the best way to control fear and fatigue.

The Uzi hanging at his back felt like a steel ton, as did his helmet and mail coat. Years of lugging fenders and quarter panels had give him strong muscles, but he still didn't have half the stamina of Chisholm's army. He couldn't help but be grateful that two of their number carried the rope, along with the heavy spikes attached to each end. The men who'd earned his gratitude walked close to the stone wall—one at the front, one at the rear—and carried the rope between them. When Ormeskirk appeared, each man would drive his spike into the wall.

Luke wasn't positive the rope would work, but he'd studied Ormeskirk thoroughly: On open land his powerful wings merely caused brisk winds, but when aided by the ocean breeze and the confines of the steep wall, they became a force strong enough to topple a man. The rope provided a brace to prevent this, and also protected them from Ormeskirk's sharp beak and claws. Luke doubted the animal would risk hitting stone just to snare an attacker.

"Ormeskirk!" the front rope bearer yelled as he spun to drive in his spike.

"Ormeskirk! Ormeskirk!" The cry traveled down the line. When it reached the last man, Luke heard metal slamming against stone. Both men had done their jobs. Swinging his Uzi to the front, Luke slipped behind the line. Hub slid in beside him. His enormous size would surely test how securely the spikes had been driven.

The line held firm.

"To the ropes!" Chisholm commanded. As a unit, the remaining soldiers hurried for their places.

Ormeskirk came from above.

Screaming with rage, he hovered in front of the drop-off. The hummingbird beat of his wings whipped Luke's hair from beneath his helmet and into his eyes, and his balance came under attack. As he'd instructed the men, he knelt on one knee and leaned into the rope. The others did the same. Again the rope held.

Setting the Uzi for bursts, Luke fired at Ormeskirk's chest. Although one or two bullets might pierce a rib, the wall of bone would deflect the rest, so he didn't expect to cause much damage. What he really wanted was a sight of the belly, but Ormeskirk kept his tail high, making that shot impossible.

Out of the corner of his eye, he saw Hub trying to draw a bead on a pterosaur eye, even a surer way to kill him than a hit to the stomach. But Ormeskirk was not only big, he was swift. He rose, then sank, then rose again. On each hover at the lip of the drop-off, he reached out a foot, seeking an enemy.

Hub's gun exploded. Ormeskirk stalled, then sank.

"A hit!" Hub bellowed with almost nauseating glee. "The lizard's a goner!"

The glee was short-lived. The pterosaur zoomed up, hovering yards above them. Though fluid dripped from the base of his crest, his eyes glared fiercely. But his position gave Luke what he needed. He fired at the underbelly.

Ormeskirk swerved, avoiding the bullets as though they traveled in slow motion. Letting out a dour cry, he sped upward, higher and higher, then vanished into the clouds.

Still braced against the rope, the column waited at the ready. When time passed and Ormeskirk didn't return, Chisholm gave the command to resume the march.

The soldiers went wild. "It worked!" they cried, one after the other. "The rope worked!"

Luke received more rib-breaking slaps than he'd ever gotten in his life. Not a man had been lost. Not even scraped, for the helmets and mail had protected them from flying pebbles. Luke supposed it was something to celebrate, but he couldn't help wishing there was another way. Each shot he'd fired had gone against his grain.

But that line of reasoning had been before Tom had been captured. He'd now gained insight into why these people prayed for Ormeskirk's death. Sometimes two different species couldn't share the same space, a fact he had to accept.

Luke went to help the front man pry his spike free, then to the end of the line to help the other. When he finished, he looked up. The sheer rock face seemed to go on forever. They'd traveled less than a quarter of the way, and the real battle would be at the top.

Luke coughed and lifted his flax scarf higher. Clouds of dust billowed from the tromping feet ahead.

"Fucking dirt," Hub grumbled after a particularly nasty choking spell.

"Don't waste your breath," Luke replied irritably, wondering why he was wasting his. His legs ached like crazy. A spot low in his back throbbed from the continual beating of the Uzi, and his sinuses were beginning to ache.

The pterosaur had appeared only once since the earlier encounter, and they'd so peppered the creature with arrows and bullets that Luke doubted he'd try again soon.

So far no one had been lost.

Foot after weary foot, Luke encountered dust. He heard tired mutters from the troops. Hub swore again. Luke adjusted the position of the Uzi one more time, pulled his scarf to eye level, then bent his head and kept on climbing.

"The dragon! The dragon approaches!"

The attack began before the ropes were secured. Deprived of their lifeline, men dove for the ground. Ormeskirk roared and screeched, swooping hazardously close to the wall. Arrows flew, muskets fired. Luke engaged the Uzi and shot off a volley of bullets. One soldier's crossbow was blown from his grip as he notched his arrow. Enraged, he stood, drew his sword, and charged at the pterosaur.

Ormeskirk snapped his head around and caught the man, then threw him back on the trail like a broken matchstick.

"The ropes are secure!" Chisholm shouted. "To the ropes, men! To the ropes!"

Soldiers backed up on hands and knees, some getting off musket shots, others still firing their bows. The wind sent an arrow askew, and it struck a hapless soldier in the arm. A chance flap of Ormeskirk's wing swept a kneeling man over the ledge. His terrified screams followed him to the ground.

Trying to block out the sound, Luke assessed the situation. They were high up in the spire now, where the trail twisted sharply, preventing the lead of the column from knowing what the rear was doing. At this rate, they'd kill each other before Ormeskirk got a chance. A memory flashed, bringing back the day Ormeskirk had come upon Caryn and him in the hills. The creature had stood above them but hadn't detected their presence.

"Ormeskirk can't see you if you don't move! Stop fighting and stay very still!" Luke shouted the order to Hub, told him to pass it down the line. Then he gave the same order to the man ahead of him, with instructions to pass it up.

This went against their Celtic warrior instincts, and Luke only hoped that after his success with the rope the men would trust him enough to obey. Just minutes later, as he had feared, a soldier positioned about three men up the column slid under the rope and leaped to his feet.

"*Tàbhachd!*" he bellowed, charging with his sword raised. Ormeskirk was mere feet away. The soldier swung down his blade and slashed through a long clawed talon. The pterosaur screamed in pain and rage, then reached out his uninjured foot and captured the man.

Out of nowhere came an arrow, striking Ormeskirk in the neck. Angrily he shook off his captive, then wrapped the offending arrow with the small fingers at his wing and plucked it free. Meanwhile the injured soldier writhed on the ground, whimpering in agony.

"Be still!" Luke hissed, although his every cell cried out to rescue the man. He hoped he hadn't made a mistake. This tactic came from the movie *Jurassic Park*, and though it worked for him and

Caryn, he didn't know if the fictional logic was correct. Even if the imaginary dinosaur's behavior was based on science, it assumed lizard physiology, while Luke was fairly certain Ormeskirk was a bird.

They waited. The animal hovered near the ledge, snapping now and again, thrusting out a foot. When some time passed without motion from the troops, he let out a wail and rose above the ledge, staring down like a specter from hell.

For the first time, Luke found himself fiercely wishing the animal were dead. Treacherous is what the folks called him, and they were right. One man dead already because of this beast. Three injured, one perhaps mortally. And two had died in Marco's attempt.

Ormeskirk soared off. Luke felt Hub move and heard similar noises up and down the line. "Wait!" he called out.

No sooner had the words left his mouth, then Ormeskirk swooped down. Close to the wall, very close, he appeared about to crash into it. But just as a collision seemed eminent, he leveled out.

Gliding high above the unit, he sped away.

When Luke was satisfied the beast wouldn't return, he gave the order to resume the march. Soldiers hurried to their fallen friends. The man thrown against the wall had a broken arm, while the one hit by friendly fire was attempting to dislodge the arrow. The third man had taken a claw to the gut. Without a twentieth-century trauma team, Luke doubted he'd survive.

Chisholm came down from the head of the line,

ordered the wounded carried to a cleft in the wall, then instructed two men to stay with them. After that was done, he approached Luke.

"I give the orders here!"

"Do you?" Luke asked indifferently.

"Aye." From some kind of inborn instinct Luke failed to understand, Chisholm's hand moved to his belt. "And ye best not forget it."

"We're all alive, aren't we?"

"Hey," a soldier called from below. "Who's the scrawny lad at the end of the column?"

Glad for the interruption, Luke turned toward the slight figure that held the rear. The guy lifted a long-bow in salute, then lowered his scarf and smiled.

"What the hell are you doing here, Caryn?"

"Shooting at Ormeskirk. What else would I be doing on Wizard's Spire?" Moving haughtily past the gaping soldiers, her longbow held loosely in one hand, she stopped beside Luke.

"Lady Caryn." Chisholm's gruff voice held shocked rebuke, and he leaned around Luke to fix her with a fierce glare. "Shocking as I find it to see ye in trews, ye went beyond the pale by donning a sporran."

"Where else did ye expect me to keep my bow-string wax, much less my powder and horn?" Lowering her bow, she took a haughty stance. "I expected gratitude, Captain. After all, 'twas *my* arrow that freed McCullough from the claws of the beast."

Stripped of her voluminous skirts, clad only in trews that revealed the narrowness of her hips and waist, Caryn suddenly seemed fragile to Luke. Never mind that Tom needed rescuing, his strongest urge was to march her to safety. Her tone of voice, however, gave a different message.

"You promised to stay behind," he said accusingly, paying little attention to Chisholm's unceasing bluster.

"Nay, I said it was settled. Ye alone put meaning to those words."

Chisholm elbowed his way between them and grabbed Caryn's arm. "Ye will come to the head of the line, Countess, and remain in my protection."

Luke pushed Chisholm's hand away. "She'll stay with me."

"Do not touch me in that manner!" Chisholm whipped a long knife from his belt.

These guys had knives and swords everywhere, Luke thought, as a foot and a half of gleaming steel rested inches below his nose. Reluctantly, almost wearily, he lifted the Uzi. "Your mail coat won't protect you, Captain. I suggest you back off."

"Captain." The soft call came from a nearby soldier. "We need Slade's strategy to succeed."

At the same time, Caryn edged forward. "Put away your dirk, Captain," she said coldly. "Though you disapprove of my actions, I am still in command of the realm until our laird says otherwise."

His face flamed red, a stark contrast to the pale metal of his helmet, but he looked away as if Caryn hadn't spoken. "Ye give wise counsel," he said to the soldier. "Fall in, men. We resume our march."

"How can you be so reckless?" Luke asked Caryn after they were again under way.

She slanted him a defiant glance. "Do not worry, Luke. Though I have no wish to offend your male dignity, I am truly a better warrior than you. Ye'll soon be glad to have me at your side."

He already was, but damned if he'd tell her so.

" 'Tis impenetrable as a palisades." Chisholm stood next to Luke with his hand on his dirk, wagging his head back and forth. A tangle of branches and dried mud surrounded the windmill, some twenty feet high if it was a foot. Overhead, a broken vane clanked against the braces. Excited utterances and curses filled the quieter spaces in between those sounds.

"That's what the grappling hooks are for." Luke held back a smile, remembering the grumbles he'd met when he handed each soldier the rope and hook.

"Ascend that monstrosity? Are ye mad?" Chisholm gazed up at the sky. "We mus'na permit Ormeskirk to take residence again."

While Chisholm pondered the sky, Caryn inched closer to the nest, studying it intently. Luke, however, looked around him. Not only was the nest high, it occupied most of the space on the plateau. No more than five or six yards encircled it, leaving little room to fight. If the entire column came up at once, they'd be shooting each other, or get bumped off the edge and fall to their deaths. Moreover, the approach to the plateau was a steep incline. They'd already had to drive the spikes so the men still below could cling to the rope to keep from sliding back down.

The broken vane struck the beam again. Luke

jerked and noticed that Chisholm did the same. Everyone's nerves were like live electric wires. The situation was grim, success unlikely.

Looking somber, Caryn backed away from the nest and returned to Luke's side. "Young Tom . . ." she said. "I fear he is lost, but we cannot give him up until we're certain."

Luke had hoped to retrieve a live boy, but the funereal bleakness of their surroundings had ripped away his last shred of faith. Except for the clank of the vane and the hissing wind, the plateau was as silent as death.

"Heeelp."

The sound appeared to be the wind, but somewhat louder. Luke looked around. Perhaps another soldier had slid down the incline.

"Pleeease . . ."

"It's Tom! He lives!" Caryn cried. "Tom lives!"

Before Luke could stop her, she shoved her bow into his hand and broke into a run.

"Caryn, don't!"

But she was climbing the nest like a monkey.

"Milady, I must implore you to—"

"Shut up, Chisholm!" Luke dropped the bow and ran after her. "Get down from there!" he demanded.

Clinging to a branch with one hand, supporting herself on another with her foot, Caryn paused and looked down. "We may not get another chance."

"Then I'll go!"

"Nay. The nest is insubstantial. A heavier person will pull branches from the mud."

"But I have a grap—" Hell, she'd started up again. "Dammit, Countess!"

Luke ripped the rope and hook off his shoulder, then turned toward the soldiers who had gathered behind him.

"Stand back!" He threw the hook at the windmill's closest crossbeam. Missed, and tried again. The third try took and he leaped onto the rope.

The nest was hard, prickly, unforgiving. Branches snapped beneath his feet, bringing soft curses from his lips. But each time one snapped, he found another. Thorns grabbed at his sleeves and trews, but he jerked them free and kept his eyes on the next few feet of rope ahead of him.

After what seemed an endless climb, he reached the top.

He caught sight of Caryn against the eastern wall, holding a sobbing Tom to her chest. Relief made him weak, and he steadied himself with the rope as he scanned the inner nest. Leaves, wool, and other debris padded the basin and reduced the distance from the rim to about half of what it was outside. As he was calculating the best method of getting Caryn and Tom up, something moved on the western side. He turned, stunned by what he saw.

The pig that Ormeskirk had snared was rooting through the foliage. Broken eggshells were scattered everywhere. Off to one side, petrified embryos the size of eagles were laid out head to foot. In the center of the basin rested a single unbroken egg.

"Aye," Caryn called up, half in awe. "Ormeskirk is female. She's protecting her last unborn. A lost cause, to be sure, but I do not think she's accepted it."

"Which makes her all the more dangerous." Bracing himself with the rope, he edged down the inner side of the nest, holding out a hand. "Quick! Hand up Tom. We've got to get out of here."

Tom apparently grasped the situation. When Caryn hoisted him, he grabbed for a nearby branch, scaling the bramble as skillfully as Caryn. When he reached Luke, he jumped so forcefully they both almost fell.

"Good boy," Luke said, half laughing after the near disaster. But Caryn didn't seem at all amused.

"I'll be back for you," he said.

"I know you will." She looked at the boy and sternly said, "Young Tom, do not be wiggling around in Sir Luke's arms, ye hear? Ye could both take a terrible tumble."

"Aye, Lady Caryn."

"I'll be waiting on the rim when ye get back."

"Hang on," Luke told Tom, feeling confident they'd all escape. "I'll need both my hands to get us down."

"Aye, sir." Wrapping his legs and arms around Luke like vises, Tom didn't talk during their descent. When they were halfway to the ground, soldiers stretched up their arms. A man made contact and murmured, "Got ye, lad."

Luke gently tried to pry Tom free, but met little success until the soldier had his hands firmly around the boy's waist. With a gasp of terror, Tom transferred his grip to the soldier's neck.

"How did ye breathe, man?" the man asked.

"With difficulty. Tell Chisholm to regroup the men. We're going to retreat."

The soldier nodded. " 'Tis the only reasonable decision."

Then Luke started back for the top. His hands stung from rope burn, but he'd already gotten used to it, and most of the way he didn't bother to brace his feet. When he was almost to the top he saw a helmet emerging over the rim, several yards to his left. "Why did you come up over there?" he asked. "The rope is here."

"I wanted a better look at that egg." She stood up and traced her way along the craggy ledge. He found it hard to get mad at her risky side trip; it was something he might do himself. Besides, the sky was clear, and they hadn't heard Ormeskirk scream for quite some time. But still . . .

"Hurry, Caryn!"

She'd come to a wide chasm in the twig and mud structure and was studying it with trepidation. Hesitating, she started to crouch, apparently planning to crawl over it.

"The dragon comes!" yelled a man on the ground.

Ormeskirk screamed. Caryn swung her head around. Already precariously balanced, she lost her equilibrium. For a hideous instant she swayed back and forth, struggling to regain it.

With a startled squeak, she toppled into the nest.

Chapter Thirty-one

Marco's ankle throbbed as he labored to make it up the sharp rise of the turn. Shouts carried on the wind, telling him he was almost there, but the high sheer wall of the spire prevented him from seeing what was going on. At the moment he had only his ears to rely on, which told him Ormeskirk was still alive, that the soldiers had little confidence they would kill him, and that something had happened to the Lady Caryn.

Rage shot through him. Why had Chisholm let her come? And how had he failed to protect her? Didn't he realize the woman was precious? Ignoring his throbbing ankle, Marco broke into a lopsided run.

Finally, he saw flashes of plaid.

"Someone approaches," called a nearby soldier, who clung to a line to keep from sliding down the incline.

Marco drove more speed from his legs, but the trail had turned to polished rock. He fell several times, nearly wrenching a shoulder in his efforts to protect his ankle.

The rear man turned and extended a hand. "Grab on."

Half crouching, Marco stumbled up the short distance. Soon he, too, was clutching the rope.

"What brings ye to this place without armor or helmet?" the first soldier asked. " 'Tis folly to face the beast without them."

Marco reached into his belt and pulled out his Walther PPK. "I got leverage."

"So, too, does the dragon slayer. Yet he devised the coats of steel. Do ye trust your weapon more than he does his?"

"Yep." What he actually trusted more was his willingness to use it.

"Must be a remarkable gun."

"Yep," Marco repeated, putting the Walther back in his belt. "Now where's the battle!"

The soldier pointed up the incline where men hung from the rope like bulbs on a strand of Christmas tree lights. "Ye'll have to get past them. From the looks of that game leg of yours, I'd say it won't be an easy task."

"I'll manage."

Grunting commands to move back, he climbed the rope. If Lady Caryn was alive, he'd find her. What's more, it was time to take out Luke and Chisholm. Who could lay blame on a stray shot fired in the heat of battle?

Arrows flew into the air, some on their mark, some going wild. A musket blasted. At the bottom of the nest was Caryn, crumpled and motionless.

"Stop shooting!" Luke bellowed down to the soldiers. "You're going to hit one of us."

He heard grumbles. Saw helpless faces staring up. But they felt no more helpless than he did.

Caryn was too far to his left, and walking over was so treacherous it would take forever. Luke glanced up at the grappling hook, checking to see if it was lodged securely enough to allow him to swing. It appeared so.

"*Tàbhachd!*" he roared, taking a deep breath and soaring toward the spot where he'd last seen Caryn.

Though good enough, his landing was rocky, but he quickly forgot about it anyway. A shadow darkened the nest. Ormeskirk had returned and was circling high above. With a screech of fury, the pterosaur dove into her nest, landing with a flutter of wings.

Luke's breath locked up, every muscle screaming to slide down the rope and get Caryn out of there. His brain reminded him that this was certain death to them both.

Apparently unaware that Tom was absent and Caryn was now in his place, Ormeskirk pulled in her wings, waddled over to the intact egg, and sat down. Her tail covered the egg completely and her knees protruded on either side of her body. While this relieved Luke's immediate worry, he was no closer to rescuing Caryn.

"Sir Luke," Chisholm shouted up from the outer base of the nest, "how fares the lady?"

Luke made a sharp motion for silence. Down there, the men looked smaller, less formidable than he remembered. How insignificant they must seem to the monster in the nest, who must regard them as they would regard a swarm of rats—as something to be exterminated.

He took in the eerie scene below. A rooting pig that should have been long ago devoured. A rotting fish. A few half-live doves. Why hadn't they been eaten? Why had Tom been spared? And what had Ormeskirk been doing with the dead sheep that day on the mountain?

Suddenly it came to him.

She was trying to replace her lost offspring. First with the pig, then with the sheep, finally with Tom. Luke felt a strong wave of pity. Lost, alone, cut off from her kind, she must be trying to build a colony.

The wind gusted, causing his rope to bow, and for a second Luke lost his footing. As he regained it, a twig snapped. Ormeskirk cocked her head, sharp eyes searched for the source of the sound. Luke forced his every muscle to stay as it was.

The pterosaur rose from the egg, clearly more clumsy on foot than by wing, and moved closer to Caryn. Just then, Caryn rolled and moaned. Ormeskirk let out a questioning peep. Although she seemed confused, and swung her head left and right, her otherwise calm behavior implied she was confident the nest protected her from danger. Then why attack them on the ascent?

Of course, Luke thought, her encounters with men on the spire had always been accompanied by an onslaught of arrows and bullets. People on the trail equaled pain, which equaled enemy. But somehow she'd never equated their actions with an attack on her lair. Until now, Luke thought. Until she realized Caryn wasn't the guest she'd invited.

"Don't move, Caryn!" he shouted.

His cry brought Ormeskirk's head in his direction, leaving him no more time to think. He yanked the Uzi forward, preparing to fire, then stopped. Bullets ricocheted. One might hit Caryn.

But bombs wouldn't, he thought, remembering the Molotov cocktails. The nest was a kindling pile, making fire almost as dangerous as bullets, but at least it didn't rebound off hard surfaces. If they could force the pterosaur from the nest for even minutes, he could get Caryn out.

"Let the bombs fly," he cried out. "Aim west and aim true!"

On the ground outside the nest, feet scurried. He could hear the scuffle of bags being opened, glass clanking against stone.

Caryn lay half-conscious beneath the animal's shadow. To think he'd even considered walking away from this woman. Who was he kidding? She'd become the heart of him, part of his soul, and the minute he had her safely in his arms, he was going to tell her so.

Just then, the pterosaur made a peep, and lowered her head. "Don't move," Luke shouted a second time, hoping to draw the beast away.

Where were those bombs?

Caryn heard Luke's warning cry, but as the blunt beak came nearer, she let out a whimper, then scrambled back on her bottom and hands until she hit the wall. She twisted and grabbed for a branch, pulling herself to her feet. There was no hope for it, no possible chance of scaling that vast expanse before the dragon ensnared her, but she scrambled up, regardless, grabbing branch after branch, praying none gave way.

She'd covered only meters when hot breath fanned the naked spot between her helmet and her mail. She turned, facing the horror head-on.

A large round eye with the quick blink of a hawk's stared at her intently, then moved up. Slowly, the beak came in view, widening to reveal rows of small teeth as pointed as a shark's. Aye, and just as sharp.

They were heading for her arm.

Above, Luke was shouting, but Caryn's blood pounded so fast and hard she couldn't hear his words. The beak closed down. She screamed, struggling to climb away, but Ormeskirk plucked her off the brambles, dangling her as a cat might a kitten. Caryn squeezed her eyes shut, whispered a prayer for God's forgiveness, and waited.

She felt herself being lifted through the air. Opening her eyes, she saw the earth beneath slowly approaching. Then Ormeskirk put her down. With soft chirps, she nosed Caryn and sent her sprawling, then turned back toward her egg.

Half-frozen in terror, Caryn stared at the retreating tail, with no idea what to make of this.

An explosion of light shattered her paralysis. The pig squealed and bolted Caryn's way. Caryn started to rise, but hesitated, transfixed.

Instead of flying away, Ormeskirk was hopping

toward the flames, which were perilously close to the unbroken egg. Another bomb hit, exploding against Ormeskirk's wing, but still the dragon protected the egg.

Caryn didn't wait to find out what happened next. She jumped onto the wall, scaling it faster than she'd ever scaled anything before.

"That's my girl," she heard Luke shouting. "Faster. Climb faster."

More explosions. But Caryn didn't look back, no, she wouldn't, couldn't, no matter how frequent the bombs, how piteous the squeals, how piercing the dragon's screams. Finally Luke had hold of her. Lifting her onto the rim, he then blasted Ormeskirk with his gun. Bombs continued to fall in the nest. A rat-a-tat-tat of bullets streamed toward the dragon, hitting her flapping wings and exposed thighs. Abruptly the staccato sound stopped, followed by empty clicks.

"Dammit!" Luke snarled, pulling out the cartridge holder and reaching into his pocket.

"What is it?" Caryn asked with alarm.

"I'm out of modern cartridges. I'll have to use the ones Joshua made."

Caryn wondered if that was bad, but he'd already slammed in the new cartridge holder and was firing again. Assaulted from all sides, Ormeskirk nudged the egg to the place Caryn had been, which so far was out of harm's way. Random fires sprouted behind the animal, sending up thick spirals of smoke. The stench of burning flesh fouled the air, and patches of the dragon's skin were raw and smoking.

Still, she hovered over the egg as though a living embryo waited to crack the shell.

The dragon's gallantry pierced something hard and unforgiving in Caryn. She had never understood Luke's fondness for this creature, but now she saw that the animal she'd called a monster loved its young and yearned for companionship. They were not so unalike, after all.

Beside her, Luke fought like the warrior on the tapestry, but she knew he took no warrior's joy in the act. He was doing it only because it needed doing. He made her feel ashamed. A sob lodged deep in her throat and escaped on her breath.

Suddenly Ormeskirk flapped her wings. With a scream of fury, she sped up and out of the nest. The barrel of Luke's gun followed her. Caryn saw what he saw: the opportunity to strike the dragon's underbelly. Had it been her with the weapon, she might have hesitated, but Luke did not. The stream of machine gun bullets hit their mark. Ormeskirk squealed and listed, plunging toward the ground. Luke released the trigger, waiting.

An instant later the animal regained her loft. Luke fired again. This time, visible holes speckled Ormeskirk's stomach. Her wings no longer moving in tandem, she somersaulted, leaving streaks of blood in her wake.

"She's finished," Luke said gruffly, shoving the rope into Caryn's hand. "Climb down."

She kissed him quickly, hard and fiercely, then shimmied down the rope.

*   *   *

Luke touched his lips almost like a talisman, then checked the sky for Ormeskirk. She struggled mightily to stay aloft, but Luke knew it was a losing battle. Such an enormous creature, yet still destroyed by the vermin called humanity.

Shouts and cheers arose from the ground. Hands reached out for Caryn. Luke climbed on the rope and scaled it a yard at a time. When his feet struck ground, Chisholm was ordering soldiers down the incline. But where was Caryn?

He found her sliding over the slope, being helped by the last man he'd expected to see.

Ormeskirk let out a piercing wailing. Luke looked up to find her spiraling toward her nest.

He ran. The men remaining on the plateau were jumping over the ridge to the trail, shouting, crawling over each other. There was no room for Luke. Backing away from the edge of the mesa, he knelt and bent over, covering the back of his helmeted head.

As over a ton of weight slammed into the nest, mud and branches whirred past him at dizzying speeds. Something struck his shoulder. A tree limb rolled to the edge of the plateau and fell off.

It was over almost as quickly as it began. Slowly, Luke turned his neck to see Ormeskirk collapsed over the outer edge of the nest, supported only by the rim. She lifted her head, gave out a plaintive peep. Then her neck gave out. Her head fell, coming so close Luke could have touched her curved snout. With a low and melancholy wail she stared at him.

On an almost human sigh, she closed her eyes.

Soon after, Luke heard footsteps behind him, but he didn't turn toward them. The corpse of the pterosaur held him spellbound.

"So you killed it, huh?" asked Marco, his raspy voice only slightly less grating than his question.

"Yeah," he replied. "I killed her."

But he took no pleasure in that fact.

Chapter Thirty-two

"Christ, Slade, you act like you just murdered your best friend." Marco pulled out his pistol, took aim, and fired a shot at the pterosaur's wing. "Hey, Hub," he shouted jubilantly. "Where are you? It's time for some target practice."

Like an insect coming out of the woodwork, Hub crawled over the rim of the mesa, then lumbered to his feet. He lifted his gun and gazed down the sights. "It's one big target, ain't it, boss? Let's see if I can get me an eye."

"Cut it out, Marco!"

Marco fired again. The bullet struck the animal's bony crest. Hub whistled and ducked as the shot deflected off the hard surface and ricocheted several times.

"You jerks!" Luke ripped away Marco's gun. "You're going to hit someone."

"Yeah?" Marco countered.

By this time, a number of the soldiers had climbed back onto the mesa, their ascent accompanied by cheering and coarse remarks about dead dragons.

Luke swept the crowd with his eyes, half smiling when he saw Caryn off to one side, frowning her own disapproval.

"Give me my gun, Slade."

"Put it away and it's yours." Luke held the weapon back just far enough to force Marco into an undignified lunge. Considering the large and rapt audience, he doubted the man would try.

"Sure. Okay. We were already getting tired of the game, weren't we, Hub?"

"Hell, I never even got a shot off." Irritably, Hub turned aside and put away his Magnum. Luke returned Marco's gun and went in search of Chisholm.

"It's time we marched back," he told the man.

"Are ye daft? My soldiers are weary from the arduous climb. They need rest and water."

Luke gestured to the nest, where smoke rose steadily. "It's a tinderbox up there."

Chisholm nodded curtly, then issued an order to fall in. Moans of protest sounded, but soon the men were down. Hub and Marco descended last, leaving only Luke, Caryn, and Chisholm.

"You next, milady." Chisholm extended his hand.

She shook her head. "I'll remain with Sir Luke." When Chisholm scowled, she squared her shoulders. "Go now. We will follow soon."

Luke touched her shoulder. "Caryn—"

"We'll stay only a moment. I need to speak with you."

With clear reluctance, Chisholm started down the incline. As soon as he was gone, Caryn turned to Luke, and stared down, twisting the Celtic ring on her finger. Her helmet was slightly askew, and her mail coat had shifted so one shoulder hung over her upper arm.

"You wanted to say something?" Luke asked, holding back the urge to check her over, make sure nothing was broken.

"I—I cannot express my regret over my deceit enough." She took his hands in hers and firmly met his eyes. 'Twas cruel and heartless, and it put Randy in grave—"

"You were thinking of your people."

"—in grave danger. Moreover, even knowing your sympathies for Ormeskirk, I urged you to kill her."

"It wasn't all your fault." Luke paid no real attention to what he was saying. He simply drank Caryn in, filled with gratitude that she'd survived. He reached out and straightened her mail coat, then lifted her hands. "Ian had reasons—Dammit, you're bleeding!"

He ran his thumb along the line of her cheekbone, then kissed her wounded palm. "When you were lying in— My God, Caryn, she was right on top of you!" He dropped her hands and cupped her face. "I knew that if you died, I might as well die with you."

" 'Twas as I felt fearing you would die in battle. Oh, Luke. I do not know how I'll survive when ye're gone from the realm."

"Gone?" asked a gravelly voice. "There's a way out?"

Marco stepped onto the rise of the mesa. Seconds later, Hub came up behind him. Both had weapons drawn.

Luke moved Caryn behind him, and Marco grinned.

"In case you hadn't noticed, Slade, the monster isn't dead."

Luke glanced at the nest. Ormeskirk's eyes were open, but blankly so, and he was sure Marco was wrong. Then she blinked. Letting out a bleat reminiscent of the sheep she'd once let fall, she closed them again.

"She's dying," Caryn said. "She poses no threat."

Marco smirked. "No? In that case, let me do that for her. Hand over the Uzi, Slade."

"What?" Luke lifted the weapon. Marco raised his gun. Hub lined up the long barrel of his forty-four.

"What do you want, Marco?" Luke asked.

"The secret to escaping this hellhole. My money. And Lady Caryn's promise to come with me."

"Boss?" Hub said. "That ain't what—"

"Shut up and get the Uzi!"

Luke stood motionless, shielding Caryn, then handed the sub-gun to Hub. When Marco stepped forward to take it, Luke moved his arms backward, covering Caryn on both sides. He didn't like the obsessive longing he saw in Marco's eyes, and knew this wasn't as much about money or getting away as it was about her. Uzi or not, the man would get her over Luke's dead body.

Clearly Caryn didn't see those signs. She swept from behind Luke and glared at Marco. "This is absurd. If ye want out, then I'll gladly give you this." She pulled off the ring and held it out. "When we get back on the ground, I'll show you how to use it, and hand over your money. Lochlorraine is well rid of you."

"I've never met a woman like you," Marco said. He took the ring, put it in his sporran, then reached for Caryn's wrist.

"Let go of me!" she demanded, unsuccessfully trying to jerk free.

Marco pointed his gun at Luke. "This thing's got a hair trigger, Lady Caryn. Accidents happen."

Luke felt sure Caryn had no idea what a hair trigger was, but her expression showed she'd gotten the message. "So what more do ye want from me?"

He stroked her cheek. "Come back with me. We'll be rich as sin. Where would you like to go? Paris? Rio? I'll give you anything you want."

It took all Luke's will not to lunge at Marco. But they were just feet from the mesa's edge. One mistake, and Caryn could get bumped off.

"Chisholm awaits below," Caryn said coldly, visibly shuddering under Marco's caress. "Ye cannot fight his army."

"I don't have to. Robert's in my pocket. With Luke dead, he'll be a hero. The soldiers will follow him when he takes over the kingdom and deposes your brother-in-law. Too bad I can't find it in myself to let him have you too." Marco smiled dreamily. "He wants you, you know. Hell, every man in the kingdom wants you. But I just can't give you up. You have to come with me."

Marco knew he was talking too much and taking unnecessary risks. He hadn't believed his ears at first, and hearing about the escape from the bubble should have made him decide to take the money and run. That was obviously what Hub wanted to do. Taking Caryn along was the height of stupidity. If Ralph were still alive, he'd undoubtedly bring up that point.

He'd say Marco should toss Luke and Caryn off the plateau and claim the dragon had done it. With victory assured for Chisholm, the man would gladly hand over the cash, and let them all go back to the city.

Marco shook his head. He couldn't leave this woman. Not her with the wild red hair, the flashing green eyes, and the smile that melted a man. And with the Uzi back in his hands, he now felt the power of his greater weaponry. If Chisholm decided to give him a fight for Caryn, well . . . one burst could mow down half a dozen soldiers.

The impact caught Marco off guard. He fell forward, unintentionally pulling Caryn with him. His Uzi bounced and clattered, landing feet away.

"Ye lying, sneaking cur!" Chisholm towered over him, face twisted with rage.

"Robert, listen," Marco said. "I was just talking. I didn't mean it."

"Do not think me a fool," the captain roared, pulling out his broadsword. "The lady is mine!"

"Back off, man!" Hub shouted, cocking his revolver. Chisholm whirled. Raising his sword like an ax, he brought it down on Hub's head. The forty-four exploded in a shot that went wild. Blood splattered everywhere. A faint gurgle escaped Hub's throat, then he collapsed.

Meanwhile, Marco belly-crawled toward the Uzi. As he reached out, he saw a flash of silver. He pulled back his hand just as the broadsword came down. When the metal struck solid stone it snapped off at the hilt. With a roar, Chisholm threw down, the sword and swept up the Uzi.

"I will not suffer ye to live!" Leaning back toward the nest, he pointed the weapon. Shit, Marco thought in panic, the man couldn't miss at this range.

"*Tàbhachd!*" Chisholm pulled the trigger, unleashing a stream of bullets.

The recoil caught him by surprise, throwing him off balance, and the shots went wild. He stumbled backward toward the nest, the Uzi falling from his fingers and landing inches from Marco's feet. But before Marco could grab the gun, Chisholm had swept it up again.

Marco threw himself on the ground, rolling, covering his head, trying not to whimper. She was watching, Caryn was watching. He couldn't disgrace himself. And his one regret as he waited for Chisholm's shot was that he'd never known her love.

He heard a click, then another.

The gun had jammed. Dear, sweet Jesus, the gun had jammed.

Chisholm stared down, perplexed.

Marco sprang to his feet. Before Chisholm knew what he was up to, before the man even had a chance to realize what was happening, Marco snatched the Uzi from his hand. Swinging it wildly, he slammed the butt into the captain's head.

Chisholm went down with a grunt. As he fell,

Marco cleared the jam, and before the captain had fully hit the ground, he fired.

The joy he felt as Chisholm jerked and bucked was unimaginable, but he restrained himself and released the trigger. He had only one course of action open to him.

Whirling, he turned on Luke and Caryn. They were together again, with him sheltering her oh-so-gallantly under his arm. Marco heard voices below; heard soldiers climbing the ropes. He had to act fast if he wanted to escape a hangman's noose. But Caryn clung to Luke's shoulder, white-faced, clearly unwilling to go.

She'd get over it. He put out his hand.

"Come on, Caryn. Come with me and I won't shoot Luke."

"The soldiers," she said. "You'll never—"

"I will if *you're* with me." He couldn't leave without her. He was nuts, he knew, but he just couldn't deal with his warring emotions. Marco impulsively charged the pair. Surprise on his side, he took Luke down with a blow from the barrel of the Uzi, then grabbed Caryn's wrist.

"Say you'll come with me," he said, "and I won't kill him."

Caryn stared at him, then looked at Luke, who had rocked to his knees but was clearly still dazed.

The sounds of the returning soldiers grew nearer. This wasn't smart. He needed to kill them both, place the blame on Chisholm, then say he shot back in self-defense.

But . . .

A whoosh of heat and flying debris flew out of nowhere.

Marco whirled and saw flames licking at the rim of the nest. The approaching soldiers screamed warnings as chunks of smoldering and flaming material rained down. The pterosaur shrieked in pain and lifted her head.

Marco clutched Caryn to him, spinning and flailing his arms, slapping out the small flames that erupted on his clothing, on her legs.

Caryn fought to escape him. Although her trews were smoldering, her helmet and mail coat protected her, and she knew Luke's protected him. But Marco was completely exposed. This was their chance for escape.

Ormeskirk let out a moan. Slowly her huge head came toward them. She closed her mouth around Marco's torso, then lifted him from the ground. He still clutched Caryn with all his might and a mew of panic left her throat as she began to rise. Her gaze locked on to his eyes, which were filled with terrified acceptance. Still he held her fast.

Suddenly, unfathomably, something soft and tender flashed across his face. In an act that was clearly a decision, he let her go.

She stumbled into Luke's waiting arms, sobs rising in her throat, staring in horror as Ormeskirk spread her wings, then rose from the nest. Marco screamed and kicked as they soared off the spire.

"We've got to get out of here," Luke said. Taking Caryn's hand, he began running toward the trail. As they shimmied down the rope until the steep surface leveled out, Marco's hideous shrieks rang in their ears.

They turned toward the loch and watched Ormeskirk fly unevenly toward Lucifer's Window. When she reached the water, she hovered overhead, Marco still flailing in her mouth.

She dropped him. His scream of terror abruptly ended in an arc of rising water.

Gliding above the churning loch, Ormeskirk let out a low, mournful sound. A second later her wings collapsed. She plummeted into the sea, swallowed by huge waves that battered the shores.

Caryn moved closer to Luke, soothed by his nearness. His arm tightened about her shoulders, and he huskily said, "Naomi's curse has been fulfilled."

His statement hung in the air, full of implications. After a long silence, Caryn spoke. "I've ne'er believed fully in the Men of Peace, but surely some power has brought about Gann's downfall." She shook her head. "I no longer know what to believe."

Luke pulled her even closer. "Neither do I."

They sat against the wall for quite some time, each lost in their own thoughts. The sun moved overhead. The chapel clock rang twelve. At one point Caryn said, "I believe I will hire young Tom to serve in the castle."

"Wise decision," Luke replied.

When the clock rang half past, footsteps pounded on the trail below. Caryn started to stand.

"Where are you going?" Luke asked.

"They're coming for us." She dusted ashes off her trews. "We must hurry lest the portal closes."

Luke slowly climbed to his feet. "It probably already has."

"Nay, it has not."

He stared at her blankly as he removed his helmet. His dark hair billowed in the ocean breeze. "How do you know?"

"A shudder passes through the land each time we move. Although it does rattle the china and pottery, otherwise the fief endures."

As the words left her mouth, a wide smile crossed Luke's face. Suddenly he laughed uproariously, evoking a burst of anger from Caryn. They just endured a hideous tragedy and her heart was breaking at the thought of him leaving. How could his spirits be so high?

"I'm delighted ye found that amusing," she said, her spine stiffening with ice. She turned, ready to go now, ready to meet the rescuers marching toward them, ready to gladly send Luke through the portal so he might never break her heart again.

Of their own volition, her shoulders sagged. A moan of anguish escaped her throat.

Instantly Luke's hand was on her back. "I'm sorry, Caryn. I'm sorry. I thought you understood I'm not going."

Afraid to believe her ears, she arched her neck to look at him. "Ye will stay in Lochlorraine?"

His smile returned. "That's what I said. That's why I was laughing. Now, finally, I learn all your secrets. Just in time to tell you I'm staying."

"Are ye certain of this?"

"Absolutely." He turned her to face him and

looked hard into her eyes. "I love you, Caryn, and Lochlorraine has become my home. Where you are, I will be. What I need to know is, do you love me, too."

His hesitancy, the imploring sadness of his deep brown eyes, took her breath away. "Aye, Luke, I love you. Beyond all reason, I love you."

His rush of relief was visible, and he ran a hand through his windswept hair as he studied her expression. A lock fell over one eye, giving him a rakish air that brought back the night in her bedchamber.

"Are you blushing?" Luke asked.

She nodded, unable to hold back a shy smile.

"Why?"

"Ask me again at the castle and I shall show you." Then she offered her mouth for a kiss.

"I'll do that." He brushed her lips, then stepped back and took off the inscribed gold ring she'd so often seen him wear.

"My class ring," he said as she looked down at it. "Or sort of . . . would've been. Where I come from a man gives it to the girl he wants to marry."

Caryn's head snapped up. "Ye wish to wed me?"

"Oh, yes, Countess. Wed and bed, and everything else that comes with marriage." He stroked her cheek. "So what do you say?"

"S-say?" Tears rushed to her eyes. "Aye. I say, aye."

"Just what I wanted to hear."

He kissed her again, lingering this time, releasing her only after someone below them cleared their throat.

Looking toward the sound, Caryn saw Ian politely directing his gaze toward the edge of the trail.

"I'm delighted to find ye two so well and happy," he said, when he noticed them staring his way. "But if we stand in this tiresome wind much longer, we'll surely be blown to the castle." He grinned mischievously. "Moreover, ye have missed the dinner hour. 'Tis most inappropriate."

"I'm not hungry," Luke and Caryn replied in unison.

"Aye, ye are."

And Ian was right.